Shutout

Shutout

AVERY KEELAN

BRAMBLE

TOR PUBLISHING GROUP
NEW YORK

This is a work of fiction. All of the characters, organizations, and events portrayed in this novel are either products of the author's imagination or are used fictitiously.

SHUTOUT

Copyright © 2023 by Avery Keelan

All rights reserved.

A Bramble Book
Published by Tom Doherty Associates / Tor Publishing Group
120 Broadway
New York, NY 10271

www.torpublishinggroup.com

Bramble™ is a trademark of Macmillan Publishing Group, LLC.

EU Representative: Macmillan Publishers Ireland Ltd, 1st Floor, The Liffey Trust Centre, 117–126 Sheriff Street Upper, Dublin 1, DO1 YC43

The Library of Congress Cataloging-in-Publication Data is available upon request.

ISBN 978-1-250-40069-7 (trade paperback)
ISBN 978-1-250-40070-3 (ebook)

The publisher of this book does not authorize the use or reproduction of any part of this book in any manner for the purpose of training artificial intelligence technologies or systems. The publisher of this book expressly reserves this book from the Text and Data Mining exception in accordance with Article 4(3) of the European Union Digital Single Market Directive 2019/790.

Our books may be purchased in bulk for specialty retail/wholesale, literacy, corporate/premium, educational, and subscription box use. Please contact MacmillanSpecialMarkets@macmillan.com.

First Bramble Paperback Edition: 2025

Printed in the United States of America

10 9 8 7 6 5 4 3 2 1

To anyone who's ever felt like too much.

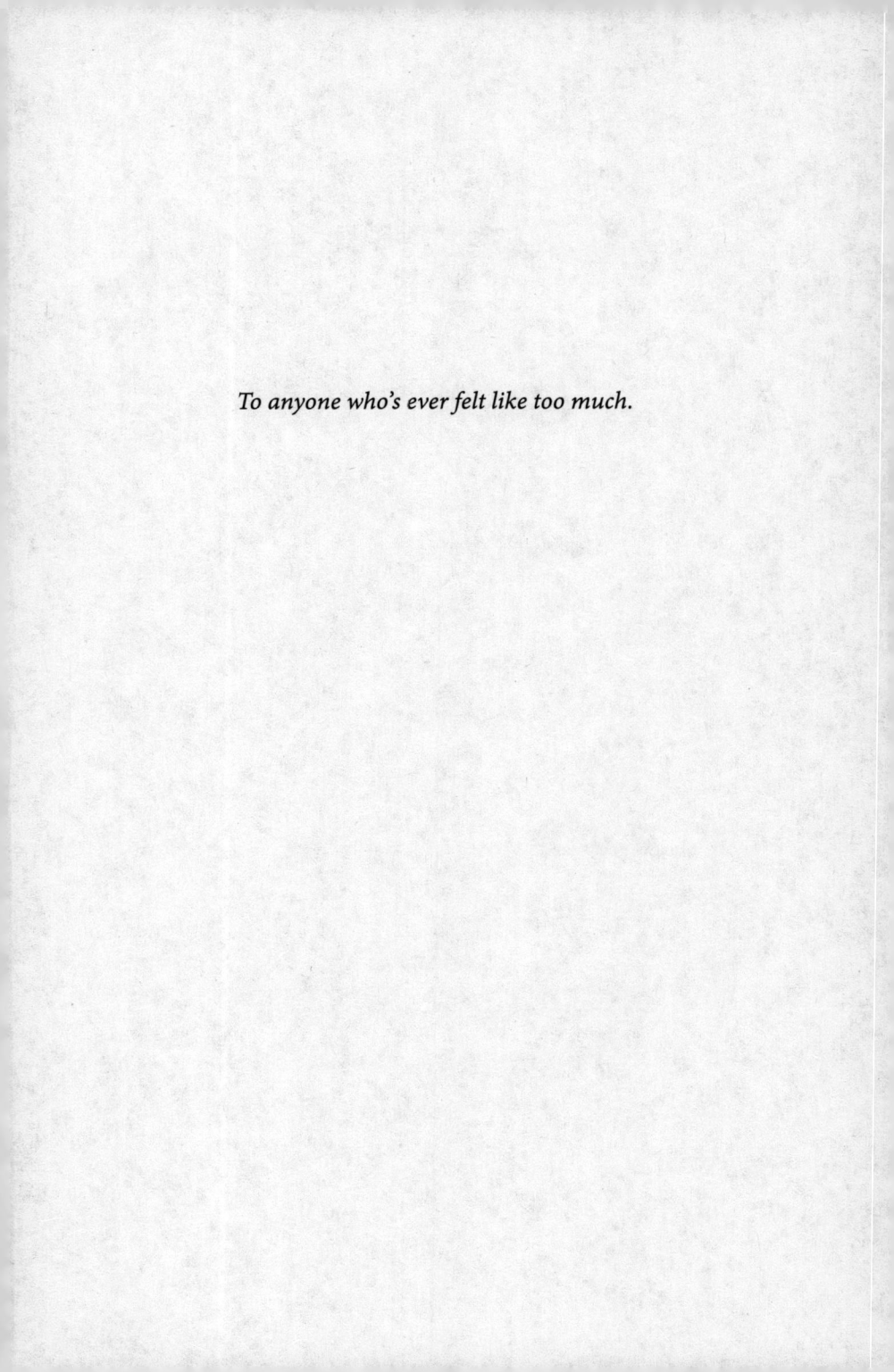

Shutout

Chapter 1
UNDER PRESSURE

TYLER

"Focus, Tyler!" My goalie coach's yell reverberates through the empty arena.

Winter break with my family in Los Angeles hasn't been much of a vacation. I've spent almost every day getting my ass kicked, and I'm about to hop on a plane back home, where I'll do it all over again tomorrow.

Giving my head a shake, I reset my position and wait for him to shoot. Mark has been running me through this puck-tracking drill for what feels like a fucking eternity. Shot-rebound-shot, over and over again. My gear is soaked with sweat, and my brain checked out ten minutes ago.

I block his next backhand, but he slips it past me on the rebound. *Fuck.* My molars clench, and my gaze darts over to the stands, where my father and brother are watching. It isn't that my dad will be angry if I don't show up well on the ice—it's that he'll be disappointed, and somehow, that's even worse.

Mark glides up to retrieve the puck from in the net. "Watch the shot come all the way in," he reminds me sternly. "When it rebounds, stay locked on it, and follow it to completion. Don't take your eyes off it even if you think it's a routine save."

I *did* have eyes on it, which is the most frustrating part. But rather than argue, I nod.

From in the crease, I watch him skate back to the top of the circle and stickhandle the white training puck while I track its every movement. It blends in with the ice, and it requires laser-like focus to separate it from the playing surface. Black regulation pucks practically glow in the dark in comparison.

The next few saves go more smoothly, and we wrap up on the rink before relocating into the fitness area for functional training. My workout is a grueling blur of one-legged squats, single-leg Romanian dead lifts, cable pulls, and side-to-side hurdles. I already know I'll be hurting later, and by the time we move on to medicine ball throws, I'm tempted to lob the forty-pound ball at Mark's head.

"Nice work." He claps me on the shoulder, then pushes to stand. "You can take a five-minute breather before we move on to myofascial release and stretching."

Breathing heavily, I wipe the sweat from my brow with my white gym towel. My eyes land on the far side of the room, where my father is standing with the phone to his ear. As a sports agent, he represents some of the biggest names in professional sports. It's how I fell in love with hockey as a kid; he took me to a client's game when I was four, and I was immediately obsessed.

Realization hits me, and my skin prickles. If my dad was on a regular work call about someone else, he'd step out into the hall. The fact he hasn't makes me think he's talking about me.

My suspicions are confirmed when he waves Mark over and they huddle together. They're too far away for me to eavesdrop, but their conversation is brief.

"What did he say?" I ask Mark as he strolls back into the stretching area.

He retrieves a black foam roller from the rack. "New York's general manager wanted to confirm that you were working on your puck tracking, because they had some concerns about it going into Christmas."

The fatigue weighing me down vanishes in a rush of adrenaline and worry. I was drafted by New York when I turned eighteen, and the team keeps close tabs on my performance and development.

"My puck tracking is fine." I tip my head back, chugging my water. "It was just a fluke run of games. Bad puck luck."

I got in my head last month and my performance went sideways for several straight games. I'm still the top goalie in the league, but it makes for a lot of pressure going into the second half of the season. If a first-line forward or defenseman has a rough stretch, the worst that'll happen is they get dropped to the second or third line temporarily. If I shit the bed, I'll be riding the bench.

Mark gestures impatiently for me to move. "Adductors, Ty."

Complying with his order, I position myself facedown on the mat, bracing on my forearms. Then I redistribute my weight to one side, placing the foam roller under my inner thigh.

"You can't luck your way out of a slump," he adds.

I hit a painful knot near my groin, inhaling sharply. "I know. That's why I've been working my ass off."

There's a delicate balance between grinding and burning out, and I walk that tightrope constantly. I'm only human, but the team doesn't care about that. The *competition* doesn't care about that. There's always someone who wants it just as badly, if not more than you—and if you take your foot off the gas pedal for even a second, they'll overtake you in a heartbeat.

◆ ◆ ◆

Once I've showered and gotten dressed, I find Jonah and my dad waiting for me in the hallway to take me to the airport. My mom and sister, Elise, are back home in Beverly Hills, and I've already said goodbye to them. With less than ninety minutes until my flight leaves, my schedule is tight. I'm starving, but I'll have to wait to grab dinner until I get past security.

Dad pockets his phone in his suit jacket, giving me an approving nod as I walk up. "I rewatched some footage of your drills from this week. You're looking sharp out there."

"Not bad, bro." Jonah punches my bicep. "Maybe someday you'll learn how to do the butterfly."

"Oh yeah?" I wrap my arm around Jonah's neck and yank him into a headlock, rubbing my knuckles on his scalp. At sixteen and six foot two, he's six years younger than me and almost as tall as I am, but it'll be a few more years before he gains enough muscle to put up a fight. "Maybe someday you'll learn how to skate."

I let him struggle against me for another second before I let him go, giving him a shove. Jonah straightens with a smirk, smoothing his unruly blond hair. He's an elite right-winger in the minors, a force to be reckoned with on the ice, and a cocky little shit to boot. If I'm being honest, I might admit the last trait runs in our family.

"You've been holding your stance more," my dad notes.

I'm relieved he noticed. "Yeah, I've been working on it with Mark."

Mark McNabb is one of the best goalie coaches in North America, with a mile-long waiting list and a six-figure price tag for one year of private training. I work with him on the side because Boyd doesn't have a dedicated goalie coach. Added to all the other money my parents have invested in my career, the sum is staggering—easily enough to buy a small house. One privilege of many I've been granted thanks to my father's profession.

There are downsides to my dad's job, however. Even though he tries not to push me, sometimes he bypasses parent mode and slips into agenting. The line between what's best for me and what's best for my career is perpetually blurry. I'm not sure I know the difference anymore myself.

When we step outside into the late-afternoon heat, my dad's all-black Lamborghini Urus is idling in a no-parking zone by the doors. We load the trunk with my equipment before piling in, and I let Jonah take shotgun while I sit in the backseat. Leaning back against the soft leather, I stare out the window, watching the palm trees fly by in a blur. Once in a while, I miss California, but it's always a relief to get back to school.

Don't get me wrong. I love my family, but they're so picture-perfect it's like something out of a sitcom. Famous sports agent father, dermatologist-to-the-stars mother. Both younger siblings on the honor roll. Sometimes it feels borderline suffocating, like there's no margin for error. One mistake on my end, and I won't be a true Donahue anymore.

As my father pulls onto the exit ramp leading to Los Angeles International Airport, he glances at me through the rearview mirror. "Remember what we talked about, Ty."

"I will."

Keep your eyes on the prize.

Hockey. Training. School. No distractions.

This year, I've been stricter with myself than ever. Lots of sleep. Nutrition on point. Perfect compliance with my training plan. This doesn't leave me with much free time, which means I hardly go out and I limit myself strictly to casual hookups. No strings, no feelings, no promises. With so much else going on, I can't offer anything more than that.

"There's a world of difference between playing at the college level and the league." Dad turns into the passenger drop-off zone and shifts into park, switching on his hazards. "Some of these guys get their asses handed to them in their first year playing pro. It shakes their confidence, and it's hard to come back from. I want to make sure you're as prepared as possible."

To his credit, he isn't agenting right now. He's in father mode. There's a protective tone to his voice, and I get the sense that he's trying to help me the best way he knows how.

"I know, and I appreciate it."

"You're almost there," he adds. "In another year and a half, all of this will have paid off."

A knot forms in my stomach, and I swallow, trying to quell it. Other athletes would kill for the chance to be in my shoes, so what the fuck is my problem?

Deep down, I know the answer to that.

When you've been given the world, everyone expects you to dominate it.

Chapter 2
HADES

SERAPHINA

I'm not sure whether I should be worried or annoyed. My brother was supposed to meet me at one o'clock to help unpack my vehicle, but I just pulled up to his place and I'm staring at an empty driveway. His black pickup is nowhere to be found.

Confused, I shift my car into park and let the engine idle while I verify the house number. Just like I thought, it matches what Chase texted me. Checking the Maps app further confirms I'm in the right place, so where the heck is he?

As I reach for my phone to call him, it lights up with a message.

> Chase: Sorry, Sera. Ran over a nail and my tire is fucked. Be there as soon as I can.
>
> Chase: If you beat me home, go ahead and let yourself in. Code is 4938.

While the delay is decidedly not his fault, I'm still irritated. Not with him, necessarily, but with life in general, or maybe with the universe. Ever since our mother's cancer diagnosis, I've eaten very little, slept even less, and my sanity is hanging on by a thread. Lately, even the most minor inconveniences feel like the end of the world. Can't one thing go right?

Heaving a sigh, I write him back and set my phone aside. Then I crane my neck, giving my new temporary home a once-over. Towering snow-covered trees frame a gray stucco two-story with sleek black trim and modern, oversized windows. It looks nice enough from the outside. Let's pray the inside doesn't smell like dirty socks and sweaty athletic gear like I suspect. Hockey players are gross, which is why I have some serious reservations about living with three of them. The bathroom situation is probably a nightmare.

I let the ignition run while I sip my decaf vanilla latte, debating whether to let myself inside. Even though Chase claims it won't be an issue, I'm worried his roommates will resent me for crashing here on zero notice. Not having my brother here makes moving in seem all that much more intimidating—but if he takes a long time, I could be sitting out here in my car for a while.

My phone rings before I can decide what to do. Instead of it being Chase like I expect, it's Abby. Stifling a yawn, I accept the call using Bluetooth.

"You're coming out with us tonight, right?" Abby's high-pitched voice booms over my speaker. I've known her since elementary school, and while she's five foot nothing, her personality is stronger than a shot of straight Everclear. "Kendra and Rachel are coming over at five to pregame."

"Would love to, Abbs, but I have to unpack."

Abby huffs. "You're no fun."

"Let me get settled, and I'll see." All this change has left me feeling unnervingly adrift. Back in Arizona, I had a solid group of friends, knew most of my professors, and could navigate the campus blindfolded. It was easy. Comfortable. Familiar.

Now I'm starting all over again.

A vise wraps around my neck, and I swallow another sip of coffee that does nothing to alleviate the tension restricting my throat. On second thought, maybe going out wouldn't be a bad idea. It would help get my mind off things, if temporarily.

"Come on, Sera." Abby's voice climbs. "It's your first night back and we need to celebrate. You can unpack tomorrow. Plus, there's an invite-only event at XS, and I can get us on the list. Maybe you'll see your sexy devil from Halloween again."

"Hades," I correct her, my face heating. The masked guy I hooked up with at a nightclub masquerade ball has reached legendary status within our friend group—probably because he gave me an impressive total of three orgasms during a quickie on the edge of a grimy bar bathroom sink.

"Fine," she says. "Your sexy Hades."

"Psh, I doubt I'll ever see him again. What are the odds of that?" Our encounter fell woefully short when it came to exchanging personal details. The only things I took away from our tryst was that he's hot (obviously), has lots of tattoos (further adding to the hotness factor), and knows where the G-spot is. Somehow, we didn't touch on where he lived, where he went to college, or much of anything else—including his name.

In all of my twenty years on this planet, I've never done something like that before. Or since, actually.

Either way, I was left with the impression that unlike me, our anonymous hookup wasn't out of character for him. He probably wouldn't even remember me. I only wish I could say the same. That night has lived in my head rent-free ever since. Toe-curling, lip-biting, panty-soaking memories I reminisce about late at night when I'm alone in bed with a battery-operated toy in one hand.

"Think it over?" Abby pleads, snapping me out of my dirty daydream. "XS will be way more fun than opening boxes."

It's hard to argue with that. As impractical as it would be, a night out sounds a lot more appealing than drowning in a sea of cardboard.

"Sure," I concede, knowing I shouldn't. "I'll come for a while."

My brother pulls up beside me and gets out of his truck. He strides around the front and raps on my window impatiently, his deep brown eyes fixed on me.

"Let's go, Sera. I have to leave for practice soon." His voice is muffled through the glass.

"Gotta run," I tell Abby, unfastening my seatbelt. "I'll text you later so we can make plans."

Ending the call, I slide out of the car and wrap my arms around my torso to combat the bitter wind howling at my back. Note to self: Buy a massive winter coat, stat. The bigger, the better.

Chase raises his dark eyebrows. "Let me guess. That was Abby?"

It isn't really a guess when she talks loud enough to render a megaphone unnecessary.

"Yup." I press the rear hatch release, watching him in my peripheral vision. He opens his mouth to speak before closing it again without saying anything further. We both know where he stands on the Abby issue. He claims she's a bad influence, but that's ironic considering the source.

"Why didn't you let yourself inside?" he asks, his tone softening. "It's your home too now."

"I don't know. I wanted to wait for you."

We circle around to the back of my SUV to find the oversized trunk and backseat crammed to the roof, which means we have our work cut out for us. In retrospect, I won't need glittery cocktail dresses from sorority formals or out-of-season linen pants any time soon. Should've left some of it in storage, but it's too late.

"Brr." I shiver, bouncing on the spot for warmth. It's the type of cold you feel right down to your bones. The minute we finish, I'm going to boil myself in an hour-long bath with an audiobook.

"Let's get this over with. If we work quickly, maybe we won't freeze to death."

My brother pinches the sleeve of my lightweight white jacket, giving me a withering look. "A real coat might help."

"I have a hoodie underneath."

"A windbreaker still won't cut it in the middle of a Massachusetts winter."

"Did you forget I'm moving from Arizona? Forgive me if I'm a little ill-prepared."

"Don't worry." He hoists up a large box with a grunt. "I'll introduce you to Dallas's girlfriend, Shiv, and you can hit the mall until your credit cards melt. Bailey will be ecstatic to be spared from shopping duty."

"It's a deal." Branching out socially would be a good idea. I love Abby, but she's a little intense, bordering on overbearing at times, and it bleeds into the dynamic with the rest of our friend group. She also parties seven nights a week, which means hanging out with her requires doing the same.

When we get inside, Chase gives me a quick tour of the main and upper levels, both of which are passably clean. A few video game controllers are strewn around the living room, and someone left a carton of orange juice on the kitchen counter, but the dirty sock smell I'd feared is blessedly absent.

Then we move on to my temporary bedroom. Located off the living area, it formerly served as an office I suspect no one ever used and the glass-panel door leaves much to be desired in terms of privacy. It also lacks a closet, which is a fairly serious deficiency in light of my shopping habits. But the price is right (as in, practically free) and both of those problems can be easily rectified by a trip to IKEA.

As we pass the main-floor bathroom, I poke my head in to find only a pedestal sink and toilet. "Um . . . where's the shower? Did I miss it?"

"Both of the upstairs bathrooms are en suites, so the closest shower is on the lower level. You'll have to share with Ty," Chase says apologetically. "But don't worry, he's not messy."

Called it. Nightmare bathroom situation confirmed.

After two more trips to unload my car, the lower level is packed with cardboard boxes, reusable shopping bags, and stray items I shoved onto the front seat. Mysteriously, my trunk is still as full as when we started.

Overwhelm barrels into me, and my stomach crumples. Now that I'm here, reality is sinking in faster than I can process it. I have so much to do in so little time. Unpacking, finishing course registrations, filling out miscellaneous paperwork, handling my change of address, learning my way around an unfamiliar campus, making new friends, attending as many doctor's appointments with Mom as possible . . .

"Sera." Chase gently touches my arm, and only then do I realize I'm crying.

I sniffle, wiping away a stray tear with my finger. "Huh?"

He steps closer and wraps me in a hug, squeezing me tightly against his oversized frame. "I know it's a lot to deal with. I'm here, and we're going to do all we can as a family. But if I'm late for practice, Coach Miller will have my ass, so let's keep this moving."

This is his nice way of telling me to suck it up. Unlike him, I wasn't blessed with expert-level compartmentalization skills. Any worries I have inevitably bleed into all areas of my life, hanging over my head until they resolve or blow up in my face.

I laugh-sob into his shoulder. "Okay."

"Have you eaten? Did you take your meds?" Chase releases me and holds me at arm's length, giving me a concerned once-over.

"Yes and yes." It's half true. Technically, I haven't eaten—unless liquid breakfast counts—but I did remember to take my ADHD medication.

He nudges an overstuffed Lululemon tote with the toe of his white sneaker. "Good. We can order dinner later. Unpacking is gonna take you a while, though. You have enough blow-dryers and curling irons to start your own salon."

"It's called self-care, Chase." My extensive collection of professional hair tools is worth every penny. Besides, you can't put a price tag on feeling good. Not a small one, at least.

"Sure." He smirks, and his gaze falls to the pile of gigantic men's shoes in the entry, recognition glancing across his face. "Hold on a sec. I didn't think anyone was home."

Brushing past me, he strides over to a closed door next to the stairs and yanks it open. He cups his mouth with his hand, leaning through the doorway. "Yo, Ty! You here? Come give me a hand bringing everything inside."

Trepidation seizes hold of me. While I've known Dallas for years, Chase's other roommate is a complete mystery.

Turning back to face me, Chase gestures with his keys. "We'll finish unpacking your car while you organize stuff in your room. That way you can stay inside where it's warm, snowflake."

Wait a minute. Who's he calling a snowflake?

The front door slams shut behind him before I can formulate a sassy retort. It's impossible to match his level of verbal agility. I've been trying ever since I learned how to talk.

Hanging up my jacket, I scan the room and try to prioritize my next sequence of tasks. Should I begin by unpacking my clothes or shoes? Or maybe I should start with my makeup stash. I have a bunch of new products I haven't unboxed yet.

Am I obsessing over minor details to distract myself from all the things in my life I can't control? Yes. Will I continue to do so? Also yes.

Heavy footsteps echo in the downstairs stairwell. Nerves spiking, I glance up as a guy steps through the open doorway. He's tall with full-sleeve tattoos on both arms visible from a distance.

Our eyes lock and I freeze, clutching a hot-pink Lululemon duffel bag in one hand.

Holy hell. My new roommate is hot enough to melt the ice on a rink. Piercing slate-gray eyes; a strong, square jawline; and a full, slightly sulky mouth. His sandy hair is cropped short at the sides, tousled on top in a way that invites you to rake your fingers through it.

Forget everything I ever said about hockey players being unappealing. He's the very definition of appealing.

Something about him is also strikingly familiar, but I can't place what it is.

My focus lingers on his face before drifting lower, methodically searching for some sort of identifying characteristic. A black fitted T-shirt stretches across his broad shoulders and clings to his lean, V-shaped torso, the sleeves showcasing sinewy biceps and forearms. Gray joggers emphasize his thick hockey thighs; that one's to be expected, since Chase said he's a goalie.

Catching myself blatantly checking him out, I force my eyes back up to meet his. He draws closer, running a hand through his hair, drawing my attention to the dark, ornate designs that run all the way along the length of both muscular arms. My gaze snags on the compass etched onto the back of his hand, and my heart comes to a screeching halt.

That tattoo. I remember it.

He might've been wearing a mask the night we met, but I'd recognize those hands anywhere.

Hades.

Chapter 3
TINKER BELL

TYLER

Fuck me.

Heart pounding, I slow to a stop in the middle of the living room, trying to reconcile the identity of the girl standing in front of me. Distinctive rose-gold hair falls around her shoulders in soft waves, framing a heart-shaped face with lush, full lips and whiskey brown eyes I'd recognize from a mile away.

When I draw a little closer, I catch sight of the small gold hoop in her right nostril, further confirming what I already know. This is supposed to be Chase's younger sister, Seraphina, but I remember her as the smoking-hot chick I fucked in a nightclub bathroom on Halloween. Granted, I was slightly inebriated, the lighting had been dim, and she was wearing a sparkly green fairy costume at the time, but it's definitely her.

"Hades?" Seraphina's eyes widen, and the bright pink gym bag she's clutching slips from her grip, landing on the floor with a dull thud.

"Hey, Tinker Bell." I flash her an easy grin, doing my best to appear unfazed. Panicking won't help anything, and judging by the look on her face, she's doing more than enough of that for both of us.

"Oh my god," she whispers. "You can't . . . this can't . . ." The words die on her lips as the front door creaks open.

Chase steps into the living room carrying an armload of stacked boxes, giving us an unimpressed look. "What is this, social hour?" He nods to the pile on the floor. "We've gotta leave soon, Ty. Let's keep it moving."

"Right." I grab the nearest crate and turn toward our former office, now Seraphina's makeshift bedroom. Her attention lingers on me, and my adrenaline surges. It's a foregone conclusion we aren't going to tell her brother what happened between us, right? If she does, being late for practice will be the least of my problems. Revealing that I "accidentally" fucked his sister would be the equivalent of starting World War III.

I hardly ever go out. What are the odds of this even happening?

Seraphina's dark lashes flutter as she blinks rapid-fire. "Sorry. We were just, uh, doing introductions." She picks up the bag she dropped but remains frozen to the spot like she can't figure out what to do next. Fortunately, Chase either doesn't seem to notice how strangely she's acting or he's attributing it to something other than my presence.

"You two can chitchat after we get back from practice." Chase nudges her with his elbow as he passes, following me down the hall. "Though I should warn you, Ty isn't the talkative type. He doesn't like people."

"I heard that," I call over my shoulder.

Chase laughs. "Where's the lie?"

For the next few minutes, I help transfer bags and boxes out of Seraphina's white Lexus SUV while she and I politely ignore each other. Or try to, at least. I keep catching myself stealing glances at her, and several times I catch her doing the same. The tension between us is so thick you could cut it with a skate.

By the time Seraphina's vehicle is almost empty, her room is so full of bags and boxes there's barely space to walk around the white daybed I helped Chase assemble this morning. There's also more pink than I've ever seen in my entire life. A pink desk chair, pink computer, pink hangers, even pink shoes. Guess this explains the pink hair . . . and the pink panties she was wearing on Halloween.

That memory sets off a sudden flashback from that night. My

lips on her lips, her hands on my body, my cock buried deep inside of her. Not to mention, those little sounds she made when she came—three times.

Inhaling sharply, I bite the inside of my cheek and force myself to think about hockey. It only partially works. That night has replayed in my brain a thousand times since. Getting out of this semester alive is going to require ironclad boundaries and a fuck-ton of willpower.

Chase sets a tall stack of books in the entry. "Mind helping Sera with the last couple of things? My tank is empty, and I need to put on my spare tire before practice. I can swing back and grab you after." He gives me an apologetic look, lowering his voice. "Sorry to put you out. She's really overwhelmed with everything and I'm trying to stop her from having a meltdown."

Maybe this is a blessing in disguise so we can clear the air. "No problem."

Once the roar of his truck's engine confirms he's gone, I head for Seraphina's room. She's perched on the edge of her bed looking down at her phone, her mouth pulled into a pout of concentration with her bottom lip poking out slightly.

Pausing in the doorway, I grant myself the briefest moment to observe her, still taken aback by how fucking pretty she is. I've never used that word to describe a girl before. Hot, sure. Cute, sometimes. But she's more than either of those. She's pretty in the way that catches your attention and refuses to let it go.

A thorn pricks at my conscience as an unfamiliar emotion overtakes me. I'm not certain whether it's guilt over my attraction to someone I can't have—or the fact I already did.

Get it together, Donohue.

I knock on the open door, and she glances up, giving me an apprehensive look that mirrors the way I feel. Neither of us wants to have this discussion. Might as well rip off the bandage now, though. God knows we'll be seeing a lot of each other.

Keeping a safe distance while we're alone seems like the best course of action, so I lean against the doorframe, crossing my arms. "Chase asked me to help you finish while he ran out for a sec, but I thought we should talk first."

"Yeah, we should." She grimaces, setting her cell on the nightstand. "This is awkward."

"I hadn't noticed," I deadpan.

Serious talks aren't my strong suit. Blame my sarcastic default setting.

Irritation flickers across her face, and her gaze darts around the room as if surveying for onlookers, then lands back on me. "You didn't think to *lead* with the fact that you play for the Falcons?"

Do I leverage my hockey career to get laid? Sometimes. It's a great way to find like-minded chicks who aren't looking for anything more than one night of meaningless fun. But for some reason, I hadn't felt compelled to disclose that information to Seraphina the night we met. Maybe I was caught up in the thrill of an anonymous encounter. Or maybe—even though I'm loath to admit it—I wanted to be desired for who I was for a change, instead of what I do.

Vulnerability nags at the edges of my mind, and I shove down the last thought.

"You and I didn't do much talking." One thing led to another, and before I knew it, I was giving her a hat trick on the edge of a sink. Not a lot of words were exchanged in the process.

An adorable flush creeps across her cheekbones, spreading all the way to the tips of her ears. "Pretty sure neither of us would've done that if we'd known who the other person was. I don't date hockey players." She clears her throat and juts her chin, squaring her shoulders. "Or fool around with them. Athletes aren't my type. Plus, Chase would flip out."

That stings a little, but she's right. I'd be six feet under within the hour.

"Let's start over," I offer. "Pretend it never happened. And I think we can both agree we don't need to tell your brother."

"Agreed on both points." Seraphina's posture softens and she offers me a smile, but it's weak. She hesitates, her teeth sinking into her bottom lip. "We can still be friends, can't we? I don't know anyone at Boyd other than Chase and my friend Abby, and it'd be nice to have another person to hang out with once in a while. Unless you think that would be weird . . ."

If she were anyone else, I would shut down this suggestion immediately. Not only am I not in the habit of befriending former one-night stands, but the number of people I'm close to can be counted on one hand—and I barely have enough time for them as it is.

Her warm brown eyes gleam with uncertainty as she looks at me, waiting for a response. She looks so hopeful; so vulnerable. I can't bring myself to say no—even if saying yes feels like skating on dangerously thin ice.

Against my better judgment, I cave. "Sure, Tink."

Chapter 4
DRY SPELL

TYLER

"Why so quiet, fucker?" Chase shoots me a questioning look as we step inside the glass double doors of Northview Arena's main entrance.

It's a fair question. I wasn't exactly good company during the drive to practice. I simply stared out a window while a chorus of "you're fucked" played through my brain on repeat to the melody of the national anthem.

"Thinking about practice," I tell him instead. "Mark is breathing down my neck about my puck tracking and rebounds." Just one reason of many I can't afford any distractions—especially not in the form of a pink-haired girl I've thought about more than I care to admit.

My reticence wouldn't be quite as obvious if Dallas wasn't checked out. As alternate captain, he always grills us about our practice plan and game strategy on the way to the arena. If you looked up "Type A personality" in the dictionary, there'd be a headshot of Dallas Ward in his hockey gear. He's been unusually preoccupied today, immersed in some kind of back-and-forth sexting marathon with his girlfriend, Siobhan.

"You sure that's all?" Chase presses.

"Yeah."

Not even a little. I'm still reeling from Seraphina's identity revelation, unsure how to handle being "friends" and stressed as fuck about the possibility of the truth getting out.

In addition, I'm stressed about *being* stressed. Playing goalie means my mental game has to be top tier. Over the years, I've carefully honed the ability to shake off errors without falling apart. Even blowout losses don't faze me as much as they did when I was younger. I don't give a shit about most things that happen on or off the ice. I've specifically trained myself not to. So why does this situation have me so rattled?

Chase's attention lingers on me, evidently unsatisfied with my response. "Are you pissed about my sister moving in? Like I said, it'll be temporary. Probably a couple of weeks at the most."

"All good. Seraphina can stay as long as she needs." My reply comes out a little too quick and a lot too eager. A thin sheen of sweat forms on the back of my neck beneath the fabric of my black T-shirt, the collar tightening around my throat. What the fuck is going on? I *never* act like this.

"I think you'll like her once you get to know her," he adds.

If only he knew.

Because I can't trust myself to behave normally, I forgo any additional verbal responses and merely grunt in assent. We move through the room, greeting the rest of the team as we pass. Dallas, still entranced by his phone, wordlessly trails behind.

Chase snickers, shrugging out of his zip-up hoodie. "Are you cranky because you're having a dry spell?"

"It's not a dry spell." Contrary to what his needling might suggest, my recent hiatus from sex has been fully self-inflicted. My encounter with Seraphina at XS was top fucking tier—and it demolished my interest in anyone else after. I took it as a sign I was spread too thin and decided to focus on other things for a while. Or on one thing, rather: hockey.

At any rate, I've ignored several booty call texts since getting back into town, including one with a topless sneak peek photo attached. I could easily get laid if I wanted to. But I haven't wanted to, and I'm not sure what that says about me.

"Whatever you say, Ty." Chase's gaze flicks over to Dallas, who's standing next to us in a daze and still hasn't removed a single item of his street clothing. At this rate, practice will start and finish without him even noticing. "Quit thirsting over your girlfriend and get dressed, Ward. Miller is gonna bag skate us if you make practice start late."

Unsurprisingly, Dallas doesn't respond. Chase leans over and shoves him. I snort a laugh as Dallas loses his balance, nearly collides with his equipment stall, and staggers half a step before steadying himself. His head jerks up, his mouth pulled into a sheepish grin.

"Shiv's been in Florida for the past week," he protests, putting away his cell. "That's a long time."

Chase narrows his eyes, shaking his head. "You whipped motherfucker."

"Like you're one to talk." Dallas flips him off.

Much to my relief, they start discussing the couples' trip they're planning for Valentine's Day next month, because they are, in fact, both whipped motherfuckers. This change in subject spares me any additional questions about my sex life or lack thereof, so I'm not complaining.

Tuning out their talk about flowers and wine and other shit they've got planned, I turn away and pretend to be focused on getting into my gear to deter anyone else from making conversation. Fortunately, my resting "fuck off" face is strong, and no one attempts to engage.

As I lace up my skates, my thoughts circle back to Seraphina. The basement is solely my domain, and I'm not used to having anyone else in my space. This means I'll have to make a few adjustments, like no more naked trips to the bathroom. Or naked sleeping in general, I guess.

Then again, Chase described her as a social butterfly and claimed she was rarely ever home. Maybe that means this clusterfuck will be a little easier to navigate.

With my luck, probably not.

"Oh, shit. Did you guys see Coach's email?" The urgency in Dallas's voice snaps me out of my thought spiral. When I glance up, he's clutching his phone again, staring at it in disbelief.

"Huh?" I ask absently, fastening my chest protector. "What email?"

Chase makes a face. "Fuck no. He sends like thirty a week. Update this, compulsory training that. Who the hell is reading all of those?"

"No, this is huge. He said—"

A wolf whistle pierces the air behind us. Startled, we whirl around to find Coach Miller standing at the front of the room next to a tall guy sporting a scarlet Falcons hoodie. A guy who does not, to the best of my knowledge, attend Boyd—because he plays on the starting line for one of our rival teams.

"What in the actual fuck?" Chase says beneath his breath, so low that only we can hear.

"That's what I was trying to tell you," Dallas hisses.

I glance over again in confusion. As Woodbine's top forward, Reid Holloway is one of the division's point leaders this season. I can hold my own in net, but there's nothing more unsettling than the sight of him barreling down the ice on a breakaway after he's weaved through our defensive line yet again. He's *that* good.

He's also a total prick, as most opposing players are. Shoots high, crashes the net, and every time we play in their barn, he leads the crowd in chanting my name to taunt me. At this point in my career, I can block it out for the most part, but it's still irritating as hell.

"Good afternoon, gentlemen. Per my email earlier today, we have a new athlete joining us this semester." Coach Miller gestures to Reid's towering figure with his red clipboard. "This is Reid Holloway, our new junior forward. Most of you are familiar with him from his time with the Panthers, where he was one of their top performers. The rest of you will get to know him over the coming days at practice.

"I expect *everyone* to welcome him with open arms and make him feel like a valued member of this team." He levels the room with a steely glare, lingering pointedly on Chase. Given how much time he spends in the sin bin whenever we play against Woodbine, Miller has a point.

Around the room, the guys offer tentative greetings and half-hearted welcomes. Beneath the forced friendliness is a definite undercurrent of reluctance. Changing up the roster in the middle of the season is almost unheard of, and for good reason. It throws off the whole team dynamic.

Reid heads for his new locker, looking about as happy as we are to see him, which is to say he looks miserable. Something catastrophic must've happened to make him transfer so abruptly. I'm mildly curious as to what it might be, but not curious enough to find out.

We finish getting dressed while Coach Miller runs us through the day's practice plan. He's already rearranged our starting forwards, placing Reid with Dallas and Chase on the first line. Chase is wholly displeased with this development and slips on his crimson jersey overhead while muttering a tirade of curses under his breath. At least I'm not directly affected on the ice. I would be pissed about that too.

Everyone else filters out of the dressing room while we hang back, intentionally dawdling to buy time. Chase watches Reid push through the swinging door, then turns back to face us in the empty dressing room. Tension stretches across his face, mirroring the way I feel.

"This is bullshit." He snatches his water bottle off the bench, clutching it like he's trying to strangle it.

"Chill, man." Dallas makes a "calm down" motion with his hands. "It'll be fine once the new lines have a chance to gel. Whether or not you want to admit it, Holloway's one of those players you hate when he's on the other side but like having on your team."

Pretty common scenario in hockey. My money's still on Reid being a dick, though.

When neither of us respond, Dallas continues. "Help me out

here, Ty. You know you'd hate Carter if you had to play against him."

"Fair enough," I admit. "He'd be the fucking worst."

Chase's head swivels to look at me and he levels me with a scowl, but his mouth twitches like he's trying not to laugh. Thanks to his physical playing style and smart-ass mouth, he can get under other people's skin like no one can. It's his God-given gift. Speaking as a goalie, players like that are a huge pain in the ass.

"Either way," Dallas adds, "you're going to have to get over it. Consider it practice for the league."

This is true, unfortunately. Players get traded mid-season in the pros all the time and when it happens, everyone has to move past any prior grudges for the sake of the team. I'm practical enough to understand that, but spiteful enough not to care at the moment.

It's also possible I'm not thinking clearly after today's earlier events. Maybe I'll be more levelheaded after some time on the ice. Practice always helps me get my head straight.

"Gonna be a long semester," Chase mutters.

I grab my helmet, pushing to stand. "Sure is."

Just not for the reasons he thinks.

Chapter 5
ONE & THE SAME

SERAPHINA

> Office of the Registrar—Boyd University
> Declaring a Major: All students must declare a major by the end of sophomore year.

I set my mug of coffee on the kitchen counter and make a face, rereading the page. While I understand the reasoning behind the policy, it strikes me as a little unfair. Unlike Chase, I didn't come out of the womb knowing what I wanted to be when I grew up. He's eaten, slept, and breathed hockey for as long as I can remember. My first memory of him is on skates.

Meanwhile, I can't even commit to a program of study, let alone a career. As a sophomore entering my second semester, it's getting down to the wire. I'm nearly finished with my general education requirements, and if I don't settle on a major soon, I could end up wasting time and money on courses that won't count. The only other alternative would be taking a break from school until I decide. That poses a very real risk I wouldn't end up going back, and I don't have a backup plan that doesn't involve college.

Then again, I don't have a plan that involves college, either. I don't have a plan, period.

Flipping through the Courses and Academic Options section, I do a gut check as I try to picture myself in various programs. English? Not unless romance novels are a major part of the curriculum. Science of any sort? Hell no. Math? An even harder no. Psychology? Maybe...

The page lands on Introduction to Creative Writing.

Curiosity piqued, I scan the course description. Writing has been one of my favorite escapes from reality ever since I was a kid. It started with devouring books at a young age and evolved into imagining my own stories. Eventually I started writing to occupy myself whenever I got dragged to one of Chase's games. Maybe that wasn't very sisterly of me, but in my defense, there were a lot of them. A girl can only watch so much hockey.

I composed countless pieces huddled on the benches of various subzero arenas over the years. Although everyone in my family thinks writing was a phase, one of my best-kept secrets is that I still do it. Mostly poetry, along with some other scraps of fiction that I've buried in the farthest depths of my hard drive, praying no one finds them should I meet an untimely end.

A seed of curiosity blooms in my brain. I've never studied writing formally. The idea is intriguing, if slightly intimidating.

Someone clears their throat behind me. I whirl around to find Tyler standing a few feet away, both freshly showered and fully shirtless. More specifically, he's got a white T-shirt slung over one muscular shoulder, but for reasons that remain unclear, he isn't wearing it. Not that I'm complaining.

Between the miles of ink, the taut muscles, and the trail of fine hair below his navel, it's impossible to look away. I'm full-on staring. I can't help it. Might be drooling a little too. I can't say for certain because I've lost all capacity for higher-order thinking.

When I don't say anything, his mouth lifts at one corner. "Hey, Tink."

Words continue to elude me, and the Boyd U undergraduate programs handbook slips through my fingers, fluttering to the floor.

"Didn't mean to startle you." He bends to pick up the booklet and hands it to me with a grin. "Just needed some coffee."

Still clutching the registration guide, I glance over to discover I've been zoning out in front of the coffeemaker. Next to me on the counter, my freshly poured coffee is now lukewarm. How long have I been standing here? When my ADHD meds kick in, the hyperfocus is no joke. It's easy to get caught up in the wrong tasks if I'm not careful. One time, I lost an entire afternoon to playing Two Dots on my phone.

Tyler tugs his shirt on overhead—which, while slightly disappointing, is probably for the best—and grabs a mug from the cupboard as I step out of his way. When he takes the carafe off the warmer, my brain finishes rebooting and comes back online.

"That's decaf," I warn him.

He stops mid-pour, his brows knit together. "Decaf? Not to be a dick, but what's the point of that?"

"I take medication that can't be mixed with caffeine. I tried once and I'm pretty sure I nearly had a heart attack. But I used to be a hard-core coffee addict and I still like the ritual of drinking it in the morning, so I switched to decaf. You can pour out the rest and start over if you want the good stuff. I don't mind." Clearly, I'm more nervous than I realized, because I just told Tyler far more than he ever wanted to know about my history with coffee. *Good move, Sera. Definitely normal friend behavior.*

"Nah, it's not a big deal. Probably wouldn't kill me to cut back anyway." With a shrug, he finishes filling his cup. Then he props a hip against the cupboard, facing me. The mug is oversized, pushing twenty ounces if I had to guess, and it still looks small compared to his hands.

Dammit, no. Don't think about his hands.

I shift my focus higher, tracing the intricate inked designs that adorn his arms and neck before I reach his face, taking in every feature. Somehow he's both intensely beautiful and powerfully masculine. He's also a lot more intimidating than I remembered.

This situation is like having psychological whiplash. My poor brain is running in circles, scrambling to catch up to what my body already instinctively knows. I'm still trying to grasp that those are the same hands that were up my dress in the bathroom just months ago. The same lips that kissed me on the dance floor until I was breathless and dizzy. And the same guy who murmured filthy, unspeakable things in my ear while he made me come so hard I saw stars.

When he brings the coffee cup to his lips, part of me envies that piece of white ceramic.

Reaching for my mug, I tear my eyes away. "I didn't think anyone else would be up yet."

"I have an early biochem lecture," he says. "Not ideal, but it was the only time they had. What about you?"

"Chronically incapable of sleeping in." My inability to snooze past seven o'clock in the morning is a royal pain in the ass. It doesn't matter how late I stay up or how much I drank the night before. The moment the hour hand hits that cursed time, I'm wide awake whether or not I want to be.

On the plus side, being an early bird means I'm already dressed and ready for the day. I'll have to remain on my primping A game for the duration of my time here. No schlubby sweatshirts with stray nail polish stains, no baggy period pajamas, and definitely no charcoal face masks anywhere outside the bathroom. Might have to burn my ratty old robe for good measure. Not because I care what Tyler thinks, but because . . . okay, I definitely do.

"Ouch. That's rough." He pretends to wince. Reaching up, he palms the back of his neck. Something flashes across his face that I don't quite catch. "Are you sticking around for Chase's birthday party?"

Like I have a choice. Much as my brother likes to pretend otherwise, he's a bit of a diva. He would hold it against me forever if I didn't attend his birthday party. And he doesn't even *like* birthdays.

I want to attend, though. Chase and I were best friends growing up. Even in high school, we hung around the same crowd, and I was hurt that we grew apart after he moved out for college.

If there's one silver lining to this situation, maybe it's that we can become closer again.

"I'll hang around for a bit. It'll be a good chance to get to know more people from Boyd." That Tyler happens to be one of them is merely a coincidence.

He opens his mouth to say something and a quiet knock at the front door cuts him off. It's quarter after seven, which means Abby is more than twenty minutes early picking me up for our 8:00 a.m. spin class. She was also supposed to text, not get out of her car to retrieve me.

"That'll be for me," I tell him, wishing I knew what he was about to say.

Tyler heads back downstairs with his coffee while I go to the entry to let in my incredibly nosy, incredibly sneaky friend. When I bailed on unpacking the other night—because let's face it, that was bound to happen—I ended up at her place being interrogated over White Claws before we went to XS. She wanted to know Tyler's life story. Unfortunately, I had little insight to offer. So far, he's no less mysterious than when he was Hades.

"This isn't a date, Abbs. You don't have to pick me up at the door." I hold it open for her, ushering her inside. Because she's ahead of schedule, I'm not ready to leave yet. I suspect that was by design.

She cranes her neck, searching the house for signs of Tyler, not even attempting to be discreet about it. I silently mouth "he's downstairs," pointing to the basement, eliciting a dramatic pout from her in response.

A few minutes later, we're out the door and her curiosity remains unsatisfied. The front door slams shut behind us, and I wince at the racket, knowing Chase and Dallas are still asleep upstairs. I'm not used to their house yet. Unlike my old apartment, where I had to drag the door shut with all my strength, this one closes itself with the force of a hurricane wind.

"I can't believe you're living with Hades," Abby screeches, pulling on my arm through my coat. Even with us outside, it's entirely possible it was loud enough for Tyler to hear. Or for the entire block to hear, for that matter.

"His name is Tyler." A frigid gust of wind kicks up as I climb into her white Range Rover, issuing a brutal reminder I still need to hit the mall for a proper winter coat. "And it's temporary."

"It's a live-in booty call, Sera. Think of how convenient that could be."

I cross my legs in the passenger seat, trying to ignore the way my body eagerly responds to her suggestion. "That would be a terrible idea."

"Please. You told me all about what happened in that bathroom. With chemistry like that, you two are totally going to fuck again." She throws the SUV into reverse, and the rear tires fishtail as she pulls onto the street.

"Doubtful. The only thing Tyler seemed to care about was making sure we don't tell Chase." I was in full agreement because I have no interest in him becoming even more overprotective than he already is. I'm not even sure what he'd do if he found out. Send me to a hotel? Stand guard outside my bedroom? String a little bell along the top of my door?

Other than the brother issue, Tyler seemed completely unfazed when he learned my identity. Like our bathroom hookup wasn't memorable or noteworthy at all. While that bruises my ego a little, maybe it's ultimately a good thing. It means it'll be easier to move on without any awkwardness.

Though if I keep drooling over him in the kitchen, it might remain awkward no matter what.

"If anything," I add, "I should find someone else to distract me from him." Entertainment in the form of another warm, willing male would get me out of the house, keep me occupied, and most importantly, take my mind off Tyler. It's a solid enough plan. Unfortunately, I have zero desire to follow through with it—especially after seeing him shirtless in the kitchen.

Abby laughs. "Come to our next mixer and we can make that happen."

For some reason, the offer doesn't sound as appealing as it usually would.

She tugs off her knit purple beanie, freeing her unruly copper curls, and launches into an update on her love life. She's caught in the middle of the most complicated love triangle I've ever heard. Or maybe it's a love quadrangle? Love square? There's a hefty amount of history between all of the parties involved, and I could use a flow chart to help keep it straight.

When she wraps up her story, she remarks, "You seem off today."

I feel her gaze on me as I look out the window, watching the snow-covered trees fly by in a blur. "I'm okay."

In truth, I'm thinking about my mom. They caught her cancer early and she's expected to make a full recovery, but it's hard not to worry. Since they live over an hour away, my stepfather Rick has been taking her to chemotherapy and I've been receiving regular updates. I'll be coming to her next follow-up appointment later this month and attending as many as I can after that. Maybe that way, I'll at least feel like I'm doing something to help.

Abby barrels toward a red light and I claw at the seat nervously, my gel nails digging into luxury leather. Her SUV skids for a few feet before coming to a stop halfway into the crosswalk. It snowed again last night, and the plows haven't come by yet. Given that she drives like a speed demon even in the poorest of conditions, I'm rethinking my decision to carpool to the gym.

The rest of our drive goes much the same. I exhale a sigh of relief as she veers into a parking spot, marking an end to our frightening journey.

She kills the ignition, shifting to look at me. "You're going to reaffiliate with Kappa, right?"

"Soon." As a transfer student, I've been given the choice between switching to early alumni status with my sorority or joining the Boyd University chapter. Reaffiliating seems like the obvious choice, but there's something holding me back from fully committing.

"I can get them to rush the application," she sings.

"It's on my to-do list."

What I don't tell her is that every time I go to draft the request email, I freeze. Maybe it's too much change all at once.

Chapter 6
99 PROBLEMS

TYLER

This is the longest round of Screw Your Neighbor I've ever played. Or maybe it just feels that way because I'm trying to stay on my best behavior and I'm not doing a great job of it. It's taking all of my effort to keep my attention focused on the game.

Laughter erupts from the adjacent living room where Seraphina is standing with Bailey and Siobhan. Something inside me stirs, and I grip my beer tighter, channeling every shred of restraint I have to keep myself from looking at her again.

Proof the universe likes to fuck with me? She's wearing one of the tiniest dresses I've ever seen. It's purple, and it looks like it's been painted on. I'd like nothing more than to be the one to peel it off at the end of the night. Since I value having my limbs in working order, that obviously isn't an option. But you can bet your ass I'll be thinking about it later when I'm alone.

My strategy of pretending we never fucked is failing miserably.

"How are you liking Boyd so far, Reid?" Siobhan drapes an arm around Dallas's neck, lowering to sit on his lap. We have more than enough chairs for everyone; they're just attached at the hip. Her plane landed while we were at practice this afternoon, and she was at our place by the time we got home. I'm just glad my room is in the basement, so I'll be spared hearing them "catch up."

Reid snatches his beer off the table, like the very question makes him want to drink. "Been a big change, but the team seems solid so far."

That's a rehearsed answer if I've ever heard one. He sounds like he's being interviewed by a reporter on TV. There's definitely a story behind why he transferred. I've heard rumors ranging from "family reasons" to a disagreement with team management to my personal favorite: having allegedly beaten the shit out of one of his teammates.

"It sure is," Dallas says cheerfully. If he picks up on the evasiveness in Reid's response, he doesn't let on. He retrieves the pile of haphazard cards and shuffles them for his turn as dealer. "We're going to crush Maine this weekend."

Unsurprisingly, Dallas is the one who talked us into inviting Reid tonight. He coined it "Operation Bury the Hatchet" and rightfully pointed out it would be a dick move not to include him when the rest of the team was already coming. Hard to argue with that, so Chase and I relented. I sort of figured Reid wouldn't come anyway, but to my surprise, he did. At least he came bearing a case of top-shelf beer, so points for that.

Ever since Reid showed up at the door, Dallas has been running interference like a man on a mission, hell-bent on smoothing over any past grudges for the sake of team harmony. It's been fine, I guess. At least his presence has taken some of the heat off of me, so no one's noticed how tense I am. Tonight is the only night this month I've scheduled to let myself cut loose, and I'm more on edge than ever.

Dallas leans forward, distributing cards around the table. My willpower glitches, and I steal another glance at Seraphina. She takes a sip of her White Claw, bringing my focus to her perfect, full lips. I shift my weight in my seat, mesmerized. It's impossible not to think of all the other ways I'd like to put her mouth to use.

Almost like she can sense me looking at her, she glances over and our eyes lock from across the room. She flashes me a flirty, knowing grin that I feel myself instinctively return.

Fuck. Way to be obvious, man.

Taking a deep breath, I force myself to look away and refocus on the conversation at the table. Sort of. Everyone is talking about some new movie, but I'm not following along enough to say which.

One by one, everyone else gets eliminated from the game until it's down to Chase and me. It's a miracle I've made it this far with Seraphina distracting me from across the room. What I still don't understand is why I'm so affected by her. It was just sex. It didn't mean anything. It never does. I've never thought twice about it after with anyone else.

"Suck it, loser." Chase throws down the winning card and reclines in his seat with a smirk.

"Yeah, yeah." I wave him off. He's the worst winner in the history of mankind. Dallas just so happens to be the worst loser, which means our house is rife with competitive clashes all the time. Neither has any chill. "Be right back. I need to grab my phone."

I set down my beer and push back my chair, heading for the kitchen to retrieve my cell from where I left it charging on the counter. Realistically, I don't give a flying fuck about my phone. I probably won't even look at my texts. It's mostly an excuse to compose myself.

When I step through the doorway, I find Seraphina standing on her tiptoes, trying in vain to retrieve something from one of the upper shelves of a cupboard. My gaze instantly drops to her full, round ass, watching the already short hem of her dress inch up as she strains to grab whatever it is she's reaching for.

Letting out a cute little sound of frustration, she leans forward and tries again, causing the fabric to ride up a little more. All the blood in my body rushes to my cock, and I fight to contain the groan rising in my chest.

Because I can't guarantee I won't do something foolish, my first instinct is to leave. She immediately turns around and notices me, which means I can't without looking like an asshole.

A smile forms on her lips. "Hi."

"Hey." My voice is huskier than usual. Fuck, I even sound turned on.

"Could you help me for a sec? I'm trying to get the straws." She points to a yellow cardboard carton, then gestures to herself, and I seize the invitation to check her out again. "I can't climb on the counter in this."

"Sure."

Seraphina moves over a few inches, barely making enough room for me to grab the box she indicated without bumping into her. I draw closer and her perfume wafts over to me, the sweet scent giving my dick all kinds of wrong—but also very right—ideas.

My arm brushes her shoulder as I reach up and grab the box off the shelf, setting it on the counter.

"Thanks," she says. If I'm not mistaken, she sounds a little breathier than normal.

"Don't mention it."

Tension coils between us, and the air crackles with electricity. We're standing close; arguably too close if she were anyone else. Despite that, neither of us takes a step back. I couldn't make myself move away if I wanted to.

Her glossy pink lips pull into a sultry smirk, and her dark, thick lashes lower, giving me a deliberate once-over. When her gaze lifts to meet mine, her amber eyes shine mischievously. I can tell she's holding back to see what I'll do.

And fuck me, I really want to do something I shouldn't.

"Hi!" A shrill greeting carries through the air, jolting me back to reality.

We're interrupted by a busty redhead with nearly waist-length hair who rushes up and throws her arms around Seraphina. She's petite, at least half a foot shorter, and wearing a pink dress that's equally as scandalous. Based on her voice alone, I'm pretty sure this is the same girl who picked up Seraphina at the house a few days ago. She's reportedly one of Sera's best friends, which is why I can't explain the uneasy feeling in my gut the moment my eyes land on her. Admittedly, I *am* irritated by the interruption, but there's something deeper to it than that.

A well-groomed older guy walks up and wraps his arms around Seraphina, drawing her into a hug. Now I'm even more irritated. His hand lingers on her lower back as he brings his mouth to her ear, saying something only she can hear. She laughs and shakes her head, swatting his arm playfully. The way he's touching her is familiar, bordering on intimate, and it's highly aggravating. Him wearing a designer suit at a house party aggravates me even more.

After a quick round of introductions, I learn they are Abby and Rob, and decide I like neither. This is further cemented when Abby tugs Seraphina away with Rob trailing behind them.

Several people try to catch my eye as I squeeze through the crowd, taking a seat at the table where Dallas and Chase are hogging the food Siobhan set out. She claims it's to help soak up the alcohol, but I think she likes the excuse to play hostess. Either way, I'm thankful for it tonight. I've never been one to eat my feelings, but it seems like a safer bet than the alternative.

"Isn't that Rob dude a dickbag?" Chase asks. His jaw is tense, the cords in his neck tight.

"Who is he, anyway?" I reach for my half-empty beer, trying to sound neutral. "Your sister's ex or something?"

"Abby's older brother. I've been looking for an excuse to beat his ass for years. He constantly hits on Sera, even though he's way too old for her. The guy is, like, twenty-nine or something. I mean, he's a fucking corporate lawyer, and he's hanging out with a bunch of chicks who still use fake IDs to get into bars."

It takes every ounce of restraint I have to keep a straight face. I *knew* I didn't like him.

Chase grabs a handful of tortilla chips before he continues. "Plus, Sera's been out every goddamn night this week. What's wrong with staying in every once in a while?"

Never thought I'd see the day where Chase sounds like a grouchy middle-aged father, but here we are.

Dallas smirks. "Gee, sounds familiar."

"I'm not like that anymore."

"Yeah, but you're also older than she is. Look at what you were doing in the middle of your sophomore year."

I suck in a sharp breath, bracing myself. A year ago, Chase was still single, getting wasted on the regular, and fucking random chicks like it was going out of style. It's not a flattering comparison.

Chase shoots upright in his seat, snatching his beer off the wooden table. "What the fuck, Ward?" He drains the remaining third in a few gulps before slamming the bottle back down. "Are you trying to make me feel worse?"

"That's, uh, not what I meant." Dallas reaches for a handful of potato chips from the bowl on the counter and takes a bite into one, gesturing with the remaining half. "What I was *trying* to say is I'm sure this whole partying thing is a phase. Lots of people go through it and come out perfectly fine in the end. Like you did."

A for effort, but he's leaving out the part where Chase only turned it around because of Bailey. If he hadn't met her, I'm not sure he'd still be on the team. Or in college, for that matter.

Chase's eyes lock onto the empty bottle in front of him, and his expression grows distant. "I worry, you know? I feel responsible for Sera. Always have since our dad died."

An unfamiliar feeling settles in the pit of my stomach: sympathy. He almost never talks about their father. It must be hard as fuck not having him around. I don't know if I'd be where I am today without mine. He's been there for me through everything, from my first pair of skates to the draft.

"Seraphina was okay at ASU without you," I remind him, trying to set his mind at ease. "I'm sure she'll be fine at Boyd. From what I know, it's a lot tamer here than it is there."

He sighs, shaking his head. "Maybe so, but I'll have gray hair by the end of the semester at this rate. She's such a goddamn handful."

Chase isn't wrong. Until recently, all of my problems were hockey related. Now, as Seraphina giggles on the other side of the room in her should-be-illegal scrap of fabric, I have ninety-nine more. And they're all the words "Seraphina Carter" repeated ninety-nine times.

Chapter 7
HISTORICALLY ACCURATE

SERAPHINA

I'm never listening to Abby again.

Thanks to her, I'm wearing a lavender dress that's more like a shirt. She assured me over FaceTime that it was perfect, but I discovered only too late that I can't sit without the possibility of giving onlookers a peek at my Victoria's Secrets. It wouldn't be as big of a deal at a club, but it's inconvenient at a house party. What am I supposed to do, remain awkwardly standing all night?

Fully worth it to see the way Tyler's jaw dropped when he saw me in this dress, though.

"I'm going to marry her." Chase leans a shoulder against the stainless refrigerator, watching his girlfriend, Bailey, on the other side of the room.

Those are four words I *never* thought I'd hear leave his mouth. But times have changed, because the birthday boy is a little drunk, a lot in love, and the result is pretty endearing—even for him.

A grin tugs at my cheeks. "Oh yeah? When are you going to do that, Romeo?" Seeing my hulking, trash-talking, pain-in-the-ass brother whipped over a girl is so amusing it almost takes my mind off my wardrobe miscalculation.

"As soon as she'll let me." Chase shifts to face me, tilting his head. "What about you? Were you dating anyone back at ASU?"

This is further confirmation he's several drinks deep. Generally, my brother would prefer to pretend that I lead the love life of a nun. Deep down, he knows that isn't the case, but the denial seems to help him sleep at night.

"Single as a Pringle. Same as always." I haven't had a boyfriend since starting college, nor have I wanted one. Based on what I've seen of my friends' experiences, college guys get complacent, gradually putting in less and less effort until you both resent each other and even the sex becomes a chore. It strikes me as a waste of time and energy, at least in this phase of my life.

I have, however, had a generous handful of hookups and a couple situationships. I doubt my brother wants to hear about those.

"Just stay away from the team," he mutters, bringing his amber bottle of beer to his lips. "Most of them are assholes to chicks."

There we go. The reason for this line of questioning has suddenly become crystal clear. Overprotective big brother mode: activated.

"That won't be a problem. I'm not into athletes, especially hockey players." My cheeks heat, and I take a sip of my vodka Sprite to hide my face. While this claim is historically accurate, it feels borderline dishonest right now. They must put something in the water at Boyd, because at least half the guys on my brother's team are hot. In addition to Tyler, they have a new transfer who looks like he could moonlight as a male model. He's a gazillion feet tall, and has tousled sun-streaked hair and a dimple in his cheek to die for.

That's not to say I'm interested in the new guy. My brain has already been hijacked by Hades, his heavily tattooed counterpart. Still, a girl can appreciate nice things.

"That's right," Chase says. "I forgot you like pretty boys."

"No, I don't." The hem of my dress rides up for the umpteenth time and I tug it down, wishing I had some kind of double-sided tape.

He cocks a brow but says nothing. Just gives me that "you're full of shit" look that he's perfected over the past two decades as my older brother.

"Maybe it's a little true," I amend. There's definitely a common theme to my past hookups. Clean-cut and preppy; probably belongs to a frat; drives something ostentatious; bound for an overpaid professional position after college thanks to parental nepotism. I'm not sure why I keep gravitating toward that type when it's like thirty-one flavors of disappointment in the bedroom. There's a reason my nightstand drawer is fully stocked. Either I have to provide explicit, step-by-step directions like some kind of sexual GPS or I give up and resort to taking matters into my own hands after the fact.

Mind you, there's one noteworthy exception to this rule—and he's sitting ten feet away.

Upon further reflection, I think I've got a new type.

"Are you sure you'll be okay while we're away next month?" Chase furrows his brow, scrutinizing my face like he doesn't believe I'll answer him honestly. "You could stay at Bailey and Shiv's if you want. Or go see Mom. She'd like that."

"Can't I just stay here?" I'm not clear on why he's asking this. He'll be out of town for several away games before this trip, and I'll be by myself then too. Does he not trust me without his supervision? Thinks I'll throw a kegger in his absence?

He lifts a shoulder. "Wasn't sure you'd want to be alone with Tyler. Don't get me wrong, he won't do anything out of line, but I get it if you'd rather take off for the weekend. I'm sure he wouldn't be offended."

Oh . . . shit.

Naturally, I hadn't given much thought to my brother's upcoming romantic getaway, which means I also hadn't considered the implications of him and Dallas both being gone; two whole nights alone with Tyler. Just the highly tattooed sex god I hooked up with on Halloween and me. No big deal. Perfectly normal, everyday situation.

"How come he isn't going with you guys?" I ask, playing dumb. Chase is more loose-lipped when he's drunk, and I'm hoping he'll give me some dirt to help fill in the blanks. What good is an older brother if you can't exploit him a little for investigative purposes?

"Ty? On a couple's trip?" He barks a laugh. "Tyler doesn't date, Sera. He mostly just fu—" He catches himself before he finishes saying what we both know he was about to say. Why, I'm not sure. I'm not innocent, and it's not like I have virgin ears. "He's more of a hookup kind of guy. But he hasn't been doing that lately either."

"Oh. I wonder why." Now I'm really pushing the envelope, but it's a chance I'm willing to take. I'm dying to know the answer.

Chase snorts, rolling his eyes. "Who knows? He's a moody fucker sometimes."

Bzzt. Thanks for nothing, elder sibling. I wanted the tea, not a glass of lukewarm tap water. The term "moody" could be used to describe the majority of guys I know.

That men somehow managed to convince the world *women* are the emotional sex is the biggest scam of all time.

"Speaking of moody." I gently touch his arm to draw his attention away from Bailey again. "How have you been?"

His expression clouds over. "Fine."

"Are you sure?" His life basically exploded at the end of last semester, and he's been dealing with the fallout ever since.

"As long as I've got Bailey, fuck it. Everything else will pass."

Fair enough. If anyone is resilient enough to make it through in one piece, it's Chase. I'm glad he has someone to lean on.

"Are you talking about me?" Bailey strolls into the kitchen wearing a little black dress that Chase called "his real birthday present" earlier when he thought I was out of earshot. Her cheeks are rosy, her hazel eyes are glassy, and she's clearly more than a little buzzed.

The way he does an immediate 180 in her presence is nothing sort of shocking. His attention zeroes in on her and his entire demeanor softens like a stick of butter over a hot stove.

Dipping his head, he brings his lips to hers. "I'm always talking about you, baby."

Okay, now we're tiptoeing into nauseating territory. He is still my brother, after all.

"Carter," she whispers, giggling. "We have an audience."

"Right..." He kisses her again before he reluctantly pulls away and wraps an arm around her waist, tucking her against him protectively.

Bailey gestures to the kitchen table with her red plastic cup. "Our game just wrapped up. Do you guys want to join us for the next round?"

It might be tempting—if I could lower myself into a seated position without committing indecent exposure. Maybe if I squeeze my thighs together tightly enough, it'll be okay.

His expression sobers when he notices her drink is empty, and he studies her with tenderness in his dark eyes. "Do you need anything, James? Should I grab you a glass of water?"

Given how they met, it's a reasonable enough question. She reportedly had too much to drink and threw up on my brother's shoes outside a nightclub. The same one where I first encountered Tyler, incidentally.

It's a cuter story than it sounds. At any rate, I find it endearing how innocent Bailey seems compared to Chase, who was doing beer bongs in our basement at sixteen.

"I already switched to water," she confirms, looking sheepish.

Abby walks up and bumps my hip with hers. "Just about ready to go, Sera?"

"Go?" Chase echoes, eyeing Abby like she's some kind of party-crasher.

"Yeah! Rob's got us on the VIP list for XS. Wanna join?"

My brother's lip raises in a none-too-subtle sneer. He looks like he'd rather have a root canal. Bailey discreetly elbows him, an unspoken reminder to be polite he'll surely disregard.

"We're good." He catches my eye and raises his eyebrows pointedly. "Don't you have an appointment with your academic advisor tomorrow? You know, to finish finalizing your course selections?"

Damn. Even I'd forgotten about that. How did he remember? Chase can barely run his own life.

"Not till later in the morning."

He works his jaw. "Uh-huh."

"Come on, Sera." Abby's cold hand wraps around mine, tugging. "Rob's waiting in the car."

Guilt overtakes me, and I hesitate with my feet frozen to the kitchen floor.

"I can stay," I tell Chase. "I don't have to go."

"Do what you need to do, Sera." He waves me off, but I can tell he's pissed.

It's a rock and a hard place for me, because no matter what I do right now, someone is going to be unhappy with me. When I made these plans, I didn't think Chase would care; clearly, I was wrong. But I promised Abby I would go out with her, and I hate breaking my word.

A fully preventable predicament—and also completely my fault.

I came to his birthday party for a couple hours, at least. That should count for something, right? Under normal circumstances, I wouldn't even be here. I'd still be back in Arizona.

Abby looks down at her phone, then up at me expectantly. "Are you coming or not?"

When I hesitate again, she drags me away, and I let her lead me to the door. She takes shotgun while I climb into the backseat of Rob's red Mercedes, greeted by new car scent mingled with his cologne. It smells good in a generic sort of way—you can tell it's likely expensive—but it doesn't affect me on a visceral level the way Tyler's did earlier in the kitchen.

Rob's dark blue eyes meet mine in the rearview mirror. "Glad you decided to come."

"Abby wouldn't take no for an answer." Literally.

Half an hour later, I'm standing in the middle of XS clutching a vodka seven. I'm strangely disheartened knowing there's no chance of bumping into Hades.

"Isn't this amazing?" Abby yells in my ear to be heard over the music, dancing on the spot to the beat.

"It's great!" If I weren't being polite, I might point out it's so crowded inside the fire marshal would have a stroke, the music is so loud it's hurting my ears, and it's oppressively humid. Normally, I'd never notice any of these things and I'd be dancing on the spot right along with her. This should be fun. Why isn't it fun?

Abby steers me over to a group of guys, immediately latching onto the hottest one and leaving me to act as her wing-woman. I have the unfortunate luck of getting stuck talking to the most obnoxious guy imaginable. He keeps calling me Sierra, and he tells me about his Tesla five times in the span of a ten-minute conversation. The real cherry on top is when he asks me if I want to see it, as if that's not obvious code for trying to fuck me in the parking lot.

I'm more than a little relieved when Rob appears from out of nowhere and rescues me from Todd. Or Tadd. Or maybe it's Brad. Not only could I not hear, but I also didn't care.

"Thank you," I tell Rob, leaning against a tall table we snagged near the dance floor.

"No prob." He shifts his weight, moving a little closer to me. Blue and green strobe lights flash in the background, illuminating his features. Everything about him is polished, from his haircut to his perfectly tailored outfit. He looks like he walked straight out of the pages of GQ. Girls have been staring at him all evening, and I can understand why.

"Circumstances aside, I'm really glad you're back, Sera."

"Me too." I'm not certain that's true; it just seems like the right thing to say. I can't objectively evaluate the situation when it hinges so heavily on my mother's cancer.

"You should let me take you out to dinner sometime," Rob adds.

Sixteen-year-old Seraphina would kill to be in my shoes right now. When I was younger, I had a massive crush on him. You know, the typical "lusting after your friend's hot older brother" scenario. Because of our age gap, this went unrequited for a long time on my end—as it rightfully should have.

Things started to shift between us as I got older. Incidental touches, lingering glances, that kind of thing. It continued to escalate until we hooked up on prom night at Abby's after-party at their parents' place. I freaked out the next day because I didn't want to hurt my friendship with her.

Now Rob and I are just friends, and I don't see him as anything more.

"Don't you have a girlfriend?" I ask, confused. "Abby told me about her. Isabel?"

He shakes his head. "We're not committed. Plus, it's different with you."

An uneasy feeling forms in my gut. This sounds like Male BS 101. Does *Isabel* know they're not committed? And "different" with me how, exactly?

Before I can ask what he means by that, Abby butts in between us and sets a fresh drink in front of me that I didn't ask for. She's got Lana and Destiny in tow, two of her sorority friends from Kappa. Both are fine in that they've been perfectly nice to me, but I can't escape the feeling there's some thinly veiled resentment going on.

Destiny flashes me a fake smile from across the table. "Hey, Serena!"

See what I mean? I've met her at least ten times.

Abby drains the last of her rum and Diet Coke and gestures to us with her empty glass. "Why are we wasting our time down here when we have VIP access? Let's go upstairs."

Somehow, that sounds even worse than staying on the main level. "I think I might go, Abbs."

"What? No!" She points to the highball glass. "I just got you a refill. C'mon, Sera. Stay for one more drink. Please?"

"Hang on." Glancing down, I check a text that just came through.

> Chase: Party wound down, FYI. Try to keep it quiet if you come back tonight.

Seems he's still a little miffed about earlier this week. Abby broke a glass in our kitchen after we got home at two in the morning and it woke him up. It was an accident, but I understand his irritation.

I lock my phone, then look back up at the table where everyone is staring at me expectantly. If I leave, I'll be alone. That includes being alone with my thoughts—and they're entirely too loud lately, especially at night.

Chapter 8
TAXI LIGHT

SERAPHINA

Maybe chase is right; maybe Abby is a bad influence.

Then again, it's not like she forced me to drink last night. I'm paying for it today, though. My head is throbbing, my mouth is desert dry, and I'm freaking exhausted.

Given my sad state of affairs, my appointment with my academic advisor to finalize course selections this morning is more than a little painful. What possessed me to schedule that the day after Chase's birthday?

I hit Starbucks to reward myself for surviving and come straight home for an emergency hangover bath. Perching on the edge of the tub, I adjust the temperature on the faucet as the water runs. While I should finish unpacking, storage space has been an issue and it looks like a clothing store exploded all over my bedroom. I'd rather not deal with that today. Or ever. Maybe if I ignore the mess long enough, everything will magically organize itself.

At least no one is home to judge me for being a sloth in the middle of the day. The unforeseen upside to having three varsity athlete roommates is that so far, they're hardly around. Tyler's even less present than Chase and Dallas because he works with some private goalie coach in addition to everything else. I also overheard him saying something about having a nutritionist and a meal plan. I don't know how they juggle everything. It seems exhausting.

My phone chimes on the counter next to me with a text from Abby. We go back and forth for a few minutes until my battery dies abruptly, cutting us short. I forgot to charge it—again.

With the tub half full, I toss in a handful of Epsom salts, a few drops of eucalyptus oil, and some fancy detoxifying peppermint bubble bath, watching the iridescent bubbles multiply on the surface of the water.

Satisfied, I light a few pillar candles on the counter and drop my white terry cloth robe before climbing into the tub. I'd normally listen to a book, but I'm too lazy to grab my charger from upstairs. I close my eyes, basking in the warmth of the water instead. All of my worries slowly melt away. Maybe I'm getting better at compartmentalizing, or maybe I'm just too tired to care.

Once the water has cooled from nearly scalding to lukewarm, I lather up one of my legs and reach for my razor. The blade is midway up my calf when the bathroom door swings open. To my horror, Tyler is standing in the doorway.

He's fully clothed . . . and I'm fully naked.

Our eyes lock and I yelp as the razor slips from my hand, disappearing into the sea of foam. A lightning-quick scan of the room reveals that my towel is on the counter, my robe is on the floor, and both are firmly out of reach. My only option is to huddle awkwardly behind the edge of the tub.

"What are you doing?" I demand, gripping the cold porcelain ledge.

Tyler freezes on the threshold and removes an earbud from one ear, his jaw practically unhinged. "I—what are *you* doing?" He gives his head a shake and averts his gaze, turning so his back is facing me.

"What does it look like? Taking a bath." At least the massive mountain of bubbles affords me some degree of privacy. They're nearly up to my neck, and I'm not sure he could even see anything from where he's standing. Although I can't say for certain that he didn't either.

"In the middle of the day?"

"Is that a crime? Didn't you hear me?"

"Hear what?" He throws his arms in the air. "You weren't making any noise."

"I'm sorry, next time I'll narrate my entire shaving process from start to finish."

Tyler chokes on a laugh. "Why didn't you lock the door?"

"Obviously, I thought I did!" I'm half-laughing too, partly from nerves and partly at the situation itself. Forgetting to lock the door is perfectly on brand for me.

Bracing one hand on the door frame, he hangs his head. A low curse leaves his lips as he scrubs his jaw with his palm, looking down at the floor. "Sorry, Tink. My goalie coach called in sick today, and I came home early to pack before we leave. I'm not used to having anyone in my space, and I wasn't paying attention. Let's implement a knocking rule, okay?"

"Deal."

He shuts the door behind him as he leaves, and once he's gone, I slip out of the tub to lock it for certain this time. Not because I think he'll come back, but for my own peace of mind.

Heaving a sigh, I sink back into the room temperature water and grab my razor again. My heart is still skittering, body buzzing. I try to console myself with the fact that he's already seen my boobs, but when you factor in my bare, sweaty face and messy, off-center bun, it's not a flattering scenario. Him seeing me naked on my own terms is an entirely different story.

I guess it could've been worse. If it had been a few minutes later, Tyler would have walked in on me awkwardly contorted while shaving my bikini line. It would be impossible to come back from him seeing that.

Maybe I should switch to waxing.

◆ ◆ ◆

"Dallas just texted and said, 'Remember to use your profile so it doesn't fuck up my Netflix recommendations.'" Siobhan glances down at her screen, letting out a tiny snort.

"I'm guessing this is a pattern?" I tear open a packet of sweet-and-sour sauce and drizzle it over my second egg roll of the evening. Bless whoever invented stretchy pants, 'cause I'm about to get my money's worth out of this elastic waistband.

"It's been known to happen from time to time." She holds her camera up to the screen, taking a picture of *Heartless Engagement* queued up ready to play. "Dare to dream, Dal. It's chick flick central up in here and it's all under your account."

The guys left a few hours ago for their first road trip of the year. Now I'm curled up on the living room couch with Bailey and Siobhan. It's only seven o'clock and we're already in our pajamas, stuffing ourselves with Chinese takeout while we debate which movie to watch first.

I can't remember the last time I stayed in on a weekend. It's kind of nice. Even though it might not be how I usually spend my Friday nights, I'm having fun, and contrary to what I expected, I don't even have the slightest hint of FOMO. Much as I love Abby, I desperately needed a break from her and the party scene.

A second later, Siobhan's phone vibrates in her hand, and she cackles. "He said, 'I'm going to spank you when I'm back.'"

"Sounds like an incentive to keep misbehaving."

"Right?" Siobhan sets aside her phone and grabs her chicken chow mein off the coffee table. She tucks her legs beneath her, gesturing with her chopsticks. "If anything, I need to step up my game. It'll keep things interesting for when he gets home."

Despite my generally cynical view of college dating, I have to admit their relationship is cute. They're reportedly nine months in and still seem to have fun together. My brother and Bailey seem pretty perfectly matched too.

Too bad those are both unicorn relationships. The exception, not the norm.

"Speaking of that, you should've seen the text Chase sent—" Bailey catches herself and buries her face in her palms, her voice muffled. "Oh my god, that's your *brother*. I'm sorry. I'd rather die than hear about my brother Derek in that context. Forget I said anything, please." The tips of her ears turn red, burning so bright they nearly match her crimson Falcons hoodie.

Siobhan pats her back soothingly. "Aww, it's okay. Chase has corrupted you a little, that's all."

Or corrupted her a lot, by the sounds of it. Even with my bedroom on the main floor, noises travel—and I've heard some things I wish I hadn't over the past couple of days. But good on Bailey for getting hers, because from what I know, her ex was a total piece of shit.

"All good," I tell her, reaching for my sesame shrimp. "I'll pretend he's not my brother anytime you mention it. It'll be the first rule of Sleepover Club."

Bailey reluctantly drops her hands, but she still looks mortified. "Thanks, Sera." She slides off the couch and stands, avoiding eye contact. "I need to pee. Be right back."

Siobhan and I watch her leave, exchanging an amused look. Bailey's slip of the tongue bothered her a thousand times more than it did me. Brother factor aside, I'm not one to judge what consenting adults do in their spare time. I mean, I did have sex with a stranger in a nightclub bathroom.

To my left, a new message pops up on my phone.

Abby: The Kappa girls are waiting for your application! They can't wait to have you as a member.

Sera: Sorry, Abbs. I completely spaced on that. Been swamped with school and unpacking, but I'll get to it as soon as I can.

Abby: Are you sure you don't want to come out? You're missing an amazing party. Lots of hot guys . . .

Sera: Maybe tomorrow. Girls' night in tonight. You know, bonding with my brother's girlfriend and all that.

Abby: Buzzkill.

Considering I've gone out with her nearly every night this week, calling me a "buzzkill" over a single evening is hardly accurate. I've been to some of the local bars so much the staff are already starting to learn my name. Irritated, I lock the screen and toss my cell aside without replying.

"Tell me, is it weird living with Tyler?" Siobhan asks, nudging me with her elbow.

"Weird?" The word comes out as a squeak, several octaves too high. I certainly *sound* weird. Drawing in a breath, I try to normalize my voice. "No, why would it be?"

She laughs, tucking a lock of glossy raven hair behind her ear. "I stayed here briefly after there was a fire at my old place, and I don't think he spoke more than a handful of sentences to me the entire time I was here."

"Ty isn't rude," Bailey interjects, sinking onto the sofa next to me. "He's just quiet. Don't scare Sera."

"I didn't mean it like that. Tyler's a bit of a dark horse, that's all. Hard to get to know."

"He's been nice so far." I cram an entire shrimp in my mouth at once so I have an excuse to stop talking.

"I'm sure the fact that you're gorgeous helps." Her mouth tugs, her blue-green eyes glinting. "You know, I bet you two would look cute together . . ."

I saw us in the mirror on Halloween and can confirm we look *great* together, especially with him between my legs.

For a brief, insane moment, I wish I could tell them the truth about what happened with Tyler. But I know I can't. It wouldn't be fair to ask either of them to keep that a secret.

Bailey playfully pokes Siobhan in the ribs. "Shiv! Stop, you're such an enabler." Fighting a smile, she leans forward and takes the last egg roll from the carton.

"He's hot," I admit. "But even if you remove the roommate part of the equation, I think Chase's head would explode if anything happened between one of his friends and me."

Still chewing her bite of egg roll, Bailey presses her lips into a line and nods emphatically, verifying what I already know. My brother would go nuclear.

"Probably, hey?" Siobhan muses. "As an only child, I didn't even think about the whole brother factor. Plus, Chase is overprotective of people he cares about. Like both of you."

I'm all too aware, which is why I deliberately shield him from certain details about my life. Even with good intentions, his execution is misguided at times.

"Tyler isn't exactly relationship material anyway," Bailey points out.

Good thing that's not what I want him for.

Knowing better than to say that out loud, I lean over and snag a throw blanket from a wicker basket next to the couch instead. I'm convinced Siobhan or Bailey must have purchased some of the décor around the house. There are a few feminine touches scattered around, like the vanilla-scented candle above the fireplace and the matching hand towels in the bathrooms.

Siobhan shrugs. "I guess that depends if you buy into the whole Taxicab Theory."

"Taxicab Theory?" Bailey echoes, her forehead creasing.

"Taxi-what?" I ask.

"It's from *Sex and the City*. I was binging reruns over winter break. Anyway, according to the theory, men are like taxis: when they're available, their light goes on. They wake up one day and decide they're ready to settle down, so they commit to the next suitable partner that comes along. By that logic, someone could have a 'one that got away' simply because the timing wasn't right." Siobhan pauses, taking a sip of her ice water.

"I don't buy that, though," she continues. "I think it's more about the right person. That's why you see those guys who date a woman for eight years without proposing. She issues an ultimatum, he refuses to pull the trigger, and they break up. Then the guy turns around and immediately gets engaged to his next girlfriend two months later. Timing has little, if anything, to do with it. When you meet The One, you won't let them get away for anything."

A memory tugs at my heart filled with bittersweet nostalgia. I swallow hard as I fidget with the cuff of my pink sweatshirt, fighting the wave of sadness creeping in. There's no question that my parents were each other's Ones. Even ten years into marriage, I remember how they slow danced in the kitchen, sneaking kisses while my brother and I rolled our eyes. My father brought flowers every time he got back from being on the road; a dozen roses for her and a single pink one for me. He always looked at her like she was the only woman in the room; in the entire universe even.

I'm not sure everyone gets to have that kind of love, though. Sometimes I think I'm too much to be someone's One. Too loud, too disorganized, too extra, too messy.

Bailey winces, twirling a lock of honey-blond hair around her finger. "I don't know . . . That seems a little harsh to the first woman in that scenario, don't you think?"

"Your relationship is walking proof of what I'm saying," Siobhan counters, scooping up a piece of broccoli from her carton. "Chase's taxi light wasn't on when you met."

"Shiv has a point." Until recently, I wasn't convinced my brother even *had* a taxi light.

"Maybe so, but I think it's more complicated than that sometimes. Circumstances can count for a lot and they're not always surmountable. You were a little gun-shy with Dallas at first, remember?"

"Then I came to my senses because I knew I couldn't lose him. All I'm saying is the light turns on for the right person."

As someone who considers her light to be firmly switched off, I wonder if that's true.

We settle in with the rest of our food and start the first movie, chatting idly during the slow spots. Ironically, it's a romcom about the hero and heroine finding their way back to one another after a series of missed chances. This sparks a debate between us about whether it's an example of the Taxicab Theory or the opposite phenomenon.

I'm on the fence. Partly because I've seen several friends accept bargain basement behavior because he "wasn't ready" or "was focusing on school." And for what? A dude who sleeps on a bare mattress and uses a ratty old towel for curtains? My father treated my mother like a queen. I'm not about to drop my standards for some guy named Tripp who can't be bothered to change an empty toilet paper roll.

That's why I'm inclined to think Siobhan is right; if those guys had been invested enough, they would've stepped up their game. But putting all your faith in the concept of The One has its downsides too. What if you find them and you screw it up? Deep down, I think this might scare me more than the possibility of never finding them at all.

Now switched to silent, my phone lights up with another text. I unlock it expecting it to be from Abby again, and my heart skips a beat when I read it.

> 555-257-9909: It's Tyler. Chase gave me your number and said we should swap in case of emergency. So now you have mine too.
>
> Sera: Only in case of emergency?
>
> 555-257-9909: Or just because.

My breaths turn shallow as I stare at the screen, trying to parse the meaning behind his words. I'm either reading too much into it or not enough. There is no in between.

Chapter 9
21 QUESTIONS

TYLER

> Tinker Bell: For clarity's sake . . . what kinds of texts qualify as 'just because' texts?
> Tinker Bell: Knock-knock jokes, maybe? Riddles? Or did you have something else in mind?

Dallas glances down at my screen. "Who the fuck is Tinker Bell?"

My phone slips from my hand in surprise, striking my kneecap before it lands on the floor. *Motherfucker, that hurts.* Wincing, I grab my throbbing knee as I look around for Chase, trying to gauge whether he heard. Relief washes over me when I spot him on the opposite side of the hotel room, immersed in a conversation with Reid and one of the other guys from the team.

"Just a chick." I quickly snatch my cell off the geometric-patterned carpet. Time to turn off my previews in case this conversation takes a more incriminating turn. Better safe than sorry.

When I straighten in my seat, Dallas is staring at me like I'm unhinged. "You okay, buddy?"

"Yeah. I'm good." A thrill runs through my body as I look down at Sera's message again. The only replies that come to mind are downright filthy, and while her tone seems flirty, it's hard to know for sure via text. I don't want to overshoot and come off as a creep.

> Hades: How about 21 questions? You start.

> Tinker Bell: Okay. Let me think . . .

Tinker Bell: Question 1: How would you be useful in a zombie apocalypse?

I stifle a laugh. It's not what I expected, but I'm not mad at it.

Hades: I'm good with a stick, which means I'd be excellent at decapitating the undead.

Tinker Bell: Plus, your goalie gear would help protect you from their bites.

Hades: That too.

"Just a chick, huh?" Dallas interrupts. I look up to find him studying me with a shit-eating grin across his face. "Is that why you're smiling like a fool?"

"Go call your girlfriend, Ward. Write her a poem or some shit." I flip him the bird and turn my back to him, returning my attention to our conversation.

Hades: Question 2: Large city, small town, or countryside?

Tinker Bell: Who do you think you're talking to, Hades? City girl all the way.

Hades: That tracks. City for me as well.

Tinker Bell: Question 3: Would you rather give or receive a gift?

Hades: Give, for sure.

Tinker Bell: Receive, obviously. *princess emoji*

Receive, huh? There are lots of things I'd like to give her, starting with . . . My cock perks up, my hand tightening around the phone. Then I glance around the room and remember where I am—as well as who I'm with. I shouldn't be texting Sera in the first place, and I definitely shouldn't be picturing the filthy things I am right now.

Giving my head a shake, I force my mind out of the gutter.

> Hades: Question 4: How much pink is too much pink?

Tinker Bell: The limit does not exist.

At her response, my mouth pulls into another goofy grin. I'm not a big texter, especially back and forth. Normally, I'd have written some half-assed reply and put my phone away for the night. Then again, normally I wouldn't have left the communication door open with my "just because" text in the first place.

> Hades: I'm not so sure about that. Think I'm gonna have to draw the line at a pink car.

Tinker Bell: No way. Look up the Porsche Taycan in Frozen Berry Metallic and tell me it isn't amazing.

> Hades: Fair enough. That's pretty sick.

Tinker Bell: #goals
Tinker Bell: Question 5: Most recent picture in your camera roll?

> Hades: image.jpg

It's a full-length shot of my left sleeve after it was touched up last week. Not overly recent, but it's the newest picture I have. In addition to not texting much, I don't take many photos. With my schedule, what would they even be of? The inside of the locker room?

An incoming call interrupts me before she replies, and my father's name comes up on the call display. While it's nearly ten o'clock here, it's not yet seven where he is in LA. I watch the screen flash for a moment before I push to stand. Dallas throws me a questioning look, and I point to the door with my phone. It's hard to get privacy on the road, especially this close to curfew.

I lean against the wall outside our room and swipe to accept, keeping my voice low. "Hey, Dad."

"Nice work out there this evening," he says warmly.

"Thanks." A shutout always feels good, but it feels even better knowing he watched the game and saw it for himself.

"Big news." Excitement laces his voice. "I just got off the phone with Gary, and New York said they've been impressed with your performance over the last couple games. If you remain consistent, they're thinking of taking you on to train with the team this summer. Personally, I think it's a lock."

Surprise overtakes me and I pause, temporarily lost for a response. I should be thrilled at this development—it's what I've been working my ass off for day in and day out—but I have some mixed feelings.

"That's great." My voice is flatter than I intend it to be. I should sound excited. I should be excited.

"I've spoken to Mark about this already, and your puck tracking has come a long way lately. We think it's time to shift your training plan. More focus on your rebounds and lateral movement . . ." He continues while I try to fake enthusiasm, still processing my abrupt change in summer plans. Just one aspect of many I have no control over when it comes to my life.

We chat for a few more minutes before he tells me I should get some sleep, even though we both know I'll be up with the guys for at least another hour. I promise to call him when I get home tomorrow so we can go over things in greater depth.

Lingering in the hallway, I mull over his news as I try to untangle my thoughts. Being invited to train with the team is a huge opportunity, and it's one that most prospects never get. Investing in an athlete this way shows the organization is serious about fostering a successful long-term relationship, which is a great sign for my future.

I should be grateful, and I am. But hockey consumes my entire life during the academic year, and extending it to the summer will eliminate the only break I get. Without some downtime, I'm worried I'll lose my edge.

It's no different than what my life will look like once I turn pro, though.

I need to suck it up. Get used to it. Cope better.

A familiar sense of anxiety creeps in. My gaze drops to my hands, then slides up to my arms. I've just about run out of blank real estate on both of them. Getting tattoos is inexplicably calming; almost like my own version of therapy. When everything else feels like it's out of my control—from my diet plan to my workouts to my future—it's one thing I have total autonomy over.

At any rate, collecting ink is a hell of a lot healthier than some of the other things I used to do to cope.

Scanning my key card, I wait for the green light to flash and tug the hotel room door open. As I step back inside, my phone vibrates.

> Tinker Bell: Hot. Can I see the rest of your tattoos sometime?
>
> Hades: Any time you want.
>
> Tinker Bell: Here's my most recent picture . . .
>
> Tinker Bell: image.jpg

When it loads, I nearly drop the phone again.

It's a selfie of her lying on her side in bed, a curtain of silky pink hair partially concealing half of her face. Espresso eyes woven with flecks of honey and gold stare back at me, her full lips slightly parted. There's the slightest hint of cleavage at the bottom of the screen, but it's not the focus of the photo.

The least explicit picture I've ever received, but by far the hottest. It's the perfect tease.

"Having fun talking to your girlfriend?" Dallas smirks, pulling off his T-shirt overhead. Mental note to strangle him with it in his sleep.

Chase strolls out of the bathroom and stops cold, his green toothbrush hanging halfway out of his mouth. "Say *what* now?"

"I don't have a girlfriend."

Dallas juts his chin at me. "Lies. He's been texting with some chick all night."

"It's not like that, Ward."

But even I'm not sure that's the case.

Chapter 10
CIRCUMSTANTIAL EVIDENCE

SERAPHINA

I've almost survived my first day of classes.

This includes successfully navigating a new campus, even though my courses are not so conveniently located around the outer boundaries of Boyd. Staying on schedule without getting lost may not sound like an impressive feat to most people, but thanks to the ADHD symptom lottery, I'm both directionally challenged and prone to time-blindness, so I'm calling it a win.

Fueled by an infatuation high, I practically skip across campus to my last lecture of the day, my first session of Introduction to Creative Writing. Tyler and I have worked up to question fourteen and our conversation shows no sign of stopping anytime soon. Despite the name of the game, I'm pretty sure we'll keep going past twenty-one.

I make a last-minute stop at the campus Starbucks en route, and while I'm not late, I'm not as early as I'd like when I arrive. The seats are already partially filled up, students scattered around the room. Obviously I don't know a single soul, so I scan the lecture hall in search of someone who looks friendly. I settle on a brunette in the middle row who's rocking a cute oversized plaid jacket. Can't explain why, I just get a good vibe from her.

She flashes me a small smile as I take the seat on her left.

Setting my decaf mocha off to the side, I quickly unpack my things from the black hole otherwise known as my bag. Judging by her array of colored pens and pencils and sticky notes, my seatmate is significantly more organized than I am.

Our instructor introduces herself as Professor Durand but insists we call her Maxine. I listen, rapt with attention as she tells us about her publishing career in fiction and nonfiction as well as the various publications she's written for, ranging from *Vogue* to *The New Yorker*. In addition to magazines, she's been featured in numerous anthologies and has several traditionally published books of poetry. I make a note to check those out later.

It's legitimately fascinating, and for the first time in my life, I don't catch myself zoning out during class even once. This feeling is what I'd hoped college would be like all along. That thirst for knowledge, the excitement to learn more. I'd all but given up on finding anything that genuinely interested me.

Maxine dismisses us a few minutes early and instructs us to introduce ourselves to our classmates with the extra time, explaining that we'll be doing some partner work for peer editing in the near future. The prospect of showing someone else my writing—let alone having them critique it—sounds more than a little terrifying, but I guess it's what I signed up for.

Turning to me, the dark-haired girl offers me a shy smile. "I'm Chloe."

"Seraphina. Sera's fine too." Or Tink, if you're Tyler. *Shut up, brain. Now isn't the time.*

"How are you liking class so far? Isn't she amazing?" Chloe nods to the front of the room, where Maxine is sliding her lecture notes into a Louis Vuitton tote. "My friend took this class last year and raved about her."

"Totally," I agree. "She reminds me of Sylvie from *Emily in Paris*, only a lot less passive-aggressive and significantly nicer."

She laughs, placing her pastel highlighters into a zippered case. "Oh my god, you're right. Are you a creative writing major?"

Until recently, I hadn't realized that was an option. I've been considering it as a serious possibility, but it's too early to say just yet. I'm not sure I'll even like this class.

"Undeclared but trying to decide soon. How about you?"

"Pre-dentistry."

"Wow. That sounds intense. Good for you." Suddenly, I feel

woefully outmatched. Bet that's heavy on science. Probably lots of math too. I wouldn't last a day.

"It's pretty demanding," Chloe admits, zipping her black book bag. "This is my one and only fun class. The rest are biology, calculus, that kind of thing."

She pushes to stand, and I do the same, leisurely walking alongside her up the staircase leading to the doors. Since this is my last class of the day, I don't need to sprint across campus like I otherwise would. It's like the fates conspired to ensure I hit my 10,000 steps a day before noon.

We linger in the foyer chatting for a few more minutes before we exchange phone numbers, then Chloe heads to her next lecture while I start for the parking lot outside. It feels nice to have a new potential friend; someone not connected to Abby or my brother. Actually, it's not all that different from what I assume dating is like—I'm a little nervous and wondering whether she actually wants to hang out with me sometime or if she was merely being polite.

Either way, for a Monday, today is shaping up better than I expected. Even the weather doesn't seem as bad as I push the doors open and brave the bitter January cold. My gigantic new parka probably helps too.

When I climb into the driver's seat, Tyler texts me again.

Hades: Question 14: What book
are you currently reading?

Tinker Bell: I plead the fifth.

Hades: attachment: voice message
"Nice try, but that's not a real answer.
Cough up the title, Tinker Bell."

Letting the engine idle in park, I press play and listen to Tyler's message for a third time, my cheeks tugging at the delicious way his voice gets a little more growly with each word. Other, much lower parts of my body are responding too.

God help me, I'm getting turned on in the middle of a strip mall parking lot.

I indulge in a fourth listen before I reluctantly lock my phone and tuck it away in my console. My stomach is full of butterflies, and I have no idea how I'll be able to look him in the eye without blushing when I see him later.

I decide to leave him hanging for a while before I reply, though. You know, to keep him on his toes. I'm also stalling because I'm in the middle of an especially smutty book at the moment, and I have to summon the courage to admit it to him. Why this particular question fazes me, I'm not sure. It makes no sense in light of everything else.

◆ ◆ ◆

My plan to leave Tyler hanging backfires—because he's unexpectedly home when I walk inside. I didn't see his vehicle parked outside, but I find him standing in the entry with his winter coat on like he's about to walk out the door. He's occupied with something on his phone, seemingly oblivious to my arrival.

Like usual, he's dressed in head-to-toe black. It seems patently unfair that a guy can get away with such a monochromatic wardrobe and still look so hot.

When the door slams shut behind me, his head snaps up and he breaks into a smile that gives me the butterflies all over again. "Hey, Tink."

"Hi." Slipping off my winter boots, I linger in the hall.

His focus stays fixed on me, and his smile gentles. "How was your day?"

"Good." One-word answers seem to be all I can formulate at the moment.

"Good." Something about his tone makes me feel warm and fuzzy, like a hug. It's new, and I like it.

Curiosity jump-starts my brain. "Are you headed out?"

Tyler looks confused for a second, then his eyes flick down to his phone like he'd forgotten it was in his hand. I'm starting to realize I affect him more than I thought. He's just better at hiding it.

"My car was being serviced at the dealer. I've been trying to book their shuttle to come pick me up, but the app is trash. I was about to call them."

"I can take you if you want."

"You sure?" His brows lift. "I don't want to make you go out of your way if you have other stuff you need to do."

Even if I did, I have no idea what they are anymore.

"I don't mind. That's what friends are for, right?"

He trails behind me into the garage, which Dallas has kindly agreed to let me use during my temporary stay, and pushes the overhead door button on his way by. We climb into my car and slam the doors behind us, sealing out the cold. The scent of his cologne fills the interior, beckoning me to get closer. Trying to be discreet, I draw in a lungful, savoring the notes of driftwood and citrus. He doesn't just smell good; he smells downright addictive, like an expensive habit I can't afford.

Shoving the last thought aside, I press the brake pedal and push the red ignition button on the dash. As the engine roars to life, so do the speakers.

"Her soaking pussy clenches around me, and I drive deeper, thrusting in perfect tempo with her moans..."

Oh no. No, no, *no*.

My stereo is connected to my phone, which is still open to my audiobook—and chapter twenty-one is Smut City.

I squeal, hitting the pause button with ninja-like reflexes. It's so quick I may break some kind of world record. The baritone voice vanishes, and the interior of the car falls unnaturally silent. Heart hammering, I grip the steering wheel, trying to steady my breath.

Exposed by Bluetooth. Goddamn technology.

Tyler chuckles. "Oh, don't turn that off on my account. Sounds like it was getting good."

He presses the illuminated play button, switching the sound

system back on. I reach for the controls, but before I can shut it off again, his large hand captures mine, handcuffing my wrist with his thumb and forefinger. My entire body comes alive at the contact.

Testing him, I make a halfhearted attempt to free myself from his grip. His expression darkens, his hold tightening. A shock of desire runs through me, liquid heat pooling in my core.

"You're not done until I say you're done."

"Sera, you naughty girl." Spoken in a husky timbre, the words are agonizingly seductive—especially with him still restraining my wrist.

Lust, desire, uncertainty; a million emotions overtake me all at once. Factoring in my mortification of moments ago, it makes for a highly confusing combination.

Steel gray eyes drop to my mouth, lingering for a beat before lifting to meet mine. Our gazes stay locked as the male narrator praises the heroine, sprinkling in hints of mild degradation. It's the icing on the dirty talk cake, both undeniably appealing and impossible to ignore.

Tyler's mouth tugs into a devilish grin. "This is why you didn't want to tell me, huh?"

My lips part as I search for a response. Nothing. I have nothing to offer. My brain has been wiped clean. Other parts of my body have seized control, and they aren't the ones responsible for sentence formation—or rational choices.

All I can do is nod.

The audiobook continues in the background. My breaths turn progressively shallower until I'm nearly panting. A needy throb settles between my thighs, growing more intense with every beat of my heart. Tyler's grin fades and he watches me intently, studying my reaction.

Suddenly, I remember the stereo dials on the steering wheel. Using my free hand, I turn the volume all the way down, silencing the naughty narrative before the hero reaches a climax that's rapidly approaching. Not a moment too soon either. I was dangerously close to having my first hands-free orgasm right along with him.

"That was highly circumstantial." I sound every bit as breathless as I feel. "There are only a handful of sex scenes in the entire book. One could say I'm a victim of bad timing."

"I was just teasing you, Tink." His calloused thumb runs along the outer edge of my palm, gently caressing. The unexpected intimacy behind the gesture makes my stomach do a cartwheel. "Though I have to admit I'm curious."

"Curious about what? Romance novels?"

"What makes you tick."

"Who said this makes me tick?"

He cocks a brow. "Why else would you be listening to it?"

"For the plot," I say, working to keep a straight face. "Obviously."

"Which happens to include the heroine getting destroyed in the bedroom. Repeatedly, if I had to guess."

Technically, the hero's railing her on the ninth hole of a golf course after hours, but I'm not about to correct him on that minor detail. Because he's right—this *is* what gets me going, which is why letting him know about it makes me feel extra vulnerable.

"Ergh." I face-palm with my free hand, hiding my face to conceal the telltale warmth spreading across my cheeks. When I peek between my fingers, he's regarding me with so much tenderness that my embarrassment abates slightly.

"It's all good, Ser. No judgment here, I promise. Knowing you listen to that stuff is fucking hot." He squeezes my hand reassuringly, then releases it. My skin turns cold without his touch, and I clamp down on the urge to reach for him again. "If it makes you feel weird, I'll drop it. I won't turn it back on again. You have my word."

I'm not sure if it's intentional on his part, but being let off the hook so easily feels like a challenge. One that I can't back down from.

Besides, I listen to steamy stories all the time while driving. I'm a certified spicy romance connoisseur. There's no reason this scene should affect me one iota more than normal simply because Tyler happens to be sitting next to me.

More than six feet of tall, heavily inked hotness.

Within arm's reach.

Close enough that I keep catching hints of his intoxicating scent.

Who am I kidding? I'm absolutely affected—both by his presence and the book itself. But it's not like I can admit that to him.

"No." I sit up, squaring my shoulders. "It's fine. We can listen to it if you want."

He hesitates for a second, like he's going to say something. Instead, he turns the audiobook back on and adjusts the volume.

"Take it," the narrator growls. *"That's right, just like that."*

"Hmm," Tyler murmurs, stroking his jaw.

I steal a glance at him as I shift into reverse. "Hmm?"

He waves me off. "Just taking notes, don't mind me."

"Good girl."

A thunderbolt of desire jolts between my legs. I squeak, slamming on the brakes halfway down the driveway. The car screeches to a halt, sending us both lurching forward, our seat belts locking up to keep us in place.

He casually places his forearm along the door and turns to face me, a ghost of a smirk playing on his lips. "You okay over there, Tink?" He juts his chin. "We can switch places so I can drive, if you need."

Nice of him to offer, but not having both of my hands occupied could make this even more hazardous. Then I might touch him—or myself.

"No, I'm fine." I clear my throat. *Chill, Sera.* "Thought I saw someone on the sidewalk behind us."

He makes no attempt to hide his smile. "Uh-huh."

Easing off the brake pedal, I slowly idle the SUV in reverse until I clear the sidewalk. Shoulder checking, I make a ninety-degree turn and start down the street while the filthy narrative continues in the background.

As I pull up to the first red light, the scene switches into the heroine's perspective.

"His fingers wrap around my throat and his grip tightens..."

Next to me, Tyler shifts in his seat. His large hands flex, the blue veins in his forearms prominent, and I suppress another squeak. If only it were possible to cross my legs while I'm operating the vehicle.

Fortunately for both of us, I manage to compose myself before the traffic signal turns green. Sort of. Except somewhere along the way, it's grown downright sweltering inside my vehicle. The climate control is still set to the same moderately warm temperature, and yet...

"Is it hot in here?" My shaky fingers land on the dial, turning down the heat until the air conditioning is on full blast—even though it's subzero outside.

A muscle in his cheek tugs. "Think that's just you, Ser."

"Could be," I rasp.

True to fiction, the hero has superhuman stamina and we're treated to a full-blown sex marathon for the entire duration of the ten-minute drive. Missionary, cowgirl, oral—you name it. By the time I pull into the dealership parking lot Tyler has directed me to, my panties are soaked and I'm so close to the edge a gentle breeze could get me off.

I shift my car into park, waiting for him to unfasten his seat belt, but he doesn't. He leans back in his seat, looking up at the roof. His chest rises and falls with a heavy sigh. A telltale bulge in his jeans tells me I'm not the only one who's hot and bothered.

"Is this the right place?" I bat my eyelashes at him, feigning innocence.

"Yeah," he mutters. "Just give me a sec."

Chapter 11
FALSE ALARM

TYLER

Edging via audiobook. That's a new one.

After I got my raging hard-on under control—no small feat after seeing Seraphina so turned on she was literally squirming in her seat—it was a quick stop to pick up my Audi, because I'd already paid for the service online. By then, it was well past five and we were both starving, so I offered to order takeout when we got back.

Half an hour later, we haven't settled on any food yet. We've been too busy talking... and flirting. It's risky to be hanging out alone with her like this, but at least Chase is crashing at Bailey's for the night, so he won't randomly walk in. I'm not sure where the hell Dallas is. He's going to have some serious questions if he comes home.

From the couch beside me, Seraphina nudges my foot with hers. Since we've gotten home, we've crept progressively closer and closer. Between playing twenty-one questions over the weekend and getting horned up listening to her spicy book earlier, I have no idea what the fuck we're doing. I don't even care. There's no one else I'd rather have sitting next to me right now.

"You don't have to buy me dinner." She grabs her iced tea, smiling around her clear glass straw as she takes a sip.

"We don't have any groceries," I remind her. Not surprisingly, food doesn't last long with three athletes under one roof. The cupboards are either totally stocked or depressingly barren.

"True." She sighs, ice cubes rattling as she stirs her drink. "You guys demolished every scrap of food we had. The fridge is pretty empty, and the freezer is even worse. Someone must've gotten desperate, because even the frozen vegetables are gone. I was going to place an order with FoodSave for delivery later. How the hell do you survive?"

"We eat at school a lot." One major perk of playing for Boyd is that the hockey team has a rotation of chefs on staff who prepare healthy breakfasts, lunches, and dinners Monday through Friday, plus pregame dinners on Saturdays. Things like protein pancakes and turkey sausage; grilled chicken wraps and raw vegetables; roasted sweet potatoes and seared steak. Being able to grab a meal or snack any time I need is a lifesaver, especially when you eat as much as I do.

"Plus, constant grocery shopping," I add. Except one of us doesn't keep up their end of the shopping bargain and by one of us, I mean her brother. "We take turns cooking when there's food."

"I like to cook, but I'm terrible at cleaning as I go, and I always end up making a huge mess. You can add me to the rotation as long as someone else is on dish duty." She wriggles out of her black cardigan to reveal a pale blue blouse with a deep V-neck. A delicate gold chain drapes around her neck, a teardrop crystal pendant hanging from it. She's dressed up more than usual. I think it's because she was nervous for her first day of classes at Boyd, but I suspect she'd never admit it.

"Sold. You cook, and I'll clean."

"Maybe one of us should think about joining Costco," she adds, pushing her half-empty iced tea aside. "You guys eat in bulk, so we might as well shop that way. I don't understand how we went through *three* bags of chips in one afternoon."

"Ask Carter and Ward. They eat junk like it's going out of style." Reaching over the coffee table, I pass her a stack of menus. Our fingers touch ever so slightly, and I try to ignore the effect it has on me, because I'm a grown-ass man who definitely shouldn't be excited by something as minor as playing handsies.

"And the entire package of cheese tortellini?"

"That one's on me," I admit. "In my defense, goalie gear is heavy. I burn a lot of calories on the ice."

Seraphina rolls her eyes, but she's fighting a smile. "Not to mention whatever happened to the string cheese, one dozen apples, two loaves of bread, the variety pack of Greek yogurt, and, most upsettingly, my emergency pint of strawberry cheesecake ice cream." She holds up a hand, ticking the items off on her slender fingers.

Shit.

"Er . . . it was my cheat day, and I didn't know that ice cream was yours. Sorry, Tink."

Her eyes widen at my confession, and she smacks my hand. "That was Häagen-Dazs, Hades. The good stuff. If you mess with my stash of pink Starburst, our friendship is officially over."

"Noted. I'll replace the Häagen-Dazs, and I won't fuck with the Starburst. Promise."

"I'm going to start keeping food in my room," she grumbles, but her foot is still resting against mine. "Maybe get a mini fridge with a lock on it."

"As long as it's pink."

"Obviously." A smile plays on her lips. "I hope you realize you owe me now."

"Name it and it's yours." It comes out before I can stop myself, and it sounds even more suggestive than I intended.

She reaches across the couch and playfully boops me on the nose. "I'll keep that in mind."

◆ ◆ ◆

Goaltending hones your patience, and right now, that's a good thing. Seraphina has been leafing through the menus for various local restaurants for over twenty minutes, flipping back and forth like it's a life-or-death decision. I'm trying not to rush her, but my stomach is growling so loudly it sounds like there's an angry rottweiler in the room and I'm going to gnaw off my own arm if I don't get something to eat soon. I'd happily take food from any or all of these restaurants at this point. Hell, we can hit up three or four places if that's easier.

She scrunches up her mouth, inclining her head as she studies a yellow-printed leaflet for Thai Boat.

"What do you want to order, Tink?" I ask.

Her head snaps up, her dark eyes wide. "I have no idea. I've never seen so many menus in my life. There are too many options." She waves a hand at the list, growing frantic. "Whenever I go to restaurants, I always check online ahead of time, because I'm indecisive and I freeze on the spot. And now there are, like, fifty restaurants to choose from."

"I can give you some suggestions to help narrow it down if you want."

"Can you just pick a place and order a few things for us to share? I'm not picky."

"Any dealbreakers?" I ask, gently prying the stack of leaflets from her hands. I'm beginning to see that she isn't quite as easygoing as she tries to make everyone else think. And I don't mind that—at all. I'm just not sure why she puts on a front.

"Mushrooms and olives." Pausing, she shudders. "No organ meats either."

It's not a lot of direction to go off, so I verify the order with her before I submit it online to make sure we've got things she'll eat. An hour later, we're surrounded by a sea of nearly empty takeout containers.

"Guess how I know you were the last one to empty the dishwasher?" I offer her the last samosa, then take it for myself when she declines.

"How?" She sets down her fork, cocking her head.

"Because you left half the cupboards open." This isn't an exaggeration. It might have been more than half.

Seraphina bursts out laughing. "That isn't my fault," she protests, gesturing with a piece of coconut naan. "That's an ADHD thing. I can't help it. It's like I legitimately don't see them."

"Honestly, I think it's cute. It's your calling card, like a reminder Tinker Bell was here." It made me smile when I saw it this morning. She leaves a little trail of destruction everywhere she goes, and I find it oddly endearing.

Don't get me started on our shared bathroom. Between the jars, vials, and tubes, there's zero counter space to be had. The entire room smells delicious 24/7, so I can't complain too much. I'd never live it down if anyone else knew I secretly sniffed her coconut shampoo every time I'm in the shower.

"Shut up, Ty." She shakes her head, still giggling.

"Question fifteen," I say, leaning my forearms on my thighs. "What's your major?"

It's the wrong use of a question. Her mouth pulls into a frown, and she looks away before answering. "I . . . don't know yet. I need to decide soon, but I haven't found the right fit."

"That's okay. There's no rush."

"Well, there kind of is." She fidgets with her napkin, refusing to meet my eyes. "I have to declare my major before the end of the semester. But like I said, I get analysis paralysis and have trouble making decisions. What about you?"

"Biochemistry."

Her brows tug, eyes shining with curiosity. "You're smart, huh?"

"I don't know about that. I just like science. It explains the way things work."

"On that note, what would your career be if you didn't play hockey?" she asks, immediately catching herself. "Oops. Question sixteen. I forgot to add that."

"In another life, I would've been pre-med with the intent to go into medical research or something surgery related. Guess that's my backup plan should I ever get injured."

"Do you worry about that?" her voice softens.

I pause, pushing the last grains of saffron rice around my plate while I debate how to respond. "Sometimes." This is something I rarely admit even to myself. Denial is a powerful drug.

"There are no guarantees I'll ever set foot on the ice in a single professional game."

That's a difficult truth to digest when you consider how much of my existence revolves around hockey. It's more than a little sickening to think I've devoted the better part of my life to pursuing something that may never come to fruition. I'm betting big on myself and praying it pays off.

Seraphina shifts to face me. "I see how hard you work, Ty. And you're crazy talented to begin with. That's coming from a girl who knows her hockey. There's no question you'll be out there someday."

"Thanks, Tink."

Thing is, only half of the players who are drafted actually make it to the pros.

My worst fear is being one of the ones who don't.

◆ ◆ ◆

Around ten, we finally stop talking long enough to clean up the empty takeout boxes and take our dirty dishes into the kitchen. Setting our plates and cutlery on the counter, I turn and open the dishwasher. Even though it's completely empty, one side of the sink is filled with dishes someone didn't bother to load. Fucking Chase.

"I can help with that," Seraphina offers.

I glance at her. "Have you ever heard of the internet meme that says, 'In every partnership, there's a person who stacks the dishwasher like a Scandinavian architect and a person who stacks the dishwasher like a raccoon on meth'?"

She narrows her eyes. "No . . ."

"I mean this in the nicest possible way, Ser, but you're the meth raccoon in this scenario."

Rather than get offended by my teasing, she smirks and swats me with a yellow dish towel. "I'll take that as your offer to assume my dish-loading duties permanently."

"Not gonna lie." I laugh. "That might be for the best."

I load our plates as Seraphina turns away to refill her glass. As she flips on the tap, a stream of water shoots from the faucet at warp speed, splashing all over the front of her blue blouse. She lets out the cutest fucking squeal I've ever heard and leaps back, fumbling with the chrome handle to shut it off.

Behind her, I try to hide a snort of laughter. I already know what happened. Someone left it switched to spray mode—otherwise known as "fire hose." It's been like this for a couple of weeks. Since Dallas's parents own our place, Dallas was supposed to arrange for someone to come take a look at it. He's been slacking on his landlord duties.

Seraphina dabs at her chest with a clean yellow dish towel, her face pulled into a scowl. Another snicker escapes me. I can't help it; she's cute when she's pissed. Sexy too, but I'm trying not to go down that particular rabbit hole.

"You think that's funny, huh?" She grabs the pull-out sprayer and wields it menacingly.

I cock a brow. "Go ahead, Ser. See where it gets you."

Unfortunately for both of us, Carters never back down from a challenge—even when they should.

Looking me straight in the eye, she pulls the trigger. A deluge of ice-cold water hits me in the chest, soaking through my black T-shirt. A yelp of nervous laughter slips through her lips, and she immediately releases the button. I drop my chin for a beat, assessing the extent of the damage. I'm drenched.

When I look back up, Seraphina is giggling like a schoolgirl. "Oops."

Goalie reflexes kicking in, I cover the ground between us in two long strides and step behind her. I wrap an arm around her waist lightning-quick and haul her into me before she can react. My large frame surrounds hers, hard muscle against soft curves.

"Rookie error, Tink." My voice is low; raspier than normal. "Don't pick fights you can't win." I pry the sprayer from her hand, aiming it directly at her cleavage. Her shirt has a few splotches of water, but it isn't soaked like mine. "What do you think? Should I even the score?"

"No!" she says between peals of laughter. "Don't, please!"

Still pinning her in place to me, I return the faucet to its holder. I've got over half a foot on her in height, and from my vantage point above, the stiff peaks of her nipples are evident through the thin fabric of her shirt. All I can think of is running my tongue along each one, and the little sounds she'd make in response.

Seraphina squirms in my grip, pretending to resist, but it's a half-assed attempt and we both know it. Suddenly, I'm hyperaware of her round ass rubbing against my rapidly hardening dick. My cock protests with need, way more turned on than I should be standing in the middle of the kitchen. I want to place her on the counter, spread her legs, and eat her for dessert.

She falls still, and I know I'm not the only one trying to repress the risqué mental movie playing through my mind. I can't even blame the audiobook from earlier. This isn't happening because listening to a racy scene got me worked up. This is because I want *her*. I've wanted her since the first time I saw her at XS—since the day she moved in.

With one foot in the present moment and the other firmly planted in the memory of our night together, it's impossible to think straight.

"You're getting me wet," she breathes.

My chuckle echoes between us. "Good to know."

"From your shirt, I mean." A flush creeps up her chest.

"Right," I say. "From my shirt."

My palms land on her hips and I spin her around to face me, reveling in the way she fits perfectly beneath my hands. While my intention is to let her go, my body has other ideas and before I know it, I've backed her up against the cupboard.

We look at one another, our soft inhales and exhales the only sound in the room. Every nerve in my body lights up as my fingertips brush the soft bit of exposed skin above the waist of her jeans. *Goddamn.* I know I'm playing with fire, but I can't seem to put away the matches.

"Question seventeen," Seraphina murmurs. "Do you ever think about that night?"

"All the fucking time." I'm not a big believer in sugarcoating the truth. Plus, I think it's pretty obvious.

"Me too." Her throat bobs, her warm brown eyes searching mine. "Do you regret it? I mean, it's made things kind of complicated now."

Complicated is an understatement. Ever since she moved in, it's been like navigating a minefield. The more time we spend together, the closer I come to doing something I shouldn't.

"No, Tink. I could never regret you."

Her pupils dilate as she peers up at me expectantly, her breaths shallow. My gaze lingers on her mouth as the tenuous hold on my restraint slips through my fingers. I still remember how every inch of her body felt beneath my hands. How those perfect, full lips taste. And the exact whimper she made when my hand dipped between her legs for the first time.

I would do anything to hear her whimper like that again.

Fuck.

My self-control hangs in the balance, my jaw tight as I fight to steady my breath. I can't. I shouldn't. I won't . . .

All of the reasons I need to keep my ass in line flash before my eyes. Her brother. The fact she's living with us. Hockey. This season is critical; one that could make or break my career. After working this hard for this long, I can't afford to derail my focus with a chick. Casual hookups are one thing—there are no emotions involved. But something tells me I can't be casual with Sera. When I'm not thinking with my dick, I know she deserves more than that too.

That doesn't make doing the right thing any easier.

Even though I know I should, I can't bring myself to pull away. Instead, I wrap my arms around Seraphina's small frame to draw her in for a hug. She freezes for a split second before she melts against me and loops her arms around my back, nestling closer. All of the chatter in my brain falls quiet as I press my cheek to the top of her head, breathing in her scent.

"You're soaked," Sera says, but she doesn't let me go.

"Sorry."

An indeterminate length of time passes, and neither of us moves. Her chest presses into mine with each inhale, her breaths slow and even. I'm not normally a touchy-feely person, which is why I can't make sense of how good holding her feels. Why is it so different?

Suddenly, a car door slams in the distance, and I snap out of my Tinker Bell-induced trance. I'm not sure whether it's Dallas or the neighbors, but it's a good reminder to wrap it up before something else happens.

"It's late, Ser. We should get to bed." Letting my hands fall to my sides, I reluctantly release her. Hurt flashes across her face, and I hate myself for it.

"Yeah." She looks away, wrapping her arms around her torso tightly. "We should."

Chapter 12
50-50

SERAPHINA

"I hate him."

At the manicure station next to me, Abby glances over with a raised brow. "Do you hate him because you wanted him to kiss you or because you didn't want him to kiss you?"

"I hate him because I wanted to kiss him and he hugged me, Abby. Like I was his grandmother."

It's been three days since the kitchen incident, and my fragile female ego is still wounded. I know Tyler wanted to kiss me. Hell, he even started to lean in. Then he stopped short like a switch flipped in his brain, and he left me hanging like a fool.

I suspect it all circles back to my older and decidedly overprotective brother—despite the fact that who I hook up with is none of his business. Chase is clam-jamming me without even realizing it.

That, or I've misread the situation to a catastrophic degree. That can't be the case, could it? Tyler admitted he still thinks about that night at XS. Unless, god forbid, he was trying to spare my feelings. Usually I'm pretty good at reading guys, but I'm starting to second-guess myself.

Maybe I friend-zoned myself when I suggested that the day I moved in. That would be ironic.

Abby shrugs. "No one ever said guys were smart."

"They definitely aren't." Which is why I've never wasted much time or effort on them, and also why I'm extra irritated I've let that change.

Despite my venting, there's no denying my stomach does a happy little somersault every time one of Tyler's messages pops up on my phone. They're like little dopamine hits throughout the day. I've been living for every single text.

Can girls be simps? Because right now, I feel like one.

Abby gives the manicurist her right hand, placing her left beneath the LED light to cure her burgundy nails. "Are you ever going to reaffiliate? I hyped you up to Allie and Gina, and they keep asking me when you're going to submit your application. Allie is the president, and she's a third-generation Kappa, which means..."

I try to follow what she's saying, but it's hard to make myself care. There are more pressing items on my plate than rejoining a sorority, like picking a major and figuring out what I want to do with my life. Worrying about my mom's health. Things that have long-term implications.

"Are you even listening to me?" Abby's voice breaks in.

"Yeah. Um, I'll try to get that Kappa paperwork done as soon as I can." I clear my throat. "Just having a bit of a rough time right now, that's all."

"Don't worry, Rob's party tonight will help you take your mind off things."

"Hopefully." I'm not overly optimistic. Not even a fresh manicure is turning this day around. My nails are transforming into the most glorious shade of pale pink, and I'm still grumpy.

I have to find some way to get over it, though. I'm taking my mom to a checkup with her oncologist after lunch, and the last thing she needs is a cranky daughter. It doesn't help that I'm running on approximately three hours of broken sleep after tossing and turning all night, dreaming up all kinds of terrible hypotheticals. I'm a nervous wreck. What if we get bad news? What if she's not responding to treatment the way they hoped? It'll be ten years this spring since my dad died. I can't lose her too.

If I'm being honest with myself, I might admit my mood has a lot more to do with all of that. But it's easier to blame Tyler.

◆ ◆ ◆

Two coffees later—a decaf white chocolate mocha for me and a hazelnut latte for my mom—I exit the Starbucks drive-through and head for the highway to her house. It's an additional twenty-minute drive from town, so I pass the time with more of my audiobook. The hero just angrily kissed the heroine in the kitchen after she was flirting with someone else. Toxic as it may be, I live for a good jealousy scene.

Unfortunately, the story only helps so much. The closer I get to my destination, the harder it is to focus on anything other than what lies ahead. In a way, I just want to get it over with, and I feel bad for that.

Mom climbs in the passenger side, and my gaze lingers on her, concern creeping in. As recently as Thanksgiving, her chestnut hair was thick and wavy, all the way down to her collarbone. Now it's wispy and short, tucked beneath a blue-patterned scarf. Her already thin frame is even thinner too. She's as beautiful as ever, but she looks fragile.

In the console, my screen lights up with a text from Tyler—or Hades, as he's listed in my phone—and a tiny thrill runs through me. It's immediately followed by a whopping dose of guilt. I should be focused on other, more serious things right now.

"You look smitten, Ser-bear. Who's the guy?" My mother teases me, her tone playful. Her cancer treatments have taken a toll on her energy level, but she still has the same upbeat attitude.

I glance over to find a knowing smile on her lips, her sparkling emerald eyes crinkling at the corners as she studies me. Either I'm being painfully obvious or mother's intuition is better than I realized. I'm hoping it's the latter.

"Oh, um . . . no one." Even if I wanted to tell her, it feels weird when we're en route to her oncology appointment. Not sure how she'd take the news that I'm living with the guy I'm crushing on, either.

"Sure seems like someone."

"Just a guy I've been talking to. It's not even a thing."

And at this rate, it never will be.

◆ ◆ ◆

"Mrs. Carter?" A petite nurse in pink scrubs stands in the doorway, scanning the waiting room until my mother stands up. "The doctor can see you now."

My heart races as I follow my mother and the nurse down the wood-paneled hallway into Dr. Wilson's office. With a sprawling glass desk and two leather guest chairs, it looks more like something I'd expect to find at a law office rather than a medical practice. But he's one of the best oncologists on the East Coast, so that might explain the decor.

The first half of the appointment involves a lot of medical jargon, some of which I didn't fully understand, but I ask questions and take ample notes because the chemo gives my mom brain fog and she likes to be able to reread things later. I relax slightly as Dr. Wilson explains that they expect her to respond well to the protocol they've designed, and her overall prognosis is excellent. For her type and stage of cancer, the rate of survival is nearly 90 percent with early aggressive treatment like she's receiving. Probably even better in her case because she was in such good health before. All things considered; she's doing great.

While everything has been encouraging until this point, the mood in the room shifts markedly when he mentions something about genetic testing, reaching for a folder on the tray next to his desk. My nerves skyrocket again, and I hold my breath, waiting for him to continue. Did they find something else wrong with her?

He clears his throat. "As we discussed, we conducted a comprehensive genetic testing panel during the diagnostic process. The results have come back, and you're positive for the BRCA1 mutation. It's helpful that your daughter is here with you today; when a patient has a positive result, we recommend testing all immediate relatives since there's a 50 percent chance they've also inherited it."

My vision tunnels, and the room turns sideways on me.

BRCA.

A 50 percent chance.

I try to make sense of what he just said, but I'm lacking critical information. I don't know what it means other than it's something bad, and I might have it too.

Mom reaches over and covers my hand with hers, giving it a squeeze. "I know it sounds scary, sweetheart, but it's better to get tested and find out. If you're negative, it'll be a weight off your shoulders." Despite her reassurance, her expression is tight, and there's fear beneath the brave face she's putting on for me. She looks more upset than when she told me about her diagnosis.

"Why? What does it mean if I'm positive?" I ask, trying to hide the wobble in my voice.

"Sera, let's not get ahead—" she starts.

"No, tell me. Please. If you don't, the first thing I'm going to do when I get home is Google it, and that'll be worse."

Dr. Wilson laces his fingers together, giving me a sympathetic look. "I need to emphasize that statistically speaking, there's an equally good chance you're *not* a carrier. With that said, individuals who carry the BRCA gene are at a higher-than-average chance of developing breast cancer and are more likely to develop it at a young age. There's an increased risk of ovarian cancer as well."

This is more or less what I expected, but somehow hearing it out loud makes it even worse.

"Routine cancer screenings begin sooner and are conducted more frequently," he adds. "Some patients may also opt for a prophylactic mastectomy and/or salpingo-oophorectomy to reduce their risk of cancer down the road. Even if you test positive, you have some time to weigh your options in that regard."

"Sal-what?" I echo, not even able to process the mastectomy

part that preceded it. When I came here today, I had no idea we might discuss anything in relation to me. Part of me wishes my mother had warned me in advance, but I also understand why she didn't. The stricken look on her face says it all—she was hoping the results would be negative and that she wouldn't need to.

"Removal of the ovaries and fallopian tubes," he clarifies.

In other words, surgically eliminating my ability to get pregnant.

Panic claws at my throat. "How much time are we talking?" I'm in no hurry to settle down, but I want to have children someday, and I assumed I had plenty of time to make that happen.

He hesitates. "It depends how aggressive the patient wants to be. Most risk reduction strategies recommend the procedures between the ages of thirty-five and forty or when childbearing is complete, whichever is sooner. The risks are incremental, and they increase with age. Statistically speaking, most women with BRCA1 develop breast cancer eventually."

The good news is the intervention timeline isn't as immediate as I feared. I'm almost twenty-one, so we're talking roughly fifteen years in the future.

The bad news is that working backward, this wouldn't give me as much time as I thought I had to start a family.

The worst news is being a carrier would mean I'm a ticking time bomb.

My chest is so tight it aches. "I see."

"Let's not get ahead of ourselves," he says, shuffling the papers on his desk. "The first step would be to book you in for testing. We can facilitate that if you'd like. After that, you can be referred out for additional genetic counseling if necessary."

"What about men? Could Chase be a carrier?" He made me promise to message him the minute we finished, but this isn't a conversation for text.

He nods. "Men can carry the gene too."

"Seraphina." My mother touches my forearm, drawing my attention to her. Her lips press into a grim line. "If you don't mind, honey, I'd like to hold off on telling him about this for now. Just for a couple weeks. He's got a lot on his plate to deal with, and I don't want to add to his stress."

I swallow the boulder sitting in my throat. "Right. I won't say a word."

We gather our things and I numbly trail behind my mom, my head spinning and ears ringing. When we step back into the lobby, I spot a woman standing at reception. She's hardly older than me—well under thirty for certain—and like my mother, she's clearly sick. A pink-and-purple scarf covers what's left of her hair and her olive complexion is wan.

My eyes dart in her direction again. She's beautiful, with wide dark eyes and full lips. I can't get over how young she looks. Twenty-four or twenty-five, if I had to guess. How old was she when she was diagnosed? Did she even suspect she might get sick? Did she do the same genetic test Mom's doctor mentioned?

Could that be me someday?

The reality of what I'm facing slams into me. People always say you have your twenties to figure everything out. I always assumed that was true, but everything seems different when you're looking down the barrel of a diagnosis.

While I have a hazy, imprecise understanding of what I want out of life, I couldn't articulate it if I tried. My plan for the future is vague and amorphous, filled with terms like "one day" and "eventually." Like an apparition you see out of the corner of your eye that vanishes when you try to grab it.

I want to get married eventually—that much I know for sure. And if I'm a carrier, that has consequences for both of us, not just me. It could even impact how many children we have. What if I can't have kids in time? Or what if I do, and then I get sick?

Deep down, I know it's irrational to get ahead of myself before I get tested and receive the results. There's a decent chance I'll be BRCA negative. But what if I'm not?

I'm spiraling and I can't help it. There are too many unknowns—and many of them are terrifying.

Fueled by a morbid sense of curiosity, I steal another peek at the young woman. A million questions swirl through my mind. I wonder how much life she got to experience before her diagnosis. Did she get the chance to fall in love? Does she have a partner to help her now? To my stepfather's credit, he's been there for my mother more than I expected, even picking up cooking and cleaning around the house. I'm not sure she'd be doing nearly as well without him.

As we pass, I overhear part of their conversation.

"Still with Cigna?" the receptionist asks.

"No, that's not—I have new insurance. We just got divorced. I'm not on his anymore." Her voice is shaky as she looks down and rifles through her purse. "I'll find it; I know it's in here somewhere."

A pang of sympathy tugs at my stomach, followed by overwhelming nausea. I can't imagine going through a divorce while battling cancer. Losing your marriage on top of everything else would be heartbreaking. I've heard it happens not infrequently. Something about the stress of the illness straining already struggling marriages. Whatever happened to in sickness and in health?

Sure, dating isn't on my current priority list—I don't need another disappointment on top of everything else. But she's older than me. She's had more time to meet someone, and a lot could change after graduation. If I'm lucky enough to find the right person later, would they stand by me through something like that?

Would they even want me in the first place? I bet it would be a dealbreaker for a lot of men.

Maybe living in the moment is the only way to keep my sanity and heart intact until I know.

"Sera?"

"Pardon?" My gaze slides over to my mom, who's looking at

me expectantly. We're standing next to my car in the parking garage beneath her doctor's office. I have no recollection of taking the elevator down.

"I said, do you want to go for dinner?"

"Sure," I say distantly. "You pick."

Chapter 13
DEAD BATTERY

TYLER

Seraphina must have been the last one in the kitchen again.

I set the groceries on the counter and unload the first bag, closing the open cabinets as I go. With a fourth person in the house, I made a point to order more than usual. We'll see how long it lasts this time. Sera consumes normal quantities of food, but Chase and Dallas are total wildcards.

Moving on to the next, I get the frozen items into the freezer before they start to melt. This includes two pints of Seraphina's favorite Häagen-Dazs to make up for my unintentional theft, plus a third pint for me. I have another cheat day soon and that cheesecake ice cream was next level.

Behind me, the front door creaks open and slams shut. My body comes alive with anticipation as I catch a glimpse of Seraphina through the kitchen doorway. Seeing her is the high point of my day lately, followed closely by our constant back and forth texts.

She kicks off her shoes and reaches up, hanging her coat on the rack. It immediately slides off the hook and falls to the ground, but she doesn't stop to pick it off the floor.

"Hey, Tink," I call, putting a box of cereal on the shelf.

"Hey." She breezes past in a blur of pink and denim, avoiding my attempt to make eye contact.

"Do you—" I start, but she's gone before I can finish.

Guess that's a no on wanting dinner, then.

Confusion overtakes me and I lean a hip against the counter, mentally replaying our interaction. What the hell just happened? There was a bit of weirdness between us earlier this week after our close call in the kitchen, but we moved past it pretty quickly. We were messaging today like everything was fine. I have no idea what changed.

Chase steps through the door a few minutes later and slips off his winter boots in the entry. "Is Sera here? She was supposed to text me after my mom's checkup, but she never did."

My stomach drops to the floor. *Shit.* Maybe the appointment went badly and that's why she's upset.

"Yeah. She got home and barreled straight for her bedroom."

"Guess that explains the coat," he mutters, kneeling to retrieve it from the floor. "I'm going to check on her."

Worry simmers in the pit of my gut. For lack of other options, I finish putting away the rest of the groceries and get started on dinner to distract myself. I bought enough steak to feed a small kingdom, which means we'll probably polish it off in one sitting.

Just as I'm putting the potatoes on to boil, Chase strolls back into the kitchen and heads to the fridge.

I give him a questioning look over the island. "All good?"

"Dunno." He cracks open a carton of strawberry-peach EnduraFuel with a frown. "She said our mom's checkup went smoothly, but she's acting weird. Wouldn't really talk to me."

Now I'm really concerned. Generally, I try to minimize messaging Sera when Chase is around. You know, as an insurance policy. But I can't stop myself from grabbing my phone and texting her.

> Hades: You okay, Tink?

Tinker Bell: Yeah, I'm fine.

> Hades: Are you sure? You seemed upset when you got home.

Tinker Bell: Just having a bad day.
School stuff. Nothing major.

"Yo, Carter." Dallas saunters into the room and lobs a small black object at Chase, who narrowly catches it before it hits him in the shoulder. "Stop putting your shit in my bag."

Chase pulls up the sleeve of his sweatshirt, pointing to the Apple Watch on his left wrist. "That's not mine, bro." He passes the other watch back to Dallas.

Dallas holds it up to the light to examine it, frowning. "Then who the hell does it belong to? And how did it get into my backpack?"

"Shoplifting, Ward?" I ask. "I know you've got expensive taste, but maybe you should get a part-time job instead."

"Ha-ha." He makes a face, flipping me the bird.

All three of our phones ping in unison. I check my texts to find a new message in our team's group chat.

FILTHY FALCONS

Reid Holloway: Anyone seen an Apple Watch? Latest model, black band. It went missing out of the locker room after practice earlier.
Reid Holloway: If this is some kind of hazing prank, you can fuck off.

Chase snorts a laugh, and even my sour mood lifts slightly.

I point to Dallas with the spatula. "See? You're so distracted texting Shiv all the time that you're stealing people's stuff now."

"Fuck. I have no idea how that happened." Groaning, he reaches for his cell. "I'll let Holloway know. I don't have time to meet up with him tonight, though. You gonna be here for a bit, Ty? I can tell him to come by and grab it."

"All night." It's been a long week and I'm fucking bagged.

Cooking takes my mind off things temporarily, but the additions of pan-seared steak and Caesar salad don't take much time to prepare, especially because Dallas pitches in to help. Dinner is ready in a flash, and I'm stuck with company I'm not particularly in the mood for.

We all have seconds—and in Chase's case, thirds. Even though I doubled the portions, there's hardly enough for one person left. Probably the perfect amount for Sera if she weren't holed up in her room.

I focus on my food while the guys talk about some movie they're going to see with their girlfriends. Apparently, it's at a brand-new theater that serves food and alcohol right to your seats. Despite my attempts to engage in conversation, my thoughts keep drifting back to Sera. Something is definitely wrong, and it's eating at me. I don't know when I suddenly developed a sense of empathy, and I'm choosing not to question it.

"Later." Chase throws me a wave as I rinse a pan under the faucet, and Dallas follows behind him out the door.

In an ideal world, the person who cooked dinner wouldn't be the one stuck doing dishes, but I'm trying not to be salty over it. It isn't like I have other plans.

The doorbell rings while I'm drying the last dish, and I look up as Seraphina darts past to answer it. Her little black dress is even more revealing than the one from Chase's birthday. It's got a lace overlay that gives the illusion of bare skin beneath, and the neckline plunges low in the back. There's no way she's wearing a bra beneath it.

I watch from where I'm standing at the sink in the kitchen island, facing the entry. It's impossible to tear my eyes away from her. Her rose-gold hair is a cascade of waves against smooth, creamy skin. Dark makeup accents her chocolate eyes. And those pink lips . . .

"Hey." She moves aside, motioning for the other person to come in. "Where's Abbs?"

My blood pressure spikes as Rob steps into the foyer, brushing snow off his wool dress coat. His hair is neatly slicked back, designer clothes perfectly pressed. I grapple with the urge to frisbee the plate I'm holding at his head. With my aim, I'd definitely inflict some serious damage. Can't actually do it, but the mental image is incredibly satisfying.

"She's having some kind of 'hair emergency' at my place," he says, making air quotes. Tension winds through my body. Even his use of air quotes is irritating. "Asked me to come grab you instead."

Seraphina takes a seat on the wooden bench, bending to fasten the straps on her metallic high heels. As she does, the fucker blatantly stares down her dress, but she doesn't seem to notice. She stands and reaches past him to pull her new winter coat off the rack. My molars grind together as Mr. Lowlife tucks her pink hair over one shoulder, helping her slip on the puffy white parka. Seeing him touch her makes every inch of my skin crawl.

Drawing in a sharp inhale, I look down and violently polish the dish I'm holding. I need to chill. It's not my place to care.

"I could've driven myself," she says. "I'll be splitting an Uber home with Abby either way."

When I glance up, he winks at her. "Or you could stay over."

Everything turns red, and the plate flies out of my hand into the sink. Fragile porcelain hits the stainless basin, shattering into pieces.

Fuck. One more thing to deal with later.

Even though I know I'm being irrational, I stride into the entry and lean against the wall, flashing Rob a not-so-friendly smile. "Have her home by nine thirty, Ron."

"Er . . . it's Rob, actually." He laughs uneasily, like he's not sure whether I'm kidding about the curfew remark. I'm not. While he's almost as tall as me and looks like he probably hits the gym on the regular, there's no way this dude has been in a fight in his life. At least, not any that he won. I could easily, and very much want to, clobber him.

"Tyler doesn't mean that. He's joking." Seraphina turns to me and widens her eyes, giving me a reproachful look.

I fold my arms, my biceps flexing. "She's right. Ten o'clock is fine."

"*Tyler.*" Her expression is half-exasperated, half-amused.

Rob opens the front door and lingers with it ajar like he's hoping it'll help expedite their departure. Cold air rushes inside, but I guess he doesn't give a shit about our heating bill—or the fact he's too old to be inviting a college sophomore for sleepovers.

Ignoring him, I hold her gaze. "Call me if you need anything, Ser."

And then she's gone.

◆ ◆ ◆

My floor is clean as fuck. My head is still a mess.

I hit the power switch on the vacuum handle to shut it off, and the whir of the motor fades out. Since Seraphina left, I've been too full of restless energy to stay still for longer than a couple of seconds. I've washed, dried, and folded every item of clothing I own; changed my sheets; and I just finished angrily vacuuming the entire lower level. Some people find stress cleaning weird, but it keeps me from resorting to other, less constructive coping strategies.

I receive two texts within quick succession, but it's false hope followed by immediate disappointment. They're both from girls I haven't spoken to in months—well before that night at XS. Why they're both hitting me up now is anyone's guess.

Alyssa: wyd? let's meet up.
Jasmine: u busy later?

Mission Control reports zero response down south. My dick is broken. Or maybe my brain is the problem because my cock worked just fine last night when I was thinking about Seraphina.

Then my phone vibrates again with another group text from the team trying to encourage me to join them. Drowning my sorrows sounds tempting, but there's a risk I'll do something after, like drunk dial Seraphina. Or punch a hole in the wall when I get home, which I was already perilously close to doing after she left.

Plus, I can't shake the nagging feeling I was supposed to do something else.

As I'm putting the vacuum back inside the hall closet on the main level, footfalls thud on the front step. For a brief, foolish second, I think maybe Seraphina changed her mind and came home early. Then the doorbell rings, and disappointment kicks me in the face.

I open the door to find Reid standing outside. Right... That's the other thing I was supposed to do.

He nods at me, his hands stuffed into the pockets of his navy winter coat. "Hey, man."

"Mind coming in for a sec?" I ask. "I have to figure out where Carter left your stuff."

Reid kicks the snow off his boots before he steps inside, shutting the door behind him. My gaze darts around the room in search of his watch, but I have no idea where Chase put it. I forgot Reid was even coming.

I scrub my jaw with my hand. "Do you want a beer? I might have to text him to ask what he did with your watch."

Ten minutes later, we're halfway into our bottles of Stella. Per Chase's text, the watch was sitting on the kitchen counter in plain sight all along. I just happened to miss it—four times. If that doesn't sum up my mental state, I don't know what does.

"You look pressed," Reid remarks.

"Little bit," I mutter, peeling the label off my beer.

"You going out with the team later?"

"Nah," I say. "Not feeling it tonight."

"Wish I could say the same. I could use at least ten drinks after today's practice."

My brows lift because I'm usually pretty dialed in, and I didn't notice anything on the ice. "Coach Miller up your ass?"

"Miller's fine. Better than fucking Grady." He rolls his

neck, reaching for his bottle. "It's hard coming in mid-season like this. A few of the second and third liners haven't exactly been welcoming. They seem to think *I'm* the reason they're not starting."

Of course they do. Some of the guys on our team are such entitled fucks. They wouldn't last a day with the pressure of being goalie.

"They're not starting because they're not good enough."

"You and I know that but try telling them." Reid smirks.

I snort. "I will if you want. I have no problem bringing them back down to reality."

On the counter where it's charging, my phone rings with an incoming call. I glance over my shoulder, confused. No one calls me, and for good reason—I never answer.

"Sorry. Hang on." I push back my chair to retrieve my cell, expecting a wrong number. When I pick it up, the display says Tinker Bell.

Nerves rattled, I swipe to accept the call. "Ser?"

"Ty? Are you there?" Seraphina's voice is nearly drowned out by pounding bass in the background. It's hard to tell, but it sounds like she's crying.

"Tink." I plug my other ear in an attempt to hear better. "I can't hear you. Are you okay?"

"I'm sorry..." She cuts out. "...loud..." The call cuts out again. "...more quiet."

Reid catches my eye and jerks a thumb to the front door, giving me a questioning look as if to ask whether he should leave. Grateful he picked up on it, I nod and silently mouth "thank you."

Trailing behind him, I lock the deadbolt and pace circles in the kitchen, waiting for Sera to continue. Seconds crawl by that feel like hours. The music slowly fades to a more manageable volume, and a door clicks shut on the other end of the line. All I can hear are her gasping breaths, interspersed with sniffles.

"Ser?" I prod.

Seraphina draws in another shaky breath. "I smoked part of a joint, and now I feel weird. The room won't stop spinning. I tried to text you, but I'm seeing double and it's too hard to type."

Icy dread grips me, and I come to a screeching halt. "Just weed or—?"

"Um... I-I think so. That's what Rob said."

I bite my knuckle, holding back a string of expletives. Of course. Should've known that fucking guy had something to do with this.

Not to mention, Rob's connections are probably about as trustworthy as he is. It could've contained anything.

Frantically scanning the room, I grab my keys off the counter and barrel down the hall into the garage. Before I can think twice, I'm sitting in the driver's seat of my car. I don't even know where I'm going.

"Where are you? I'll come get you." I press the control on the overhead console to open the garage door and watch it creak open in the rearview mirror.

Seraphina hiccups. "Rob's p-penthouse downtown."

Oh, so he supplied *and* hosted. My grip on the steering wheel tightens until I think it might disintegrate beneath my fingers. Not because I'm upset with her, but because I want to pummel Rob into next week.

"Send me a pin with your location. I'm leaving right now."

Something clatters on the other end of the line. "... shit!" There's rustling. "Sorry, I dropped my phone. M-my dying's battery. I mean, my battery's dying, but I'll try. Gimme a sec."

Pinching the bridge of my nose, I draw in a slow, deep breath to calm myself. The good news is she's talking to me, and she's safe—for now. But she's having a bad trip, and she's in a potentially dangerous situation surrounded by a bunch of strangers. I don't trust the people she *does* know there either.

A few seconds later, a link to her location appears in our text thread.

"Got it," I confirm, backing out of the garage.

"I'm scared, Ty." She whimpers, triggering some kind of primal instinct I've never felt before. Testosterone, adrenaline, it's a biochemical cascade. All I want is to fix whatever is making her feel this way.

"You'll be okay." The reassurance is for myself as much as her. "Just stay on the phone with me until I—"

Suddenly, the background noise on the other end of the line vanishes.

My Bluetooth beeps and the display reads, "Call Failed."

Heart racing, I call her back. It goes straight to voicemail, and I receive an automated message informing me hers hasn't been set up yet. I try again. Voicemail.

I can't do anything until I get there.

I'm completely powerless, and it's one of the worst feelings I've ever had.

Chapter 14
GRAVITY

TYLER

I make what should be a twenty-minute drive in less than ten and pull up to the curb of a swanky apartment building, leaving my Audi running in a no-parking zone. They won't have enough time to tow me, and I don't give a flying fuck if I get a ticket.

Cold winter air whips at my cheeks as I slide out of my SUV, the wind biting my bare forearms. In twenty-two degrees, a coat would've been a smart idea, but I wasn't exactly thinking when I left. When I step onto the sidewalk, I spot a uniformed doorman standing outside the glass double doors, and trepidation seizes me. Dammit. Getting past him might be an issue.

Like I predicted, saying I'm here to see "my friend Rob, who lives in the penthouse" gives me zero credibility in the eyes of the middle-aged building attendant, who side-eyes my tattoos and refuses to let me pass without Rob's last name. In my mind, it's Pieceofshit, but this guy won't buy that. When I try to argue, he tells me to "call Rob" if I have a problem with it. If I had his fucking number, I'd do that in a heartbeat. In fact, I'd tell him to come downstairs so we can have a chat fist-to-face outside.

After more unsuccessful attempts to negotiate, I resort to bribing the doorman to get upstairs—and it isn't cheap. A private elevator whisks me up to the penthouse on the twenty-fifth floor. Rap music tumbles inside as the doors spring open, unveiling bachelor bro central. Everything is chrome, and I do mean everything.

Sidestepping a couple making out in the entry, I scan the room for Seraphina's distinctive rose-gold hair. A cluster of well-dressed people are lounging on white leather couches in the living area. Another handful of partygoers have gathered around the coffee table in the center of the room, snorting lines off the glass.

Abby spots me in the crowd and sashays over, clutching a martini glass in one hand. Her eyes are glassy, and her expression tells me she's more than a little fucked up. I guess Seraphina isn't the only one.

"Hi, Hades. I mean, Tyler." She giggles. "What are you doing here? Did Sera invite you?"

"Where is she?" Glancing over her shoulder, I survey the sprawling apartment again. It's packed with bodies, but I don't see Sera.

"Chill." Abby rolls her eyes, twirling a lock of copper hair around her finger. "I saw her not too long ago. She's around here somewhere."

Her blasé attitude only pisses me off further. I hate knowing Seraphina has a friend this shitty.

"How long ago?" I demand. "She just called me freaking out."

"Sera did? Why?"

"Because she's high as fuck and she's scared." Another scan of the room leaves me frustratingly empty-handed. My irritation spikes, and I turn back to face Abby. "Don't you have some kind of girl code? Aren't you supposed to look out for each other?"

She waves me off. "Sera's a big girl. She's been to plenty of parties before."

"Hopefully not like this."

"It's no big—"

I storm away from her mid-reply and stalk through the apartment, yanking open every door I can find. Three bedrooms, one closet, several couples in various states of undress, and no Seraphina. The more I search, the more worried I become—because I haven't seen Rob yet either. If I find him anywhere near her while she's in this state, I'm going to kill him with my bare hands.

Finally, I reach a locked door at the end of the hall with a light pouring out beneath it. Tentative hope sparks within me. *Please let her be in here, and please let her be alone.*

"Ser?" I knock on the door, putting my ear against it. "Are you in there? It's Tyler."

The lock rattles, and the door swings open to reveal her standing on the other side. I heave a sigh of relief as all the worst-case scenarios I'd been imagining dissolve into thin air.

Before I can get a good look at her, she launches herself at me and wraps her arms around my waist. Her perfume surrounds me as her body radiates heat through my clothes.

She buries her face in my chest, sobbing. "Thank you."

"Of course." I return the hug, rubbing her back to calm her.

A few people are staring at us from the other end of the hallway, so I slowly walk her backward into the bathroom and close the door behind me to get some privacy.

"I'm sorry..." Seraphina draws in a jagged inhale, tears seeping through the cotton fabric of my shirt. "I felt so sick, and I didn't know what to do."

"You don't need to apologize."

Her breathing slows after another minute or two. She gradually relaxes in my arms, but she doesn't let me go. Resting my cheek on the crown of her head, I inhale the tropical scent of her shampoo and wait until I'm confident her panic attack has passed.

"Look at me for a sec, Tink." Tilting her chin, I gently angle her face up to mine so I can see better in the bathroom lighting.

Her pupils flicker, darting back and forth as she tries to focus on me. "You're scaring me," she murmurs.

"Just making sure you're okay." There's a pang in my gut as I study her face. The whites of her eyes are bloodshot, and her skin is red and blotchy from crying, remnants of black mascara trailing down her cheeks. She looks terrified.

And she's still beautiful—ruined makeup and all.

I've drifted from assessing her into admiring her. *Not the time or place, Tyler.*

"Hold on. I don't want you to rub makeup in your eyes." I grab a tissue off the counter, wet it under the tap, and carefully remove the dark streaks marring her face. Once I'm finished, I reluctantly drop my hand. "How are you feeling?"

Seraphina takes a fresh tissue from the box and wipes her nose. "Awful. I wanna go home."

"Come on," I tell her. "Let's go find your coat."

Opening the bathroom door, I place a hand on her lower back to guide her into the hall. She teeters in her heels, and my arm wraps around her waist to keep her steady. Rob glares at me as we leave, clearly pissed. As the elevator doors slide closed, I throw him a middle finger with my free hand. Sera is too out of it to notice.

◆ ◆ ◆

"Did you mix the joint with anything else, Tink?" My gaze flicks over to Seraphina, trying to gauge her sobriety level. She's curled up using a spare hoodie I found in the backseat as a pillow, and she hasn't said a word for the entire fifteen minutes we've been in the car. I've tried to let her rest, but I also need to know.

"Um . . . when I didn't feel good, Abby told me to go see Rob and he gave me a vodka seven. It tasted strong. Might've been a double."

My jaw clenches, but I hold my tongue.

"Is that bad?" she asks in a tiny voice.

"Not ideal, but you'll be fine. We'll need to hydrate you once we're home, though."

Silence cloaks the interior of my vehicle. In addition to the bloodthirsty vendetta against Rob that I'm fostering, I'm concerned about her because I'm not sure what drove her to do this in the first place. Judging by how things went down, it seems like she was way out of her depth. She's bold, a little wild even, and I like that about her. Putting herself in a situation like that verges on reckless.

There are a few possible explanations for what happened. She's inexperienced and simply smoked too much. There was something else in the joint. Or someone—potentially Rob—spiked her drink. With the kind of people she was hanging out with, it's anyone's guess. And without any form of proof, that's how it'll stay. A big fucking question mark that'll haunt me.

Slowing to a stop at a red light, I glance at her again. "What happened earlier today, Ser?"

Seraphina doesn't look at me. "Like I said, I was having a bad day."

I don't want to upset her, so I drop it.

She leans against the window and falls quiet for a few seconds. "Question twenty-one: Have you ever done any drugs?"

"I've done lots of things," I say, giving her a pass for misnumbering the question; we're up to twenty-two now. "But not anymore."

Much to my relief, the house is completely dark when I pull up. Hanging out upstairs obviously isn't an option, so I shuttle Seraphina into my bedroom as soon as we get inside. I'm not sure what my longer-term plan is for tonight, but I'll worry about that later. Right now, I'm in triage mode.

Steering Seraphina across the room to my bed, I hang her coat on my computer chair and light the desk lamp on the way by. She perches on the edge of my mattress, still wearing her gold heels. Sympathy washes over me. Something tells me she doesn't have the coordination to undo the tiny buckles holding the straps together.

"Let me get your shoes off, Tink."

She nods wordlessly and leans back, bracing her palms behind her on the bed. I kneel on the carpet in front of her, and when I glance up, she's watching me intently. Soft brown eyes fix on me, full lips slightly parted. Even with me in a subservient position, she seems vulnerable, defenseless.

Making a point to be gentle, I take her left foot in my hand and prop it on my knee to hold it steady. Her foot is perfectly pedicured; her toenails painted light pink. Fuck, even her feet are pretty.

My fingertips brush her skin as I carefully unfasten the delicate clasp, and she draws in a soft breath, goose bumps coasting down her bare legs. It's hard to ignore how intimate this feels. It's even harder knowing I can't act on it.

"Are you sure no one will come downstairs?"

"No one ever does." It's an unspoken rule. The only exception is when we're having a party and people are playing beer pong down here. Even then, I rarely allow it.

When I'm finished, I head for the closet to change. I tug off my jeans and T-shirt—which is still damp from her tears—and toss both in the hamper. Then I grab a pair of black athletic shorts and pull them on. Briefly, I debate whether I should put on a shirt too, but my bedroom runs stiflingly hot and I suspect Sera doesn't care.

"Scale of one to ten," she says, absentmindedly dragging her bare toes along the gray carpet. "Ten being the worst. How much of a mess do I look like right now?"

"Zero."

A breathy laugh escapes her lips. "You're sweet, but you're a liar."

Her gaze shifts to my bedroom door, and her nose crinkles. She pushes to stand, still slightly off balance. "I need to wash my face. I feel icky."

Taking Seraphina by the elbow, I help her to the bathroom. We both brush our teeth, then I wait outside while she finishes up before guiding her back to my room. Once I'm convinced she'll be okay on her own for a minute, I jog upstairs to grab water for myself and a sports drink for her. Thankfully, the house is still otherwise empty. Maybe Chase and Dallas will crash at the girls' place tonight. That would make handling this so much easier.

Handing her the plastic bottle, I lower to sit next to her on my bed. "Drink this."

"Why?" She looks at me, her brows knit together.

"Because both cannabis and alcohol are diuretics, which—" Catching myself, I stop before I launch into a science lecture I'm sure she has no interest in hearing, least of all right now. "Just drink some for me, Ser. You'll thank me tomorrow."

"Fine." She unscrews the cap and takes a few sips before resealing it. Her phone lights up from where it's charging on the nightstand next to us, and a text from Abby appears.

I snort. "How nice of her to finally check in." The words slip out before I can censor myself. I can't help it—I'm pissed at her and her snake of a brother.

"Ty."

"She had no idea where you were, Tink," I say, softening my tone. The last thing I want to do is pick a fight with her on top of everything else. "What if some creep had found you?"

"It's not like I was passed out."

"Abby didn't know that."

She presses her lips together and studies me for a beat, scrutinizing me like a puzzle she's trying to fit together. The annoyance on her face gives way to amusement.

"You like me," she says in a singsong voice.

Obviously. But what can I do about that? Sweet fuck all, that's what.

"I don't want anything to happen to you."

Her mouth tugs into a grin. "Because you like me."

"Yeah, Ser. I do."

A door slams upstairs. Someone barges into the kitchen, stomping like a goddamn elephant. The TV switches on, volume up high, followed by a burst of female laughter. *Shit.* Dallas and Chase just got home, and they brought Shiv and Bailey with them.

"Shit!" Seraphina clamps a hand over her mouth, frantically

scanning the room like she's looking for an escape route. "What the hell am I supposed to do? I can't see my brother like this."

There's a loud crash above us that sounds like a kitchen chair tipping over. Based on the racket they're making, they're probably too drunk to realize she's higher than the International Space Station, but I understand her concern. If I were in her shoes, I wouldn't want to face them either.

Racking my brain, I land on the only solution I can think of. "You can sleep down here. In the morning, change into your robe before you go upstairs and pretend you were in the shower. If anyone asks, say you got home after everyone else was asleep."

"Yeah . . ." She nods slowly. "That'll work, right?"

"I'm sure it will," I tell her, turning away to set my water bottle on the nightstand.

It's a lie to keep her calm. There's a non-zero chance this sleepover could backfire. At least the basement door squeaks like a motherfucker. It annoys the shit out of me, but it makes for a good early warning system.

Seraphina pushes to stand, fanning herself. "Oh my god, it's boiling in here."

My mouth goes dry as she unzips her dress at the side and slips it off one shoulder, evidently unfazed that I'm standing right in front of her. I hate that I have to stop her, but I do.

"Whoa, Tink. Let me give you—"

She lets the fabric go and it drops to the floor, revealing her perfect, full breasts and a tiny pair of see-through black panties. My cock stirs as I suppress a groan, and I immediately tear my gaze away. Even from the split-second glance I got, the image has been permanently etched into my memory. Pert, rosy nipples pebbled and begging to be touched; the dip of her waist leading to the swell of her hips; and the outline of her pussy visible through the thin fabric of her underwear.

Under normal circumstances, this would be too much temptation to handle. Right now, it verges on torture.

"What's the big deal?" Playfulness tinges her tone. "Nothing you haven't seen before."

No need to remind me. I only replay it in my head a hundred times a day.

"*You're* not wearing a shirt," she adds. "With how hot it is in here, I assumed clothing was optional."

"In that case," I manage, voice strained, "maybe we should both put on shirts."

I open my closet and find a worn black concert T-shirt, handing it to her. It's slightly faded, but it's broken in and the fabric is softer than the rest. I may or may not have fantasized about her wearing it, albeit under dramatically different circumstances. Then I grab a white T-shirt for myself. Fair's fair, I guess.

Making no attempt to hurry, Seraphina leisurely pulls on my shirt while I channel every shed of my self-control to keep myself from looking directly at her. Once she's dressed, I know I'm really in trouble. She looks just as hot in my shirt as she did naked.

My dick perks up again as she walks over to the bed with the dark fabric draped perfectly over her body, hitting at mid-thigh. He clearly hasn't gotten the memo about sex being off the table tonight, and he's in for a world of disappointment.

I pull back the covers, sliding over to make room for her. She crawls all the way to my side and wraps herself around my torso, clinging to me koala-style. Her neediness is one reason I'm glad she's not around Rob right now. I'd never take advantage of her, but I doubt the same can be said for him.

"You smell nice." She sighs, resting her cheek on my chest. "You always do."

She always smells edible, but I can't say that out loud.

It suddenly occurs to me that I don't know what to do with my hands. Even snuggled up together like this, I'm trying to be respectful. Not touching her seems weird but touching her too much seems opportunistic. It might also give my overly optimistic cock the wrong idea. I settle for resting one palm on her shoulder, placing the other on the bed beside me.

"Could you pet me? Play with my hair, maybe?" Seraphina asks, her voice small.

Even high, she's cute as hell.

Brushing the silky strands off her forehead, I rake my fingers through her rose-gold waves. She lets out a happy little sound, a cross between a sigh and a groan, nestling against me. Her full breasts press into my side, smooth legs intertwined with mine. This arrangement isn't helping me fight my attraction to her. It's become a losing battle at this point, like resisting gravity.

She sighs. "I feel a lot better than I did earlier."

"I'm glad, Tink."

"Do your hands get sore from playing? My dad's always did. He used to have a lot of hand and wrist pain." Seraphina takes my free hand in hers and presses her thumb into the fleshy part of my palm, massaging in small circles. An appreciative moan escapes the back of my throat. I should be the one taking care of her, but her touch is incredibly relaxing.

"Everything is always sore. Kinda goes with the territory."

"Hmm," she hums. "Bet I could make it feel better."

I chuckle. "I'm sure you could."

We lay in the dimly lit room while she tells me about her freshman year at Arizona and I tickle her arms at her request. Then she asks me random questions about being a goalie, like what possesses me to throw myself in the path of a puck traveling eighty to ninety miles per hour. That one's a little hard to answer, because I'm not too sure myself.

It feels like it's only been a handful of minutes, but when I check the clock it's been over an hour. Having anyone else wrapped around my body for this long would've made me claustrophobic. Hell, if she were anyone else, I wouldn't even *be* here. I'd have made sure the other person wasn't dying and left them to fend for themselves. I might've left them a bottle of water on my way out.

But she isn't anyone else, and that's the problem.

Her voice grows drowsy, and her responses start to come slower and slower. Just when I start to think she's fallen asleep, she pipes up.

"Question twenty-two: Why don't you date, Hades?"

Reasons line up in my brain. Not surprisingly, they all trace back to hockey.

There are countless factors beyond my control, like whether our defense plays well and how strong the other team's offense is. What I can control is my level of effort and preparation, and it isn't possible to focus on those the way I need to if I start adding other variables into the equation. I only have so much bandwidth.

Not to mention, a relationship would pose a serious risk of fucking with my mindset. Playing goal is one of the most psychologically demanding positions of any sport, and I don't have the bandwidth to handle any additional stress. If Chase fumbles a pass or Dallas misses a shot, people may not even notice—but *everyone* knows when I make a mistake.

I clear my throat. "Too busy. No time."

"You never know." She yawns. "Maybe your taxi light just hasn't come on yet."

I have no idea what that means, but I'd gladly listen to her all night.

Chapter 15
IN CHECK

SERAPHINA

After a night of sleeping next to Tyler with zero release, my vibrating Sonicare toothbrush is starting to look more tempting than it should.

Shaking off the thought, I lean over the bathroom counter to examine my face in the mirror. I don't look as rough as I expected. Not great, but not like someone who had to be rescued from a bathroom at a party after a series of poor decisions.

The aftermath of last night's events becomes more evident as I run through my skincare routine. My skin is drier than the Sahara, thirstily soaking up layers of serum and moisturizer almost instantly. I dab some Aquaphor on the worst spots for good measure before moving on to brush my teeth. The sooner I banish my morning breath, the better.

Midway through brushing, there's a soft knock on the bathroom door. "Ser?"

I open the door with my free hand to find a rumpled, half-awake Tyler. My heart flutters, and a rush of giddiness courses through me. At some point during the night, he must've gotten hot and taken off his shirt. Now he's got this sexy-cute thing going on, all tattoos and bedhead.

He ducks his head to catch my eye. "How are you feeling, Tink?"

"Pretty good," I mumble, giving him a thumbs-up with my toothbrush still in my mouth. Despite what happened last night, I feel relatively normal this morning. No worse than a normal hangover, at least.

Wildly confused about what the two of us are doing, however.

Did I embarrass myself in front of him last night? Turn him off forever? I think I remember most of what happened, but I can't be sure there aren't any key, humiliating details I've conveniently forgotten. If taking off my dress was the worst thing I did, I can live with that. It doesn't seem fatal.

"Mind if I . . . ?" He points to his toothbrush on the counter, raising his eyebrows. When I nod, he squeezes past me and his palm presses to my lower back. My stomach flutters with butterflies, but to my dismay, he doesn't let it linger.

My toothbrush vibrates in my hand, telling me it's time to switch sides as he grabs his off the counter, wetting it beneath the tap before dabbing a pearl of blue gel on top. Brushing our teeth together feels oddly domestic. I like it more than I should.

The timer goes off, and I set the handle back on its base to charge. "Did I wake you?"

"Kinda." The word is muffled by his blue toothbrush.

"Sorry. Like I said, I can't sleep in."

He waves me off, leaning over the sink to spit. "All good. Bed just felt a little empty suddenly, that's all."

Hearing that does something to me it shouldn't.

When I step back into his room, my heart sinks at the knowledge I should sneak upstairs while I still can. No one else is awake yet and it's the perfect opportunity. Even knowing that, I can't bring myself to leave. Tyler and I have been in this cozy little bubble since we got home last night, and once it ends, I'm scared things will never be the same between us again.

Instead, I waste time gathering my shoes, my dress, and a few items that spilled out of my clutch onto his desk. Best not to leave evidence behind. Not that anything happened.

I don't know what's holding him back—whether he won't make a move because of Chase or if there's something else I'm missing. I could give him a pass for last night, but he'd had other opportunities and still . . . nothing. It's frustrating as hell. I can only throw myself at him so much before giving up.

Tyler returns a moment later and lowers to sit on the edge of the bed. Every inch of his body looks like it was carved from marble—from his chiseled upper body to the curved obliques disappearing beneath the waistband of his black athletic shorts.

Setting my things in a heap on his desk chair, I draw in a breath and summon the courage to give it one last-ditch effort. At least this way, I'll know for sure.

I come to stand before him, painfully aware of how little I'm wearing. I'm not shy—but right now I feel naked in more ways than one.

"Are you mad at me?" I ask softly.

Tenderness gleams in his gray eyes as he looks up at me. "Why would I be mad at you?"

Why won't you kiss me?

Swallowing the words I want to say, I settle on something else.

"I thought maybe I ruined your plans last night."

My breath catches as his warm, calloused palms wrap around the backs of my thighs, gripping just below where his borrowed T-shirt ends.

"No, Ser. I'm glad you called. And when you're ready to tell me what happened before you went out last night, I'm here to listen."

"Thank you," I murmur, placing my hands on his broad shoulders. "For everything."

Electricity thrums between us as the energy in the room shifts.

His gaze darkens, blazing a heated path down my body before lifting to meet mine, and his lips tug. "I like you in my shirt."

Taking the hem in his hands, he gently tugs me closer. It's subtle, more of a question than a demand, but I don't need much encouragement.

Suddenly, we're face-to-face and I'm straddling him with my

bare legs bracketing his. He's solid beneath me, a frame of firm muscle and taut skin. I could spend all day mapping every single inch, committing each ridge and indentation to memory.

When our eyes lock, I feel high all over again.

"Guess I'm the one who owes you now, huh?" My words are breathy.

"We don't need to keep track," Tyler murmurs, tucking a lock of hair behind my ear. He scans my face, and I lean into his touch as he caresses my cheek. "You're so fucking pretty."

At that, my heart stutters. "Even first thing in the morning?"

"Especially first thing in the morning."

Almost as if it's subconscious, his fingertips slip under the hem of my shirt and his rough palm claims my hip. My pulse races as his thumb dips beneath the waistband of my panties, stroking my lower stomach. There's an insistent throb between my thighs that only he can satisfy, and I'm so wet I'm sure he can feel it through the fabric separating us.

Our lips hover mere inches apart, warm breath and mint toothpaste mingling. Nothing else exists in this moment. The house could burn down around us, and I wouldn't even care.

His nose brushes mine, and his eyelids hood. "This is dangerous, Tink."

"Why?" I whisper.

"I don't know if I can keep myself in check."

"So don't."

One hand slides up to the back of my neck, and his mouth captures mine, soft and firm and perfect. Sparks shoot down my spine, a whimper escaping the back of my throat. His hold on me tightens and he lets out a low, impatient growl as his tongue glides along the seam of my lips, demanding entrance. Whatever was holding him back before has vanished; this is the same strong, dominant guy who fucked me senseless in a nightclub bathroom.

My lips part, yielding to him as he threads his fingers in my hair and angles my face. When his tongue brushes mine, we both groan, needily grasping at one another. Now I remember how we ended up with me on the counter and his cock buried inside of me. One kiss, and I'm completely under his spell. I'd let him do anything he wanted right now.

Heat floods my body as he nips at my neck. It's followed by a trail of searing open-mouthed kisses before his teeth sink into my skin again, hard enough to leave a mark this time. Between the friction between our bodies and the skill of his lips, it's pleasure overload. I whimper, my nails clawing at his back. He's going to make me come, and he hasn't even taken my clothes off.

"Ser," he rasps against my throat. "I've waited months to hear you make those sounds."

And I've waited months for him to touch me again.

Strong hands dig into my waist with a crushing grip. I rock against him again, hungry and frantic with need, reveling in the way he hardens even more.

An appreciative sound rumbles in his chest. "Are you going to come for me like a good girl?"

"Uh-huh," I cry into his mouth.

Our kiss grows wetter, sloppier as I reach the point of no return. I swivel my hips, chasing the release I desperately crave. When he thrusts up to meet me, euphoria sparks in my core, and my vision tunnels.

My head tips back, my lips parting on a gasp. "Oh, god. Tyler, I—"

Suddenly, the doorbell rings upstairs and we startle, jolting apart. Every part of my body protests at the abrupt loss of stimulation. I'm breathless and fevered, literally aching to come.

Is it possible to die from being edged? It feels like a legitimate possibility at the moment.

Tyler glances up at the ceiling, his brows drawn together. "Who the fuck would be here this early?"

"I think I might have an idea." But I sincerely hope I'm wrong.

He releases me and I scramble off his lap to open his bedroom door, poking my head out to hear what's happening upstairs.

Blood roars in my ears as I listen, trying to catch my breath. Footfalls sound, followed by hinges creaking open.

"Hi!" Abby's muffled voice travels through the floor above. "Is Sera awake yet?"

"Fuuuuck." Tyler falls back on the bed, throwing an arm over his eyes. His position draws attention to the very large, very angry erection straining to break free from his black boxer briefs. Desire pulses like a heartbeat between my thighs. The temptation to finish what we started is almost too much to resist.

"You tell me. I thought she was with you," Chase says to Abby, his voice flat.

"Oh. Um, can you check her room, maybe?"

Shit. She's going to blow my cover.

He pulls himself upright onto one elbow. "It'll be okay, Ser. Just stick to the plan like we discussed. Go upstairs and act like everything is normal."

"Plan," I repeat. "Normal. Right."

Except under our original plan, I wasn't interrupted in the middle of an orgasm and completely discombobulated.

I run to his nightstand and grab my cell, frantically composing a message.

> Sera: Just got out of the shower. Give me a sec and I'll be right up.

Abby: No prob.

Bolting for the bathroom, I strip out of Tyler's shirt and quickly tug on my white terry cloth robe, tying it at the waist. What I really need is a pair of clean underwear, because mine are drenched, but beggars can't be choosers. At this point, I'll settle for not getting caught.

Then I put my hair up, splash some water on my face to emulate a freshly showered look, and pray as I climb the stairs.

They're both standing in the entry waiting for me as I step upstairs.

"Sorry," I tell Chase. "I was getting out of the shower when I heard the doorbell, and I couldn't dry off in time."

"No worries, Sera." His attention swivels to Abby, and irritation flashes across his face. "Just text her next time instead, Abby. Don't ring the fucking doorbell. I know you might not relate, but some of us have actual lives and responsibilities and need our sleep."

It's a little harsh, but I can't fault him for being annoyed. Sometimes it seems like her thought process is either focused solely on herself or entirely nonexistent.

"Sorry," she says, but it rings insincere.

I jerk my thumb at the hall leading to my room, then gesture to myself. "I'm not decent. Let's go into my room so I can finish getting dressed."

"I brought you an apology coffee." She offers me one of the cups from the cardboard tray. I take it from her hand, noting that it's not decaf. Mixing this with my meds will launch me to the moon. But it's the thought that counts . . . I guess.

"Thanks."

Chase's eyebrows lift. Not only is he nosy, but he also never misses a thing. "Apology for what?"

I cut in before Abby can respond. "Oh, we had a silly little argument last night. Nothing major. You know, girl stuff."

Girl stuff? I don't make any sense right now. Hopefully he's too tired to notice.

"Right. Whatever." He stomps back upstairs muttering something beneath his breath. I don't love that he'll be crabby with me for a while, but it's still better than the alternative of being found out.

Head spinning, I usher Abby into my room and close the door behind her. I'm still kind of pissed at her, but also trying to process everything that's happened in the past twenty-four hours. I almost can't decide how upset I should be. Shouldn't I be able to look out for myself?

Abby flops onto my bed, giving me an expectant look. "What's going on, missy?"

For once in her life, she's actually whispering.

"Nothing," I hiss back.

Rifling through my drawers, I search for something to wear. I still haven't fully unpacked, and I can't find a single thing lately. I'm drowning in clothes—and I have a few more deliveries on the way. I should declare a shopping hiatus. Will I? Probably not.

"Bullshit. You left with Hades. Something had to have happened."

"I left because I wasn't feeling good, Abbs. Tyler wouldn't take advantage of me like that."

"If you say so . . ." She purses her lips, studying me. Then her green eyes fly open with sudden realization. "Wait. Something happened with you two this morning."

How does she know that? Oh my god. Is it written on my face? Does Chase know?

"Shh!" I hush her. Not only do I not want my brother to hear, but there's also a tiny part of me that doesn't fully trust Abby with this information. I can't explain it; she's supposed to be one of my best friends. I've known her since we were little.

Lately, there's this nagging friction between us that she doesn't seem to notice. It's not clear whether she's changed or I have. Maybe we're just growing apart. But who does that leave me with? I hardly know anyone here. Siobhan and Bailey are lovely, but maybe they feel obligated to hang out with me as part of some girlfriendly duty.

"Did you guys fuck?"

"No. You interrupted us." Much to my dismay. A tiny part of me was worried I'd built Tyler up too much in my head. That time and imagination had distorted my memory of our night together, twisting reality into some kind of impossible fantasy. That the real thing couldn't possibly live up to what I remembered.

I was wrong. It's so much better.

Abby grimaces. "Oops."

Turning away, I step into some clean underwear, then put on a matching pink bra. It seems wrong to get dressed before I've even showered, but I can't even begin to think about going back downstairs and seeing Tyler after what just happened.

"And you almost busted me with Chase," I add, slipping a tank top over my head. "Just text next time, Abbs."

"You're not going to get a boyfriend and turn boring on me, are you?"

Excuse me?

Tugging on a pair of yoga pants, I glance up at her. "Why would a boyfriend make me boring?" There's an edge to my tone I can't hide.

She lifts a shoulder. "Because then you won't want to go out and do fun things anymore."

"Last night wasn't exactly fun for me. Where were you, anyway?"

What upsets me most of all about this scenario is that I would never do the same to her. In fact, I've taken care of Abby countless times, both back in high school as well as when I came back home for visits in college.

"I was in the living room the whole time. I would've helped you if I had known. I'm sure it would've passed quickly if you waited it out."

I'm not so sure that the first part is true. Abby isn't exactly the nurturing type. She might have patted my back for a minute, but would she have really stayed with me until I calmed down? Either way, there's no chance I could've stayed at the party. With the lights, music, and people, it was complete sensory overload.

Shame seeps into the pit of my stomach. Why did I do that, anyway? I've *never* taken hard drugs before. In the moment, I'd been overwhelmed by everything that had happened at the doctor.

Fear, grief, sadness, anxiety. It was too much; all I wanted was for it to stop.

In retrospect, it seems like such an irresponsible choice.

Does Tyler think less of me now? Ugh. I always screw things up.

"I need to cut back on going out anyway, Abbs. I have to pick a major ASAP and I need to make sure my grades stay up." Although this is a legitimate concern, it isn't the only reason. I'm more than a little annoyed with her after last night. And if that's an average weekend outing for Abby, I'm not sure we'll be hanging out much.

"Psh." She waves a hand dismissively. "Who cares about all that? Just get an M-R-S degree."

"M-R-S?"

"Yeah," she says. "A Mrs. degree. A.k.a., marry rich."

I groan. "Abby . . ."

"What? That's my plan." Abby tips back her coffee. "I guess it's different when you already have lots of money like you do. You can become a sugar mama and have a rotation of hot pool boys."

While that idea might appeal to her, it sounds highly depressing to me. My father left me an inheritance to ensure I would be financially stable and could pursue my dreams, not loaf around and pay hot younger men for sexual favors.

Thinking about the future brings me back to what happened at the doctor's office yesterday. My stomach sinks to the floor. What if the test comes back positive? I'm sure that would be a great icebreaker on dates.

"By the way, I'm nearly guaranteed to develop cancer, and I need to have children sooner than later."

No pressure there, right?

I hate that I have to think about this right now. I hate that Mom is sick in the first place.

All the emotions from yesterday start to well up again. I draw in a breath, holding it for a beat before I exhale slowly, counting to five inside my head. It doesn't help. My entire body is brimming with anxiety, threatening to overflow.

Clearing my throat, I paste on a neutral expression as I work to conceal the turmoil inside. "I hate to kick you out, Abbs, but I have a ton of schoolwork to do."

She makes a face. "What? It's not even noon."

"Yeah," I lie. "Super swamped." In truth, none of my assignments should take overly long. I need some time by myself to process everything. Or try to, at least.

Once I escort a protesting Abby out the door, I go back into my room and lock myself inside. A sigh of relief slips through my lips. She seemed more than a little miffed, but I don't particularly care.

Instead of feeling better like I expected, my thoughts grow a thousand times more upsetting the moment I'm alone. The doctor. My mom. BRCA. Tyler. School. Picking a major. Everything circles in my brain as my mind races, panic ramping up a notch. I'm on the verge of having an epic meltdown. Whether that's another anxiety attack or crying or something else, I can't be sure. Maybe all of the above.

Grabbing my noise-canceling headphones, I sit crisscross on my bed and pull out my MacBook. Then I start to free write, channeling everything onto the page. At first, it dredges up everything I'm trying to hide from, and I feel a thousand times worse, but with more time and more words, I slowly start to feel better. Not happy—but lighter, at least.

My calendar pops up at the bottom of my page reminding me about my creative writing assignment due tomorrow. Normally, I wouldn't start on this for another few hours. I put the "pro" in "procrastination," and I work best under pressure. Since I need the distraction, I retrieve my textbook and read the first two chapters as assigned. Then I submit a response paragraph including my "Writer's Purpose Statement" to the online forum for class discussion.

An iMessage notification appears on-screen from Tyler.

> Hades: Grabbed you breakfast. I knocked but you didn't answer. Wasn't sure if you were sleeping.
>
> Tinker Bell: Sorry, I didn't hear it.
>
> Hades: I'm at your door.

I practically pole-vault off the bed, then catch myself and realize I'm being overly eager. *Relax, Sera. You saw the guy, like, an hour ago.*

When I pull open the door, Tyler is standing there with a latte in one hand and a brown paper bag in the other. My stomach does a twirl. Then it hits me that I'm still unshowered, but too late now. I'll get on that next.

His mouth lifts at one corner. "Strawberry muffin. I thought you should eat. And since it's decaf, I figured you can never have too much coffee."

"Thank you." The bag crinkles as I take it from him, then the coffee. Tension crackles between us, the by-product of unresolved desires and unspoken questions.

"Ty!" Dallas calls in the background. "I'm leaving without you if you don't get in the fucking car."

"Gotta go. We have dryland. I'll text you later." He winks at me, and a tiny thrill runs through my body.

"Sounds good."

The past twenty-four hours have been some of the best and worst of my life.

Chapter 16

WORK-LIFE BALANCE

TYLER

The first half of my week is uneventful, if slightly unfocused. Turns out, reminiscing about Seraphina grinding against my cock is a lot more interesting than learning about molecular biochemistry and nucleotides.

I can't stop thinking about that kiss. Her soft inhale when our lips finally met and every pretty little sound that followed until the fucking doorbell rang. Unsurprisingly, taking matters into my own hands hasn't been remotely satisfying. I'm so horny I can barely function, and I have a full day ahead of me before I can do anything about it.

So much for compartmentalizing.

It's bitterly cold as I cut across campus on my way back to the arena for afternoon skate. Even with my gloves, my fingers are stiff as I pull out my phone to answer an incoming call.

"Hey, Dad." I jam my free hand back into my fleece-lined coat pocket for warmth, scanning the quad in search of a place to duck inside.

"Tyler." His voice is warm like always, but there's a note of something I can't identify. Hesitancy, or maybe concern. "Do you have a minute?"

"Sure. What's up?"

He pauses. "I thought you should know there's been some chatter about New York talking to Caleb Brown."

"*What?*" My heart smashes into my rib cage, and I come to a halt in the middle of the sidewalk. A guy walking behind me nearly plows straight into my back. He grumbles at me, veering left at the last minute, and I narrowly bite back a retort telling him to keep his head up.

Based on New York's current depth chart, everything is perfectly aligned for me to step in after their current goaltender retires in a couple more years. Or it *was*, anyway. This development is a massive, hockey-stick-sized wrench in my career path.

"I wanted to let you know in case you heard it through the grapevine."

"I hadn't," I mutter, pinching the bridge of my nose. Surely I would've soon, though, and we both know that. Him sheltering me is pointless, especially given how invasive social media is. Everyone knows everything in the industry. There are no secrets.

"Take a breath, Ty. Remember, this isn't personal. You know how the business works. They're not replacing you; they're acquiring a tradable asset."

"Caleb isn't some random player." Chest tight, I take a sharp left to duck inside the campus food court. It's too fucking cold to stand out here and have a serious conversation. "He's another goalie."

More specifically, Caleb is another third-year Division I goalie who's sitting two spots below me in the standings. I'm still leading the league, but it's a tight race.

Warm air envelops me as I step inside the cafeteria commons. It's more crowded than usual, and there's a line at the coffee shop nearly out the door. I'm going to chance it. I need a caffeine fix.

"You've been a top prospect your whole career. He's a kid having one banner year. The team is hedging their bets. If you stay strong, they can package him as part of a deal later to make the team better."

And if I don't, they can run with Caleb and relegate me to the farm team for the rest of my days.

A text from Seraphina comes through.

> Tinker Bell: Question 26: Your go-to way to relieve stress?

I blink at the screen, trying to decipher if this is an honest question or her roundabout way of initiating sexting. My brain is legitimately too fried to tell.

Dad's voice comes through on the speaker again, and I place it back to my ear.

"On paper and on the ice, you're stronger. You've been on fire since getting back after Christmas."

Exactly. So why is New York sniffing around another goalie prospect?

Except I know why. It's a business, and at the end of the day, I'm a product.

"Feels like a lot of pressure to keep it that way," I admit.

"There are always going to be ups and downs. All that matters is your consistency. Don't let this take you out of your head this weekend."

Little late for that. I'm in a tailspin. Hopefully, I'll have my shit together before Friday. That's a few days away still.

"Just so I'm clear," I say carefully, "does New York still want me for training over the summer?"

"Last I heard, it was looking good. That alone is a great sign, and it's why you shouldn't worry. Focus on what you can control."

He's right. That's all I can do.

Ending the call, I get into line for a coffee before I haul ass to the rink. Practice is a shit show, at least inwardly. My performance is strong, but my mental game sucks. I'm rattled after every single shot that gets past me—even though very few of them do.

When I meet Mark for off-ice training afterward, I already know I'm in for a rough ride.

"Have you been practicing your drills?" He looks at me over his shoulder as he grabs the yellow reaction ball from where it rolled out of my reach. Again. Its unpredictable trajectory is perfect for training reflexes and agility. It also makes it painfully obvious when I'm not in the zone.

"Daily, like you said."

He grunts. "I was watching you on the ice. You've been distracted all day."

Who wouldn't be? Between New York looking at picking up another goalie and what happened with Seraphina a few days ago, my head is anywhere but here.

That isn't an excuse. In fact, it's pretty goddamn weak.

"Sorry," I say, taking the six-sided ball from Mark's palm.

Fucking focus.

Drawing in a deep breath to center myself, I reset my stance before I release the ball again. It bounces off the floor and veers sharply to the right. This time, my hand snatches out of midair on the first try.

It takes more effort than usual, but I manage to pull my act together for the rest of our tactical skills training. Then we move into the stretching area for some much-needed mindfulness, breathwork, and visualization. It requires stellar emotional regulation to perform well under pressure. I can't win games, but I can sure as fuck lose them. I'm the hero or the scapegoat, depending how things play out. Either way, *everyone* knows how I played.

"Let's do a quick nutrition check-in." Mark shuffles the stack of papers on his lap and glances up at me. "Latest DEXA scan looks good. Your muscle mass is great. Body fat percentage is right in the range of where we want it to be, though it's trending down slightly. Make sure you're eating enough. We don't want you to get too lean."

"I'm not sure I could eat more if I tried." At this point, it feels like a part-time job.

My stomach growls angrily as if the subject summoned my appetite.

"On that note," he says, "what do you say we grab a cheat meal off-campus? We can have a chat about a few things."

I know from experience this is his way of using fried food to lure me into a false sense of security before he delivers a tough-love pep talk. After how shaky I was at the start of training, I can't say I'm surprised.

"Sure. Let me swing by my locker to grab a few things and I can meet you in half an hour."

♦ ♦ ♦

Halfway to the Overtime to meet Mark, I get delayed behind a massive accident. After sitting at a full stop for ten minutes, there's no chance I'll make it on time. I'm supposed to be there already.

When I hit the button on my hands-free controls to call and let him know, it says no phone is connected. Huh?

I reach into the console for my phone and find it empty. *Great.* Must've left it in my locker. At least, I hope that's where it is; that, or it fell out of my pocket on the way to my car. If I lost it, that'll be the last straw for the day.

Either way, I'm late—which I fucking hate—and I can't even let Mark know. Then I realize I never got the chance to write Seraphina back. Shit. She probably thinks I'm blowing her off.

Mark already has a booth in the corner when I finally walk inside the wooden double doors to Overtime. He gives me a nod, and I tug off my gloves, weaving around the tables over to him.

"Sorry," I say, sliding off my winter coat. "One of those days. Got stuck in traffic, and I don't have my phone on me. I have no idea where it is."

Something that looks like concern glances across his face. "No worries, Ty."

He lets me borrow his phone to sign in to iCloud on his browser. According to the little blinking circle on the map, my phone appears to be at the arena like I thought. On the off chance it's sitting out somewhere and not in my locker, I put it into lost mode until I'm able to go grab it.

Our server runs us through the daily specials before she takes our drink orders and leaves us with the menus. Scanning the list of dishes, I debate whether to stay on plan. I've been diligent about my eating habits this season. A lot less beer and alcohol, and a lot more nutrient-dense calories to fuel me through practices and games. Worth it for the resulting performance gains on the ice, but I can't deny that it sucks to see Chase and Dallas hoover whatever they want without a second thought. They have a lot more leeway than I do. Teams have more than twenty players but only one starting goalie. Our career paths are not the same.

"I meant what I said about the cheat meal." Mark looks at me pointedly over the top of his menu. "Don't even think about trying to order something like grilled fish and rice."

That's all the excuse I need. I settle on a loaded bacon cheeseburger with fries and a salad. Mark orders the same, minus the fries, and we split nachos to start.

"Circling back to your issues focusing earlier, have you been meditating daily like we discussed?" he confirms, raising his blond eyebrows.

"Yep." Trying to stay still for five minutes verged on agony when I first started. Now I can sit for more than half an hour without getting too restless. I rarely have that much time, though.

"Make sure you're getting enough rest. Not just physically, but mentally."

"I'm getting plenty of sleep."

"Not what I mean, Ty. You need downtime when you're awake too."

That's a nice idea in theory. In reality, my brain never shuts off.

Going into games, I prepare by cataloging the other team's players and their tendencies for passing and shooting. Once

I'm standing between the pipes, I'm constantly tracking everything happening on the ice even when the play is in the other zone. Monitoring my position; keeping tabs on the opposing team; checking in with my teammates; trying to predict where the play will go next. And always, *always* keeping eyes on the puck.

After all is said and done, I run through everything that happened. What worked, what didn't. Victories and failures, lessons and takeaways. I have a running inner monologue twenty-four hours a day, seven days a week. I even dream about hockey.

The only time I feel some semblance of calm is when I'm with Seraphina. Then it's like all the other noise disappears, if only for the brief sliver of time we're together. Her effect is a double-edged sword. It also means she has the potential to divert my attention when it counts.

That's on me. I need to do a better job at keeping everything separate.

Movement on the other side of the room catches my eye, and I spot Seraphina walking through the doors with a dark-haired girl. Speak of the devil. Her rose-gold hair is pulled back in a ponytail for a change, the loose curls tied with a black bow.

My eyes travel lower, taking in the tiny plaid miniskirt poking out beneath the bottom of her bulky winter coat. She looks innocent yet naughty, and it's hot as fuck. I'd like nothing more than to hike up that skirt and rail her in a bar bathroom for a second time.

I continue to watch her, transfixed. She's deep in conversation with her friend as they take a vacant table on the far side of the room, lowering into their seats. Should I go say hi? That wouldn't be weird, right? It would be weird if I saw her and *didn't* say anything. But I don't want to interrupt them . . .

"Thinking about something other than hockey once in a while wouldn't hurt." Mark's voice brings me hurtling back to reality.

I glance at him. "Oh, that's just my roommate."

"I see." He gives me an amused look, because I was drooling, and we both know it. "All I'm saying is, it's important to have some work-life balance."

It isn't that I disagree with him. It's that I have no idea how to do that.

Chapter 17
AGGRAVATINGLY PERFECT

SERAPHINA

Overtime is busier than usual, and empty tables are in scarce supply when Chloe and I arrive in the middle of the dinner rush. There are a few seats scattered on the opposite end of the bar, but we spot a bunch of obnoxious-looking frat boys nearby and decide to steer clear. Abby would've dragged me straight over and insisted we sit near, if not with, them.

Truthfully, I'm thrilled to be out with someone who's *not* Abby. Chloe and I have been able to carry on real conversations about meaningful things beyond bars and boys. Music, current events, activities to do around town. I still like fun, frivolous things too, but sometimes it's nice to discuss topics of actual substance instead of debating which nightclub has the best VIP section.

A little company is exactly what I needed today, especially because Tyler is ignoring me. Okay, maybe that's a little dramatic. I texted him a few hours ago—six, but who's counting?—and he never wrote me back. That wouldn't be as concerning if not for the fact I know he saw it. I know it sounds needy, maybe verging on insane, but this is the longest he's ever left me on read without replying.

Is he getting tired of all our messages back and forth? Has the appeal of our twenty-one (now twenty-six and counting) questions with me worn off? I know I'm overthinking, but it's impossible not to with a legitimately overactive brain.

Finally, Chloe and I find a small table near the pool tables at the back and snag it before anyone else can.

She slips off her navy jacket across from me. "Your poem today was amazing, Sera."

Heat laces my cheeks. "Thank you."

All of my writing is personal to me, but the one she's referring to is about my mom's cancer and BRCA. Although the true meaning is shrouded in heavy amounts of symbolism, it's the most naked thing I've ever put down on the page.

"I loved it. The part where you used the wind as a metaphor gave me chills."

"Really?" Her validation eases some of the tightness I've been carrying in my shoulders. "Oh, thank god. I was worried it wouldn't make sense."

"No, it totally did. How was it sharing your work? Was it terrifying?"

Surprising even myself, I voluntarily offered up some of my writing to workshop in class today. Everyone will have to do it at least twice this semester, so I figured I might as well get used to it. After the initial moments of terror passed, it wasn't as bad as I expected. All of my classmates were nice, and I got some useful feedback.

"I was a nervous wreck," I confess. "But I'm really glad I did it. I'm surprised how much I've been loving class so far."

"Me too. Though I'm not looking forward to next week. The syllabus says we're studying love poems in honor of Valentine's Day." Chloe makes a face. "Might as well study fairy tales."

"You don't believe in love?"

She scoffs. "About as much as I believe in the Easter Bunny. I mean, it's a nice concept. I'm sure it's out there for other people. For me? No. I've abandoned that idea. Love, dating, all of it. Plus, between work and school, I don't have time to date. Like, at all."

"That last part sounds like Tyler," I muse. "I mean, my roommate."

Worry glimmers in the back of my mind again. Why didn't he write me back? If he's blowing me off, I can live with that; I'd just like to know. Actually, that's a lie. A big, fat lie. If he's blowing me off, I'll be crushed.

Our server takes our drink orders, and once she disappears, we agree to split a bunch of appetizers instead of getting entrees. It's one of my favorite things to do at a restaurant. My bottomless pit of a brother is the first person who introduced me to it. Somehow, it feels vaguely naughty in a fun way—like you're a little kid who's bending the rules by not eating a "proper" meal.

We quickly settle on spinach-and-artichoke dip, buffalo chicken wings, pulled pork sliders, and chili-garlic shrimp, vowing to split the white chocolate brownie after if we still have any room left. It helps that we planned ahead; I got to preview the menu online ahead of time, thereby avoiding the usual overwhelm I run into when I'm put on the spot to make a decision.

Chloe sets down her Diet Coke, catching my eye. "Before I forget, there's a writing contest through *Revolve Magazine* I meant to tell you about. There are a few different categories, and I think the grand prize is five thousand dollars or something. The winners will be compiled into their yearly anthology, which is a huge deal. Maxine's been featured in it multiple times."

"Anything Maxine has done is goals, for sure. Are you going to enter?"

"No, silly. I meant you should."

"Me? That's nice of you to say, but I can't see how I'd ever have a shot at something like that." While I've always gotten by in school, I've never been an exemplary student. I don't get straight As, I don't make the honor roll, and I definitely don't win contests for my work. Those accolades are for organized, prepared types of people who have their acts together. In other words, not me.

She angles her head, leveling me with a look that says she doesn't understand. "Why not? You said you've been writing for a while. It's not like you're new."

"I'm new to writing *properly*," I counter, biting into a piece of spicy shrimp.

"There's no right or wrong with poetry. Remember what Maxine said in class today? 'Good poetry makes you feel something.' Your poem definitely made me feel something, and I'm not the only one."

Cautious hope blossoms within me. Chloe seems to believe what she's saying, but that doesn't make it true. It's possible she's just being supportive.

"Thanks, Chloe. I'll give it some thought." Can't see myself actually going through with entering, but it's nice of her to think of me.

We plow through our food in short order, making it to the famed white chocolate brownie topped with vanilla ice cream, whipped cream, and chocolate sauce. It's ridiculously over the top and decadent and I inhale my half with zero regrets.

When the server brings our bill, I grab the black leather folio and stick my credit card inside. "I got it."

"What?" she protests. "No, you don't have to do that."

"You picked me up, so I'll pay. Don't worry about it." Based on some of our conversations, I've gathered that finances are tight for her, which is why she works full-time while juggling school.

She opens her mouth like she's going to argue, then closes it again. "Okay, but only if you're sure. Thank you." Her gaze lands off in the distance over my shoulder. "Actually, I need to hit the restroom before we go. Be right back."

Chloe excuses herself to use the restroom before we leave. As soon as she's out of sight, I unlock my phone again to check my messages. My hopes crash and burn when I find several new texts from Abby and none from Tyler.

Footfalls thud beside me as someone approaches the table. I lift my chin expecting to see Chloe, and my heart does a twirl when I lock eyes with Hades himself.

A fitted black Henley drapes across his firm chest, long sleeves pushed partway up to reveal his inked forearms; a pair of perfectly broken-in jeans emphasize his strong hockey thighs;

and the leather watch he's wearing somehow makes it all ten times hotter.

He looks absolutely, aggravatingly perfect.

"Hey, Ser." Tyler stuffs his hands in his pockets, giving me a boyish grin that makes my insides turn to mush. If I didn't know better, I might think he's nervous. Not sure why he would be when he's the one who left me hanging.

I paste on a smile I hope looks more genuine than it feels. "Hi."

"I'm sorry I didn't write you back earlier. Forgot my phone at the arena after practice." Tension stretches across his face, and he forks a hand through his sandy hair, mussing it. "It's been a day."

A paradox of emotions hits me. Relief, giddiness, along with a strong undercurrent of embarrassment at how I overreacted. I feel silly, even though no one else knows I did.

"That's okay," I say. "Are you here with the team?"

"Just finished up with my goalie coach. We grabbed some dinner after training."

Chloe speed walks up to the table, her gaze glued to the phone in her hand. She's so frazzled she doesn't seem to register Tyler's presence.

"I'm sorry, Sera. There's an emergency at work, and they need me to come in right away. It's on the other side of town, so I'll drive you home quickly, and then—"

"I got it," Tyler interjects. "I'm heading home anyway. I can drive her."

Her attention lifts from her screen and lands on him, her mouth parting in a little "O" of confusion. I didn't mention having a boyfriend, and that's probably what she's assuming right now. Or she thinks I'm about to leave with some random guy.

I gesture between them. "Chloe, this is Tyler, my roommate. Hence the driving-home offer. Tyler, this is Chloe. We have a class together."

Her shoulders sag with relief. "Would you mind? My boss

is such a jackass. I feel terrible. It's probably something like a clogged toilet he can't be bothered to plunge himself. Again."

"All good," I assure her. I'm more excited about Tyler driving me home than a normal person should be. It's a ride home, not a date. Then again, we've already had one eventful car ride with my audiobook.

Once I get my credit card back from the server, we walk Chloe to her car where it's parked near the back of the lot.

Tyler turns to me as she pulls away. "Mind if we make a quick stop at the rink to grab my phone?" His words are puffs of steam against the frosty night air.

"No, that's fine." Like I'd turn down a chance to be alone with him longer. The minute we get home, we're going to go our separate ways and act like we hardly know each other, then send a bunch of texts back and forth until we fall asleep.

We fall into step together as he expertly navigates across campus, teaching me several new shortcuts along the way. The chill nips at my ears, and I pull up my hood, but it doesn't help enough. Between my admittedly impractical outfit and my failure to pack a beanie or earmuffs this morning, I'm frozen and I'm starting to shiver.

"Here, Tink." Slowing to a stop beneath a streetlamp, Tyler pulls something out of his backpack. Then he tugs down my hood and carefully slides his black Falcons beanie over my head, his touch light, like he's trying to ensure he doesn't ruin my hair. The thick wool covers my ears and buffers the wind on my face, instantly cutting some of the chill.

He studies me for a beat, like he's inspecting his own handiwork, and one side of his mouth tips up. "You're cute."

"Cute?" I pout.

"Among other things." His gaze does a slow coast down my body before he catches himself. Inclining his head, he gestures for us to start walking again. We pick up our pace as Northview Arena comes into sight in the distance, so close but so far from the sweet relief of being indoors.

Tyler opens the oversized glass door and holds it open, motioning for me to go first. Warm air washes over my face as I step inside, and he follows.

"For reference, my answer to your question is cleaning."

"Cleaning?" I can't remember what my question was.

"You asked what I do when I'm stressed out," he says, taking a left to lead me down a hallway. "I clean. Or when I have more time on my hands, I get tattoos."

Picturing Tyler with a mop in one hand is both oddly cute and surprisingly endearing. I hadn't pegged him for the domestic type.

"Does that also include the occasional piercing?" I ask.

I nearly fell over when my hand wrapped around his cock in the bathroom at XS to find not one, not two, but three silver barbells at the base. A full-on Jacob's Ladder. I'd never been with a guy who had piercings before, and let's just say I'm a newly converted believer. It hit the spot—literally.

"Just the once." A grin tugs at his cheeks. "No plans for any more of those, I don't think. Your turn to answer."

"Truthfully? Probably go out with my friends and pretend whatever's stressing me out doesn't exist, but as you know, that strategy doesn't seem to be working out so well for me lately. It looks like shopping is going to be my coping mechanism moving forward. I'm big into retail therapy."

"The constant carousel of online deliveries gave me some idea," he says wryly. "As did the fact you've started to take over the hallway."

"I'll organize my room . . . someday." I really need to finish unpacking. Maybe I can pay someone to come help me. How much do professional organizers cost? Probably worth it.

"Hopefully before you move out."

I groan at the reminder. "Oh, god. Things have been so crazy that I haven't even *looked* for an apartment." It's one of the billion balls I've dropped since moving. Others include working out and eating an adequate amount of fruits and vegetables. At the rate I'm going, the guys are going to get sick of me long before I manage to find a place to live.

"I'm not in a big hurry to see you go, Ser." His voice softens, melting me right along with it.

In a few more turns, we reach the doorway to the Falcons locker room. Finally warm enough, I slip off Tyler's beanie and tuck it in my purse. I smooth my static flyaways while I hang back, waiting for him to enter his ID for access. He holds open the crimson-painted door for me, and I brush past him, savoring the familiarity of his masculine, clean scent.

Much to my surprise, the locker room smells fresh, tinged with a hint of Windex and cleaning solution—a far cry from what I assume it smells like after a game. The door clicks shut behind us as he flips a switch on the wall and a three-dimensional Falcons logo in the center of the ceiling lights up, illuminating the space. It's spotless; sleek and modern, all shades of red, black, and gray.

Equipment cubbies run along both sides with padded leather benches in front and stainless-steel name plaques marking each player's spot. To the right is a wall listing of alumni who played professionally after attending Boyd. I run my fingertips across the embossed metal plaques, scanning their names, some familiar and some not.

"You'll be up here soon," I tell him.

He winks at me. "That's the plan." Striding to the opposite end of the room, he opens a red locker and emerges with his phone. A moment later, he comes to stand in front of me, an indecipherable look across his face. "Do you need to get home?"

Excitement crackles beneath my skin. "No, why?"

"I want to show you something."

Taking me by the wrist, he leads me to the door, and we step back into the hall. I'm equal parts confused and disappointed. Our sneaky locker room break-in had my mind going in a dramatically different, far dirtier direction, and I thought "showing me" was code for something else.

A heavy, muscular arm slides around my waist as he wordlessly steers me down the corridor, his grip casual, like it's the most natural thing in the world for the two of us to be this close. I've been so desperate for him to make a move; I'm on the verge of hyperventilating now that he is.

Two flights of stairs later, we come to stand before another locked door. Tyler punches in a code and pushes it open to reveal a small room filled with audiovisual equipment. Wide panes of glass along one wall look out onto the arena, a faint, blue-tinted glow from the emergency lighting system filtering through. He closes the door behind us, but he doesn't flip on the lights.

"The announcer's box?" I guess, scanning the array of dormant electronics.

"My dad brought me up here when I decided to attend Boyd. He gave me this long inspirational speech about how proud he was of me. I always looked up to the athletes he worked with when I was kid, and this was the moment when I felt like I'd finally made it to the next level."

"You and your dad are close, huh?" My throat tightens at the reminder of everything I've missed with mine. Losing him in that helicopter crash when I was nine changed everything. It changed me.

"Yeah," he says. "We talk all the time. I think we're a lot alike."

"What's the rest of your family like?"

"My younger brother, Jonah, plays hockey too. He's good, though maybe not quite as good as he thinks." Tyler smirks. "Then my mom's a doctor, and my sister, Elise, is into competitive gymnastics. It's like a whole family tree of overachievers."

This doesn't come as a huge surprise, and it's starting to shed some light on why he pushes himself so much.

"Were you close to your dad?" he asks softly.

A familiar pang of longing sets in. "I was a total daddy's girl."

His eyes hold mine. "I'm sorry, Ser."

I can tell he wants to say something more, but he doesn't. Dead parents make even the most well-intentioned people uncomfortable. I don't hold it against anyone. If they haven't experienced it themselves, it's impossible for them to relate.

"It's okay." I step closer to the bank of windows, taking in everything from our elevated vantage point. Down below, the spectator stands are completely empty, the playing surface vacant aside from the painted lines and massive Boyd U Falcons symbol beneath the ice. This perspective from above drives home the massive scale of the seventeen-thousand-person arena, which is bigger than some professional hockey venues.

"Nice view," I murmur. "Everything looks so small from up here."

"Feels a lot bigger when you're standing down there in front of the net." He comes to stand beside me, the heat of his body warming mine. Our fingers brush, and my heart skips a beat as he threads them together. I have no idea how something so small can have such a big effect on me.

"Did you always want to play goal?"

He nods, his gaze focused on the other side of the glass. "The first time I stood in that crease, I knew."

"Makes sense. Goalies are built different. Some people say they're a little cr—"

"Watch it, Tink." Tyler pokes me in the ribs, and I yelp, trying to scoot out of his reach. He pulls me toward him instead, easily overpowering me. Pivoting, he walks me backward a few steps until I'm trapped between a table and his broad, solid body. My skin thrums in response to his proximity, the throb in my core growing stronger by the second. I'm wound so tightly I can hardly breathe.

Cupping my chin, he tilts my face up to his. "Care to finish what you were going to say?" Slate eyes peer down at me, gleaming with a mixture of desire and amusement.

"Goalies are crazily talented?"

He tsks, fighting a smile. "You're a brat, you know that?"

"I try."

For a few tense breaths, neither of us moves. His calloused

thumb runs across my cheek, caressing, and his gaze falls to my mouth, darkening to a smolder that lights a fire low in my belly. My heart skips a beat as he lowers his lips to mine until they're almost touching. I circle my arms around his neck to pull him closer, and he draws in a jagged breath, covering my mouth with his.

Finally.

Exhilaration floods my veins, and I let out a sigh, twining my fingers in the soft hair at his nape. He takes my bottom lip between his teeth, biting gently, then licks where he just nipped me. This is different than last time; more deliberate and controlled, like he's savoring every second.

Strong hands cup my ass and set me on the table behind us. He nudges my legs apart, then pulls me to the edge until there's no space between our bodies. Our centers aligned perfectly, my hips move into his, and I feel him harden against me. The empty ache in my core is nearly unbearable.

My palms smooth up his chest to his shoulders, impatiently urging off his jacket. Without breaking our kiss, he shrugs it off, then removes mine. The room fills with breathy moans and the rustling of clothes, murmurs, and the clanging of his buckle. We're on a mission to see this through to completion, neither wasting time on foreplay after we got left hanging last time.

Fumbling, I unfasten his jeans while he yanks up the hem of my skirt. His fingertips hook onto the sides of my panties, yanking them off in one decisive swoop. Rough palms smooth up my bare legs until he reaches the apex of my thighs. Cupping where I'm heated and aching for him, he strokes my clit, and a feral growl rumbles in his chest.

"Such a perfect pussy." His finger dips inside my entrance and strokes my inner wall, curling to apply perfect pressure.

"Ty." I groan, writhing as he teases me again. Pleasure sparks in my core, flickering in and out while he deliberately keeps me hanging on the edge.

My hand slips beneath the band of his boxer briefs, skimming past his smooth, taut abs to grasp his cock. He's even bigger than I remembered, thick and heavy in my palm. His breaths grow shallow as my fingertips skim down his shaft, tracing the three piercings at the bottom.

When my fist wraps around the base, his hips jerk, and he groans into my neck. "Fuck, Ser. I can't control myself with you."

"Condom," I manage, panting and desperate and soaked. "In my purse over there."

In a blink, he's sheathed and settled between my legs again. My back arches, fingertips greedily scrabbling to pull him closer. He grips himself, rubbing the head of his cock up and down along my swollen, sensitive clit.

I whimper. "Don't tease me."

He kisses me as he thrusts forward, swallowing my cry. It's a snug fit that fills me completely, leaving me lost for words. He pushes into me until he meets resistance, the base of his pelvis rubbing my clit.

Euphoria floods my core, and my legs wrap around his waist. "Oh, god."

"*Shit.*" His hips stutter and he grabs my waist roughly, dropping his forehead to my shoulder. He falls still for a moment, exhaling slowly like he's channeling his control. "You feel so goddamn good, Tink. So fucking tight."

Once his composure returns a second later, his lips tug into a wicked smirk. He lowers his mouth to my ear and his warm breath skirts my skin. "I'm going to fuck you nice and hard, and you're going to be quiet for me like a good girl, aren't you?"

"Uh-huh." My voice is breathy, my body desperate for him to start moving.

He eases his length out before he thrusts inside me, rattling the equipment behind us. My eyes squeeze shut, overwhelmed by the sudden rush of pleasure. Our bodies align together so perfectly it's like it was by design. It's so much more intense than anything I've experienced with anyone else.

"Do you feel how hard I am for you?" He plunges into me, nudging my G-spot.

"Yes." I gasp as my walls clench around him, embarrassingly close to coming already.

With the next snap of his hips, my purse falls off the table beside us and crashes to the floor, its contents scattering all over.

"Leave it," I beg. "Don't stop."

His growl tells me he had no intention of stopping. Body rolling, he rocks into me, going deeper and creating friction where I need it most. He hits the perfect spot inside over and over, relentlessly dragging me up to the peak as I hold on to him for dear life.

Pleasure coils in my core as I teeter on the edge, entirely at his mercy. A string of pleas slips through my lips, desperate for release—and then he gives it to me, expertly fucking me through an earth-shattering orgasm.

When he's finished, I'm reduced to a quivering, boneless mess, and I'm so sensitive I can't handle another second of stimulation.

"Give me a sec." Sighing, I slump against him.

He huffs a low laugh and kisses the crown of my head. "Only one."

Chapter 18
LIKE THAT

TYLER

There's nothing hotter than watching Seraphina unravel beneath me.

I have no idea how I held it together while she came all over my cock, especially when it's been a few months since I last had sex. Since *we* had sex, specifically, because I haven't been with anyone else. Maybe all my mental training from hockey has paid off in other areas.

She rests her head on my shoulder, her rose-gold hair spilling in a curtain against my dark shirt. Somewhere along the way, I must've pulled out the bow holding her ponytail together. I have no idea when—or where it went.

Her chest heaves with a contented sigh as I rub her back, waiting for her to recover. She's soft and warm in my arms, her wet pussy gripping me so tightly I could easily bust on the spot if I let myself. My cock twitches impatiently, but I know she's overstimulated and needs a breather.

Another couple of seconds pass and Seraphina pulls herself upright, giving me an expectant look. Her rosy lips are kiss-swollen, her cheeks flushed, and her eyelids are heavy with pleasure.

She inches forward slightly, bringing her lips to mine. "Keep going. Fuck me."

I love how unabashed she is. It's one of my favorite things about her.

"I have a better idea." Reaching beneath her bare thighs, I lift her off the table without disconnecting our bodies. She holds on to me as I shuffle a few steps backward and lower to sit in a nearby chair so she's straddling me.

Her chocolate eyes flash with understanding, and her fingertips land on my jaw as she brings her mouth to mine. "Gonna make me do all the work now, Hades?"

"I've been picturing you riding my cock ever since that morning in my room." I brush my lips against hers as my hands coast up her bare rib cage to cup her tits. They're a perfect handful, supple and weighty in my palms. My fingers pinch her nipples through the lace of her bra, reveling in the way they harden beneath my touch. "Actually, I've been thinking about it ever since XS."

Placing her hands on my shoulders, she rises onto her knees until we're nearly separated. My body protests and my hips lift reflexively, driven by the primal urge to stay balls deep inside of her. Her mouth tugs into a coy smile as she pauses, driving me crazy with anticipation.

"You mean like this?" She sinks down, taking me fully, and it's so good I swear I nearly black out.

"Fuck, yes." The words are a tortured groan across my lips. "Just like that."

This is like living out every fantasy I've ever had. I've been imagining her, dreaming about her, and jerking off to her for weeks, and the reality is even better. I've never been so hard in my life. Her little miniskirt takes the hotness of this whole equation to the next level.

Hiking up the plaid fabric covering her lower half, I look down at where our bodies are joined. My dick hardens even more at the sight of her wrapped around me, her folds pink and swollen and slick with her arousal.

"That's it," I husk, watching her glistening pussy slide up and down my cock. "Look how pretty you are taking all of me. Every single inch."

That earns me a breathy moan, because she likes being praised and I know it. She picks up speed, somehow taking me even deeper, and I bottom out inside of her, groaning her name. As much as I'd like to break our three-orgasm record, tonight isn't going to be the night that happens.

Seraphina grinds against me again, swirling her hips. She feels like heaven, and I'm dangerously close to losing control. All I can hope for is making sure she gets there again first.

Bracketing her waist with my hands, I thrust up to meet her so the base of my cock gives her the friction she needs.

Her mouth falls open in a soft gasp. "It's too good, Ty. I—ah, I can't."

"Yes, you can. We both know you've got more than one in you." Slipping one hand between our bodies, I tease her clit, slowly rubbing and circling while her body trembles, her pussy throbbing around my dick.

With a few more strokes of my fingers, her breath hitches.

"Oh." She cries out, louder than we should be, but I can't bring myself to care. "*Oh, god.*"

"Good girl." Pleasure builds at the base of my spine. It's a warning signal to slow down, but she's too far gone for me to stop her. "Come on my cock."

Her walls clench around me and squeeze so tightly, I can't hold back. White-hot pleasure tears through me, and my hold on her waist tightens until I know I'll leave marks on her skin later.

My mouth angles against hers, muffling her scream as we both fall apart. I come harder than I ever have before, pulsing and twitching inside of her, spilling into the condom while she kisses me frantically, her nails digging into my back. It's frenzied and needy, desperate and wild, like hurtling toward some kind of oblivion.

Panting, she rides out every last wave until we're both too spent to move.

"Wow." She drapes herself over me, her heart thudding against my chest.

My arms wrap around her and pull her closer. "I'm ruined, Tink. Fucking ruined."

A better person probably would harbor some degree of guilt for crossing a line. All I feel is a deep sense of primal satisfaction for having claimed her. All I want is to do it again.

Once we both come back to our senses, we reluctantly untangle ourselves and get dressed. Seraphina looks down and slips on her panties, pulling them up beneath her skirt while I kneel to pick up the items that fell out of her purse when it fell: a tube of lip gloss, a couple pens, a pink highlighter, her keychain, my black Falcons beanie, and her phone—luckily unscathed.

As I shove the items back into her bag, I catch sight of her black hair ribbon sitting underneath a chair and I grab it. At least we won't be leaving behind any evidence... other than the used condom in the garbage.

Passing Seraphina her purse, I lower my lips to hers for another brief kiss. And another. Being around other people without doing this is going to suck. Then again, I'm not sure what the hell "this" is.

I hold up her coat and help her slip into it. When she turns back to face me, my first instinct is to kiss her again. It's hard not to. With something else swirling in the back of my mind, I have to broach that first.

"What are we doing, Tink?" Maybe it's unfair of me to put her on the spot like this, but it's a legitimate question when I have no idea myself.

Her forehead crinkles and she pauses. "Why do we have to call it anything? Can't we just have some fun and enjoy things for what they are? We can be friends who kiss... and do a little more than that sometimes. Which is nobody else's business, for the record."

"Yeah?" Relief winds through me. Lately, she's the calm in the shitstorm otherwise known as my life. We have a good thing going, and I don't want to ruin it.

"Yeah." Pale pink fingernails trail down my chest, her soft lips finding my jaw.

I groan as my cock stiffens. "Easy, unless you're angling for round two."

Seraphina giggles. "Already?"

"I'm a twenty-one-year-old athlete, Ser, and you're fucking gorgeous."

My phone vibrates in my pocket, and when I pull it out to check the message, I notice the time. We've been in here longer than we should have been. It's a miracle we didn't get caught.

"We should get out of here before we land ourselves in trouble," I add.

The moment we step outside, Seraphina opens her leather purse and fishes out my beanie, tugging it over her rose-gold waves. Instantly, I feel myself break into one of those dumbass grins only she can elicit.

"I hope you know I'm keeping this," she says, smoothing her hair.

"I was hoping you would."

◆ ◆ ◆

One unintended benefit of ending my celibacy streak? I slept better than I have in months. Years, even. It was hard to drag myself out of bed.

A savory, smoky scent wafts through the air as I ascend the stairs, and my stomach growls in response. Through the doorway, I spot Dallas tending to a pan on the stove. *Score.* The only thing better than bacon is bacon you didn't have to cook yourself, especially at seven in the morning.

"What are you doing up so early?" I step into the kitchen, craning my neck to gauge the status of the food.

"I have a dentist appointment downtown," Dallas says. "Bacon should be ready in five."

I grab a mug from the cupboard and fill it at the coffeemaker as Seraphina darts into the room. Dallas's back is turned, so I leverage the opportunity to let my gaze linger on her longer than I should, taking in her black cropped hoodie, skintight black workout leggings, and hot pink Nikes.

Knowing what she looks like beneath those clothes is a special kind of torture. Can't afford to let my brain take a stroll down that particular memory lane while I'm wearing these sweats, though, or it's gonna get really awkward between Dallas and me really fast.

"Morning, Tink."

"Hey." She doesn't glance in my direction, kneeling to rummage through the cupboard. The most likely explanation is that she's distracted because she's running late, as usual. Still, I can't help but wonder if there's more to it than that.

Fuck. I'm overthinking again. Hard not to, given the situation. Every time I close my eyes, all I can see is Seraphina riding my cock in that little skirt with her head tipped back, her face contorted with pleasure. Are we good after last night?

Questions continue to play through my head while I reach into the fridge to grab the carton of milk. Thinking better of it, I put it back and close the door with my hip. Fuck cereal, I'm going to mooch some of Dallas's bacon.

Leaning against the counter, I steal a glance at Seraphina again. She pushes to stand with a frown, clutching an oversized pink travel tumbler like it's her lifeline, and makes a beeline for the coffeemaker to fill it. Maybe it's wishful thinking, but she seems more preoccupied than upset.

"Is this fresh coffee?" She brings it to her mouth and takes a sip, her brow creasing at the taste.

"Yeah," Dallas offers over his shoulder. "I tossed the other batch. Tasted like ass."

I bark a laugh because that's such a Dallas thing to do. He's particular about nearly everything, coffee included. Hell, he's almost more high maintenance than Seraphina, and that's saying something.

She's less amused with this turn of events. In fact, she looks positively crestfallen—like a little kid whose ice cream fell on the pavement on a hot summer's day. Then I realize why.

Decaf.

Guilt overtakes me and I bring a fist to my mouth, trying to pretend I was coughing. I hadn't expected her to take the loss of her coffee quite that hard, and I don't find her being sad funny. In fact, I fucking hate it.

Her warm brown eyes flicker over to the clock on the wall, then back to the coffeemaker, but she says nothing. Just heaves a quiet, disappointed sigh as she pours the contents of the mug into the sink. Judging by her outfit and the time, I'm fairly certain she's due to be at her usual seven o'clock workout class in five minutes—and the fitness studio is fifteen minutes away.

"Uh, Ward?" I say delicately. "That was Seraphina's decaf, just FYI."

"Her what?" Dallas sets down the tongs, turning to face us. His eyes widen as he processes what I'd just said, and he winces. "Oh shit. Sorry, Sera. I can make you some more if you want. It just didn't taste like it usually does, so I thought someone fucked it up. And by someone, I mean Tyler."

"To be clear, I make great coffee. It's just too strong for your wimpy ass."

"Thanks, but it's okay." She quickly rinses out the mug and dumps it in the sink. "I have to get going. I can hit the drive-through on my way to campus after the gym . . ." The waver in her voice tells me it's anything but okay.

Tossing us a wave and a mumbled good-bye, she brushes past us on her way out of the kitchen, resolutely avoiding eye contact. My chest pulls tight as I watch her leave. Conflict wars within me, a bloody battle between my conscience and my mind. The urge to go after her is strong, but I can't tell whether she wants to talk—and I don't want to make things worse if she doesn't. More specifically, I don't want to make it worse if I'm one of the things that's upsetting her.

Dallas throws me a remorseful look before turning back to tend the sizzling bacon on the stove. "Now I feel like a dick."

"It was an accident. Besides, I don't think that was about coffee."

"Dammit!" Sera's voice carries into the kitchen from the foyer. The distress in her voice is like a knife to the gut.

Fueled by pure instinct, I'm halfway to her before I even realize it.

"What's going on, Tink?" I ask, drawing closer. She's got her puffy winter coat on, and her purse is slung over one shoulder, but she's pacing in frantic circles, picking up random objects and looking beneath them. If she doesn't want to talk, at least I can say I tried.

She sets down a pair of noise-canceling headphones someone left on the couch and throws her hands in the air. "I can't find my fucking keys!"

Okay, we're in full-on meltdown mode. Noted.

"Where'd you last see them?" I ask. "I can help you look."

"If I knew where they were last, I'd have them right now!" Pivoting on her heel, she bumps the glass lamp on the entry table with her padded elbow, sending it toppling off the console. Immediately, my hand shoots out and I catch it before it hits the ground. Goalie instincts have their uses.

I set the lamp back before coming to stand in front of her. "Breathe, Ser." I keep my voice soft, my fingertips gently touching her arm through her coat.

Lifting her chin, she peers up at me, her chest heaving with ragged inhales and exhales. We stay that way for a couple more breaths, wordless. There's something so raw, so vulnerable written across her face. It takes all the self-restraint I have not to reach up and cup her chin like I want to. With Dallas in the next room, I can't risk it.

"You don't understand! If I'm more than ten minutes late, they won't let me into the class, and they'll charge me a late cancellation fee and the roads are bad and—"

"Realistically, you're not going to make it in time. That's okay. Maybe this is the universe's way of saying you need a rest day. We all do once in a while." The fee is something like ten bucks, and her family is loaded. This isn't about the coffee or the money. This is a stress spiral because of everything she's dealing with between the move and her mom.

Seraphina looks marginally less agitated, but that isn't saying much. "I'm supposed to meet Abby there."

"I'm sure if you text her and explain what happened, she'll understand."

She scrunches up her mouth and she pauses, considering. I can see her softening, little by little. The panic in her eyes fades, leaving behind a resigned weariness. She looks tired, like she didn't sleep much last night.

"My whole morning has been thrown off. I was going to shower at the gym."

If there's one thing I've noticed, it's that she does not cope well with change, however minor it might be. Unfortunately, she's been dealing with a lot of it.

"Why don't you go shower while I make you some more coffee? I can cook some breakfast too, while I'm at it. We can look for your keys after that. Everything is easier on a full stomach, and they have to be around here somewhere."

Seraphina heaves a sigh. "Okay . . ."

Reluctantly, she heads downstairs while I go into the kitchen. I drain the last of my mug and refill it before washing out the machine to make her decaf. Despite what I may have led her to believe to spare her feelings, I need caffeine like I need air.

Dallas frowns, sliding the cooked bacon onto a paper-towel-covered plate to absorb the grease. "She okay?"

"Think so. She's dealing with a lot."

"No doubt. I'm sorry about their mom." Pausing, he studies my face. The room turns oppressively silent. His pale blue eyes feel like laser beams aimed at mine, searching for any hint of a lie. "Is there anything you want to tell me?"

"What do you mean?" I deflect, playing dumb.

"You two seem awfully close."

Bringing my cup of coffee to my lips, I take a sip to buy myself time before I answer. "We're friends."

"'Tink' doesn't happen to be short for Tinker Bell, does it?"

Holy shit, did I call her Tink when Dallas was in the kitchen?

"No."

He points at me with the spatula. "She's the one you were texting with at our hotel when you were acting all goofy a while ago, isn't she?"

This keeps getting worse and worse.

I have no idea how to respond to that, so I drink my coffee instead.

"Dude." He throws his head back and stares up at the ceiling like he's pleading with the heavens, muttering a string of pleas and expletives beneath his breath. When he looks at me again, his expression is a combination of desperation and reproach.

"For the love of hockey and all that is holy," his voice is barely above a whisper, "tell me you're not fucking Carter's sister."

For the briefest second, I almost wish I could tell him the truth. Wish I could admit to someone, anyone, that I'm in over my head. That I can't think straight when she's around—and that she's all I think about when she's not.

"What do you want me to say here, Ward?" There's a friendship hierarchy within the house, and Dallas is closer to Chase than he is to me. They've been friends for longer. I know that. He knows that. And we *both* know how Chase would take this.

Dallas groans and tugs at his dark hair. When he withdraws his hand, it stands straight on end. "For both of our sakes, this conversation never happened."

After he eats, he clears out of the kitchen with a promise never to throw away coffee again and his grudging blessing to eat the leftover bacon. I cut up fruit, scramble eggs, and make toast while I wait for Seraphina. I'd make extra for Chase, but he'll probably be asleep for a few more hours. On brand as ever, he pulled an all-nighter writing a paper at the last possible minute.

Seraphina appears in the doorway changed into a fuzzy white sweater and jeans, her hair still damp from the shower. It's a darker shade of pink when it's wet, a stark contrast against her fair skin. She looks beautiful. There's something

I like about getting to see her in these everyday moments. It feels special somehow. Like a part of her most other people don't get access to.

"Guess what I found?" She dangles the key fob from her fingers with a guilty look. "They were sitting on the bathroom counter downstairs. I feel so ridiculous."

There's a pang in my gut at her last words.

"Don't, Ser. I've done the same thing before."

She shrugs off my remark and averts her gaze. When she notices the food sitting on the counter, her eyes brighten. "Thank you for breakfast. I'll return the favor sometime."

"Careful or I might take you up on that."

The energy in the room shifts from comfortable to almost unbearably tense. Her eyelids hood as she steps closer, coming to stand almost toe to toe with me. The sweet scent of her freshly applied perfume drifts over to me, mingled with her tropical-scented shampoo, and my cock perks up in anticipation.

"You could, you know."

I fight a grin. "That would be a bad idea right now." The reminder is for me as much as her. If I had my way, I'd be eating her for breakfast instead.

"Sometimes those are the best kind."

We manage to pull apart before anything more inappropriate happens. My dick is more than a little angry with me at the lack of follow-through. I'll be taking matters into my own hands the minute she leaves for class—and when I do, the scenario that just transpired is going to play out differently in my mind.

Channeling what little restraint I have left, I turn my thoughts to hockey and begin to mentally recount my stats from this season. *Save percentage, goals against average, shutouts*... I wait until Sera has plated her food before fixing my own, then join her at the table.

"I can't believe I got that upset over coffee." She scrunches up her mouth, pushing her scrambled eggs around with her fork.

"How embarrassing. It's just—you know when you're really, *really* looking forward to something and then you don't get it?"

Part of me knows.

"That's okay, Ser. I understand, and you shouldn't be embarrassed. Everyone has those mornings once in a while."

Her hand wraps around her mug. "My morning cup of coffee is one of my favorite things, and if that goes off the rails, so does the rest of the day."

"Are you sure this isn't about something else?" I ask gently.

Seraphina huffs and picks up her toast, looking away. "It probably is. Take your pick. Switching schools, dead father, sick mother, brother dealing with his own issues, undeclared major, and zero direction in life . . ." Her voice wobbles as she trails off, and my stomach sinks.

Without thinking, I cover her hand with my palm. "Tink."

"It's fine. Probably just PMS. Maybe I need to go stuff my face with chocolate and cry in my room."

Hard for me to argue with that. I know precisely zero about female hormones.

"Not to dismiss that hypothesis, but you do have a lot on your plate. I get being stressed, and those feelings are totally valid. Please don't be hard on yourself, though. You don't have zero direction in life."

Even though I don't want to, I remove my hand from hers. My entire body protests at the loss of contact. Instead, I grab my coffee to stop myself from reaching for her again and take a sip.

She spears a piece of pineapple and points at me with her fork. "How do I not? I have no idea what I want to do."

"Lots of people don't. Your perspective is probably skewed because you grew up around a bunch of hockey lifers. On average, people change jobs something like seven times in their lifetime. It's okay not to know, and even once you pick something, it's okay to change your mind about that too."

"I guess," she says quietly. "I just feel lost sometimes."

"So do I." It's the first time I've ever admitted this out loud.

"What do you mean? You've already been drafted." Seraphina sets down her fork, tilting her head.

The muscles in my jaw tighten. "New York is looking at picking up another goalie prospect."

"Oh... I'm sorry, Ty." She frowns, and this time she's the one who covers my hand.

"Could end up being nothing. Or it could end up derailing the way I thought my whole career would play out. Either way, I know where I want to go, but it feels like it's completely out of my hands sometimes." Words I've held inside for the better part of my college career start to pour out, and once they do, I can't seem to rein them in. "Sometimes instead of motivating me, all the outside pressure kills my love for the sport, and I'm left wondering why I'm doing it. There are days when I stand in front of the net going through the motions because I'm somewhere else mentally. I want to *want* to play hockey, not be forced into it because I have to. Does that make sense?"

Seraphina must have one hell of an effect on me, because I'm admitting things out loud that I haven't even admitted to myself, let alone anyone else. Things I've been in deep, deep denial about for almost as long as I can remember.

"Yeah," she says softly. "It does."

Her response is more comforting than I expected. I rarely talk about my feelings, which means I never get much validation either. I didn't realize how much I needed it.

"Would you ever want to do something else instead?"

"That's the worst part. It feels like a catch-22. Even though it makes me miserable sometimes, I can't picture my life without hockey. I just need to find a way to enjoy it again."

My focus falls to her mouth as she bites her lip thoughtfully, and I swallow an agonized sound rising in my throat. It's impossible to keep my mind on task when she does things like that.

"I think you can," she says. "It's not like you're trying to be somebody else. You're simply trying to reconnect with a piece of yourself that you've lost touch with. It's still in there, it's just gotten buried under some other junk."

"Then it's buried pretty fucking deep."

"I know the outside pressure is real, but have you considered that some of it might be the pressure you're putting on yourself?" Her mouth tugs into a patient smile. "I'm not sure whether you've noticed, but you're a little intense when it comes to hockey."

What she's saying makes sense, objectively, but I didn't get to where I am by coasting.

"Let's circle back to you for a sec. You're smart and funny and feisty as hell, Tink. I know you'll kick ass at whatever you end up doing someday, whether that means one career or seven. It's okay if you don't have it all figured out yet."

This advice probably applies to me too. Maybe if I take it one day at a time, I'll learn to chill the fuck out. Somehow.

Seraphina sidles closer in her chair and angles her body toward me, looping her arms around my waist for a hug. Warmth floods my body, and I slide my hands to her back. She lets out a contented sigh as she squeezes me, burying her face in my chest.

Seconds pass, but neither of us moves. It's a little risky with Chase home, but I can't bring myself to care. I'm a newly converted hugger, and I never want this moment to end. Besides, if hugging is the worst thing he catches us doing, I'll call it a win.

"Thanks, Hades," she says, the words half-muffled by the fabric of my shirt.

"Any time, Tinker Bell."

Chapter 19
MULTIPLE CHOICE

TYLER

You'd think having sex would reduce my horniness level, not increase it. That has not been the case. I feel like a goddamn teenager all over again.

As I tug off my shirt in the locker room for our afternoon skate, my phone lights up from the shelf in my stall. A rush runs through my body, and I immediately grab it.

> Tinker Bell: Question 29: How should I get myself off later? Fingers or toy?

Holy shit. I stand frozen to the spot, blinking at the screen for a good couple of seconds while I process her text. I can think of a couple other suggestions, starting with my mouth. Or my cock. Fuck, let's go with both—in that order. For now, I'll answer her question.

> Hades: Fingers, then toy. And let me watch.

> Tinker Bell: Can't. *sad emoji*
> Everyone will be home tonight.

Dammit, she's right. Dallas said he has some test to study for, and Chase is finishing a paper. Why can't they go do their work at the library like everyone else? Maybe I can convince them it's a good idea; plant the seed somehow. Wishful thinking, I'm sure.

> Hades: FaceTime me, then.

Tinker Bell: Only if you're a good boy.

Hades: If it means I get to watch you make yourself come, I'll be a fucking saint.

"Ended your dry spell, huh?" Chase remarks from behind me.

My heart leaps into my throat, and I lock my phone, whipping around to face him.

"What?" Did he see my screen? He's, like, six feet away. That's not close enough to read such small text, is it?

"The scratch marks on your back?" He gestures at me like it should be obvious. Behind him, Dallas's eyes widen, and he turns away, pretending to be busy with his gear. "They're all over, dude."

Scratch marks? I have no idea what he's talking about. Craning my neck, I twist to look over my shoulder. Sure enough, there are a handful of red, raised streaks trailing along each side of my spine. I was so caught up in the moment, I didn't feel Sera do it.

Didn't realize how long I'd been standing here staring at my phone either. I'm still in my street clothes, and nearly everyone else is dressed.

"Oh, right. I forgot about those."

At least he has no way of knowing who made them.

Chase sits on the bench and reaches for his skates. "Speaking of that, Sera"—I nearly stroke out as his mention of her name—"is staying at Abby's while we're gone, so you'll have the place all to yourself. You know, for you and whoever."

Wait . . . what? She's staying at Abby's while Chase and Dallas are away? Why?

It's a given I'd like the opportunity to fuck her without anyone else home. Beyond that, I hate the idea of her spending an entire weekend with that so-called friend. Between her losing track of Sera at that party and interrupting us the next day, Abby has earned a permanent spot on my shit list. Sera deserves so much better than that kind of treatment—but for some reason, she doesn't seem to see it.

I run my thumb along the button on the side of my case, debating whether I should text and ask her what the deal is. Is it even any of my business? Before I can decide, my phone vibrates in my hand.

Tinker Bell: BTW, I told my brother I'm staying at Abby's this weekend.

Hades: But you aren't?

Tinker Bell: Not a chance, silly.

Thank fuck. The only thing on my to-do list this weekend is her.

With that settled, I give my head a figurative shake and hurriedly yank on my gear in an attempt to catch up to the rest of the team. It's more obvious if I'm late than it is with the other players. Coach Miller won't bag skate me, but he *will* tear me a new one.

Ezra Jameson saunters over to us and lets out a low, appreciative whistle. "Your sister is a dime, Carter."

I stop cold, glancing up from tying my skates. Dallas fastens his shoulder pad and silently mouths, "Here we go." I'm not sure whether he's more concerned about my reaction or Chase's.

Chase's dark eyes narrow, but he says nothing. Just glowers at Ezra. As a senior defenseman, Ezra could easily hold his own against the average player. At six foot three and one of the league's most intimidating athletes, Chase would clobber him.

Pretending to be disinterested, I reach into my cubby for the rest of my equipment.

"I mean, respectfully." Ezra reaches up, rubbing the back of his neck. "Would it be okay if I asked her out?"

No, it fucking wouldn't.

The protest comes from inside my head, not Chase's mouth. Waiting for him to voice the same sentiment out loud, I fasten the buckles running the length of my left pad.

To my surprise, he merely shrugs and tips back his water bottle, swallowing. "All good, man."

It's like sandpaper against my brain.

I grit my teeth and look down, mentally kicking myself. Regardless of what happened between us last night, it's not like I have some claim to Seraphina.

"Really?" Ezra studies him warily.

"Sure," Chase says, his expression unreadable. "I know how to hide a body."

Ezra laughs uneasily, but it dies on his lips when Chase doesn't do the same.

"Noted." He tosses him a salute and retreats to his corner of the dressing room.

"Carter." Dallas nudges Chase with his elbow, lowering his voice. "I know you want to protect Sera, but you've got to let her live her life too."

"Ezra is the kind of dude who'd rather die than commit to someone, Ward. I don't want him within ten feet of my sister. Sera deserves someone who will treat her like a princess, not string her along."

This doesn't bode well for me, but I also don't think everything is as black and white as Chase makes it out to be. Commitment can take different forms. Even if we're not in a relationship, it's not like I have any intention of sleeping with anyone else. If Sera and I are on the same page about what we're doing, that's all that matters. Right?

Somehow, I doubt he'd agree.

◆ ◆ ◆

It's been a long fucking day. Off-ice training, classes, team practice, goalie coaching. Now it's time for the figurative cookie I've been waiting for: phone sex.

When I walk in the door after my evening training, Chase and Dallas are sitting in the living room playing *Call of Duty*. The volume is turned up ear-splittingly high, which I suppose is a bonus in this case. It'll help muffle any sounds Seraphina makes while she gives me the best private show of my life.

There's a huge explosion on-screen and Dallas curses into the microphone. "Fuck you, Holloway."

Chase steals a glance at me, still shooting. "Hey, man."

Guilt sparks in the back of my mind. It's a little hard to look him in the face knowing I'm about to go jerk off to his sister.

I'd be lying if I said the whole secret thing wasn't hot, though. That's probably a little fucked up on my part, but it is what it is.

"Aren't you guys supposed to be doing homework?" I ask him.

"Yeah, but what are you gonna do?" He leans forward on the couch, squinting to concentrate as he aims a rocket launcher. "You want in?"

"Thanks, but I'm good. Still need to shower." Sometimes, when the Boyd U ice is booked, Mark and I train at another municipal arena. It's a lot older than our school's facilities, and not nearly as clean. Ice is still ice, but the dressing rooms are gross.

I take the stairs two at a time and strip down in the bathroom. Like a creep, I snag Sera's bottle of shampoo off the shelf and sniff it while the water heats up. The tropical scent invades my nostrils, and my cock stirs impatiently. God help me, I'll never be able to smell coconut without getting turned on again.

It's one of the quickest showers I've ever taken, efficient and to the point. I wash my hair and scrub myself down in record time, then turn off the water. Stepping out of the shower, I towel off my hair before wrapping it around my waist. Through the steam, my gaze falls to my phone on the counter. There are three missed calls from my father. It's unusual for him to call more than once. I'm tempted to ignore him but thinking better of it, opt to call him back.

"Hey, Dad. Everything okay?"

"I just heard from Gary. New York is taking you for offseason training. It's a go."

"Really?" I ask, momentarily distracted from my one-track thoughts about Sera. This is huge. It's also a little challenging to process with inadequate blood flow to my brain. Faintly, I know this means I'll be away for most of the summer. The repercussions beyond that are escaping me. I'm not sure I'm grasping the enormity of this news.

"Management needs you to work on rebounds and lateral movements if you're going to make the jump next year..." Clearly thrilled, he carries on for two solid minutes without any chance for me to interrupt him. I pull the phone away from my ear and shoot Sera a quick text.

> Hades: Sorry Tink. Gimme 2.

Tinker Bell: image.jpg

Fuck. Me.

It's a selfie of Sera kneeling in front of a mirror wearing nothing but tiny white booty shorts. She's covering her breasts with one arm with her back arched and her round ass sticking out, silky pink hair around her shoulders. I want nothing more than to march upstairs, throw her down on the bed, and fuck her until she can't walk straight tomorrow.

"Listen, Dad," I cut him off mid-sentence as I walk into my room. Part of me feels bad because he's so excited, but a bigger part of me—the one below my waist—needs to wrap this up. "That all sounds great, but I have a big test tomorrow that I need to study for. Mind if I call you back tomorrow so we can talk about it some more?"

"Sure thing," he says. "Proud of you, son."

"Thanks. Talk soon."

Towel still wrapped low around my hips, I ease onto the bed to FaceTime Seraphina. My heart thuds as I hit send, and I tell myself it's impatience rather than nerves.

After two rings, her face pops up on screen.

"Hi." She gives me a soft smile, resting against her headboard with a stack of pillows propped behind her. There's music playing low in the background. I want to say it's Taylor Swift, but I'm not certain.

"Hey." My eyes flit over her face, taking in her gold-flecked eyes and perfect, full mouth. Even though we live together, she's so stunning it leaves me a little awestruck every time. I'm not sure I'll ever get used to it.

At the bottom of the frame, I catch a sliver of white tank top that tells me she's gotten dressed. Shit.

"Sorry, Tink. My dad called me three times in a row, and I had to take it. I thought it might be an emergency."

"Was it?" Her brows pull together, expression sobering.

"It wasn't." I drop my voice. "Did you wait for me?"

She bites back a grin. "No."

All the blood in my body rushes straight to my dick at the mental image of Seraphina getting herself off upstairs in her room. With everyone else home, the staircase represents an impossible divide. It's divine agony knowing she's so close yet so far away.

"You gonna get off again for me?"

"Hmm . . ." she brings a finger to her plush lips, pretending to think. "Maybe if you ask nicely."

Let's get one thing straight: I have never—not once—used the word "please" in the bedroom. But I'd sell my soul for a front-row seat to a show with Sera and her sex toy. I'll get down on my knees and beg if I have to.

Groaning, I grip myself over the terry cloth. "Fuck, Ser. I'm so hard for you. Please let me watch you play with that pretty pussy of yours."

"Since you said 'please' . . ." Seraphina's hand disappears offscreen. She lets out a breathy sigh and her eyelids flutter, forehead crinkling. I'm mesmerized, entranced. I've never seen anything more sensual in my life.

"That's it," I praise. "Just like that." Keeping my eyes fixed on her, I untie the towel with a single tug. My dick springs free impatiently, and my fist wraps around the base. Having her mouth or pussy would be even better, but this is pretty goddamn good.

She pouts. "I wish you were touching me."

"You have no idea how badly I want to touch you." My voice is hoarse. "Let me see your pussy, baby."

As soon as the words leave my mouth, the tiny part of my brain that's still functional wonders if I'm escalating too quickly. After several hours of foreplay via sext message, I'm so fucking keyed up that I don't have a single shred of self-control left.

My worries immediately ease as the camera pans down, moving past the swells of her breasts straining against her thin white crop top and the dip of her smooth, bare stomach. Little white shorts rest low on her hips, obscuring what I want to see most.

She's a fucking tease, and I love it.

"Ditch the shorts, Tinker Bell."

Seraphina brings the camera back up to her face and tsks, smirking. "So bossy."

Placing the phone down on the bed, she gives me a full view of her body. The bedding rustles, camera jostles as she lifts her hips and shimmies the waistband down, deliberately moving as slowly as possible. My dick hardens even more with anticipation. I watch the material slide lower and lower, leaving me with a view of the cleft between her closed thighs.

"Good girl. Now spread your legs and show me how wet you are."

I watch as she parts her knees, exposing all of herself to me. Her pretty cunt is swollen and ready, her slit begging for me to slide my cock inside.

Cursing, I tighten my grip on my shaft. "Your pussy is perfect, Ser. So fucking perfect."

Her fingertips circle her clit, purple-pink folds glistening with her arousal. When she whimpers, it's the prettiest sound I've ever heard. Tension coils in my core as I come dangerously close to unfurling. I stop abruptly, pinching my cock at the base to hold myself off. No way am I coming before the grand finale.

Seraphina juts her chin at the screen. "Don't I get to see?"

Well, fuck. If that's what she wants, I'm not shy. I tilt the phone to show her what she's doing to me. My cock is engorged and leaking in my hand, ready to explode.

Her teeth snag her bottom lip, pupils dilating. "Damn," she murmurs, staring at the screen. "I wish we were alone."

I husk a low laugh and set down the phone like she did, creating equal viewing opportunity. "Me too."

Seraphina gives me a coy look, but I can tell she's only playing shy. "Do you want me to get my toy?"

"You know I do."

A hot pink dildo comes into the frame, her slender fingers wrapped around the shaft. It's a generous size—though using her hand for scale, it's not as big as yours truly—and realistic, with fake veins running the length and balls hanging down. I bite down on my lip as she brings it to her pussy and rubs it along her slick entrance, teasing without penetrating herself.

"Fuck yourself with it and pretend it's me," I tell her.

"I always pretend it's you."

Those words nearly undo me on the spot.

A low, tortured growl reverberates in my chest as the pink silicone slips inside of her, slowly disappearing.

"Look how pretty you are taking that dick, baby. You look even better when you're taking mine." I slowly start to stroke myself again, imagining it's my cock inside her instead. Remembering how tight and wet she was when I sank inside of her, and the way her walls clenched around me as she came.

"Oh, god." Seraphina lets out a breathy moan, and the way she's squirming tells me she's getting close. "That's good. Keep talking, please."

"When I get you alone this weekend, I'm going to eat your pussy until your legs start to shake and you're begging me for release, and then I'm going to make you come so hard you make a dripping mess." A drop of pre-cum beads at the tip of my cock and I brush my thumb over it as I keep stroking. My tempo increases, and she follows my lead, thrusting the toy faster. "And once I'm finished, I'm going to kiss you so you can taste how sweet you are."

She sucks in a sharp breath, her cheeks flushed. "Then what?"

"I'm going to fuck that perfect little pussy like it's mine."

Her mouth falls open in a silent cry and her back arches off the bed, her head tipping back against the pillow. I follow right behind her as my hips jerk, warm release coating my hand. All of the tension that's been brewing between us explodes in a blur of moans and breaths, whimpers and pleas.

It's good—too fucking good, and exactly what I needed.

Seraphina picks up her phone and I do the same, putting us face-to-face on screen.

"Hi." Her voice is breathy, her expression sated. A subtle sheen glistens across her forehead, her espresso eyes glassy and dazed. It's nothing compared to what she's going to look like when I'm finished with her this weekend. I'm going to fucking ruin her, and then I'm going to do it all over again.

"That's going to live rent-free in my head for the rest of my life, Ser."

She giggles. "It better."

The post-orgasm haze clears completely, and my thought process returns to normal as my vitals regulate. It hits me that I don't want to end our call. What I really want is to have her beside me, and I hate that I can't.

"Time out?" I ask her.

"Deal."

Setting down my phone, I quickly clean up and get dressed while she does the same. When I pick it up, she crawls onto her bed and gets beneath the covers, pulling them up to her chest. Her dark brown eyes fix on the screen, her expression pensive.

"So . . ." She trails off.

"So," I say, leaning back against my pillows, "tell me about your day, Tink."

Chapter 20
A LITTLE EXTRA

SERAPHINA

Google is not my friend.

I should have waited until I had the results back from the genetic testing. Instead, I went ahead and dove headfirst into the scary side of the internet. Now I'm home alone while the guys are gone for a road game, and I'm freaking out.

Some preliminary research I've conducted says that if I have the BRCA mutation, my risk of developing breast cancer in my lifetime could be as high as almost 80 percent. That's not including my chance of developing ovarian cancer, which would also be significant.

I throw myself down on the pile of clean clothes covering my duvet and hug a pillow to my chest, staring up at the ceiling while Dr. Wilson's words echo through my head.

Fifty-fifty. That's it. A simple coin toss.

It's been weighing on me ever since that day in his office. I've tried to stuff it to the back of my mind as much as possible. Tried to pretend it never happened. Tried to believe everything will work out.

And I've been failing miserably.

Panic seizes hold of me and I reach for my phone, swiping into my message thread with Abby. I start to compose a text to her before I catch myself, holding down the backspace button to delete it in a single swoop. Navigating life-or-death decisions isn't her forte. It's not like she wouldn't try, but she has no frame of reference for what I'm going through, and I can't escape the feeling that she wouldn't quite get it.

I stare at the screen for a few more seconds, debating whether to call one of my friends in Arizona instead. That doesn't feel right either. We've drifted apart in the short time since I've been here, and this seems like heavy subject matter to throw at someone I haven't spoken to much lately.

Chase isn't an option, obviously. That leaves Tyler. I almost wish I could tell him, but for what? I don't even know one way or the other yet. He's made it abundantly clear how much pressure he's under, and I can't see him wanting to add to that with my hypothetical problems.

Plus, something this heavy seems like it might be a little beyond his pay grade. He's my friend—not my boyfriend. Part of me is afraid it might scare him away.

Then I remember a support website Dr. Wilson recommended to my mother during her appointment. Opening my MacBook, I enter the name into the search engine and pull it up, skimming through the posts in the aptly named "Limbo Land" forum. Everything I read confirms my gut instinct to do the testing. After all, I could be negative, which means I'd be able to move on with my life and focus on helping my mother get through her own treatment.

Or... I could be positive. Could be faced with the decision whether to wait and see if cancer catches up with me or take drastic preventative measures.

Either way, I need to know. The uncertainty will hang over my head until I do.

As I'm about to exit the site, another forum titled "Family and Relationships" catches my eye. I pause with my mouse hovering over the link, and curiosity compels me to click it.

After another couple of minutes sifting through the threads, my already fragile state of mind sails straight off a cliff. Post after post from women whose boyfriends and husbands bailed after finding out they were BRCA carriers. The details are different, but the underlying themes are all the same. They couldn't empathize with the trauma of the diagnosis. Couldn't face the prospect of their wife having major surgery. Couldn't handle the caretaking after the procedure.

I wish I could say I'm surprised, but the news that so many men are lacking an empathy chip hardly comes as a shock.

Sure, there are exceptions. When I dig a little deeper, I find the occasional story from a user whose partner stood by her side, took care of her through everything, and was her rock. One man shaved his head when his wife was going through chemo as a gesture of solidarity while another took a leave of absence from work until his girlfriend was fully recovered from a double mastectomy.

I know unicorn men like that exist because that's exactly how my brother would be if anything were to happen to Bailey. But in a sea of thousands of message board threads, those happy endings remain the exceptions—by a wide margin.

Seriously ill women divorce at a rate of more than 20 percent versus 3 percent for men. Wait, what? That can't be right. Blinking, I reread the statistic again. A one in five possibility of losing your partner while you're sick. My stomach balls into a knot at the potential implications.

Is that going to happen to my mother and Rick? Is he going to decide things are too difficult and bail when she's at her most vulnerable? Even though I've never been a big fan of the guy, I like to think he's better than that. No, he *has* to be better than that. She already lost my father; she can't go through that again, least of all right now.

Blowing out a heavy exhale, I lean back in my desk chair. My breathing turns shaky, and the screen before me turns into a blur.

In my communications class last semester, we covered how the internet has a negativity bias. People are more likely to share and complain when things go wrong, and far less likely to engage to share positive news. That means, in this case, if someone has successfully navigated their BRCA diagnosis and has gone on to live a happy and fulfilled life, they're less inclined to post about it. They're too busy doing all of those other things.

Knowing that doesn't make me feel any better.

I know I need to book that testing appointment, and I will. Just not today.

The doorbell rings, snapping me out of my daze, and I sit up. I don't think I'm expecting any deliveries. I've tried to curb my online shopping lately, at least until I get more organized.

Closing my laptop, I wait for footfalls to confirm the person has left. I'll check and see what the parcel is as soon as they're gone. Then the doorbell rings again. I resign myself to answering and push to stand. Fine. Maybe it's a delivery someone needs to sign for.

When I open the front door, Abby is standing on the step, and I am deeply confused. She's more decked out than a Christmas tree. Her blue sequined dress is short, sparkly, and dangerously low-cut with a neckline that plunges to a V in the center. If that wasn't enough, she's paired it with a smoky eye, coaxed her copper hair into loose waves, and topped it all off with the slightest hint of shimmery bronzer.

She gives me a once-over, clearly also confused. Because she looks hot—and I look like the "before" on a makeover television reality show. I'm wearing baggy gray sweatpants and an oversized ASU T-shirt, with zero makeup and my hair in a messy bun. Since the guys are gone, I thought I'd take advantage and go into sloth mode. *Advanced* sloth mode.

"Hey." A gust of winter air kicks up, freezing my bare toes. "What's up?"

"We had plans. Remember?"

Stepping aside, I motion for her to come in while I frantically rack my brain. Plans . . . Finally, I land on what she's referring to. There's a DJ spinning at some club downtown tonight, and I agreed to go with her ages ago.

"Of course." My attempt to sound cheerful comes out fake. "Come in, I'm just running a little behind schedule."

A trickle of guilt creeps in for having forgotten. I've been preoccupied lately, and maybe I haven't been the best friend. Then again, neither has Abby. When was the last time she texted to check in with me about my mom? Or about anything other than getting drunk?

I don't know how we grew up attached at the hip only to end up like this. What happened to the Abby I used to have sleepovers with? The one who stayed up with me past bedtime giggling in the dark until our parents yelled at us to go to sleep? We used to do things like play with the Ouija board and paint each other's nails. Or we'd invent silly dances and try to bake cookies without following a recipe (an epic fail every time, unsurprisingly). Sometimes we'd spy on Chase just to annoy him.

Obviously, we grew up, and I don't expect to do all of those things anymore—least of all spy on my brother—but the dynamic itself has shifted too. Abby was the first person I told when I got my period, and she brought me a tampon when I was trapped in a bathroom stall at school. Now I can't even trust her not to lose track of me at a party.

Knowing she doesn't have my back is unsettling. I've always had hers.

"We have lots of time," she says breezily. "Lana and Destiny said to be at their place around eight. DJ Banner isn't even on the program until ten, and he always starts late."

I have no idea who DJ Banner is, and I'm not particularly excited at the prospect of going out tonight, least of all with Destiny and Lana. Still, I lead her into my room and reluctantly go through the motions of getting ready while she flits around, sifting through my makeup and clothes.

Abby holds up my black patent Louboutin pumps, examining the red soles. They were a birthday present from my mom last year; a splurge I'd never buy for myself. I reserve them for only the most special occasions, and I'm relieved her feet are way too small for her to ask if she can borrow them.

"You're not going to rejoin Kappa, are you?" She tosses my shoes aside, and I cringe inwardly. "I mean, I don't know why I'm even asking. It's too late now. We're well into the semester."

"In the interest of total transparency, the whole sorority thing hasn't even been on my radar."

"See?" Glittery pink nails sparkle as she gestures to me. "This is what I was talking about. You got a boyfriend, and now you don't want to do anything anymore."

"Tyler isn't my boyfriend."

"Fuck buddy. Whatever." She rolls her eyes. "Same thing."

By definition, they are not. But it seems pointless to argue.

Rifling through my closet, I try to settle on something to wear. Nothing appeals to me. I take out an emerald-green halter dress and hold it up to myself, then immediately put it back. Then I do the same with three more dresses. Maybe I could get away with wearing jeans.

We're interrupted when the doorbell rings again. Unless Chloe is standing at my front door, I don't have any friends left that it could be. Which is a little sad, upon further reflection.

This time it *is* a delivery. The van roars away in the distance as I haul the oversized brown Amazon box inside, studying the label. It's addressed to me, but I haven't placed any orders there recently, let alone one for something this big.

Abby rushes up, peeking over my shoulder. "What is it?"

"No idea."

She trails behind me as I bring the parcel into the kitchen. It isn't very heavy, but there's something reasonably large sliding around inside. Taking the kitchen scissors, I run them along the length of the packing tape to open the cardboard flaps. A flimsy white slip that looks like a receipt sits on of the top brown packing paper, face down. I turn it over and read the printed message, angling it away so Abby can't see.

"A gift for you from: Hades."

Blinking, I read it again to make sure I'm not hallucinating. What kind of gift? Hopefully not a dirty one with Abby standing right next to me watching my every move.

I shove the gift receipt in my pocket and lift the packing paper. A smile pulls at my lips when I spot a second, slightly smaller box. A coffeemaker.

And it's pink.

In addition to that, there's a pound of organic decaffeinated coffee and a massive bag of pink Starburst. I'm shocked Tyler even remembered the last one. I'm fairly sure I only mentioned it to him once in passing.

My heart swells and an unfamiliar feeling brews within me. One I can't identify; one I've never felt.

"What's this?" Abby pokes around in the packing box, sifting through the contents because she has zero concept of privacy. She pulls the appliance out with a smirk. "A pink coffeemaker, Sera? That's a little extra, even for you."

"What's wrong with being extra?" I snap, taking it from her hands. That's it: I'm reclaiming the word "extra." Everyone says it like it's a bad thing, right up there with "basic." Both terms get wielded against me by other people, and I'm tired of it.

"I like pink. It makes me happy. Why does everything have to hinge on what other people think? Yucking someone else's yum is shitty."

"Damn, girl. I was kidding. I meant that your brother and his friends might not want a bunch of pink stuff taking over the house."

"I sincerely doubt they care." Turning away, I set the box on the counter and take a deep breath, counting to five. Bailey and Siobhan invited me to watch the guys' game with them on TV at their place, and their offer is looking better by the minute. So is staying home alone and eating pizza by myself. Or a million other things that don't involve being trapped in a sweaty night-club while Abby drags me around trying to get her attention fix.

"You know what?" I whirl around to face her. "I feel a headache coming on."

She arches a brow, studying me skeptically. "A headache, huh? Seems awfully sudden."

"Must be PMS. Could even turn into a migraine. I'd better nip it in the bud before it does."

"You know, you've been super flaky lately."

My body tenses like a steel trap, and it takes a significant restraint to keep my tone level. "You haven't been so great yourself. I'm going through a lot right now, and it doesn't seem like you even care."

"Everyone has problems, Sera."

Of course they do. Does that make mine less valid?

Tears spring to my eyes, and I grit my teeth to hold them back. "I think you should go."

Abby storms out in a huff, and the aftermath of our confrontation leaves me spinning.

Our friendship is more on the rocks than ever. Does it even count as a friendship at this point? Do I care?

Once she's gone, I unpack the coffee maker before putting the candy and coffee in the cupboard. Standing in the kitchen, I look at Tyler's gift again, and some of the turmoil in me eases. My life feels like it's going in ten drastically different directions. Some things are going better than I could've ever imagined, and others are going down in flames.

I grab my phone to send him a message, knowing he'll be getting on the ice soon.

> Tinker Bell: I got your present. Thank you. That was really sweet.

Hades: Any time, Tink. Now Ward can't fuck up your decaf again.

Hades: Question 30: If you had a time machine, would you go back to the past or ahead to the future?

A heavy ache settles into the pit of my stomach because I'd give anything to see my dad again.

> Tinker Bell: The past. You?

Hades: Neither. Too afraid of the butterfly effect.

> Tinker Bell: Question 31: What's something everyone else loves, but you find overrated?

Hades: This one might sound weird, but in the spirit of the game, I'll be honest.

> Tinker Bell: Well, now you have to spill.

Hades: Until I tried your Haagen Dazs, I would've said ice cream. Now I'm addicted, and that shit is expensive.

> Tinker Bell: Worth it though.
> Tinker Bell: Kissing is overrated. Except with you, I mean.

He reads my message immediately, eliminating any chance I have of unsending it. Did I really just write that? What am I doing? Granted, it's true. A lot of other guys try to eat your face, and it's not a good time. Or there's an *aggressive* amount of tongue.

With Tyler, it's another story. Maybe because it feels like he's kissing *me* instead of *kissing* me. It's a subtle, but important, distinction. In the former scenario, it's an unspoken form of communication; an act of giving and taking. He knows when to deepen the kiss and when to pull back. It always feels like he's fully in the moment, responding to me as things unfold.

In the latter instance, it's someone jamming their tongue down your throat.

I'm still not sure I should've told him that. Every so often, I let something TMI like this slip around him. Now I'm staring at our text thread trying not to cringe.

> Tinker Bell: Now I'm the one who sounds weird, but I stand by what I said.

SHUTOUT • 179

Hades: Glad to be the lone exception on that. I'm with you. As a concept, overrated. With you, I'd gladly do it all day.
Hades: I'd kiss you right now if I could. We can make up for lost time when I'm back.

I think my heart just exploded.

Chapter 21
PUCK DROP

TYLER

The only thing more stressful than games are the moments directly leading up to them.

Around the locker room, my teammates joke and laugh while I sit off to the side, tuning them out. Everyone knows the deal by now. Once we get to the arena, no one talks to me until we're on the ice.

Closing my eyes, I visualize the entire game from puck drop to the buzzer. All the plays and each possible scenario that could result. Passes, takeaways, giveaways. Every shot and how I'll make that save. I picture every single detail: the weight of my gear, the ice beneath my skates, the bright LED lights shining down, and the roar of the crowd after each blocked shot.

Did Seraphina text me back yet?

Fuck, Tyler. Get your shit together.

"How do you feel about facing your old team?" Dallas asks, clearly talking to Reid.

Since I've already been derailed, I allow myself to sneak a peek to see his reaction.

"Not fucking great," he grumbles, dragging the toe of his skate along the gray-speckled rubber flooring. "I'm worried about Grady. He knows my moves, and their D will be all over me."

Steve Grady—head coach of the Woodbine Rams—was a hockey legend in the making until an injury forced him into early retirement at twenty-six and he became one of the youngest coaches at the college level. He also used to be Reid's mentor, and my working theory is that Grady has something to do with why he left.

"If they are, that'll leave me and Ward wide open. Either way, we'll fuck them up nicely; don't worry." Chase tips back his head, squirting his water bottle into his mouth.

"I'm sure we will, but I like scoring too," Reid says dryly.

"That's what she said!" one of the guys yells. Raucous laughter breaks out, and the room gets ten times rowdier, filled with whoops and hollers, dirty jokes, and excessively detailed blow job stories.

Irritation seizes me when I realize I'm more off track than ever, and I clamp down on the urge to tell them all to shut the fuck up. Not only would they not listen, breaking my no-talking rule would set a bad precedent.

On a normal day, I wouldn't be able to hear any of this. I'd be completely in the zone and utterly oblivious to the circus around me. Right now, I can't concentrate for shit. All I can think about is the texts Seraphina and I exchanged back and forth all day. The first thing I'm going to do when I get off the ice is check my phone for the next.

I look down at the floor and try to focus on counting my breaths, but it doesn't work. I'll be standing in front of the net in a matter of minutes, and for the first time in my life, I'm rattled over something that has nothing to do with hockey.

◆ ◆ ◆

Halfway into the second, we're tied. If I needed something to force my head into the game, I got it. Woodbine's offense has been fucking hammering me for twenty-nine minutes. After facing over forty shots on net, I've only let in two goals. Both were bad bounces, one of which was completely out of my control. Puck luck hasn't been on our side tonight, and rebounds are our defense's weakness.

A shot bounces off the crossbar with a clink, sliding into the crease. Reflexes kicking in, I throw myself to the ice and cover it with my glove to stop the play. Or at least, the play should stop—but the officials have swallowed their goddamn whistles.

Woodbine's forward, Burgess, wedges his stick beneath my glove, digging to knock the puck loose. It's times like this I wish goalies could fight according to hockey code, because right now, I want to get up and pummel this dick. Everyone knows you don't mess with the goaltender after a save. Not only is it cheap as hell, it's pointless. Any resulting goal will immediately get called back.

As I glance up to see what the fuck is going on with the refs, Burgess jabs my hand, followed by a slash to my wrist. The blade lands above the cuff of my glove, hitting bone. I drop my head, gritting my teeth as white-hot pain radiates up my forearm.

Dirty move, dick. I already know I'll be feeling the effects of that for a few days at a minimum.

Reid skates over, cross-checking Burgess out of the way. "Back the fuck off."

"What's your problem, Holloway?" Burgess throws down his stick and skates forward, getting in his face.

The whistle finally sounds, but it's too late. After a heated period, the tension has boiled over. I push to stand as the rest of the players talk shit and shove each other, escalating into a full-blown scrum. Even our scrawniest freshman is getting into it with one of their smaller guys. Chase is yelling encouragement at our team from the bench, no doubt wishing he'd been on the ice to participate. Since I'll get pulled if I get anywhere near it, I keep a wide berth.

"Touch our goalie again, and you'll be leaving on a stretcher," Reid spits.

"Cry about it, bitch." Smirking, Burgess brings a glove to his chin, pretending to ponder. "Think they'll let you switch schools again when you shit the bed here too?"

Even I'm about to take a swing at this guy.

Without a moment's hesitation, Reid tosses his gloves aside and grabs the front of Burgess's jersey, roughly yanking him forward. Reid's fist connects with his nose, making an audible crack. I can't lie; it's highly satisfying to watch. They exchange a few more swings back and forth, with most of the successful ones coming from Reid before the officials manage to pry them apart. He's immediately ejected from the game while Burgess goes to the penalty box.

Not surprisingly, the commotion on the ice amps up the crowd, and the atmosphere in the arena feels more like the playoffs than the regular season. It's a brutal, physical grind with penalties left and right for both sides, as well as a shit ton of goalie interference against me that keeps going uncalled.

The score remains tied until the last ninety seconds, when Dallas sinks a shot between the five hole, narrowly sparing us from a round of overtime. Thank fuck.

By the time we make it into the locker room, we're drenched and bagged. Reid is pulling on his charcoal dress socks, having already showered and gotten dressed while waiting for the game to wrap up. He's also sporting a nasty bruise beneath his right eye, but it pales compared to what he did to the other guy.

"Congrats, man." Chase claps him on the back as he passes. "You're officially a Falcon now."

Reid snorts a laugh, fastening the cuffs of his light blue dress shirt. "Glad I finally passed my initiation."

I fist-bump his shoulder on the way by. "Thanks for defending my honor, Holloway. You're a true gentleman."

"You wish. I've been looking for an excuse to kick that guy's ass for three goddamn years."

"Always awkward when you can't stand someone on your team," I agree, jerking my thumb at Chase. "I mean, we all have to put up with that guy. Yikes."

Chase stops untying his skates and flips me off with both hands.

When I reach my stall, I hang up my helmet and tug my drenched jersey overhead. While the average set of hockey equipment clocks in around twenty to twenty-five pounds, my goalie gear weighs twice that by the end of a game. I'm sweaty, exhausted, and I need a gallon of electrolytes followed by a day's worth of food. I have a nagging pain in my hip that tells me I need to get my hands on an ice pack, stat... and I'm itching to look at my phone.

Obviously, that's what I do before I even finish taking off my equipment.

> Tinker Bell: It makes me happy to know I'm also the kissing exception.
> Tinker Bell: Killer game, Hades. That save at the end was *fire emoji*

She was watching? Shit, I'm kind of glad I didn't know. Silly as it may be, that would've made me more nervous than a stadium of eighteen thousand fans and a myriad of faceless cable television viewers.

> Hades: Thanks, Tink.
> Tinker Bell: Wish I could wear your jersey for good luck, but it might raise some eyebrows.
> Hades: You can always wear it alone for me.
> Tinker Bell: With nothing underneath, right? Just want to make sure I understand the assignment.
> Hades: Fuck. Yes, please.
> Tinker Bell: Wouldn't want to get it wrong and make you have to spank me.
> Hades: Standing in the middle of the locker room here. You're killing me.
> Tinker Bell: *angel emoji*

◆ ◆ ◆

Post-win celebrations at our hotel carry on until Coach Miller orders everyone back to their respective rooms. Because he's happy with our performance, he lets things go a solid hour later than usual, and it's after eleven before everyone calls it a night.

Chase and Dallas peace out to their place across the hall, leaving me alone with Reid, who's wasted. Not just drunk; he's swaying and slurring and bumping into inanimate objects. I'm fully sober other than the adrenaline high from a good game.

Realistically, we should both get to bed, but it doesn't seem like sleep is anywhere in sight for either of us. I'm trying to read, and Reid is stumbling around our room getting undressed.

"Saw you with Carter's sister the other day," Reid remarks, nearly losing his balance as he tugs off his dress pants.

My blood turns to ice, and I set my copy of *Atomic Habits* next to me on the bed. "You did?"

"Yeah. You two were leaving the arena after dark. She's got pink hair, super hot? That's her, right? I remember her from Chase's party." He casually tosses his dress shirt onto the desk chair, seemingly unaware of the fact he's sitting on information that could blow up my life.

Panic takes hold, and my thoughts start to race. I was definitely more handsy with Seraphina than I should've been on our way back to my car after our encounter in the announcer's box. Thinking with my dick yet again, even after we'd already had sex.

If Reid saw us, who else did? Has he mentioned this to Chase? Or to anyone?

"Listen," I start. "That's complicated."

Smooth, dumbass. Reid is so drunk I could tell him I'm an astronaut and he'd probably buy it. Yet I chose to go the worst possible route: admitting guilt *and* making it seem like an even bigger deal than it is.

"Complicated how?"

I've already dug myself this deep; might as well keep excavating. "Carter doesn't know, and you'd be doing me a solid if you helped keep it that way."

He flops onto his bed next to mine, stretching out his legs. "Fair enough. I won't say anything."

"You won't?"

"Nah." Reid scans my face, a grin springing across his. "Relax, man. You look like you're about to have a heart attack."

"Just didn't think we'd out ourselves like that. Sloppy on my part."

It's tricky to navigate, because I like spending time with Seraphina and doing things together. Actually, the two of us in public isn't the issue; it's that I need to keep my hands to myself when we are. Easier said than done. She's so soft, and she smells so good . . .

"I take it Carter wouldn't approve?"

"Chase would blow a fucking gasket. Besides, he doesn't need to know. We're not dating, we're just . . ."

"Fucking?" he supplies.

My stomach clenches. Categorizing it that way feels wrong.

"Friends with benefits, basically." Well, fuck. That doesn't sound great either. "We both have a lot going on right now."

Reid drains the last of his Stella and sets it on the nightstand next to the alarm clock. "Smart. All of the advantages without any of the drawbacks. Makes it easier on you if things go sideways."

"I don't think they'll go sideways."

He snorts. "That's what I thought, and then she fucked Grady."

My head whips to look at him. "What?"

I pick up my book and slip a metal bookmark inside to hold my page, setting it on the bedside table. Suddenly, it all makes sense. This is why Reid transferred in the middle of the season. This is why he's been so tight-lipped about the circumstances around it. And this is why he's shown zero interest in all the chicks who've been throwing themselves at him since he arrived. His girlfriend cheated on him with his team's head coach. Dude got burned. *Bad.*

"Fuck my life." Reid runs a hand down his face. "I'm not s'pposed to be talking about this."

"I think you already did, dude. You can tell me if you want.

Remember, you've got leverage on me too. Consider it a vow of mutually assured destruction."

He stares at the patterned bedspread, drumming his fingers on his thigh, then his gaze snaps up to mine. "Fine. Grady fucked my girlfriend. That's why I transferred. One day I went to his office after hours to ask him about something, and he had Michelle bent over his desk. Some mentor, right?"

"Holy fuck. What did you do?"

The very thought of seeing Seraphina with someone else like that makes my stomach lurch. I was pissed enough about Rob picking her up and trying to convince her to spend the night. I have a newly discovered jealous streak a mile wide when it comes to her. If I found someone else fucking her, I'd end up in jail.

"What do you think I did? I waited for him to get his pants on and then I kicked his ass. His fighting skills must've been rusty, because it was pretty one-sided." He laughs, but it's bitter. "Woodbine was more worried about keeping everything under wraps, so no one pressed any charges. Guess they figured it'd be a bad look if people found out their thirty-year-old head coach was fucking undergrads, especially his star player's nineteen-year-old girlfriend."

"That's brutal, Holloway. I'm sorry." My empathy skills leave a lot to be desired, but I feel for him in this case. I'd have done the same thing in his shoes.

"I couldn't stay there and play for him after that happened. I couldn't even look at him. They made me sign an NDA in exchange for helping me transfer. All I had to do was leave quietly and keep my mouth shut, which I'd been doing a good job of until I had all this beer and now . . . fuck. Telling you puts me in breach of contract."

He blows out a breath, sagging against the wooden headboard. "It feels kind of good to get it off my chest, though. The only other people who know are my parents, and they seem to think I should forgive Michelle. We'd been together since high school, man. How the fuck do you forgive that?"

"You don't. At least, not in my world." As I reach for my bottled water, an unpleasant realization hits me. Seraphina and I haven't talked about other people. Haven't even tiptoed around the subject. Deep down, I don't think she would hook up with anyone else, but it's unsettling to know she wouldn't technically be breaking any rules if she did.

The heat kicks on and warm air rolls across my bare upper body from the nearby vent. It starts to feel uncomfortably warm, and I'm not sure if it's due to the climate control or the disturbing mental image I'm holding in my head.

"Right?" Reid slumps in his bed and lies flat, pulling the covers over his body. He stares at the ceiling as he continues. "We were together for over three years. Three goddamn wasted years of my life. She even came to Woodbine to be with me. I had no idea anything was going on behind my back. Who knows, maybe I was too focused on my own shit."

"You can't blame yourself for her behavior. Even if you were, there are a million other ways she could've handled it instead of cheating."

"Either way, joke's on me. I thought we were going to get married. And now I am never, ever fucking dating again." His words slur together. "It's not worth it, man."

When I switch off the lights, Reid passes out instantly. I'm not as lucky. My mind refuses to shut off. I lay in the dark, staring at the crack of moonlight pouring in through the gap between the curtains and the wall. Is he right? Is this thing with Seraphina going to go sideways on me? What happens when she moves out? Or when I leave for the summer?

She said we should enjoy ourselves and take things as they come. Easier said than done when that's not in my nature. I've never *not* had a plan.

Chapter 22
VALENTINE'S DAY

SERAPHINA

This week has flown by. Not only have I been incredibly busy with school, but I also went to the new Reese Witherspoon movie with Chloe, hit up the mall with Siobhan, took my mom to two different medical appointments, and made a respectable dent in unpacking and organizing my things. Admittedly, the last one is still ongoing, but I can see the floor again, so that's progress.

Tyler's been even busier than I have. We haven't had any time together aside from a handful of stolen kisses and daily marathon text sessions. Luckily, our drought is about to end. Chase and Dallas left for their couples' weekend an hour ago, and I'm at home waiting for Tyler to get back from working with his goalie coach. We've flat out abandoned our questions today in favor of torturing each other via the dirtiest messages possible in preparation for later.

> Hades: I can't stop picturing you fucking yourself with that toy.

> Tinker Bell: I can't wait until you're the one fucking me instead.

I'm what some might call excessively prepared for this occasion. I've shaved everything from the neck down, applied perfume (including behind my knees), opted for waterproof mascara so it'll hold up better during sex, and selected the sexiest matching bra and underwear I own. Not that I expect either of those to stay on for very long.

According to the clock, I still have nearly two hours to wait. I settle onto the couch with a cup of coffee and my lap desk, opening my laptop. I've been secretly working on a poem for the magazine contest Chloe told me about. No one else knows yet, and depending how things play out, it's possible they never will.

Forty-five minutes in, my coffee is empty and so is my brain. I've been tinkering with the same three lines over and over again, trying to arrange the words for maximum oomph. Biting my lip, I reread the stanza. Something is off, but I can't place it.

I check my email and find a message alerting me to new grades in the student portal. Maxine was sick last week, so she was late marking our first assignment. We've since handed in our second, and I'm so nervous about them both it hurts.

Holding my breath, I wait for it to load.

Seraphina Carter, Student ID 29989797
Introduction to Creative Writing
Assignment 1: 91
Assignment 2: 92

No way. My hand flies to my mouth, and I let out a happy little squeak. According to the class's grading scale, those are both As. For some people, this is a regular occurrence. Possibly even an expectation. For me, it's an anomaly. I rarely get As. I don't get all that many Cs either. My grades tend to hover within a nice, predictable B-to-B+ range.

Though it is only an introductory class. Maybe she's an easy grader.

Closing my browser, I navigate back into the word processor and pull up the thesaurus bar on the right in hopes it will help solve my wording woes. It's tempting to get fancy with vocabulary sometimes, but I also have to be careful not to fall prey to substituting synonyms that aren't strictly identical in meaning.

I read through the passage again, lingering on the part that isn't working. *His face* . . . No, maybe it should be *His features* . . .

That isn't quite the same, though. Neither is right. Is there really only one word for "face" in the English language? How limiting.

"Tink." A deep voice startles me.

I jump in my seat, slamming the laptop shut. "Hi!"

Tyler studies me, a smile playing on his lips. He's freshly showered and changed into his street clothes in his omnipresent shades of black and gray. As irrational as it may sound, I can tell just by looking at him that he smells amazing.

"Looking at something naughty?" He nods to the gold MacBook in front of me. "I said your name three times and you didn't even react."

"Um, I was . . ." I flounder. Any of the alternative explanations I can formulate seem even worse than the truth. "Writing, actually. It's a poem I've been working on for class."

My face heats and I stop talking. Why didn't I just leave it at "doing schoolwork"? I haven't told anyone outside of class about my writing, and for good reason. It's unlikely anything will ever come of it.

He lifts his eyebrows. "Really?"

"Yeah." I wipe my palms on my skirt. Why are they so sweaty? Not cute.

"That's cool, Ser." He lowers onto the couch and rests a hand on my knee, warmth radiating from his palm onto my skin. "Can I ask what it's about?"

The curiosity in his tone almost makes me want to open up. Almost.

"It's a secret." This particular poem may or may not contain elements that were heavily inspired by him, and that's why he'll never, *ever* read it.

"So I was close, then. You're *writing* something naughty." His mouth tips up at one corner in that delicious way that makes me want to grab his face and press my lips to his.

"Define naughty," I hedge.

"Does it contain any of the things you let me do to you in the announcer's box?"

"Not this one, but some of them might. Maybe I'm using you for sexy poem research."

He chuckles. "Use away. Do you write often?"

"A lot, actually." *What the hell, Seraphina?* No one knows this. Now that I've flung open Pandora's box of secrets, I can't seem to close the lid.

Maybe it's the mixture of admiration and desire on his face, tinged with a hint of tenderness. No one has ever looked at me this way before.

My ears burn and I untuck my hair to hide it. "Until now, writing has been something I did for myself. This class is the first time I've ever shared it with anyone."

"I won't pressure you, but I'd always be down to read something if you felt comfortable."

That's more terrifying than sharing it with my class. Maybe someday.

"Let's see how far I get on this one. It's giving me a bit of trouble."

Tyler's expression shifts like he only just realized we're alone. He takes the closed laptop from me, setting it on the coffee table. Then he pushes the lap desk aside and picks me up, hauling me to sit on him. He smells every bit as good as I expected.

He nudges my nose with his affectionately. "How are things, Tink? I feel like I barely saw you all week."

"Better now."

A contented sound reverberates deep in his throat, and his lips press to my jaw, then my cheek. I shift a little more, turning fully toward him. One hand snakes up to grip my face and he kisses me, long and deliberate and deep.

When he pulls away, I'm on cloud nine.

Instead of kissing me again like I expect, his gray eyes bounce back and forth between mine. "We never get to sit like this. It's kinda nice."

I rest my head on his shoulder. "It is."

Something in me eases slightly; a tension I hadn't realized I was carrying. As much as I've been eager for him to rail me, it's oddly reassuring that isn't the only reason we're talking at the moment. I legitimately consider him one of my friends. In fact, I trust him more than some of my "friends." I like to think we'd hang out together even if the sexual element between us wasn't there.

Tyler runs his hands through my hair, and I nearly start purring at how good it feels. Asking him to pet me that night in his room gave him insight into one of my biggest weaknesses; an unfair advantage he didn't need.

"What color is this, technically?" he asks. "I know it's pink, but there's some gold in here too."

"Most people call it rose-gold, but my hairdresser back in Arizona called it strawberry champagne. It's a little brighter and pinker than a regular rose-gold. She blended the color specifically for me."

A low laugh rumbles in his chest. "Of course you have a custom hair color, princess."

"You got a problem with that?" I wriggle upright, pretending to glare at him.

"No, I love your hair." He holds up a section, studying it in the light. "You know, it looks different depending on the lighting and the angle."

If by "different" he means "brassy," then he's correct. Beneath the living room lamp, it's mostly copper with hints of rose. Red-based tones fade quickly, and even with special color-preserving shampoos and UV-protective styling products, I pay a hefty coloring fee on the regular to keep it looking the way I want. But having pink hair makes me happy, so it's worth it.

"Probably because the color is starting to fade. I'm overdue for a touch-up. I need to find a salon here to make me pretty again."

"You're always pretty, Tink." His mouth tugs into a crooked grin.

If humans could melt, I'd be a puddle on the floor.

"I have an idea," he adds, still running his fingers through the strands.

"What's that?"

"We've both had a long week. Let's go grab something to eat."

My stomach practically gurgles at the very suggestion. It's nearly six, and I haven't eaten since noon. Hanger territory is looming in plain sight. There's one tiny snag with his plan, however.

"It's Valentine's Day, Hades. All the restaurants will be packed."

He lifts a broad shoulder. "Yeah, but how often do we get the chance to do things together?"

True. It's a lot harder to coordinate hanging out in *or* out of the house during the week, whether it's due to our schedules, living situation, or all the other things standing in our way. Weekends are even less workable because he always has games both nights. This weekend is one of the only breaks they have.

Lately, I've been wondering if it would be simpler to bring our friendship out of the closet to everyone. There's a risk they might do the math on the rest. It's not that I think we're doing anything wrong, it's that I don't think my brother would understand. Nor does he need to.

"I don't think we'll be able to get a table unless we're talking about something like McDonald's or Chipotle. But I'm good with something like that too. Anything works."

"Let me see. I'll check OpenTable to see what's available." Broad hands shift me on his lap, readjusting us. He grabs his phone and enters the passcode to unlock it, then taps at the screen. Brow furrowed, he scrolls with his thumb. "No . . . All-you-can-eat sushi sounds dicey. No . . . Definitely not. What the fuck is Bob's Pancake and Taco Bar? Wait . . . There. We can get a table at Rouge. There's one reservation for two open at eight o'clock. Someone must've canceled at the last minute."

"Rouge?" I echo. "Isn't that really fancy? And expensive?" I'm vaguely familiar with it because Chase took Bailey there a while back, and while it was reportedly amazing, she confessed to me over Christmas that she'd had sticker shock at the prices.

Then again, money isn't an issue for Tyler, and we both know it. His father is one of the most famous sports agents in the entire country. Chase knew who Tyler's dad was from hockey industry news long before he ever met Tyler.

"Here's my take," he says. "You've been working hard at school, you haven't been out much lately, and I think you're due for some fun. And I've been killing myself with hockey. If you ask me, we both deserve the break."

"Gotta admit, I like your logic." I'm a big fan of treating myself. If anything, I do it a little too much. Did a page of homework? Chocolate. Went to the gym? Celebration smoothie on the way out. Passed a final? Sephora time. I can justify anything. And it's especially hard to turn down doing something with Tyler.

It does sound an awful lot like a date, though. Is that against the rules? I guess the nice part of our arrangement is we get to make our own.

"Unless you don't want to be seen in public with me," he says, teasing. "In which case we can order a heart-shaped pizza and it should arrive in approximately three to five hours according to the internet."

"Going out it is."

Chapter 23
VALENTINE'S NIGHT

SERAPHINA

I change a grand total of seven times before deciding on a dress to wear out for dinner.

Extra? Fully, and I'm embracing it.

Color is the biggest sticking point. I debate between pink and black for longer than any rational person should. Eventually, I settle on the quintessential little black dress paired with my black patent Louboutins. Can't go wrong with either.

Then I pull up Rouge's website on my laptop and scope out the menu to ward off decision overwhelm at the table. Agonizing over my wardrobe and menu choices doesn't leave as much buffer as I'd hoped for makeup, but I'm already dolled-up from my primping session earlier. A quick sweep of some darker eyeshadow and a bit more blush does the trick, and I'm ready with one minute to spare until we have to leave. Impressively early in my world.

Inhaling, I give myself a final once-over in the mirror. I'm nervous, likely because I don't have a lot of experience going on actual dates. College hookups really aren't the same thing. Even with the rapport Tyler and I have, something about this feels like a big deal.

Ugh. I'm reading too much into it. We're supposed to be having fun together, and we are. It doesn't have to be anything more than that.

I close my bedroom door behind me and turn down the hall. Tyler is sitting in the living room with his forearms resting against his thighs, his gaze glued to a sports channel on television. Part amusing, part exasperating. He's never not in "work" mode.

Like me, he's also changed his clothes. It's like he's identified every weakness of mine and exploited it accordingly. His black dress shirt stretches across his wide shoulders, the collar left open at the very top to reveal the edges of several dark tattoos, and his sleeves rolled up halfway to reveal even more. It's harder to see his lower half, but I already know whatever he's wearing will be perfectly tailored to every inch of the hard-earned muscles that clad his frame.

My heels click on the hardwood floor as I draw closer. He turns to look at me and freezes. The remote slips out of his hand, landing on the couch. It's difficult to interpret the expression on his face. I like to *think* I'm getting a positive reaction, but I can't be sure when he isn't blinking. He may not even be breathing. Did I break him?

"Ty?" I prod after another couple of seconds pass.

"Huh?" His eyes rocket up to mine, his voice hoarse. "You look . . ." Another stretch of stunned silence follows. He runs a hand along his jaw. "If I hadn't snagged that reservation already, there's no way we'd be leaving this house."

My nervousness abates, and the energy coursing through me morphs into something closer to excitement. Note to self: When he glitches, it's a good thing.

Pushing to stand, he picks up the remote and shuts off the television. Then he angles his head, studying my feet. "I've never considered myself much of a shoe guy, but those are fucking hot."

See? My Round Chick Altas never fail. I'm convinced they have magical powers.

"Selfie?" I dangle my phone between my fingers. "You've gotta admit, we both look good."

He hesitates for a second before agreeing. It's not a huge shock that he's not a selfie kind of guy. Sometimes he's too serious for his own good.

We end up taking a few, ranging from goofy to kissing to a standard smiling shot. The goofy one is my favorite.

Tyler's black Audi SUV is idling in front of the house when we step outside, which is a nice touch. With as cold as it's been lately, it would be like climbing into an igloo if he hadn't started it ahead of time. Probably wouldn't bother the guy who spends nearly half his life on the ice, but I appreciate not freezing to death in my dress.

He opens the passenger door for me and waits until I climb in before he shuts it, walking around to the driver's side. I'm convinced there's something drastically wrong with me that I nearly salivate when his large hand wraps around the leather gearshift handle. It's like a form of competence porn, the appeal of which I can't fully explain. All I know is he looks like he knows what he's doing, and it's hot.

Same with when I watched him play on television the other night. With a father who played professional hockey and a brother on the same career trajectory, I had previously considered myself immune to the mysterious phenomenon that causes some women to swoon over hockey players. Not so. It turns out that I am very much susceptible, at least when it comes to Tyler. Seeing him out there on the ice did things to me it shouldn't.

"You get a chance to look at the menu, Ser?" His gaze cuts to me as he slows to a stop at a red light.

My heart swells at him remembering this tiny, admittedly neurotic, detail.

"Sure did."

He squeezes my thigh affectionately. "Good."

The restaurant has a valet out front when we pull up. Tyler hands off the car, then steps up onto the sidewalk and slides an arm around my waist, tucking me into him as he steers me inside.

Rouge is even more impressive than I expected, stylishly decorated in dark jewel tones, upscale without being pretentious. The small space is dotted with tables of varying sizes, dim lamps and candles providing the only sources of light.

Music throbs low in the background as the hostess leads us

through the restaurant, Tyler's hand resting along my back the entire way. She takes us to a small leather booth in a corner off to the back. Whoever canceled this reservation sure gave up some prime seating. It's cozy, and the ambience is to die for.

A thoughtful look crosses his face as the hostess disappears, leaving us alone. He takes my hand beneath the table, his thumb skimming the thin skin of my inner wrist.

"What I meant to say earlier was you look beautiful, Tink."

I don't need a mirror to know I'm blushing. "Thank you, Hades."

For my first Valentine's Day with a guy *and* my first non-date date, the bar has been raised impossibly high.

We skim the menus while we wait, and Tyler orders a beer for himself and a glass of sauvignon blanc for me at my request. I like white wine every now and then. As much as I've tried, I haven't been able to acquire a taste for red.

"Question forty." Half a glass in, I'm feeling it ever so slightly due to the lack of food in my system. "What's your worst habit?"

He considers for a beat. "Being too competitive."

"You?" I tease. "Competitive?"

"More with myself than anything, but obviously with other goalies as well. It's good fuel as long as I don't let it get out of hand. Which does happen from time to time."

When he looks at me expectantly, I suddenly realize I'll have to answer too. Asking things I want to know about him cuts both ways.

"Mine's self-sabotage. I know I do it, and I can't seem to stop myself." Procrastination is the worst way it manifests. Others include denial and failure to prioritize properly.

"Do you know why you do it?" There's no judgment in his tone, only concern.

"No," I say honestly, rubbing the crystal stem of the glass between my fingertips. "Well, maybe. It could be linked to the whole ADHD thing. I've read they often go hand in hand."

Tyler looks down at the table like he's deciding what to say.

and it takes so long for him to speak that I start to worry about what it's going to be.

"Have you ever considered hanging out with someone like Abby could be a form of that? Like putting yourself in situations where you're not fully comfortable and trying to compensate?"

Is it? I've never thought about it like that before. Smaller house parties and bars like Overtime are fun, but I'm not sure I'm ever truly at ease at those crowded nightclubs and frat parties. My friends like them, so I've always gone along for fear of seeming boring or potentially losing friendships. Clearly not the right reason to do things, and deep down, I know that.

"Maybe . . ." I trail off. "How do you—how did you figure? That's such a specific thing to say. I'm not saying I'm mad or I disagree, but it's never occurred to me before."

"I used to do things like that. It wasn't exactly the same, but I didn't cope well with the stress I was under, and I compensated in destructive ways. Which brings us back to the stress cleaning and the tattoos, like I said before." He points to the elaborate compass inked onto his other hand. "I got this one as a reminder to myself to focus on where I want to go, not get caught in the weeds."

That tattoo is the first thing that made his identity click for me. I love it even more now that I know what it symbolizes.

"You're the most focused person I know, Ty."

We're interrupted by the server setting down our crab cakes and ahi tuna tower to start. Seafood is too hard to prepare properly at home—or, at least, I haven't mastered it—but I always order it when I go out to higher-end places. And as we dive in, Rouge does not disappoint.

"Oh, god. That's so good." I take another bite of ahi tuna and Asian slaw, letting out a moan. It's heaven on a fork. The fact I'm starving makes everything taste that much better.

Tyler eyes me over the rim of his glass. "You can't make those noises, Ser."

"Why? Getting dirty ideas?"

"Getting?" His eyes gleam with dark amusement. "More like actively trying to stop myself from acting on them."

We talk nonstop throughout our meal, interspersed heavily with flirting and innuendo. While Tyler also seems to be enjoying the food, his attention is mostly fixed on me while we eat.

By the time we've ordered a dark chocolate soufflé to share for dessert, we're both on edge.

Beneath the tablecloth, his hand creeps beneath the hem of my dress and comes to rest scandalously high on my bare thigh, fueling the anticipation that's been simmering within me all night. He isn't actively *doing* anything, but that's the point.

If he's going to dish it, he'd better be prepared to take it.

I slide closer to him in the booth and press my thigh to his, ensuring he can see right down the front of my low-cut dress. His gaze slowly, leisurely tracks a path down my face to the intended target, and a muscle in his jaw flexes.

"What's wrong?" I bat my eyelashes at him.

"Tink..." he warns.

"You seem tense. Didn't you enjoy the food?"

"Not as much as I'm going to enjoy eating your pussy when we're done."

A shock of desire jolts through me. If there's any justice in this world, I'll get to experience that at least once in my lifetime.

Tingles run down my spine as he brushes my hair away from my ear and leans in. "Remember what I said on FaceTime?"

Who could forget? Those words have been permanently imprinted in my brain. *"I'm going to make you come so hard you make a dripping mess. Once I'm finished, I'm going to kiss you so you can taste how sweet you are."*

My thighs clench around his hand, which is still several inches south of where I'd like it to be. I wriggle impatiently, growing more frustrated by the second. I've been waiting all day for him to touch me. If he doesn't do something soon, I might do it myself.

A teasing smirk appears on his face. "You want to be a good girl for me, don't you?"

I nod. "Mmm-hmm."

"Then take off your panties and give them to me."

"You want me to do that here?" I whisper, glancing around. Our table is partially shielded by one of several towering floor-to-ceiling fireplaces, and our lower bodies are concealed by the tablecloth in the way. No one is within hearing distance. "In the middle of the restaurant?"

"Or I can do it for you, but I promise I'll be a lot less discreet."

Tyler looks at me expectantly while I feign shyness. He thinks he has the upper hand here. Little does he know, I impulsively slipped off my underwear while I was getting dressed. Hence, no panties to give.

"Can't. I'm not wearing any."

Dark desire flashes across his face. He pushes my legs apart with his hand and cups my center. My back arches, my breath snagging as one broad finger slides along my soaking, heated entrance.

Warmth floods my body, and I gasp quietly. "Ty."

As much as I wanted him to touch me, I'm not sure I can be quiet enough to let him continue.

Shadows cast across his handsome face, determination in his eyes. "Stop thinking, Ser. I've got you."

Two fingers slide inside me, the sudden fullness delivering a massive dose of pleasure. Bliss rolls through my body, and I grip the edge of the table, fighting to keep my hips from rocking.

"Good girl." He hums with approval. "You're doing so well for me."

His focus stays glued to me, intently watching my reaction as his fingers pump in and out, the heel of his palm rubbing my clit. My breaths turn shaky, and the rest of the room fades away.

With a few more strokes of his skilled fingers, I'm at the top of a roller coaster staring down at the drop below. I look at him helplessly, teetering on the brink of no return.

"Just like that, baby. Show me what you're going to do to my cock when we get home."

White-hot pleasure crashes over me, and I bite my bottom lip to keep myself from crying out. My orgasm ebbs and flows, seemingly going on forever before it finally fades out. When it becomes too much and I'm fully sated, my hand flies to grasp his under the table, halting him.

"What do you know?" He gently withdraws his fingers and dips his head, kissing my cheek. "You came before dessert did."

Chapter 24
FUCK-ME HEELS

TYLER

Is it possible to be fuckdrunk prior to having fucked? Neither of us had more than one drink, yet we're both acting completely inebriated. Just driving home was a challenge for me.

Tugging open the front door, I hold it for Seraphina to enter first. My cock stiffens at the scent of her perfume in the air as she brushes by. I'm so hard I can't see straight, and she's barely even touched me.

I turn to hang up our coats, and she trips on a stray shoe sitting on the entry mat.

My free arm shoots out to keep her upright. "You okay, Tink?"

For once, she looks legitimately bashful. "You've got me too worked up to balance. I need to sit down and take these off before I break an ankle." She points to her glossy black heels. They're fuck-me shoes, and she knew *exactly* what she was doing when she wore them tonight.

Before she can lower herself onto the hallway bench, I slowly walk her backward until she's pressed against the wall. Taking her wrists in my hands, I pin them above her head as my lips capture hers. A soft, breathy laugh of surprise escapes before she angles her head, kissing me back. Her soft tongue sweeps against mine, the taste of her mixing with traces of chocolate from dessert, and an involuntary growl rumbles in my chest. I meant what I said about kissing her. It's one of my favorite things.

Dipping my head, I trail my nose along the side of her throat, inhaling her scent. *Fuck.* There are countless things I want to do, but I know exactly where I'm going to start.

"I'll get your shoes."

Seraphina giggles. "You don't have to."

I gently bite the flesh where her neck meets her shoulder. "I want to."

My palms drag down the sides of her body, shaping to the dip of her waist and the swell of her hips, moving lower until I come to kneel before her. She leans against the wall and shifts her weight to one foot, offering the other to me. It's familiar in some ways, yet dramatically different in others.

Lowering my mouth to her calf, I place a soft kiss along her skin before I unfasten each buckle and set aside both heels. Then I push up the fabric of her black dress to expose her bare lower half. A groan echoes in my throat at the sight of her pretty pussy on display for me.

"Because last time . . ." I nudge her legs wider, kissing and nibbling my way up her inner thigh. Her breath hitches, her body tensing with anticipation when I stop short of where she wants me most. "I couldn't do this."

My mouth closes over her center, and I lick her in one long, languid stroke. Seraphina cries out, sinking her fingers into my hair.

"Oh, *fuck.*" Her head rolls back, and her purse falls from her other hand.

She trembles as I swirl her clit with my tongue, slipping two fingers inside her tight, wet heat. I stroke her walls, working in perfect rhythm with my mouth until she's a begging, shaking mess above me.

As she gets close to coming, she gets even wetter, dripping with sweet, heady arousal. My dick hardens until it verges on painful, and I'm torn between the need to sink inside of her and never wanting this moment to end.

Hips swaying, she grinds against my face, tugging harder on my hair. I read her cues, keeping pace with the way she's moving against me, and with a few more lashes of my tongue, she utters a mix of breathy pleas and needy whimpers as she goes over the edge.

I ease her down gradually, giving her one soft, final lick before I rise to stand. Seraphina sags against the wall, pliant in my arms. Supporting her weight, I bring my mouth to hers and wedge my knee between her legs. A desperate moan escapes her lips as my thigh rubs against her sensitive, swollen clit.

"Ty." Her pelvis tips forward, instinctively seeking more. "I'm going to make a mess all over your pants."

"Good." I press harder because that's an incentive if I've ever heard one.

"Let's go to my room," she begs. "Please."

Smoothing my palms down her bare backside, I hoist her up and wrap her legs around me, carrying her down the hall. I turn on her bedside lamp, then lower her onto the mattress. She blinks up at me, her heart-shaped lips slightly parted. It's the most gorgeous fucking sight.

Her slender fingers trail down my chest and travel past my belt, gripping me over my pants. I grunt, the muscles in my abdomen tensing. The effect she has on me is unreal.

"See how fucking hard I am? You did that to me."

"What else should I do to you?" She looks up at me from beneath her long, dark lashes as she slowly unbuttons my shirt.

Shrugging out of it, I help her slide it off. "Get down on your knees and take out my cock."

I push to stand as Seraphina slides off the bed and kneels on the carpet in her little black dress. My breaths grow shallow as she unbuckles my belt and unfastens my pants, tugging everything down.

Her small hand wraps around my length, pumping. "Now what?"

"Give me that pretty mouth of yours."

She hums as if considering. "You want my mouth?" Her lips

hover over the head of my dick, her breath warm against my skin, but she doesn't do as I said.

"Yes." I groan, tipping my head back as she strokes me up and down, teasing me. "Fuck, yes."

"Say please."

"Please suck my cock, Ser." There's zero hesitation in my response. Right now, I would do anything to have those plump, kiss-bruised lips wrapped around my shaft.

"That's better." Her pink tongue darts out and swirls around the tip, leisurely licking me like an ice cream cone. Every pass is sweet torture. I gently gather her hair out of the way, urging her on. Finally, her lips wrap around the head, taking me fully into her warm, wet mouth. A moan escapes my throat, and I clamp down on the urge to thrust forward. With my piercings, I need to take it easy for her sake.

"Suck it," I tell her. "Take it all the way. Good girl."

She looks up at me through watery eyes, tempting every last shred of my self-restraint. The sight of Seraphina on her knees with her mouth full of my dick is enough to make me lose it on the spot. I don't know what it is about her, but it's like getting a blow job for the first time.

When she takes me even deeper, I hit the back of her throat. A familiar tingling forms at the base of my spine.

"Tink." I tighten my grip at her roots as a warning. "I'd love to come in your mouth another time, but tonight I need your pussy."

Instead of stopping, she slowly, torturously slides her lips all the way to the head and lingers there, working with her tongue. *Oh, fuck.* I won't last much longer if she keeps doing that.

She releases me with a smirk, and I haul her to stand.

Fighting a grin, I kiss her. "Brat."

"Oh yeah?" Seraphina slips out of her dress and lets it drop to the floor, leaving herself totally naked before me. Every single thought vacates my brain as I take it all in. Full, perky breasts; luscious hips; smooth, creamy skin.

That's it. I'm done. I can't wait anymore.

I shove her down onto the bed, and my lips cover hers as we frantically tug off all my clothing. It's a scramble of lips and hands, kissing and groaning. The effect she has on me is like nothing I've ever experienced. It's better than any drug ever could be.

Once there's nothing left between us, she arches her back, rubbing her wet pussy along the length of my dick. With every roll of her hips, the additional lubrication brings me a little closer to slipping inside. It takes superhuman self-control not to let my hips snap forward.

She moves beneath me again, and the tip of my cock nudges her soaking entrance.

"Easy," I rasp, fighting to hold myself still above her. My skin is fevered, muscles tense, body begging me to move.

Seraphina kisses the edge of my jaw. "Fuck me."

The urge to do exactly as she says is nearly impossible to resist. It would be all too easy to erase the distance between us with a single thrust, giving in to what we both desperately want. And believe me, I want it a *lot*.

Before I do something reckless, I sit back on my knees. "Condom, Tink."

She directs me to her nightstand, and I'm back between her legs in record time. When I sink into her, she lets out the prettiest gasp I've ever heard, tightening around me. My hips jerk forward, my body claiming hers completely.

Her mouth felt amazing, but her pussy? It's fucking heaven.

"Fuck, Ser." I thrust again, reveling in the way her tits bounce. "You're going to make me come so hard."

She claws at my arms as my hips rock against her, nudging the spot that makes her eyes roll back in her head. Going into tonight, I had told myself I'd take my time fucking her. Now that I'm finally inside her hot, wet cunt, I'm wild with lust.

Channeling my self-control, I force myself to hold back, watching her every reaction. The changes in her breathing pattern; her little sighs and sounds; the way her eyes squeeze shut when it hits just right. I lose myself in her completely, fucking her exactly the way she begs me to.

Seraphina squirms beneath me, her skin taking on a rosy flush, and I know she's almost there. I tilt my hips, changing the angle slightly. Her mouth falls open as her back arches off the bed.

"Oh, god." She whimpers, tightening her legs around my waist. "I'm coming. Come with me. Please. I need you to."

The moment she says that it's game fucking over.

My mouth crashes down on hers, and my hands fly to her waist, pinning her to the mattress. When I slam into her again, she falls apart with a cry. My abs tense, my body stiffens, and I fall right behind her, my cock throbbing with long-awaited release. It feels so good that I'm pretty sure my brain might actually be melting.

Hanging my head, I try to catch my breath. My heart hammers against my rib cage, aftershocks wracking my body. I'm far more tired than I should be as an athlete, and I'm going to chalk that up to all the anticipation leading up to the main event.

When I glance back up, our eyes lock, and her mouth tugs into a smile. She looks part-sated, part-smug—probably because by now, she knows exactly what she does to me.

"For the record," I say, still breathing heavily, "don't tell me to come unless you want it to happen immediately."

She giggles. "I'm definitely going to abuse that knowledge."

"You wouldn't dare." I pinch her ass, and she laughs even harder.

Later that night, Seraphina falls asleep first. I lay in bed with her naked body wrapped around mine, listening to her slow, even breaths in the quiet room.

That's when it hits me: I haven't thought about hockey all night.

◆ ◆ ◆

My toxic trait is that I like to know everything—even when it doesn't serve me. Keeping tabs on my own stats is only logical, but monitoring the competition is a great way to fuck up my mental health.

Case in point: Caleb Brown is up a spot in the standings, putting us squarely neck and neck. I'm still first, but the gap dividing us is rapidly shrinking.

Fuck.

I stare at the tiny numbers on my screen until they turn into a blur. The rational part of me knows it's more than a little ridiculous to stress over first versus second place in the entire league. The rest of me doesn't care—especially not when my longer-term career is potentially in jeopardy.

Seraphina walks up, studying my face with a frown. "You okay, Hades? You look like you want to kill someone."

She's not wrong. I have a bad mood brewing beneath the surface, but now that I'm looking at her, I'm trying hard to let it go. It's already Saturday evening, and it feels like the weekend is slipping through my fingers like grains of sand. I don't want to waste a single second.

"Yeah, just looking at—"

"Hockey," she finishes, gently prying the phone from my hands. "You promised we'd watch a movie."

"That I did." I even promised she could pick a girly one. It helps that she asked me in the middle of the dirtiest shower I've ever taken. Every time I see that detachable showerhead I'm going to picture it between Seraphina's legs.

She lowers onto the couch next to me and drapes her legs across my lap. Her pink-and-white pajama set she just changed into makes me want to do anything *but* sleep. The ribbed crop top hits above her navel, exposing a tempting sliver of bare skin, and the shorts barely cover her ass cheeks.

Leaning forward, she fishes a pink Starburst out of the bag on the coffee table while I open the movie store app.

"By the way," she says, "you didn't tell me your birthday was coming up."

I pause with the remote still aimed at the television. "Who told you that?"

It isn't that it's a secret; it's that someone talking about my birthday automatically makes me suspicious.

Her head snaps up, and her eyes widen. "Er... no one." She shoves a Starburst in her mouth.

Yep. Just like I thought. Not hard to guess what's going on here.

"Is Dallas trying to throw me a surprise party?"

Seraphina chews the candy slowly like she's trying to buy herself some time to think. "I don't know if it was meant to be a *surprise* per se, but I may have been instructed not to tell you about it." She grimaces. "I'm terrible at keeping secrets. Sorry."

I'm not a big fan of surprises, and I'm even less fond of surprise parties. But with the dirt Dallas is holding over my head, it's not like I can complain. Plus, it's well-intentioned. As the extrovert of the house, sometimes he forgets not everyone is wired the same way.

"It's fine," I tell her. "I'd rather know. As long as we can sneak off for some birthday sex."

Her mouth tips up at the corner. "We can definitely sneak off for some birthday sex."

After a moment's debate—though I suspect she secretly knew what she wanted all along—Seraphina chooses *Legally Blonde* because I haven't seen it and she claims it's the holy grail of movies. I hit play, then take her left foot in my hands and dig my thumb into the arch, massaging.

"Ooh, that's good." She leans back into the cushions, letting out a sigh that sounds borderline sexual. "I could get used to this."

Halfway through the movie, she's out cold on my chest. The frame stills as I hit pause to hold our place. Sundays are my only day off from all forms of training, and there's a chance we'll have time to finish tomorrow before Chase and Dallas get back

While I wouldn't have watched this on my own, now I'm invested. Warner is a total douchecanoe, and I'm rooting for his downfall.

There's something else about the movie that resonates with me too. I think I can see why Seraphina relates to it, and that gives me a little more insight into her.

Switching the TV to ESPN, I dial down the volume until it's nearly inaudible. Then I glance down at Sera, debating whether to move her into bed or let her sleep a little longer before I try. Her lips are parted slightly, her dark lashes resting against her upper cheeks. A sense of protectiveness washes over me, followed by massive confusion.

What the fuck am I doing?

Caleb is figuratively breathing down my neck, New York has a wandering eye when it comes to goalies, and the Falcons are fighting to secure a playoff spot this season. I can't let anyone down, least of all myself, and I need to focus now more than ever. Yet I just spent the better part of the last twenty-four hours taking a vacation from reality, pretending none of those priorities exist.

Getting involved with someone like this is the last thing I should do. What's worse is I don't even know if I can help it. I'm weak when it comes to Seraphina—and it's not because I like the sex.

This realization conjures up a deluge of feelings I don't want to face and questions I don't want to answer. Instead, I reach for my phone and pull up my email. There's a new message from Mark titled *EnduraFuel Invitational Weekend*. I read the body of the email, my body tensing as I do.

> *I know we're still two weeks out, but just touching base to make sure you saw the flight confirmation emails. Your direct flight departs from here at 9:15 a.m. Friday, and your return flight departs from LAX at 7:10 a.m. Monday morning.*

EnduraFuel is the official hydration partner of the league, and their annual invitational is a Big Fucking Deal. It's exclusively for high-end prospects who've already been drafted or are likely to get picked up in the near future. Just being there is a flex. There's a skills competition, a three-on-three mini-tournament, and a bunch of other events that people can buy tickets to come and watch. Essentially, it's one big dick swinging contest, and the media is all over it—which means I need to be on my A game.

For the next two weeks, I need to be sharp both mentally and physically. Extra sleep. Minimal stress. Extra tactical work...

Seraphina stirs, cracking open one eye sleepily. "Hi, Hades."

"Hey, Tink." Locking my phone, I set it aside. "Want to go to bed?"

I can't afford the distraction, but what if it's too late?

Chapter 25
CARE AND CONSIDERATION

SERAPHINA

In honor of getting through another week, I'm doing two things that frighten me today, the first of which is submitting my poem to the *Revolve Magazine* contest. I'm even submitting it early, which is incredibly off brand for me.

With a few more keystrokes, my application form is complete. I hold my breath and pray as I click "submit." The page reloads with a confirmation it's been received.

I had a last-minute change of heart and used the poem I workshopped in class as my contest entry. After all the feedback I received, I made some fairly substantial changes. Chloe helped me with a few more tweaks, and Maxine gave me some feedback as well. Still no way to know if it's what the judges are looking for, but it's easily the rawest thing I've ever written. I bled all over that page. Even if I don't win—which is likely—at least I know I gave it my all.

The second, and current, frightening item on my agenda is booking my BRCA testing. Or trying to book it, anyway. I've been sitting in my room looking at my phone for more than ten minutes, trying to will myself to hit the green call button.

My thumb hovers over the screen, my heart roaring in my ears. I swallow hard and tap it, waiting for the line to connect. It takes all the strength I have not to end the call before it does.

A female receptionist answers after one ring, well before I'm prepared to speak.

"North End Medical Center. How can I help you?"

Nausea slams into me, and the thought of hanging up crosses my mind but I force myself not to.

"Um, hi." I clear my throat. "Doctor Wilson's office referred me for some genetic testing. It should be under Seraphina Carter?"

"Hold please." A moment later, she comes back on the line. "Yes, we have all your paperwork right here. Normally, we book a few weeks out, but we had a last-minute cancellation and there's a spot available this morning. Would you be able to come in then?"

"Sure." There is no part of me that wants to do this today, but something tells me if I don't take the opening, I'm going to put it off forever. "What time?"

"Eleven thirty. I realize that's short notice. I can look at the next available appointment if that doesn't work for you."

Terror threads around my throat, and I force myself to reply. "That works."

Two hours later, I'm sitting outside the testing center in my car on the verge of having a nervous breakdown. Even driving as slowly as the limits of safety and common courtesy would allow, I'm five minutes early. Some latent, self-destructive part of me was secretly hoping I'd be late and miss the appointment.

I turn off the ignition, and the motor dies. *Get out, Sera. Get it over with. It could be negative. Everything might be fine. Remember the power of positive thinking.*

Gritting my teeth, I reach for the door handle, then immediately withdraw my hand. The sooner I know, the sooner I can deal with it whether it's positive or negative. So why can't I make myself get out of the vehicle?

I should have brought someone here with me; should have told someone, at a minimum. That way when I leave here after, I could've called them to tell them how it went.

I've never felt more alone, and it's probably because I am.

◆ ◆ ◆

"Thanks again for letting me reschedule on you." I set down the tray of coffee, pulling out a red plastic chair next to Chloe in the Communications common area. There's a regular latte for me instead of decaf sitting next to hers, which is how you know things are dire. I'm tired in the way sleep won't fix. Even my bones are weary.

"No problem. Is everything okay?" Her dark brows tug. "Not to be nosy, it's just . . . you look like you've been crying."

Concealer can only hide so much, and it can't camouflage the fact I had a half-hour crying session in my car when I got to school. It's makeup, not magic.

"Um, well—" my voice cracks, and so does something else. I don't know how or why it happens, but suddenly, everything I've been holding back breaks free in a torrential downpour of emotion. All of the fear; uncertainty; hope; doubt; sadness; grief; worry; *anger*. I haven't even scratched the surface when it comes to the last one, and I'm terrified to find out what's beneath.

Tears overflow, spilling down my cheeks as sobs wrack my chest. Embarrassment adds to the intensity of everything else I'm feeling, and I'm sorely tempted to run away, lock myself in a bathroom, and drop creative writing so I don't have to see Chloe ever again. Who has a meltdown in the middle of the foyer? We're surrounded by people, and *all* of them are staring.

"Sera. Oh my gosh. Is there something I can do?" Chloe hands me a handful of tissues, scooting her chair closer in an effort to partially block me from sight of everyone else. My nose is pouring snot, I can't catch my breath, and my mascara is running into my eyes.

"No, it's just—" I gasp. "Medical. Mom. Cancer."

She touches my arm. "Your mom has cancer?"

I nod, burying my face in my palms. For weeks, I've been repressing everything, and now that I've started crying, I can't seem to stop. It's like the floodgates opened earlier today and everything keeps gushing out.

"Here." She gathers our things and helps me stand, carrying the tray of coffee for me. "Let's go somewhere else where there are fewer people around."

Chloe leads me down a hallway I'm not familiar with, into another, older building that's connected to the one where we just were. With another left-hand turn, we're sitting on a bench near a bunch of vacant classrooms. She gets me a bottle of water from the vending machine and sits with me as I cry, saying nothing. In a strange way, it helps. Even not talking, having someone hold space for me is surprisingly comforting.

Once I'm finally calm enough to speak in full sentences again, I glance up at her. "Thank you. And I'm so sorry, I didn't mean—I don't know where that came from."

There's sympathy across her face as she looks at me over her white plastic cup. "Can I ask what kind of cancer she has?"

"Breast cancer. Stage three. She's undergoing treatment and she's doing really well, but they found she tested positive for BRCA1."

The last piece of information hangs between us; words I didn't mean to say. I'm not sure if Chloe even knows what BRCA means, but the way her face immediately falls tells me she does. Or at least, she must know enough to know it's bad.

"Oh my god, Sera. I am so sorry."

I grind my molars together, swallowing hard. Validation is comforting and upsetting all at once. "I got tested to see if I'm a carrier today, and now I have to wait to get the results."

In other words, my entire future hangs in the balance and it's literally a coin toss.

"I can't even imagine. No wonder you're upset." Chloe's expression shifts into recognition. "Wait. Can I ask—is that what the poem was about? Sorry, I just put two and two together and..."

Sniffling, I dab at my nose with a soggy tissue. I pocket it and take out a new one, wiping my eyes. "Yeah, it is. Speaking of that, I wanted to tell you I entered the contest with that. So thank you for all your help."

"You did?" Her voice brightens. "I'm so happy to hear that. I've got my fingers crossed for you. It's a strong piece. I mean, I think so anyway."

We sit and talk for a few more minutes. She tells me how her father is in remission for prostate cancer, and knowing she's been through some of the same things makes me feel a lot more understood. It's a strange role reversal being the one to worry about your parent as a child. It's stressful and confusing, and people who haven't experienced it don't understand.

When Chloe has to leave for her next lecture, I'm calm enough that I can safely drive home. In retrospect, I probably shouldn't have driven *to* school. While I wasn't crying then, my brain definitely wasn't all there.

She wraps me in a hug before we part ways. "Let me know if there's anything I can do, okay? Anything at all, even if it's just to bring by food or if you need someone to talk to."

"Thanks, Chloe. I appreciate that."

As I walk to my car, all I can think about is the fact Chloe showed me more care and consideration than a so-called friend I've known for more than half my life, and I've known Chloe for less than two months.

◆ ◆ ◆

Having a meltdown at school must have been somewhat cathartic because my mental state improves marginally after that.

After I get home, I collapse into bed and take a two-hour nap. I sleep like the dead, and when I wake up it almost feels like a new day—which is fortunate, because I agreed to go watch the guys play tonight at Northview Arena.

I poke my head out of my room to find the house empty. I'd forgotten how superstitious hockey players are. Apparently, Chase, Dallas, and Tyler have an elaborate game day routine that starts the moment they wake up, stretches into the afternoon, and carries them all the way to puck drop. My brain took a minivacation when Chase tried to explain the specifics, but I gather that it involves a pregame nap, a meal at a specific restaurant, and a handful of assorted other eccentricities. Hence why they're not home.

Tyler is allegedly the most superstitious of them all, as goalies tend to be. That probably explains why he's been distant all day via text. His stress levels show some days more than others. He hasn't been playing along much with twenty-one questions today, and I'm trying not to take it personally.

I microwave some leftover spaghetti and meatballs, then check my missed texts from when I was asleep. There's one from Abby I promptly ignore without reading it, and another from Bailey confirming our plans tonight.

> Bailey: Do you still want to come to the game with us?
>
> Sera: Yep. What time?
>
> Bailey: Shiv and I can pick you up at 6:30.

When they pull up to get me in Siobhan's car, I'm oddly nervous. Not having a matching jersey like they both do makes me feel like the odd one out. I should have stolen some of Chase's Falcons gear, but it's too late now. The Falcons beanie I stole from Tyler will have to suffice. It'll also help keep me warm because Bailey tells me Northview Arena is freezing.

Traffic is a nightmare as we draw closer to the venue, and parking is even worse. When we step inside, it's swarming with people. It might sound silly, but I'd forgotten how big of a deal college hockey is at some schools. It wasn't much of a thing at ASU. At Boyd, hockey players are full-on celebrities.

Because a hockey game isn't a hockey game without snacks, we grab popcorn, candy, and drinks at the concession before pushing through the crowd to our seats. We're early enough to catch the end of warm-ups, and a little buzz of excitement runs through me when I spot Tyler standing in front of the net as the guys take practice shots on him. I'm not sure whether he's happy I'm here or not. It was a little hard to get a read on his reaction when I told him I was coming.

The arena, like Bailey warned me ahead of time, is freaking

freezing. It may even be colder than it is outside. Thankfully, I wore extra layers, including one of the warmest wool sweaters I own.

"Who are they playing tonight again?" I ask, turning to face the girls. Bailey is in the middle of us, and Siobhan is seated on her other side.

Bailey makes a face as she reaches for another hand of popcorn. "Callingwood. My school."

"Oh, shit. Is that awkward for you? Because your brother . . . ?" Who would I cheer for if Chase and Tyler were on opposite sides, anyway? Tough call. Chase is my brother and all, but he can be a real pain in the ass.

"A little." She shrugs. "I'm used to it by now. It's sort of a win-win. Or I guess it's lose-lose, depending how you look at it."

"Boyd versus Callingwood games are always bloodbaths," Shiv chimes in. "Expect a lot of penalties, especially from your brother."

Chase takes a lot of penalties to begin with, so that's really saying something.

Siobhan isn't wrong. The game is a total barn burner. High scoring, high penalty minutes, and high drama on the ice. It's clear the teams hate each other, as evidenced by the constant sneaky shots and cheap jabs they both keep taking at one another. I even catch some things directed at Tyler, which is considered extra dirty as far as hockey code goes. He gets annoyed enough to slash one guy in return, but the officials seem to miss it.

Halfway in, the score is tied 3–3. Even at a distance, I can tell Tyler's upset. His body language makes that much clear. It isn't solely his doing; there are a lot of factors at play. Both teams are playing sloppy, which includes nonexistent defense, and the goalies are being hung out to dry. Tyler is a phenomenal goalie, and he's having an off night.

The game takes an even worse turn after the third period starts. Callingwood scores again, but it gets called back due to goalie interference. Somehow, I don't think that's of any comfort to Tyler. Knowing him, he's beating himself up for letting another puck get by.

"He's getting hammered out there," I say, watching him reset his position between the posts. It's incredibly hard to watch. I've never seen things from the goalie's perspective the way I do now. Every time a shot slips past him, I feel a little sick.

"Do you think they'll pull Ty?" Siobhan tears open a package of Skittles, offering us some.

Bailey shakes her head, her gaze still glued to the play. "No."

"Probably not," I reply at the same time.

Though I'm not sure which is worse: getting pulled or getting lit up like he is right now.

Siobhan's forehead creases. "Really? He's let in a lot of goals. I mean, I love the guy, but mathematically speaking."

"So has the other goalie," Bailey explains. "When the score is close like this, coaches usually let it ride."

I squint, leaning forward. "What the hell is Chase doing?"

My brother just missed the most basic pass imaginable. None of the team is showing up well tonight. It's frustrating for me, and I'm not even on the ice. I can only imagine how Tyler feels right now.

As the third period winds to a close, the score is tied 5–5, and we're sitting on the edges of our seats. If it ends in a tie, it goes into sudden-death overtime. And if that carries on long enough, it goes into a shootout—which is probably one of the highest-pressure scenarios imaginable for a goalie.

The play carries down to our side of the net, and there's a ton of traffic in front. I crane my head, trying to see where the puck is.

"Can you see?" I ask. "I see Dallas, but some guy is blocking Tyler."

"Why isn't their defense clearing the net?" Bailey gestures with her drink. "They're letting Callingwood stand there cherry-picking."

The fun part about Bailey is she knows as much, if not more about hockey than the guys. Since she's invested in both teams tonight, we've been getting a detailed running commentary the entire time. It's highly entertaining. For someone who's largely soft-spoken and reserved, hockey really gets her fired up.

Our attention stays fixed on our net, waiting to see if Boyd clears the puck. There's a huge commotion out front, blocking Tyler from my line of sight, and the buzzer sounds to signify another goal.

Bailey stands up, her eyes darting between the scoreboard and the ice. "What? That was goalie interference again. And they're just going to let it go?"

"I couldn't see what happened," I admit, hoping she's right. Maybe it would be some small consolation for him, even if it wasn't called.

My stomach aches as Callingwood skates off to their end, exchanging fist bumps and hollering with excitement. Boyd's team surrounds the net to give Tyler props, but the mood is decidedly somber.

More than anything, I want to hug him right now, and I can't.

Chapter 26
ALL THE LITTLE PIECES

TYLER

Sometimes I think losing by one goal is worse than a blowout. If I'd just played a little better, been more on my game, and stopped that *one* fucking shot...

The rest of the team admittedly played like shit tonight, but even that feels like my fault. Letting in that initial goal so early in the first period shook our morale and left us playing catch up for the rest of the game. For all my talk about being able to shake off bad losses, it's a lot harder to do when one rests squarely on my shoulders.

Sitting on my bed, I open the game tape from tonight on my phone and cue up all the goals I let in from start to finish. Easy to do when I know exactly what time each of them was scored. It happens every time I let a puck slip past me. The numbers on the clock are seared into my brain.

One or two of tonight's goals could be chalked up to bad luck, and there's a third I'll give myself a pass on because it was a shot anyone would've struggled to stop, but the other three are the result of definite errors on my part. Shrinking down instead of holding my form, thereby creating more openings for the other team to target. Staying too far back into the crease when I should've been cutting down the angle. In short, not playing well enough.

The second time I watch the goals, I'm even more pissed at myself. The fourth goal was so fucking weak I can't believe I let it in. The fifth, borderline embarrassing. What was I doing out there?

Since Christmas, I've been rock solid. Three shutouts and

several more wins. This is *one* loss, and somehow it's still fucking with my head.

A soft knock draws my attention, and I pause the video, glancing up. "Yeah?"

"Can I come in?" Seraphina opens the door partway, peeking inside.

I don't hesitate. "Always."

Expression cautious, she quietly closes the door and crosses the room to me. She's changed for bed, wearing a dark purple tank top and matching shorts, and her face is freshly washed. I hate how hesitant she looks; like she's not sure I want her here. The truth is that I always do, but it felt wrong to seek her out when I'm in such a dark state of mind. I know I'm not great company at the moment.

As soon as she's within reach, I wrap my arms around her and pull her onto my lap. Her body is soft and warm, fitting perfectly against mine. Fuck, she smells amazing. Faint traces of her perfume, hints of her cherry-scented lip balm she must've put on after brushing her teeth, along with something that's just uniquely her.

"Everyone else went upstairs, so I thought I'd check on you," she says softly.

Tension winds through me, and I choose my next words with care. "I mean this in the nicest way possible, but I don't want to talk about the game, Tink."

"That's okay. We don't have to talk." Soft hands grasp mine, sliding the phone out of my grip. The screen darkens as she locks it, setting it on my nightstand. "Maybe you should put this away for the night, though. It's late."

She leans against me without saying anything more. The longer I hold her, the more I relax. Her presence calms the storm that's been brewing inside me since I let in that first weak goal. As stress from earlier melts away, all that remains is exhaustion on every level. It's heavy, like an anchor dragging me down.

"Can you stay?" I ask. It's a selfish request and I know it. It means she'll have to sneak back upstairs early in the morning.

"Only if you give me a shirt to sleep in."

"Of course. Take anything you want."

Seraphina opens my closet and rifles through the shirts before settling on the same one from the night when I took care of her. Turning to face me, she sheds her tank top, then her shorts, left in nothing but a small cotton pair of white panties. They're different from her usual sexy fare, but no less hot.

Once she pulls on my T-shirt, she climbs back into bed with me and I pull her into my arms. We lay tangled together, half-spooning.

"I had a bad day too," she says, her voice hushed.

There's a pang in my chest because I had no idea. "Sorry, Tink. Wanna talk about it?"

"Not right now."

We're quiet for a few more moments. It's a comfortable silence, and I'm thankful she gives it to me. I've never had anyone here like this with me after a loss. Obviously, I've been with girls after bad games before, but it was more about forgetting via fucking. Having someone hold space for you is different. It feels deeper.

"Do you want me to pet you?" she asks.

Only she could make me laugh right now. "I won't turn it down."

Her pink nails trail down my arm, going back and forth lightly. It's one step below tickling, and it feels nice.

A tired groan resonates in the back of my throat. "Now I see why you like this."

Even though sex was the last thing on my mind when I saw her standing at my door, and even though we're not doing anything overtly sexual, my body responds to her proximity. She knows it, too, because it's impossible to miss.

The covers rustle as she shifts onto her side, facing me. Her warm brown eyes scan my face like she's trying to get a read on my mood. It's a given that I'm *always* in the mood for her.

I slide my hand around the back of her neck, drawing her to me for a kiss. Her breath catches before she lets out a soft sigh, melting in my arms. Everything that happened earlier vanishes. In this moment, the only thing that exists is the two of us, her soft curves beneath my hands, the heat of her body warming mine.

Burying my fingers in her hair, I angle her head, deepening the kiss. Her hand curls around my neck as her cherry-scented lips part, granting me access. When our tongues meet, a cascade of fireworks erupts in my body from head to toe. My blood heats with desire, and I grip her tighter in response. Every time I kiss her, it feels like I've never kissed a woman before. I'm starved, crazed; each taste I get leaves me hungry for more.

A giggle bursts through her lips as I push her onto her back, repositioning us so I'm between her legs. I kiss that spot beneath her ear that makes her moan, then continue on my mission south.

Seraphina hums happily, running her fingers through my hair. "I'm supposed to be the one taking care of you."

"Nothing turns me on more than making you feel good, Ser." I hike up the hem of my shirt she's wearing, revealing her tits. My lips trail over the swell of her breasts before I take each perfect nipple into my mouth one at a time, my tongue swirling until they harden into peaks.

"All the little pieces of you no one else gets?" I say, running my palms down her stomach. "Those are my favorite."

I'm not sure I'm talking about sex anymore.

Leaning on my elbows, I spread her legs wider as I drink in one of my favorite views. My mouth lands on her center, kissing through her white panties.

Her thighs clench. "Ty." My name is a moan across her lips, and it isn't quiet. We've been taking more risks than we should lately, but it's hard to care about that when I'm about to make her come all over my face.

She watches me, her pupils dilated as I slide off her underwear and toss them aside. I leave my shirt on her because I'm a dirty fucker and I've jerked off to this very mental image at least a dozen times: Seraphina in my shirt, her perfect pussy on full display.

I tease her mercilessly, kissing and licking everywhere except for the spot she wants it most. She's patient at first, then starts to wriggle to urge me on. When I think she's sufficiently frustrated, I sweep my tongue against her clit, deliberate and slow. Her breath catches and her back arches, silently begging for more.

"You're so wet, Ser." I tsk, dragging a finger along her soaking slit. My cock is so hard it hurts, and I can't wait to be buried deep inside her next. "Such a good girl for me. And what do good girls get?"

"To come?" she pleads.

"That's right." Gripping her thigh with one hand to keep her legs spread wide, I slip a finger inside her, followed by another. When I curl them to caress her G-spot in a perfect echo of my mouth, her legs jolt and she grows even wetter.

"Oh." She twitches, digging her nails into my shoulder. "There."

I slide my other arm underneath her thigh and wrap it around, locking her in place against me. Splaying my palm on her lower stomach, I press down while my fingers stroke her, my tongue flicking over her sensitive bundle of nerves. Fuck, she tastes like heaven. I think I'm addicted to her.

Her breaths quicken, coming in smaller bursts. When I suck her clit, her entire body tenses, and another desperate whimper wrenches from her lips. But this whimper is different; it's the point-of-no-return sound she makes, and it drives me fucking wild.

She gasps, and her feet press into the mattress, hips lifting. "Oh, god."

Soft moans mingle with not-so-quiet cries as she writhes beneath me, falling apart, and I devour her until she's a quivering, dripping mess. Once she gets giggly from the overstimulation, I slow my movements to let her down gradually. Planting a kiss on her soft inner thigh, I smooth my hands up her body, and cup her breasts, feeling her heart beat wildly against my palm for a few beats. Knowing I did that to her has an effect on me I can't even explain.

I come to hover above her, bracing on my forearms. Her cheeks are flushed, lips rosy, and she looks completely blissed out.

Ducking my head, I bring my mouth to hers. "Hi, Tinker Bell."

"Hi, Hades." She meets me halfway, smiling into our kiss.

It's at this moment that I realize I'm well and truly fucked, because this doesn't feel like just sex. I'm not sure it ever did.

Chapter 27
TROUBLE

SERAPHINA

I've been tasked with an impossible assignment tonight. We're going out with everyone for Tyler's birthday, and we have to act like nothing is going on between us. No flirting, no obvious glances, and no touching.

Naturally, we decide to start off the evening with a quickie. Sneaking in a tryst is risky in and of itself but should help cut down on the tension between us all evening. Or at least, that's my story and I'm sticking to it.

While Chase and Dallas are preoccupied playing video games upstairs, I sneak into the basement to see Tyler like we agreed. With the way those two are glued to the screen, a bomb could go off and they wouldn't notice. The volume is up so high the walls practically shake with each explosion on screen. Bailey and Siobhan haven't arrived yet, so as long as we make this fast, we should be okay.

"Is this skirt too short?" I do a slow twirl in the middle of Tyler's room, reveling in the way his gaze hungrily trails down my body, lingering on my legs. I've already gotten ready to go out, but I'll have to touch up once we're through. He likes to pull my hair, and it shows.

His mouth tips up at one corner. "No. You look hot."

"Are you sure?" I smooth my hands down the black chiffon. I'm half-teasing, half-legitimately asking. It's on the short side even for me, but I couldn't tell that when I ordered it online because I have no concept of inches in terms of measurements. It's cute, though, so I'd like to keep it and not return it.

He draws me into him and dips his head, nudging my nose

with his. "Wear whatever you want, Tink. I know how to fight."

Large hands bracket my jaw, holding my face as he kisses me. Really kisses me, like he's been waiting for this all day. When he pulls back, I'm breathless and dazed.

His lips trail along my neck, sending a thrill through my body from head to toe. "How should I fuck you?"

"Fuck me like I'm in trouble."

That earns me a throaty, guttural sound of appreciation, and his mouth presses to mine again. My fingertips slide up his arms, gripping his biceps to urge him on, and heat stokes in my center as his hand travels up the back of my bare thighs, squeezing my ass over the thin lace of my panties.

He withdraws his touch, and I look up at him, confused.

Craving flashes in his eyes. "Bend over and put your hands on the bed."

It's an order, not a request.

My gaze slides to his king-sized bed, neatly made with a dark gray comforter. It sits on a modern, low-profile platform bedframe, and it's hardly higher than the thickness of the mattress off the floor. Doing as he says will put me ass-up, which is exactly why he wants me to.

Facing him, I maintain eye contact as I take a few steps toward it. "You don't want me to get naked first?"

He shakes his head. "The skirt stays on."

My calves hit the mattress behind me, and I come to a stop. I love the way he's looking at me right now. Desire, tinged with possession.

"What about my panties?"

"Lose them."

He watches, rapt with attention as I slowly reach beneath the ruffled edges of my skirt and shimmy the scrap of lace down my legs, toeing it to the side. They're sexy underwear that I bought recently to wear for him, so hopefully they'll get some airtime later tonight when we get home.

Pivoting, I follow his instructions and place my palms down on the firm mattress. My shoulders are well below my waist, placing me nearly in a downward dog position. I'm completely exposed. Even I feel a little self-conscious, but I suppose that's his intention.

My body tenses with anticipation as he comes to stand behind me. Somehow, the energy of his body is palpable even without us touching. He slowly gathers up my skirt and pushes it out of the way. Craning my neck, I peek over my shoulder to see what he's going to do next.

He slaps my ass with a loud crack, massaging where he just spanked me. "Face down, Tink."

At that, my core clenches.

I do as he says, grabbing a pillow for my head as he smooths his palms along the sides of my bare ass. My breaths grow uneven as I wait, wondering where he's going with this. Then his hands part my thighs, pulling them wider, and one finger glides across my clit. My hips sway in response, my fingertips bunching the bedding.

"Your pussy is so pretty, baby." He strokes me again. "All pink and wet."

One broad palm settles on my lower back, holding me firmly in place as his other hand works between my legs, skillfully teasing until I'm trembling against him. He brings me close to orgasm over and over again, but he won't let me come. It's a carefully executed pattern of building and sudden withdrawal that leaves me more frustrated with each repetition. If he keeps this up, they're going to hear me upstairs no matter how loud the video games are.

He reduces me to a quaking mess as I claw at the sheets and arch my back, frantic with need. Cold air skirts my skin as he stops touching me entirely, which is the opposite of what I'm trying to achieve.

"Ty," I whine, wriggling shamelessly.

"Tell me how much you want my cock."

Without hesitating, I say, "I want your cock."

Two fingers plunge inside me, and I gasp at the sudden fullness as he thrusts them deeper. My nerves light up, core clenching. If he can just keep doing that a little longer...

"Ah." He tsks. "You do want it."

When he pulls away, I nearly grab his hand and force it back. Then I hear the clang of his belt, the ripping of foil, and he's behind me. Strong fingers span my waist and dig into my hips, roughly yanking them higher. My breath catches as he thrusts inside, shoving me into the mattress with his hand twined in my hair.

I cry out, muffled by the bedding. At this angle, he's even deeper than usual, impossibly hard and thick as he stretches me. Each thrust steals the air from my lungs, probably because it feels like he's almost hitting them.

"Fuck, Ser. I wish you could see how good you look right now."

He finds my clit, expertly stroking as his hips push forward into me again. In no time, I unravel around him, my walls clenching as I bury my pleas in his pillow. My knees shake as the last of the pleasure fades out, and I sag against the bed to keep myself upright.

Rather than let me recover, he keeps going, and another orgasm starts to build in my center almost immediately. Placing my wrists behind my back, I offer them to him in a show of unspoken submission. He lets out a low, feral growl of approval and pins them together with one hand. His other hand wraps around my shoulder, pinning me down against the bed, and his movements pick up speed, hitting deeper.

The sound of our bodies slapping together fills the room, interspersed with grunts and groans, moans and whimpers. Unlike last night, which was soft and slow, he's fucking me—hard.

"Good job," he praises, sinking deeper. "You take my dick so well."

Pleasure seizes hold of my body and my legs tremble, my

voice failing. I can't respond. All I can do is hold on for dear life while he owns me at a punishing pace, unleashing a string of praise alternating with dirty talk that would make even me blush under other circumstances.

As the delicious tension in my core winds even tighter, I feel myself approach the point of no return. He releases my hands and seizes me by the waist, pulling me into him. I fist the bedding, my calves quivering. It's even more overwhelming than the first time. It's good, almost too good, and I never want it to end.

"Ty." Air fills my lungs with a sharp gasp, my hips jolting. "Oh, god. I'm coming. Come with me, please."

That earns me another spank that echoes through the air, this one hard enough to sting. He groans my name, slamming into me one more time. His body lurches forward, and his heavy frame covers mine, pushing me into the mattress as we both come undone.

"Fuck." Breathing heavily, he collapses over me. He husks a laugh, burying his face in my neck. "You did that on purpose, didn't you?"

"Maybe." As the last ebbs of my orgasm fade away, giddiness overtakes me, and I burst into a fit of laughter. I can only assume it's a peculiar side effect of orgasming so hard that I nearly blacked out. Factoring in my legs like jelly, he's reduced me to a giggly, jiggly pile of goo.

Gentle kisses land along my shoulder, traveling up the curve of my neck. He nuzzles my cheek. "How are you doing? Talk to me, Tink."

Another burst of laughter escapes my lips, partially muted by the pillow beneath me. I don't even know why I'm laughing. I've heard of people crying after sex—something about disinhibition within certain parts of the brain—but never giggling uncontrollably. For some reason, I can't stop.

"I'm sorry." I lift my head, my eyes filling with tears. "I think you broke my brain."

"Damn right I did."

We untangle ourselves and he helps clean me up, his touch suddenly tender and careful and sweet. You'd never guess he was uttering filthy, nearly unspeakable things to me only moments ago.

Pulling me to him on his bed, he kisses my temple and runs his fingers through my hair from root to end. I nestle into his chest, happy and tired, willfully ignoring the outside world.

After a few more minutes, I whisper, "I should sneak back upstairs before they notice something is up."

"Yeah." But he doesn't let me go.

I'm not in a hurry to leave either. After a few more minutes, I know I have to. Stealing another quick kiss, we part ways and I dart into the bathroom to fix my hair. Or I try to—because when I open Tyler's door, Siobhan is standing at the bottom of the stairs holding a case of coolers.

She freezes. I freeze. We gape at one another.

Obviously incriminating circumstances aside, I'm sure I *look* like I just got fucked. Thoroughly.

This is bad, isn't it? On a scale of one to ten, how likely is this to make it back to my brother?

Siobhan recovers first. "Um, sorry. Dallas said there were more White Claws in the basement fridge. He's still playing *COD* so I came down here to grab them. I didn't realize you were down here."

"Tyler and I were just . . . talking." I jerk my thumb behind me to his room. "In there."

A knowing smile forms on her lips. "Right. Talking."

Evidently having heard our voices, Tyler steps through the doorway, and shock crosses his face. "Shiv."

"Please don't tell anyone," I say.

She holds up her hand, pretending to shield her eyes. "I saw nothing. I know nothing."

"Thanks, Shiv," we both say.

◆ ◆ ◆

Overtime is crammed when we walk into the doors just past nine to meet the rest of the team for Tyler's birthday. It's been hard to look him in the eye without getting giddy. That he can rail me so thoroughly sometimes and be so adorable and gentle at others is a paradox that leaves me wondering in the best possible way. I never know what I'm going to get.

Though, even when he's being dirty, he's still sweet beneath it.

We grab empty seats at the table, placing me with Shiv and Bailey while the guys cluster together. Siobhan has been extra-nice to me all evening, probably compensating for one of the more embarrassing ways to get caught of all time.

My eyes land on the bar, and I spot Chloe standing at the register. I'd forgotten she got a new job waiting tables here. Too bad she's working and can't join us. I have no idea when she has the time to sleep.

When it looks like she's got a free minute, I squeeze up to say hello. "Hey, how's the new job going?"

Chloe's face brightens. "Good. Much better than the old one. They don't steal my tips, and they actually pay me on time. No flagrant human rights or health and safety violations, and no one has sexually harassed me so far. Massive upgrade."

"That's great," I say. "When are you done? Any chance you can join us after?"

A few feet away, one of the side entrances opens. Reid appears in the doorway wearing a dark wool dress coat and a black scarf. He spots me and he offers me a friendly grin as he weaves past the tables to join the guys. Chloe falls unusually silent. Her green eyes track him until he disappears, then her attention returns to me.

"That's Reid," I tell her. "One of the guys on my brother's team. He's cute, hey?"

"Huh?" A dismissive wave shuts me down, and she makes a face. "No, no. I was just looking at him because he's very..." Her gaze darts to our table again, where Reid is now sitting beside Tyler. "Tall."

Chloe's right: He is tall. He also happens to be panty-meltingly hot, and I suspect that's the real draw.

"It's okay to look, even if you don't want to touch."

She huffs. "I definitely don't."

Methinks she's protesting too much, but I don't want to push. I'm sure she has her reasons for being averse to dating, and I understand that. Plus, I don't want to be nosy and overbearing like Abby. It's better if you let people open up in their own time.

One of the other servers waves to Chloe as if to tell her to get back to work.

"Sorry," I say. "I didn't mean to keep you. If you want to join us on your break or after you're finished for the night, come find me, okay?"

Chloe grabs her tray and tucks it under her arm, flashing me a smile. "I should get one in about an hour. I'll try to come find you then."

Starting for our table, I change my mind mid-step and take a detour to grab a drink first. The bar is crowded with people who have the same idea, forcing me to sidle down to the far end. I lean over the wooden counter, trying to get the bartender's attention, but I'm invisible in a sea of forty other people waving fistfuls of cash.

"Sera." A familiar male voice cuts in. "Thought I saw you there."

Ambivalence grips me, and I glance over to see Rob giving me a friendly grin. When I look a little closer, he's drunk. His eyes are glassy, his posture a little looser than normal. You wouldn't know it at first glance; his designer dress shirt has a few buttons at the top undone and his clothes are still neatly pressed.

"Hey . . ." Abby and I still haven't cleared the air since our falling out. Since I mostly see and speak to him in association to her, it's more than a little awkward. Is she here too? I hope not.

He shoves his hands into his pants pockets, stepping closer. "Can we talk for a second?"

My phone vibrates in my purse, a reminder I need to get back to our table. But I don't want to be rude, so I can make it quick. It's probably about Abby, anyway. He's played peacemaker with us before in the past when we've had fights. This isn't an ordinary fight, though. No amount of mediating is going to make me less upset about how she's been treating me. I'm fairly certain we're on the cusp of a friendship breakup, or that it's already happened.

"Sure," I concede. "But only for a second. Chase is going to wonder where I am." *And Tyler.*

Rob leans a hip against the bar, facing me. "I've missed you, Sera."

My stomach does a flip-flop. Wait, what? This isn't how I thought the conversation would go.

"Don't you have a girlfriend?" I remind him again. Abby confirmed as much prior to our fight. His claims of "not being committed" didn't pass my fact check.

Irritation flickers across his face, gone in a blink. "Like I said, we have an understanding."

"Rob—" I start, then mentally stumble. Can't tell him about Tyler, so I'll offer the rest of the truth instead. "Look, there seems to be some confusion. I don't see you that way. You're my friend. That's it."

"You know there's something between us. There always has been." His hand lands on my wrist, and my heart jumps.

When I yank it away, he offers no resistance. "Don't. You're being inappropriate."

Rob moves closer. A deluge of his cologne surrounds me, along with whiskey or some other hard liquor he's been drinking. My hands are shaking, my pulse rocketing off the charts. At least we're not alone. In fact, we're surrounded by people, and I'm worried one of the wrong ones is going to see.

"Take the hint, Rob. I'm not interested."

He tsks. "Come on, Sera. No one dresses like that unless they're looking for attention."

"Fuck you!" It may not be wise to snap at him given the circumstances, but my filter slips away before I can stop myself. "We're supposed to be friends, and then you go and say something like that to me? What's wrong with you?"

Instead of getting angry like I expect, he huffs a laugh and steps closer. "Calm down. I was kidding."

Kidding. Right. Otherwise known as the go-to gaslighting method of misogynists everywhere. They're joking—until they mean it.

"Come on, Sera. Don't be mad."

I don't know how it happens, or how I fail to react in time, but suddenly he's moved even closer, he's touching my face, and his lips are on mine. He's kissing me. Trying to, anyway, since I'm not kissing him back. Shock holds me frozen, and while I want to move—know I should move—nothing is happening.

"Stop it." I pull my head away and try to push him back, but he doesn't budge.

He scoffs, leaning in again. "What, now you're playing hard to get all of the sudden?"

"What the *fuck*?" a familiar voice roars.

Everything happens in slow motion. A tattooed hand lands on my chest, gently pushing me back a few steps. I look up in time to see a fist connect with Rob's face, making a sickening crunch. My eyes come into focus on Tyler's. Slate eyes blaze with anger, a vein in his forehead prominent. He looks like he's strongly considering homicide as a valid course of action.

I've never seen him so angry, and I'm scared he's going to get himself in trouble because of me.

"Ty—" I start.

Gripping Rob by the front of his shirt, Tyler places his free hand on my shoulder and wordlessly moves me farther to the side. His attention remains laser-focused on Rob. Heeding Tyler's nonverbal warning, I move a little farther out of their radius.

People surrounding us stop talking, some gathering to watch. None intervene.

"What the fuck is your damage, you psycho?" Rob jerks in Tyler's grip, fighting unsuccessfully to liberate himself.

"What's *yours*? You heard her tell you to stop." Tyler lets go of the fabric and hits him again, connecting with his nose this time. Rob stumbles back, clutching his face. Then he takes a run at Tyler, and they get tangled in a scuffle.

"Whoa, whoa, whoa." Dallas jogs up and puts himself in the middle of them, holding them apart. "Donohue, dude. Take a beat. What the hell is going on?"

"This fucker was all over her, and he wasn't taking no for an answer." Tyler tries to step around Dallas again, and Dallas stops him. Barely.

Panicked, I glance over my shoulder, because it's only a matter of time before Chase notices this scene. There's no chance this is going to get resolved before he does.

"I should press charges," Rob says, grabbing a handful of napkins off the bar. There's blood splattered across the front of his shirt. "This is assault."

"Go ahead." Tyler snorts. "Then we can tell the cops that you were trying to force yourself on a girl who's not even old enough to legally drink. Bet your law firm would love to hear it too."

Rob laughs dryly. "They're not going to care about some slut."

I flinch. This time, Tyler almost gets past Dallas. He's clearly expending all of his strength to hold Tyler back, and neither of them is small.

"Ty. He isn't worth it." I touch his forearm to get his attention, gently squeezing.

He glances down at me, and some of the anger across his face recedes, replaced with worry. His steel-gray eyes hold mine for a beat, a million unspoken questions across his face that I'm not ready to answer. Then he looks back at Rob, and fury reignites in his eyes.

Rob pinches his nose, his voice strained. "You should listen to your girlfriend."

"Someone better tell me what the *fuck* is going on," Chase snarls.

When I turn around, I find my brother staring at us with betrayal all over his face.

Chapter 28
SEVERED TIES

SERAPHINA

We endure the most uncomfortable ride home I've ever experienced. In retrospect, taking separate Ubers would have been preferable. Finding my own apartment in the near future isn't looking like a bad idea either.

Tyler's arm rests around my shoulders because, well, it's a little late to keep up pretenses now. Chase won't look at either one of us. Bailey talks to him soothingly, trying to calm him down. And Dallas and Siobhan compensate by making conversation with everyone, but it mostly ends up being the two of them talking to each other.

I exchange a few texts back and forth with Chloe, who saw the whole thing from afar and wanted to make sure I was okay. It's too hard to explain via text, so I make plans with her to hang out tomorrow when the guys have practice.

As the Uber pulls away from the curb, Chase storms past everyone and unlocks the front door, letting it slam shut behind him without waiting for anyone else. My stomach balls into a fist. I don't want to fight with him.

The rest of us filter inside, hanging up our coats and slipping off our shoes. Bailey takes Chase's hand, saying something into his ear that I can't hear. He shakes his head and murmurs something back. She presses her lips together, giving him a reproachful look. He heaves a sigh that's more than a little resentful. Bailey elbows him. Hard.

"I'm going to let you two have some time alone," Chase says, his voice flat. "But we're *all* going to have a chat tomorrow."

The doorbell rings, followed by a sharp, insistent banging on the door. We all exchange confused looks. It goes without saying that we left Overtime in a hurry. No one else from the team was invited back here.

Since I'm closest to the door, I answer it. Abby is on the other side—and she looks furious. I'm sure I know why.

"Your boyfriend beat up my brother? What was that lowlife thinking?" She places her fists on her hips, though the effect isn't all that intimidating given her short stature. Not that I think we're about to get into a physical fight but if we did, it wouldn't be much of a match.

My temper flares. Not wanting to put on a spectacle, I turn back to face everyone else rather than respond. "We're going to take this to my room."

To my relief, Chase and Bailey go to his room while Dallas and Shiv go to his. That means no one will be in the living room where they could potentially overhear this conversation. Or argument, realistically.

Tyler hangs back and takes my hand, ducking his head to catch my eye. "Are you okay, Ser?"

"I'm fine," I tell him, squeezing his hand. "I'll come see you after."

Abby follows me into my room, and I step around her, closing the door for added privacy. All I want is for this conversation to be over so I can go downstairs and see Tyler.

"Before you get all worked up, you should know that Rob kissed me, Abby. He was being really aggressive, and he wouldn't take no for an answer." Still facing her, I unzip my skirt and set it aside. I take a pair of black joggers from my dresser and tug them on, waiting for her to reply. Her eyes slowly travel up and down my body, and her eyelids lower in what I can only describe as a "mean girl" look.

"Rob would never do that. You're just saying that because you're jealous he's never wanted you."

My Carter temper gets the best of me, and I feel my internal filter evaporate into thin air for the second time this evening. I know I shouldn't say the words, yet they tumble out anyway.

"That's why I lost my virginity to him then, huh?"

Abby disappears from my line of sight as I put my arms through a purple tank top. Once it's over my head, she's scowling at me with her arms crossed.

"What the hell are you talking about?"

"Prom night ring a bell? You were too busy doing whatever it is you were doing with Joey Marcello to notice I was gone. Rob and I slept together that night, and we decided not to tell you. I convinced him to keep it a secret because I didn't want to hurt you."

The last words ring false as I say them. I always thought keeping it under wraps was my idea, but *was* it? Or did Rob manipulate me into thinking that? It wasn't exactly a level playing field when you factor in our ages.

"You're lying." She huffs, glowering at me.

"Why would I lie about that? Rob has been hitting on me ever since I turned sixteen. He's still doing it now that I've moved back, even though he has a freaking girlfriend, Abbs! I know he's your brother, but that's a shitty thing to do no matter how you slice it."

Abby blinks rapidly, but she doesn't say anything. What can she say? Cheating is indefensible, even when it's your sibling.

Emboldened by what I got off my chest, I continue. "On top of all that, you've been a terrible friend to me lately. You never ask about my mom or how I'm doing, and you never want to hang out with me unless it's to get drunk and go pick up guys. I've been there for you for years, Abby. I was there through your eating disorder. When your parents divorced. When you had that douchebag boyfriend Kent who kept breaking your heart. I've been there for every single thing, holding your hand, listening to you, and supporting you. Where the hell have you been now that I actually need you for a change?" Rage mingles with sadness, and I'm inundated by the most frustrating urge to cry. I might later, but I certainly won't let her see it now. Tamping down on my emotions, I ball my fists until my nails dig into my palms.

"This isn't how a friendship is supposed to work," I add. "This isn't *even* a friendship."

That's not including the things she doesn't know, like the BRCA test. No wonder I haven't told her. She clearly wouldn't care.

"Oh, so you're perfect now and I'm the bad guy?" Abby's voice climbs until I'm sure everyone in the house can hear.

This feels like a lover's quarrel, and it's arguably even more frustrating than one.

I sink onto my bed and grab a pillow, squeezing it to channel my anger. "I know I'm not perfect, but at least I care about my friends."

"Do you think you're somehow better than me because of this little hookup situation you have going on? That's never going to last, Sera. There's a reason Tyler doesn't want to be your boyfriend."

It lands like a slap.

"You don't know what you're talking about right now." The waver in my voice betrays my hurt feelings.

Abby rolls her eyes. "Keep telling yourself that. Don't come crying to me when it fails." She turns away and flounces out of my room, slamming the door behind her.

"Good!" I call. "Glad we're on the same page!"

Trying to get the last word feels immature, and I immediately regret having bothered.

The front door bangs, followed by silence. My anger fades, leaving me alone with Abby's words. And the longer I sit, the more I start to wonder if what she said about Tyler was right.

Chapter 29
WRONG TARGET

TYLER

Seraphina is in my room again, only this time, it isn't a secret.

"I brought you some ice." She pads over to the bed where I'm sitting in my boxer briefs and hands me a gel pack wrapped in a dishcloth. "I hope you didn't hurt your hand when you hit him."

"Thanks, Ser." I arrange the ice pack on my knuckles with a wince, wrapping the cloth around my fist to hold it in place. While I'm well-versed in how to throw a punch properly, my lizard brain wasn't concerned with that earlier. I was only thinking of inflicting maximum damage—not protecting my hands for hockey.

Climbing onto me, she tips up my chin, examining my face. I know from the bathroom mirror that there's a small bruise blooming, but it's minor compared to what I did to him.

"Oof. Does that hurt?" Soft fingertips trail along the mark, tracing it.

"Nah. You shoulda seen the other guy." Even then, Rob got off easy. He deserves so much worse. What if they'd been somewhere else? What if they'd been alone? Just thinking about it makes me sick.

"I appreciate that you care, but you shouldn't have done that because of me," she adds. "I'd hate for you to get in trouble."

"After that dirtbag did that? Couldn't have stopped myself if I tried. Probably wasn't the best way to tell your brother about us, though."

"Tomorrow's problem. I'm an adult, and Chase can get over it."

Questions simmer inside of me, heating until they come to a boil and I can't hold it in any longer. "What's the deal with Rob, anyway? Can you give me a little backstory?"

She hesitates. "We hooked up a long time ago, but it was a one-time thing. I always thought he was my friend, but clearly I misread that and ignored a bunch of red flags."

A long time ago? What does that even mean? Two years? Three? She's only twenty now. I'm left with more questions than answers.

"What do you mean 'a long time ago'?"

"Senior prom."

What the fuck? It takes all my strength to keep a straight face. Had I known this earlier, I wouldn't have let Dallas hold me back.

"Did you tell anyone about this?" I ask carefully. "Like Chase?"

"Rob is still alive, isn't he? I didn't want Chase to get in trouble. That was a long time ago and I'm past it. All good now. Aside from this mess that I caused tonight."

"This isn't your fault, Ser." Setting the ice pack aside, I cup her cheek. "Are you sure you're okay?" I get the impression she's come down here to make me feel better, but I'm not the one who deserves the concern.

Her mouth twitches. "I'm fine. It's not a big deal. Rob was just drunk."

That she's downplaying what he did makes me exponentially angrier with him because it *is* a big deal.

"Drunk or not, no asshole has the right to touch you without your permission. Especially not a guy who's supposed to be your 'friend.'" The words come out more harshly than I intend. "I'm sorry. I can't stand the idea of someone hurting you."

Seraphina shrugs off my comment, shifting closer to me on my lap. Her palms land on my shoulders as her lips lower to mine. My entire body fires up in response, and my dick perks up, making for a confusing combination of emotions when added to the primal anger coursing through my veins. As much as I love having her here, I'm fucking furious. I'm going to stay furious for a good couple of days, if not longer.

And if I ever see Rob again, he's going to wish I hadn't.

As if sensing my anger, she tears away from our kiss. Her breasts brush my chest, then my abs, as she slides to the floor and her knees hit the carpet.

"I don't want to talk about him anymore, okay?" Her chocolate eyes look up at me, almost pleading. More paradoxical feelings arise. It's a face that's impossible to say no to. It's also the person I have the strongest urge to protect, and that's why I'm so pissed.

"Okay, Tink." I'm not going to argue with her over that asshole.

"Do you want your birthday present now?" Her hands coast up my thighs, past my hips, then tug at my waistband.

"What is it?" I tease, smoothing her hair.

She dips her head, kissing the tip of my cock through the black material of my boxer briefs. "Whatever you want."

◆ ◆ ◆

The good: Seraphina slept in my room last night without any sneaking out required.

The bad: Chase hasn't said a single word to me all day.

Instead of carpooling with Dallas and me to the arena—which has been our routine for as long as I can remember—he left the house without telling either of us and drove alone. He beat us there, changed in silence, and stalked out of the locker room, making a point to ignore both of us entirely.

This whole silent treatment thing is unnerving. I expected a heated confrontation, or maybe an ass kicking. Instead, he's been quiet. Too quiet for someone who's normally loud and outspoken.

It feels like the calm before the storm, and I have no idea when the sky is going to erupt or what the magnitude will be.

The longer this drags on, the worse I suspect the fallout will be when it hits.

"You good, Donohue?" Reid nudges me with his padded elbow. Most of the team is already out on the ice, save for us and a handful of stragglers. I'm in no hurry to step onto the ice, even if it means Miller is going to chew me out for being late.

I grab my goalie helmet from my stall without looking at him. "Yeah."

"Carter's pissed, huh?"

"That's an understatement." Beneath my equipment, my chest heaves with a sigh. "Pretty sure he's plotting my murder as we speak."

Jokes aside, a physical altercation isn't what I'm worried about. It's that I fucked up our friendship. Fucked up my living situation in the process. And potentially fucked up the team dynamic along the way.

Even worse, I dragged Seraphina into it. I can live with Chase being angry with me but him icing Sera out would break her heart, and one thing I *can't* live with is hurting her.

"He'll get over it," Reid says, grabbing his gloves. "He just needs some time."

"Have you met Carter? He's not exactly the forgive-and-forget type."

"At the end of the day, he wants his sister to be happy. If you're good to her, he'll have no choice other than to be okay with it eventually."

Will he, though? Not sure he'll ever be on board with our nebulous "having fun" arrangement.

"I suppose that depends how you define 'eventually.' In a couple years, sure. Maybe. Any time soon, probably not."

I start for the door and Reid deftly steps in front of me, blocking my path. While I'm broader than he is with my equipment on, he's got a slight height advantage, and he's clearly not going to budge until he deems this conversation finished.

"Would you take it back?" he asks.

I shuffle back a step. "What?"

"If you could go back in time, would you change anything with you and Sera? Telling Carter doesn't count. I'm talking about you guys."

Everything flashes before my eyes in a single breath. The first time I laid eyes on her dressed as Tinker Bell at XS. Move-in day. Our near kiss in the kitchen. Picking her up from Rob's the night she called me. The time she lost her keys. The way her nose scrunches up when she laughs. Movie nights. Twenty-one questions. Falling asleep with her in my arms. Coconut shampoo. And so much pink.

"No. I wouldn't change a single thing."

"Exactly, so drop the fucking pity party. If he wants to stew, let him. His feelings are his issue. Problem ownership, my friend."

"Sounds like you've had a lot of therapy."

He grunts. "You don't know the half of it."

The first half of practice goes smoothly. The second half, not so much. Coach Miller breaks us into groups to run drills, and he sticks Chase and me together at the net for shot practice. As we skate over to our end, Chase refuses to even acknowledge me.

My eyes track the puck as he approaches, and I mentally calculate his next move. Knowing Chase, he's either going to toe drag and snap it five-hole or fake me out and pull it across backhand. To my surprise, he does neither and levels me with a screamer of a slap shot instead. It narrowly misses my neck, one of the most vulnerable spots for a goalie.

I'm used to pucks barreling toward me traveling over ninety miles per hour, and the close call is still unsettling.

His second shot hits above my knee, where there's a gap in my padding.

"Fuck!" I double over with a hiss, trying to breathe through the blinding pain. Getting hit is never particularly pleasurable, but some places hurt more than others—and this is one of them.

Resetting my position, I wait as Chase snags another puck

and approaches the net again. He's one of our best shooters, which is why I'm trying to give him the benefit of the doubt regarding his questionable aim. Maybe he's off his game after everything that happened last night.

After his third shot nearly takes off my head, I know it wasn't an accident.

"You know you're supposed to shoot at the *net*, right?" I yell, gesturing with my stick.

He flies up to the crease and stops abruptly, digging in his skates to spray me with shaved ice. If someone from another team snowed me during a game, he'd be the one kicking their ass.

Gripping his Bauer in both hands, he gives me a look that says he wishes it was my neck he was strangling instead. "And *you're* not supposed to fuck your friend's sister, but that didn't stop you."

Here we go. He's had all morning to explode, and now he's doing it at practice.

"Come on, man. That has nothing to do with you."

"On what fucking planet does Seraphina have nothing to do with me?"

Dallas skates up behind Chase and pivots, wedging himself between us. Stealing a glance over his shoulder, he carefully pushes us apart. "Cut it out, you guys. Miller is watching. Do you want to get the whole team bag skated?"

"Frankly, Ward, I don't give a shit," Chase says through clenched teeth.

"That's nice, but the rest of us do. We need to leave some gas in the tank for our game tomorrow." Dallas spreads his arms wider, increasing the distance between Chase and me to his full wingspan. "Obviously, you two have a lot to talk about, and we can deal with that once we're off the ice. The only thing you should be worried about until then is working on your snipe, and the only thing Ty should be focused on is blocking it."

Chase glowers at me. "Fine."

He stops actively trying to decapitate me, but the rest of his shots are still excessively forceful considering it's only a practice. By the end, I know I'm going to have several bruises on my shoulders and knees to show for it.

With some significant effort on Dallas's part, Chase reluctantly agrees to meet us for a drink after we hit the showers. He reiterates that he's not promising anything and he's only staying for one beer. Guess it gives me a small window of opportunity to smooth things over.

My nerves jangle as Dallas and I pull into the parking lot of Overtime. It's a small miracle I'm not banned from here after hitting Rob, but one of the bartenders caught the tail end of our altercation and realized who was at fault.

We grab a table and wait, making small talk while avoiding the topics of Chase, Seraphina, and anything related. Chase rolls in more than fifteen minutes late, probably to make a point because he's still sulking. Knowing him, he sat in the parking lot to intentionally kill time.

He takes his sweet-ass time crossing the bar to us. Then he reluctantly flops into the seat across from me like being here is some massive inconvenience. Love the guy, but sometimes he can be a man-child.

Once the server brings our drink orders, Dallas takes his beer and pushes to stand. He lingers at the head of the small table, leveling us both with a reproachful look. "Now that we're all here, do I need to stick around and play mediator, or are you two capable of talking it out like adults?"

"Adults," Chase and I mumble in unison.

"Good. Then I'll be over there watching the game, enjoying my nice cold beer, and making sure you fools don't kill each other." He points to a nearby table facing the bank of widescreen TVs. "If I have to get up to intervene, someone's getting bitch-slapped."

"Way to take my side, Ward," Chase snaps.

Dallas gives him a pitying look. "You know I love you, Carter.

But if you're too stubborn to see what's really going on here, that's on you."

"What the fuck is that supposed to mean?" He gestures with his beer in hand. Dallas's back is already turned and he's halfway to his seat.

I'm not sure what he meant either.

Chase and I look at each other from across the table while he shoots daggers at me with his eyes. Guilt wanders into my mind, because he's one of my closest friends and I didn't intend for things to turn out like this. I'm not sure what my intention was.

A heavy silence fills the air between us.

"What's going on between you and Sera? Explain." Chase raises his dark eyebrows expectantly.

"Sera and I—"

"What the hell were you thinking?" He places his forearms on the table and his glare takes on a venomous quality. "You know my sister has been in a vulnerable place with the move and our mother being sick."

I wrap my hand around the cold bottle of beer, channeling my patience. "Let me start at the—"

"Like, fuck, man. I thought I could trust you."

My teeth clench together so hard they're at the risk of grinding into dust. I'm not clear on what I'm supposed to do when he clearly has no interest in hearing me out. No surprise there. Arguing with Chase is about as worthwhile as arguing with a wall, and I knew that going in.

"Are you going to let me talk, or would you rather interrogate me?" I ask. "Or maybe you'd prefer to sit here and bitch at me until you run out of breath? Just trying to determine how to proceed on my end."

His nostrils flare. "Let me guess, this little arrangement was your bright idea?"

That question puts me in an impossible position. Not like I can tell him it was Sera who suggested it after we had sex in the announcer's box.

"I don't know how to answer that," I tell him honestly. "I'm trying to walk the line between being respectful to her and truthful with you." Emphasis on the former. Seraphina's privacy and her feelings matter more to me than anything.

"Respectful," he says mockingly. "Right."

"Yes. Anything she and I are doing or not doing is fully mutual. Whether or not you believe it, I care about her. A lot. She's one of my friends."

"A friend you happen to be fucking, because you don't *believe* in dating."

"That isn't . . ." I suppose technically that isn't false. But it sounds bad when he puts it that way.

"In other words, you're using her."

Everything in my body recoils.

"Not the fucking case, Carter." My response verges on a snarl. His assumptions regarding my motives are wearing on my last nerve. I think the world of Seraphina and she knows it, which is ultimately all that matters.

He huffs. "How is it not? You're sleeping together and you supposedly care about her, but you won't commit? The math doesn't add up. Nothing could keep me from being with Bailey. And don't give me that whiny 'it's different because I'm a goalie' bullshit."

I'll give Chase credit, he's great at pushing people's buttons. World fucking class. While I'm technically in the wrong here and I'm trying to defuse the situation, he isn't making it easy for me to stay calm.

"It *is* different. The pressure you and I face isn't the same. It just isn't. I'm fighting for one of thirty-two spots in the entire league."

"So what? You're going to let that rule your life off the ice too? Boo-fucking-hoo, it's 'too stressful' so let's compound that by making hockey the center of my universe and refusing to get close to anyone."

Harsh, but not surprising. If there's anyone who sucks more

than I do at empathy and tact, it's the guy sitting across the table.

"That's some nice logic there, bro." Chase snorts, pointing at me with the neck of his half-full beer. "That way you'll have nothing left during the shitty times with your sport. Real smart."

A dull throb forms in my temples. "Has it occurred to you that Sera might not want to be with *me*?"

"What?"

"Like I said. She's an adult. This isn't some evil scheme I masterminded all on my own."

His jaw slackens. "Holy shit."

"Huh?" I glance around the pub, searching for the cause of his sudden change in demeanor, but he's looking at me. Staring at me, actually, and he isn't blinking.

"You sad sonofabitch," he murmurs.

"I'm not following," I admit.

Chase was frustrating when he was tearing into me, but this is almost more unsettling.

"The karma bus hit you good, didn't it?"

"Er . . . no?"

I watch warily as he reaches across the table. Instead of hitting me—which I'm halfway expecting—he pats my hand, almost like I'm a small child. It's the most bizarre thing I've ever experienced.

"You know what?" Chase crosses his arms and leans back in his seat with a smirk. "Nah. You and I are good."

Chuckling, he waves to get Dallas's attention and motions for him to come join us. I'm still trying to figure out how we went from Chase wanting to tear my head off to him being amused with the situation.

"All sorted?" Dallas sinks into the seat next to me, his gaze darting back and forth between us.

"Yeah." Chase picks up a menu and flips it open. "Let's get some food."

I have no idea what the fuck just happened.

Chapter 30
SUDDEN STOP

TYLER

My father "dropping by" on his way home from New Jersey is setting off all kinds of alarm bells in my brain. Ever since he texted this morning to tell me, I've been in a tailspin.

It doesn't help that I've lost the last four games in a row, starting with the one Seraphina attended. The EnduraFuel tournament is this weekend and going into that on a losing streak is one of the worst possible scenarios.

"How many left?" I grunt, trying to ignore the searing fatigue throughout my abs. I'm so distracted, I can't even count my fucking sit-ups today.

"Two more," Mark urges.

My heart feels like it's going to explode in my chest. To say I've been overdoing coffee would be an understatement. But without it, I would be horizontal. I've been trying to get extra sleep to compensate for all the stress, and the irony is I'm sleeping less than ever. It's turned into a vicious cycle of caffeine and fatigue that I can't seem to break.

A knock at the training room door interrupts us, and the door beeps as someone enters the keycode. When my father steps inside, there's something across his face I can't read—or maybe I don't want to, because then I'd have to admit it's bad.

"Can I talk to Mark for a second, son?"

They step out into the hallway and have a hushed discussion that drags on for longer than I expect. I make a halfhearted attempt to eavesdrop, but their voices are low, and the metal door is thick. It's impossible to make out what they're saying.

Breath heavy, I reach for my phone, navigating back into the text Seraphina sent me earlier today.

Tinker Bell: Question 40: Worst fear?

It's a little too on the nose for me to comfortably answer at the moment. Worst fear? I'm going to go with disappointing everyone in an epic fashion, wasting my parents' time and money, and nuking my career before it starts. Oh, wait. That's already happening.

Panic winds around my body like a rope, tightening its hold until it feels like my ribs might crack. It's easier to maintain where you are than to make a comeback if you fall. I'm close to falling, if not already there.

The door reopens, and my father enters, but Mark doesn't rejoin us.

"What's up?" I grab my water bottle and drain the rest of it.

Dad slips off his navy suit jacket and drapes it over the back of a nearby chair, then lowers to sit in it. His expression tells me we're in parent mode right now, ramping up my level of anxiety to a record high.

"Normally, I wouldn't distract you during a weekend like this, but I want you to hear the news from me before it breaks."

My mouth turns drier than the Sahara. "What news?"

"New York picked up Caleb Brown."

I glance around the training room, because there's a 95 percent chance I am actually going to vomit. "You're kidding."

Pushing to stand, I start doing laps. My heart is racing, my mind is going even faster.

This is happening. It's actually happening. He's taking my spot on the depth chart.

"Son." He stands in my path, and I come to a halt. "I'm not trying to upset you. But it's all over social media. I didn't want you to see it for yourself or hear it from a friend. We can talk this out. Your career is going to be just fine."

"How do you know that? Do you have a crystal ball? 'Cause I could sure fucking use one."

"Tyler." My father claps me on the arm, then drops his hand. His shoulders rise, and he heaves the heaviest sigh I've ever heard. "Let's have a chat. And not just about hockey."

"What do you mean?" Reluctantly, I let him steer me to sit in the green plastic chair next to the one he was sitting in, and he reclaims the seat beside it.

"I've been pushing you too hard. You've been pushing yourself too hard. This isn't healthy. When you were younger, you were always so driven and I wanted to encourage it, but I've done you a disservice in the process."

"I'm fine," I insist, picking up my water bottle. It's empty. Leaning over, I steal a bottle of mixed berry EnduraFuel from the nearby mini fridge. In a few swallows, I drain half and set it aside.

"You're not, and it's my fault. I can absolutely own that. But now that I see the trajectory this is taking, I have to intervene and try to help you as your father. Not as your agent, and not as your career advisor." He pauses and his dark gray eyes probe mine. "What's going on in your personal life?"

"Nothing," I say automatically.

Eyes on the prize. *Hockey. Training. School.*

My chest aches because I know those pieces aren't enough on their own.

"Are you seeing someone?"

A vise wraps around my neck. Mark must've mentioned something to him.

"Yes," I say. "No. I don't know."

"Tyler—"

"Look, Dad. I appreciate all the concern, and I understand where you're coming from. I even see your point. I don't disagree with you, but I need to survive this EnduraFuel event first. Can you let me do that? My bandwidth is fully maxed. I can't take on anything additional, even if it's supposed to help me in the long run. Let me focus on the invitational, and I promise you we can figure out this work-life balance and mental health stuff later."

My father studies me. "It's a deal, but we're not dropping this."

"I know. I just need to get through this weekend."

Chapter 31
UNSCHEDULED

SERAPHINA

I'm not vibing with these prompts for my creative writing class's short-form fiction assignment. Invisibility potions; monsters swimming beneath ships; finding a genie in a bottle. One of the things I like about writing is that I get to pick what it's about. Being fenced in like this makes me strangely resentful. They're all sort of science-fiction, adventure, or thriller themed too. Couldn't one of them at least leave room for me to include a little romance? I suppose monster romance is a thing. Maybe I could do that...

The front door slams, and I glance up from my laptop eagerly.

Tyler steps inside a moment later, crossing the room to me. He's dressed in head-to-toe training gear like he has been all week, not even bothering to change into street clothes. Just clean sets of training clothes in steady rotation like it's the literal only thing on his mind.

Drawing closer, he plants a kiss on the top of my head. "Hey, Ser."

"Hi." I move to close the laptop, but before I can, he's already halfway out of the room. Not sure why I expected otherwise; he gave me a thorough rundown of his schedule for the week.

I'm not part of it.

He didn't directly say that. He didn't need to. There's no free time left between all his off-ice coaching, team practices, studying, and extra training he's crammed in there in advance of this hockey invitational he's attending this weekend.

Heart aching, I lean back against the leather couch and reopen the homework I was working on. This week has been awful. One for the record books in the worst possible way. My friendship with Abby is finished, which means I have one less friend here, and I didn't have all that many to begin with. Even if she sucked, she made my life look better on paper.

I'm also still waiting on the BRCA test results. Enough said.

Then Chase gave me a speech about how I shouldn't have lied to him and hid things from him for so long. It came from more of an "I'm not mad, I'm disappointed" angle, and somehow that made me feel a million times worse than if he'd been angry with me.

And, as evidenced by what happened two minutes ago, Tyler has been distant all week. He's hardly initiated texts, doesn't seem present when we're together, and all around seems, well, disinterested in me. Maybe it's more distraction than lack of interest, but it's been several days, and it's hard not to take it personally at this point.

When I try to talk about it, he *claims* it's about hockey. How can I believe that when he won't elaborate beyond that?

I thought being outed in front of everyone would make being with him easier, not worse.

Maybe that's where I went wrong. Technically, I'm not "with" him in the first place.

Not long after, Tyler is out the door again, this time with Dallas and Chase for team practice. Bailey and Siobhan have come over for a movie night, but it's pretty clear my mind is somewhere else. We pause the movie halfway through and end up talking instead.

It's mostly me talking. And crying.

Bailey inclines her head sympathetically. "He's on a losing streak, Sera. I don't think he intends for it to be personal."

I sniffle, wiping my nose with a tissue. "It feels personal." Shouldn't he want me to be there for him if something is wrong? He opened up so much to me about hockey before and now, he's like a vault. That he's pushing me away makes me feel like there has to be something more to it.

"I'm sorry." Shiv's hand lands on my arm, rubbing. "For what it's worth, I've seen the way he looks at you, and let me tell you, that man is obsessed."

"Ha. Doubtful." Adding my crumpled tissue to the mountain beside me, I reach for my bowl of popcorn. Might as well drown my feelings in food. Though at this point, it'll take an Olympic swimming pool's worth of snacks to make a dent.

"Not to brag," she says, "but my people-reading skills are top notch. I knew something was going on between you guys *long* before I caught you."

I pause with a handful of popcorn in my hand, and one falls back into the bowl. "You did?"

"Of course. Even at Chase's birthday, Tyler was staring at you all night." Siobhan waves her Twizzler at me as if to emphasize. "Every time I came over, I noticed the same thing. He looks at you like you're the only person in the room."

It's not lost on me that's exactly how I'd describe the way my dad used to look at my mom.

"Shiv's right," Bailey chimes in. "Even I had started to think something was up after Valentine's Day. Chase mentioned it to me once or twice too. He thought Tyler had a crush on you, but he didn't realize something was actually going on."

My stomach churns because I want to believe what they're saying, but I'm scared to let myself. If what they're saying is true, he certainly isn't showing it.

Then again, why should he? It isn't like he owes me anything.

Even worse, I created this mess by telling him we should "just have fun." My ability to separate sex from emotion has fallen woefully flat when it comes to him. Now I'm tangled in a web of feelings I'm not sure he returns—or is even capable of returning. He's made it more than clear hockey is his priority.

Suddenly, an email pops up on my phone. Thinking it'll be my latest creative writing grade, I swipe into it.

From: admin@northendtesting.com
Subject: North End Medical Center Appointment Confirmation
Message: Seraphina Carter
Genetic Counseling Appointment
Tuesday at 2:00 P.M.

What? Oh my god. They didn't call me. Does this mean they just went ahead and booked me in? My test results must be back.

Blood roars in my ears as I look at the screen. Tuesday. I'll know by Tuesday.

"Give him some time," Siobhan says, snapping my attention back to her. "Sometimes it takes people awhile to realize their taxicab light has turned on."

Chapter 32
CRUISING ALTITUDE

TYLER

The timing of this fucking EnduraFuel hockey weekend leaves much to be desired.

The first day is okay, but not stellar. There are drills and mini-games, and I come out in the upper tier—though not first, where I arguably should be. After the action wraps up, I meet my dad and we attend the afterparty, where we mingle with league officials, meet the other guys, and woo brand sponsors. As nice as the professional paychecks are, the real money is in endorsements.

The second day, everything falls apart. Caleb Jones happens to also be in attendance, and he's playing on our opposing team for the three-on-three game. It could not be more ironic to have the two of us literally facing off during a match. I'm in my head, and it shows during practice. Shot by shot slip by me, the vast majority of which shouldn't.

Resetting my position between the posts, I draw in a breath and try again. The next drill isn't any better. Nausea roils in my stomach throughout the practice, and near the end, I'm dangerously close to needing the garbage can to throw up in. This weekend is huge, and I'm fucking choking.

When it wraps up, Mark practically yanks me off the ice by my jersey for an emergency pep talk in my hotel room.

"What's going on, Tyler?" He paces the floor in front of me, still dressed in his black training polo and gray slacks.

"I don't know." I rake a hand through my hair, still damp from the showers. The next game isn't until later tonight, and there are more social events scheduled first. That's why I need to get my shit together so I can go rub elbows and pretend everything is fine.

"This is about Brown, isn't it?"

"I mean, yes?" Clasping my fingers together, I stretch out my shoulders, but it doesn't help alleviate the tension all over my body. "I have some personal shit to deal with too. It's just not great timing for all of this."

Since I got here, I've been kicking myself for brushing off Seraphina all week. It isn't that I meant to; I've been so stressed out that I can't focus on a single fucking thing. I spent all week running myself ragged and making everything worse in every imaginable way. It's the definition of self-defeating. I should be able to juggle all of this, and I'm failing miserably.

Mark rolls his lips into a line, his expression sympathetic but stern. "It's never great timing. You'll have to get used to that. Hockey doesn't wait for life, and life doesn't wait for hockey."

He launches into what's meant to be an inspirational speech but somehow manages to be discouraging. It's clear he concurs with my father about me needing a better balance between hockey and the rest of my life. They think that's ultimately to blame for what's happening right now.

In other words, this is still my fault.

Familiar anxiety sets in, and my adrenaline surges.

"Can I take five alone, Mark?"

He nods. "Take all the time you need."

As soon as the door clicks shut behind him, I pick up my phone and call Seraphina. She answers on the third ring with a note of surprise to her voice, probably because I haven't been great about texting.

"Hey," she says. "How's the showcase?"

"Not fucking good." I catch myself. Part of me wants to open up to her about everything that's going on, but another part of me is afraid I'll work myself up even more by talking about it.

Why did I call her? Selfishly, it's because I want her near. I need her *here* right now. The phone isn't the same.

Fuck. I feel so needy—like I'm taking more than I can give her in return.

"I'm sorry, Hades. What happened?"

"Just a bit of a rough start, that's all. I needed to hear your voice. How are you doing?"

There's a pause. "I'm okay. Actually, I was hoping we could talk about something..." She trails off. "But if now isn't a good time, I understand. I'd been planning to wait until you got home."

"Gotta be honest with you, I'm not in a great headspace right now, and Mark is standing outside waiting for me. Can it wait?" I'll be more use to her once I get home. Once this weekend is done with, my head won't be spinning like it is right now. I just need to survive the next two days.

"Um, yeah. It can."

When we end the call, I feel even worse than when I started.

◆ ◆ ◆

The rest of the weekend is a grind. Not an abject failure like I feared, but hardly a success. I was mid at best. Caleb crushed it.

At my request several weeks ago, Mark booked an additional night in LA for me to stay with my family. It ends up being a waste. Too grouchy to visit, I snap at everyone throughout family dinner and put myself to bed earlier than most toddlers. Then I lie awake for several hours beating myself up mentally for all the things I should have done differently on the ice.

The next morning, my dad gives me another fatherly talk about how there's more to life than hockey on his way to drop me off at LAX at the crack of dawn. Despondent, I watch his Lamborghini roar away from the curb. All I want is to be back home, not 3,000 miles across the country from Seraphina. Who, by the way, hasn't so much as texted me since our call.

I navigate the airport like I'm sleepwalking. Check my luggage and my gear. Clear security. Hit Starbucks. Find the gate. Doomscroll on my phone. That last one is a huge mistake, because all the media coverage from this weekend talks about how mediocre my performance was.

When I board, I have an entire first-class row to myself, which is the sole silver lining to this otherwise shitty day. Across the aisle from me, the other row is occupied by a couple, and they're all over each other. I overhear them telling the flight attendant they're headed to Europe for their honeymoon. Seeing the way they are together reminds me of Seraphina all over again.

As we taxi the runway, I close my eyes and lean back in my seat, playing my favorite way to drive myself crazy: the game of What If. This is counterproductive at best, damaging at worst, and I do it all the time.

What if New York picks Caleb over me? What if they pick me over him? What if I get stuck down on the farm team forever? I go from best case to worst case and back again inside my head. In every hypothetical I run myself through, there's a common denominator staring me right in the face.

Tink.

When I picture the rest of my life five years down the line, I can't help but insert her in it. My brain does it automatically. She's everywhere.

What if I make it to the league? Wake up next to Seraphina before hitting the arena for practice. Come home after and see her again if I'm lucky. Call it a night after a local game and come home to her, or FaceTime her from the road.

What if I end up down on the farm team? Pretty much the same, only with a lot less money and fame. Seraphina's still there.

The longer I play What If, the more one thing becomes painfully clear: I can live with it if my career doesn't go where I want it to. But I can't live with not having her.

It's completely illogical considering we haven't talked about a future. She's not even my girlfriend, if we're being strict about labels. Somewhere along the line, my mind realized that she's it for me, and now it refuses to accept otherwise.

Then it hits me that a good portion of what's been stressing me out has nothing to do with hockey at all. I've been committing some world-class projection. Because my worst fear isn't what I thought it was.

It has nothing to do with hockey at all.

It's losing her.

And like an asshole, I've been blowing her off all week for things that not only aren't her fault, but they also have nothing to do with her. Fuck. What did she want to talk to me about on Saturday? I was too caught up in feeling sorry for myself, and I should've told Mark to wait. The first thing I'm going to do when I get home is apologize.

Over the intercom, the flight attendant announces we've reached cruising altitude. This means I can put down my tray and pull out my laptop to watch game tape, like I always do.

Instead, I scroll through my photos. I start with the first selfie she ever sent me when I was on the road. Then I keep swiping into the rest. Seraphina naked in my bed, the covers strategically hiding her body. A random mirror selfie I snagged of us brushing our teeth one morning. Another selfie she took of us kissing. A shot of her clutching a cup of coffee outside, her cheeks rosy from the cold. One of her pretending to bite my face the night we went out for dinner at Rouge. Even now, that one makes me laugh.

We look so fucking happy.

Scrolling back, I set the first photo she ever sent me as my wallpaper and lock my phone. Then I hit the side button to keep the backlight on, tracing every single line and detail of her face. Big brown eyes I could get lost in. Plump lips with a perfect Cupid's bow at the top. A cute little nose that scrunches up when she laughs. She's so fucking beautiful it hurts.

She's even more beautiful beneath the surface. Quick-witted

and smart. Silly and bold. Caring and patient, even when I don't deserve it.

As I stare at the picture in my hand, everything clicks. It's like putting on glasses and seeing things clearly for the first time.

I'm not just falling for her; I'm already there. Have been for a while.

I love her.

That final realization hits hardest of all, and it runs through my head on repeat for the rest of the flight.

Chapter 33
ONE IN TWO

SERAPHINA

Monday morning has taken an unnerving turn.

> From: admin@northendtesting.com
> Subject: North End Medical Center Patient Portal Update
> Message: A new test result is available in your patient portal. To view it, click here or download our app here.

Overwhelming nausea barrels into me as I read the email again.

This has to be some kind of technical error. The nurse I spoke to this morning said they don't give test results of this nature over the phone, and that's why I received an emailed appointment confirmation over the weekend.

Given that, it makes no sense they'd upload my results onto the internet for someone to see by themselves. Unless this is a good sign. Maybe it means it's negative. There would be no harm in putting a negative test result up for the patient to see before their appointment, right?

Hands shaking, I navigate into the app and enter my login information. Before the landing page can load, I lose my nerve and swipe out.

I should wait.

My heart thunders in my ears as I stare at the screen. I can't breathe. I can't think. I know I shouldn't look, but I won't be able to accomplish anything until I see that result.

Fifty-fifty.

One in two.

I hold my breath, watching the little rainbow wheel spin around and around as the page loads.

Please be negative. Please be negative. Please be negative.

It's not.

Chapter 34
PRIORITIES

TYLER

The remainder of my flight feels like forty hours instead of four. I text Seraphina when I land, but she doesn't answer. Again. She hasn't answered me since last night. I'm well past worried.

Baggage claim takes for-fucking-ever. I low-key resent every person whose bag appears before mine on the carousel. My equipment bag finally emerges on the conveyor belt, followed by my luggage. Grabbing it, I turn and haul ass to the parking garage to get my car. As I make the drive home, all I can think of is those last thirty seconds of a shutout when the pressure is more intense than it's ever been—everything comes down to the final second where you either walk away with the win or get denied that big moment.

Seraphina still hasn't written me back by the time I pull in. Entering the keycode, I go through the garage to put away my gear. Her SUV is sitting parked inside. My worry ramps up another notch. If she's not in class, why hasn't she answered any of my texts? Is she upset with me? Is she okay?

The house is silent when I step inside.

"Ser?" I call.

No answer.

With my duffel bag on one shoulder, I go down the hall to check her bedroom and find it empty. Could she be out with someone else? Maybe Chloe picked her up for school today.

I open the door to downstairs, greeted by the sound of water rushing through the pipes. Cautious relief sets in. If she's in the shower, that would explain why she didn't hear me come home.

Still doesn't explain why she hasn't answered any of my texts all day, though.

My gut says something is wrong, and I no longer think it has anything to do with her being angry at me. I can't explain it. I just know.

Adrenaline spiking, I take the stairs two at a time. When I reach the bottom, I ditch my bag and jog to the bathroom. The door is closed when I reach it.

Placing my ear to the door, I knock softly. "Tink?"

She doesn't answer.

"Ser." I knock harder this time, but I still don't receive a response.

Give me something. Anything. Tell me to go away. Yell at me. Be mad at me. Just answer me.

Growing desperate, I try the handle and find no resistance. It isn't locked.

"I'm going to come in for a second, okay?" I say through the door. "I want to make sure you're all right."

When I open the door, it's like a knife to the gut.

Seraphina is sitting in the tub next to the faucet with her knees pulled up to her chest. Her gaze is fixed down, and her eyes are vacant. Above her head, the running shower pours down on the tiles. The shower curtain is half-closed like it was an afterthought, and there are puddles all over the floor.

Panic courses through my veins, and cold water seeps through my socks as I rush over to her. As I draw closer, a few stray droplets from the spray hit my face and bare forearms. Even though the dial is set to warm, the spray is cold too. Our hot water tank lasts for three or four showers, sometimes more. That means she's been in there for at least an hour.

How long has she been in there under the cold water?

Kneeling by the side of the tub, I shut off the faucet and try to catch her eye to no avail. Her fair skin is dotted with goose bumps all over, her lips are pale, and she's shivering. I'm fairly certain she's in shock, and I have no idea why.

I've never been more scared in my entire life, but I need to stay calm for her.

"Ser." I touch her shoulder to get her attention, finding her skin chilled to the touch. Her eyes lock onto mine, but she doesn't react. "You're frozen, baby. I'm going to dry you off and get you warmed up, okay?"

She nods silently, but she doesn't look at me.

Turning away, I grab a stack of fluffy white towels from under the sink, draping one over my shoulder. While she doesn't resist my efforts to dry her off, she doesn't help me either. It takes some maneuvering, but eventually I manage to wrap her in two of the towels before I lift her up, bridal style. She sags against my chest as I carry her into my room.

Holding her up with one arm, I rearrange my pillows and prop them at the head of the bed before I set her down against them. "I need to get you into some clothes, Tink."

I get her dressed as quickly as possible, narrating everything as I go even though it feels like I'm talking to myself. She wordlessly cooperates as I tug my black T-shirt over her head, then lay the spare towel over her shoulders to stop the cold water in her wet hair from dripping onto her shoulders and back. Then I help her into the warmest pair of sweats I own and slip on a pair of thick socks for her feet. It's all several sizes big for her, but at least she's insulated.

Taking the extra towel, I gently blot as much moisture from her hair as I can, trying to make sure I don't pull it.

"Tell me if I hurt you," I murmur, but I know she won't. She's like a zombie. I have no idea what's going on. I suspect no one does; Chase would be here if he did.

Once her hair is dried to damp, I grab a newer Falcons hoodie that still has lots of its fleece lining left from my closet and put that over her head. Her skin is slowly warming, and she isn't shivering anymore. She looks better—but she still hasn't said a word.

Nearly out of my mind with worry, I lower to my knees on the floor in front of her. A million scenarios are flying through my brain, ranging from terrible to catastrophic. All I want is to know she's okay. I need to know she's okay.

"What happened, Ser?" I take her hands in mine, relieved by how much they've warmed since I got her out of the shower.

Her eyes glitter with unshed tears as she looks at me. My clothes drown her, and the combination makes her seem especially vulnerable. She looks so small; fragile.

"Did something happen with your mom?"

She shakes her head. "No."

This eliminates the most obvious explanation, leaving me more confused than ever.

"Then what is it? Talk to me," I beg. "Please."

Seconds pass, and she doesn't reply. She draws her hands into the sleeves of my sweatshirt, hiding them, and wraps her arms around her body, hugging herself.

"You can tell me anything." My palms smooth up her back, squeezing reassuringly. "I promise I'll have your back. But I can't help if I don't know what's going on."

"It's me," she finally says. "The test was positive." Her voice cracks, and my heart breaks along with it.

"What test?" I crane my neck and try to get a glimpse of her face, but she won't look at me. "Are you pregnant?"

She hides her face in her hands, a sob wracking her body. My mind whirls as I process the implications of what a positive pregnancy test means for us. Pregnancy. A baby. Parenthood. A little scary, and a lot sooner than I imagined during my What If game earlier, but we can handle it. I'd do anything for her, shifting timelines included.

Crawling up to sit beside her on the bed, I wrap my arms around her as she continues to cry. "It's okay, Tink. We can figure it out together. I'm not going anywhere. A pregnancy—"

She looks up at me, stricken. "No, Ty. The genetic test. My mom has a BRCA mutation, and I found out this morning that I do too."

"BRCA?" I echo, not understanding and hating myself for it.

"It's a cancer gene," she says, another sob wracking her small frame. "It's bad. Really bad. It means I'm more than likely to develop cancer in the future. I have—I have an appointment tomorrow to find out more."

It's like a bomb detonating in my brain. Seraphina. Cancer gene. The concepts wedge themselves in my mind, stuck as abstract ideas beyond my comprehension. I can't reconcile it. I don't want to accept that something could happen to her—that she could get sick like that.

Of all the explanations I'd been worried about, this one hadn't even entered my mind as a possibility. I didn't even know she got tested. Why didn't she tell me?

Then it hits me: she tried to.

"Ser." Now it's my voice that's cracking. "I'm so fucking sorry. I should've been here for you. I wish I'd known." My chest aches so intensely I think my ribcage might break open. All the shit I've been worried about lately seems inconsequential in comparison to this.

Seraphina tears her gaze away from mine again. "I guess . . . I-I wasn't sure you'd want to hear about it. You were so busy with hockey, and stressed out with your own stuff, and—"

That guts me all over again. If she believes that, I fucked up majorly along the way.

"Of course I'd want to know, Tink. I love you." The words leap from my mouth before I can think it through. I don't know if this is the right time or if she even wants to hear it. It's just the truth.

"You what?" She turns to look at me with surprise across her face.

"I love you," I tell her, tucking a lock of damp hair behind her ear. "So fucking much. And I'm sorry if I ever made you feel like I don't. None of that other stuff means a thing without you."

Her bottom lip wobbles. "You don't have to say that just because you think you should."

"I'm saying it because it's true. I know what we agreed to

going into this, but I want more, Ser. I want you. All of you. The label, a future, you name it."

Tears spill down her cheeks, and she hides her face in my chest, crying even harder than before. Knowing she was hurting like this alone kills me. I tighten my arms around her, wishing more than anything I could fix things and cursing the fact I can't.

"Y-you still want to be with me?" She can barely get the words out between her gulps for air. "Even if I might get sick or have to get surgery or—"

Her last sentence cuts me to the bone. Not because *I* don't want to deal with that, but because it kills me to think of it happening to her. Fuck. Why is life so unfair?

"No matter what. I'm all in, Ser. I'd do anything for you. Name it and it's yours."

She clings to me, bawling, while I fight the lump forming in my throat. How long has she been dealing with this alone?

"Does this have anything to do with what happened at Rob's?" I ask quietly. The timing would explain everything.

"Uh-huh." She gasps as she nods against me, clutching my shirt with her fingers.

Fuck. She's had this hanging over her head a long time.

"You don't have to go through this alone anymore, okay? I'm here."

Seraphina hiccups. "Okay."

An indeterminate length of time passes as I hold her, rubbing her back and trying to calm her down. It hurts me on every level to see how much pain she's in knowing there's so little I can do about it. It's a visceral ache down to my bones.

I wait until she's cried herself out and her sobs start to subside.

"Have you eaten?" I ask, stroking her hair.

"No," she admits. "Not since yesterday."

Dammit. I should've asked her this sooner. It's well into the afternoon, and this means she's long overdue for a meal.

I lean over and grab my phone off the nightstand. "Let me order some food. I'm going to shoot Mark a quick text too. I want to give him some notice."

Seraphina peers up at me, her lashes still wet with tears. "Notice?"

"Yeah. I'm giving him the week off. With that much time, he might want to fly out of town or go do something."

"What?" She releases me and scoots back on my bed. "No, I can't hog you all week."

"Tink." I press a finger to her lips. Training is the least important thing in the world on the heels of learning this. "Hockey can wait. Right now, you're my only priority. I'm clearing my schedule. I'll tell coach I'm out for tomorrow too. Then I can come to your appointment if you want. Or I can be waiting for you when you get home. Either way, I'm here and I'm not going anywhere."

Between the cold shower and skipping several meals, Seraphina worked up an appetite. She eats nearly as much as I do once our food arrives, and that's saying something because I'm fucking famished.

"By the way..." she sets down her nearly finished chicken clubhouse, wincing. "Chase doesn't know."

"I sort of figured. Is there a reason you haven't talked to him?" They're pretty close, so I'm surprised she hasn't.

She bites her lip briefly, then releases it. "Men can be carriers too, but my mom wanted to talk to him about it when the time was right."

"I understand." I grab another french fry from the middle where we're sharing. It goes without saying that I'm saying fuck it to worrying about my diet this week. No real plans to attend class, either. "Can you tell me more about what being positive for BRCA means, Ser?"

Obviously, I'm going to go down the research rabbit hole when I get the chance, but for now, I need her to give me the quick and dirty about what we're dealing with.

Her hand tightens around her iced tea. "It's BRCA1, which

means I have a significantly increased risk of breast and ovarian cancer."

My heart clenches at those words.

"Is there anything they can do about that? Extra screening?" My unspoken question is, can we throw money at this to help her? Sky's the limit.

"Um, well . . ." Seraphina scrunches up her mouth. "The recommendation is to have preventative surgery around age thirty-five to forty. In other words I have to decide how old I want to be before I let them cut me open and take out my ovaries and cut off my boobs. What's a good age for that?" Her voice wavers more and more as she speaks, breaking again.

I hate the idea of her undergoing something that invasive, even if it's necessary.

"Ser. I'm sorry." I set down my food and shift closer on the couch, hugging her to me. She's still dressed head to toe in my clothing. While I'd normally find it cute, it makes me sad when I know why.

"Obviously, that decision affects other things too. Like having kids. We haven't really talked about that. Do you even want any?"

"Yeah." My mouth tugs at the thought of a family with her someday. "I definitely do."

"When I was at my checkup, I asked my gynecologist about my options if the test comes back positive, and she said my best bet is to start a family in my twenties. You know, in case there are any fertility issues and it takes a while to get pregnant. I guess if you wait until thirty to start trying and things don't pan out, it doesn't leave you much time to work with given the surgery timeline."

She seems nervous to tell me this, and I'm not entirely sure why. It all seems logical enough given the circumstances.

"That makes sense."

Seraphina pulls away from me, reaching for her last bite of sandwich, and finishes it before she replies. "I'm already *in* my twenties, Ty. Barely, but still. That's kind of terrifying, isn't it?

None of this was even on my radar a few months ago. Now I have to plan out my entire life. Everything is evolving so quickly; my brain hasn't had the opportunity to catch up."

"I get why you'd be overwhelmed, but you're not alone. We'll figure it out together." There are a lot of other things out of my hands. Supporting her, at least, is something I can help with.

Her eyes narrow. "I'm talking about pregnancy and babies to you. Most guys would run for the hills. Why aren't you freaking out?"

If someone told me I'd be having this conversation, I might've expected that reaction from myself as well. When I look at things in perspective, that isn't the part that scares me.

I wipe my hands with a napkin before I reach for her, cupping her face. "I want a future with you. The details are negotiable. What's important is that you're happy and healthy, Ser. We'll do what's best for you, whatever that looks like."

Tears well in her eyes again. "I love you."

"I love you, Tink."

Her eyelids turn heavy, and she presses her forehead to mine. I almost think she might fall asleep on the spot.

"God, I'm exhausted. Do you mind if I go take a nap?"

"Go ahead," I say, kissing her forehead. "I'll clean up."

Once she's in her room, I put away our garbage and straighten up the living room. Then I empty out my suitcase and do my laundry. She's still asleep when Chase gets home after five.

I glance up from the pile of clean clothes I'm sorting. "Hey."

Even after our talk at Overtime, our relationship has been strained. Artificially cordial at best and missing the usual level of comfort longtime friends have around each other. Awkward, basically.

"Hey." He looks around, hesitating. "Anyone else home?"

"Sera is, but she's napping. Not feeling well." Partially true, at least.

Chase nods and stuffs his hands into the pockets of his red Falcons hoodie. "Can we talk?"

"What's up?" I gesture for him to sit. Is he going to ream me out again?

When he lowers onto the couch across from me, resting his arms on his spread thighs, his expression isn't confrontational.

"Look, I don't want to have this weird tension between us. I'm willing to admit I *may* have overreacted slightly." He gives me a tired half-smirk. "But you caught me by surprise, dude. When I talked to you that night at Overtime, it was clear that you care about Sera, and that's all I want. I freaked out a little at first because I know you've never had a girlfriend. I don't want to see her get hurt."

"You'd never had a girlfriend before Bailey," I point out, setting a pair of socks aside.

Not sure which one of us would've qualified as the least likely candidate to end up in a committed relationship. It would have been a close race, to be sure. Yet here we are: two whipped motherfuckers who are loving every minute of it.

"That's why I'm giving you the benefit of the doubt. You have my blessing. Conditionally. Because if you hurt her—"

"You'll fucking kill me," I finish, laughing.

"I won't make it fast, either. It'll be long and painful." He's jarringly cheerful as he says this, probably because he means every single word.

"Trust me, I have no intention of ever hurting her." Reaching into the basket, I search for another matching pair of socks. I'm nearly done folding everything, and Sera is still asleep. Poor Tink. I should go check on her.

"Good." He pushes to stand, dusting off his hands "By the way, you're invited to family dinner this weekend."

I give him a questioning look. "Does Seraphina know about this?"

"She will."

Guess I can consider that his formal stamp of approval. I'll take it.

Abandoning the folded laundry in the living room, I opt to

go see if Seraphina's awake yet. When I push open the door to her room, it squeaks, and she stirs. *Shit.*

She stretches and rolls over in bed, turning to face me. "Hi, Hades."

"I didn't mean to wake you," I say, my voice hushed. "How are you feeling?"

"As okay as can be, I guess." Pulling herself upright, she beckons to me to come closer. "I have something for you, actually."

"You do?" I sit down next to her, the mattress dipping beneath my weight.

"It's a birthday present. And not another blow job." She laughs. "I didn't get the chance to give it to you after everything went sideways that night. I may have chickened out because I wasn't sure if you'd like it."

"I already know I'll love anything you give me."

Seraphina leans over and turns on her lamp. Then she tugs open her nightstand, emerging with something wrapped in sparkly silver paper. It's not overly big; maybe the size of a soda can. I carefully tear away the wrapping to find a miniature replica of Northview Arena. It's identical down to every last detail, including the logo beneath the ice. When I look closer, there's a tiny heart rhinestone embedded in the window of the announcer's box.

"I found a company who makes custom replicas," she says shyly. "This way you'll always remember where everything started."

"Ser." I glance up at her, struggling to find the right words. It's cute and thoughtful and it's so characteristically her. There are several meanings behind it, and all of them are important to me. "This is amazing. I love it."

"Even the heart?"

This is clearly the part that made her nervous, and it's my favorite detail of them all.

"Especially the heart." Carefully setting it aside, I lean in and kiss her cheek. "Thank you. It's perfect."

My phone rings in my pocket, interrupting us. I check it to find another call from my dad, who's called five times already—probably wanting to know why I gave Mark the week off without telling him. I've been avoiding his calls while I let everything sink in. If I don't answer soon, he's going to get worried and hop on a plane here to find out what the fuck is going on.

"Mind if I take this? It's my dad."

"Go ahead. I should check online and see what I missed in class today."

She grabs her laptop while I answer the call next to her, not bothering to step out. I don't plan to make this a long conversation.

"Hey, Dad." I reach over with my free hand, raking my fingers through Seraphina's hair. She angles her head appreciatively, leaning into my touch.

"Tyler." Concern tints his voice, laced with an undertone of restrained panic. "I spoke to Mark. Is everything okay?"

"It's fine. Just need to take a few personal days to focus on some other things." While my father is generally understanding, I'm not sure how he's going to take this—or whether he's going to press me for details.

"You thought about what I said then?"

"I did, and you're right."

A relieved sigh sounds on the other end of the line. "I'm sorry if I overstepped or pressured you too much, Ty. Hockey isn't the only important thing, and I don't want you to miss out on the rest of your life because you're too narrowly focused on it. I'm glad you're prioritizing other things. Or a relationship, as the case may be. I want you to be happy."

I glance over at Seraphina. She's studying the computer screen, her mouth tugged into her trademark pout of concentration. A now-familiar feeling blooms in my chest, and all of those what-ifs flash through my mind again. They all start and end with her.

"I am," I tell him. "I can't wait for you to meet her."

Chapter 35
STILL US

SERAPHINA

"Ready, Tink?" Tyler reaches across the leather console, taking my hand in his.

Dread floods the pit of my stomach. "No."

Through the windshield of his SUV, North End Medical Center towers above us. Concrete and glass and everything I don't want to face. We've been sitting here talking for over ten minutes and my appointment is rapidly approaching. It's time to go inside, but I'm not sure I can. If I do, all of this will become real.

Rather than try to convince me, he kills the ignition and climbs out of his seat, shutting the door behind him. I fidget with the strap of my purse as he strides around the vehicle and opens the passenger side door. He doesn't say anything—just embraces me, enveloping me in the warmth of his body. I inhale his familiar scent, burrowing against him.

"I don't want to do this," I say into his coat.

He hugs me tighter. "I know. I'm sorry, Ser. I love you, and I'll be here every step of the way."

After a few more seconds, some of the tension I've been holding eases slightly. Reluctantly, I unfasten my seatbelt and take his hand, sliding out of the passenger side. Delaying won't change anything, much as I wish it would.

Tyler wraps his arm around my shoulders as we walk through the parking lot, cold air lashing at our faces. The closer we get to our destination, the higher my heart rate climbs. By the time he pulls open the door to the office, my pulse is roaring in my ears and my hands are shaking. I don't want to do this. Don't want to face this. Don't want to deal with what's ahead.

As soon as we check in with reception, we're whisked away to an appointment room with soft leather chairs and windows looking out onto a cluster of snow-covered trees. Tyler moves his seat closer to mine, then reaches over to interlace our fingers. My throat tightens, and I squeeze his hand. I've never been more thankful to have someone in my entire life.

The genetic counselor introduces herself to us, and everything kicks into warp speed. Overwhelm seizes me as I'm inundated with information. Statistics, surgeries, and survival rates. Numbers, data, and recommendations. My future flashes before my eyes as she explains, and I mentally play out the potential courses of action and outcomes that could result from each. I have choices, but all of them are scary.

Within a matter of minutes, it becomes clear Tyler is better prepared than I am. It helps that he has a science background; he's done his homework and it shows. He listens, asks questions and takes notes, and checks in with me repeatedly. It's the perfect balance of being supportive without being overbearing.

When she wraps up, I'm somewhere between denial and shock. Most of what she told me isn't new, but it's a lot to take in all at once, and it's different hearing it firsthand rather than reading about it on the internet. Knowing life-altering surgery in my future is troubling, even if it's far off.

"Any questions?" the genetic counselor asks, lacing her fingers together over the polished wood desk.

I have a million questions, none of which she can help me with. They're all too personal. When should I start a family? What's the perfect age to get preventative surgery? What will my body be like after I do?

"No." I clear my throat. "Not right now."

She offers me a sympathetic smile. "I'll give you my card and some information to take home. It's not uncommon to have some additional questions after you've had time to process everything."

"Thank you." Pushing to stand, I take the bundle of pamphlets as well as her business card. They slip from my trembling fingers and fall to the floor, scattering all over. *Shit.* Embarrassment and frustration bubble up, a sudden barrage of tears threatening to overflow. Before I can grab them, Tyler kneels to pick them up and holds on to them for me so I don't drop them again.

It's a blur leaving the office. When we step back into the cold winter afternoon, exhaustion slams into me. I'm too tired to even bother trying to make conversation, and he seems to sense that.

We slow to a stop in front of the passenger side of his SUV, and he pauses before he opens the door.

"Are you okay, Tink?" A crease forms between his brows as he studies me.

When I don't answer, his arms wrap around me and pull me closer. I swallow, resting my head on his chest. In the wake of some of the worst news of my life, he's been more caring than I could've ever imagined. His presence has been like a light of hope shining on the darkest depths of my thoughts.

"As okay as someone in my shoes could be," I finally reply.

"You're strong, and you've got this." He presses his lips to my temple. "We'll get through it together."

Hearing that does something to me I can't explain.

"Thanks, Hades."

◆ ◆ ◆

For the rest of the day, Tyler doesn't leave my side. He lets me pick all of the television shows. Rubs my feet. Plays Scrabble with me. Cooks dinner. Doesn't check his phone even once. And we snuggle nonstop.

We're cuddled up beneath a blanket rewatching *Legally Blonde* when Chase gets home and asks if we can talk. Tyler presses a kiss to my cheek before he pushes to stand, leaving me with my brother.

Apprehension creeps in as Chase sinks onto the chair next to my couch. My mother broke the news to him earlier and filled him in about everything. I'm not sure whether I'm about to receive sympathy or a lecture for not telling him about the BRCA test. Knowing him, probably both.

He crosses an ankle over his knee, shifting to face me. "How was the appointment?"

"It was okay." I shrug. "Mostly things I already knew from doing my own research online. No major revelations."

"I'm sorry this is happening, Sera. It's so fucking unfair."

That's been one of the hardest things to come to terms with. It was luck of the draw, and luck wasn't on my side.

"Yeah." Gritting my teeth, I swallow hard and tuck my hands in the cuffs of Tyler's red hoodie that I borrowed when we got home.

"Mom told me she asked you to keep the BRCA thing quiet," Chase says, looking down at the floor. His gaze lifts to mine, his dark eyes gleaming with sadness. "I understand why, but I hate that you didn't let me be there for you. If you'd told me, you wouldn't have been handling this on your own."

The guilt this stirs up is almost too much to bear. Looking away, I reach for my half-full mug of chamomile tea, wrapping my hands around the warm ceramic.

"I'm not alone anymore."

He shakes his head. "You never were. You can always talk to me, and that includes other things too."

That only amplifies my guilt for not telling him about Tyler.

"Are you going to get tested?" I've thought about that constantly since my positive result. More than anything, I want his to be negative.

"Yeah. Already booked an appointment." He pauses. "Can we talk about you and Ty for a minute?"

While I knew this was coming, part of me hoped it never would. I dislike confrontation at the best of times, and Chase is impossible to argue with.

"If this is going to be a lecture, today is not—"

"It's not," he cuts in, holding up a hand. "Promise."

"Okay." I take another sip of my tea and wait for him to continue.

Chase leans closer, and I can tell he's trying to temper whatever he says next. For someone who lacks a filter, it takes a lot of effort on his part.

"Why didn't you tell me about you guys? Why did you keep it a secret?" His tone is more wounded than accusatory.

Setting down my mug, I weigh how to answer. "The two of us hooking up wasn't any of your business. Besides, how would you have taken the news?"

"Fair." He laughs. "Probably not well. I realize I can be a bit of a protective dick, but that's only because I care about you and I don't want you to get hurt."

"I know. You're a good big brother, Chase." For all his flaws, many of them come from a place of good intentions.

Silence hangs between us for a few seconds.

He runs a hand along his jaw. "You and Ty, huh?"

"Are you still mad?" I readjust the blanket over my legs. Hopefully, he's starting to move past it. Otherwise it's going to be awkward around the house for everyone, including Dallas.

"Nah. When I talked to him at Overtime, I realized Ty had it bad for you. Think I knew before he did, actually. Seeing the way he is with you now lets me know you're in good hands."

"Oh, I am." I won the boyfriend lottery when I was least expecting it.

Chase frowns, and he looks thoughtful for a beat. "Still a little surprised, but I guess Bailey caught me by surprise too."

Him falling for Bailey caught us *all* by surprise, but I'm glad he did. He's been happier for it.

"Like they say, the taxicab light comes on for the right person."

"The what?" His forehead wrinkles.

"Er, never mind." I can't even begin to explain that theory to him right now.

He leans over and pulls me into a hug. "Talk to me next time something like this happens, Sera. Please."

"I will."

Chase heads upstairs to shower while I go downstairs to see

what Tyler's doing. When I peek into his room, I find him studying on his bed with a bunch of notebooks and textbooks scattered around. Something about it is endearing, and I can't help but smile. He's focusing so intently that I have to knock to get his attention.

His eyes light up when he sees me standing in the doorway, and he sets the books aside as I walk over and sit next to him

"How'd the brother-sister talk go?"

"Good," I tell him, resting a hand on his thigh. "Thank you for today. I don't think I said that earlier, and I should have."

"Of course, Ser." He cups my face and kisses me. It's tender and sweet, a question and an answer all at once. I shift on the bed, moving closer, but he doesn't escalate further. He's being gentle—almost too gentle, like he's afraid he'll break me.

When we pull apart, I look up at him.

"Ty," I whisper.

"Yeah?" Dark gray eyes peer into mine, shining with a mixture of affection and worry.

"Don't treat me differently because of this. Please." Vulnerability pours out of me. "I need to feel like I'm still desirable. Like I'm still me, and we're still us."

He raises a brow. "What you're saying is, you want me to pull your hair while I tell you to shut the fuck up and take my dick like a good girl?"

I giggle. "Something like that."

Suddenly, I'm on my back and he's between my legs, his weight pressing me into the mattress. His lips find mine, extinguishing my laughter, and everything in my body lights up. This kiss isn't gentle; it's demanding and claiming, erasing every single thought from my mind.

And in this moment, I know we're still us—and we always will be.

Chapter 36
QUESTION 53

SERAPHINA

I made an exception to my self-imposed shopping hiatus. It was for a worthy cause.

Bailey nods at me with a knowing smile. "Bet Tyler loved the jersey, Sera."

"Hope so." I glance down at my scarlet Falcons jersey that matches the one she's wearing, save for the name on the back. It was a surprise for Tyler, which means he didn't see it until we were in the stands before the game. He threw me a wave and a giant grin during warm-ups, but I haven't seen him off the ice yet.

We take a left down the hallway toward the team's dressing room, weaving past throngs of fans traveling in the other direction to exit Northview Arena. After taking several days off hockey to be with me this week, he crushed it out there on the ice. Boyd just defeated Woodbine 4–0, complete with a shutout for him, two goals for Dallas, plus a goal and an assist for my brother.

"Can I just say that you two are freaking adorable?" Siobhan clasps her fingers together, letting out a little squeal. "Maybe it's the romantic in me, but I love it. Now we can triple date."

"Let's see how Chase adjusts before we get too carried away." Even though we're not hiding things anymore, Tyler and I have kept PDA to a minimum and have stuck to sleepovers in his bedroom. Mine is too close to the living areas, running the risk of making things even more awkward than they already are.

"He's coming around," Bailey says. "Happy to report he's

past the freak out stage and is moving into acceptance. I'll keep working on him."

Stepping off to the side, we wait for the guys to come out. Chase is first, followed by Dallas. Tyler steps through the dressing room door a second later wearing one of his game day suits, and my heart flutters. He's dressed in rich navy paired with a crisp white dress shirt, both perfectly tailored to his lean frame.

When his eyes land on me, he breaks into one of the biggest smiles I've ever seen. He cuts through the crowd and heads straight for me, taking me by the wrist to tug me around the corner. Once we're out of sight, he spins me in a 360-degree turn to show him the name on the back, then fences me in against the red-and-black cinder-block wall.

He nudges my nose with his. "Nice jersey, Tink."

"You like it?" I ask, wrapping my arms around his waist. He smells delicious as ever, and the clean scent of his cologne is going straight to my head.

"Fuck yeah. I'm going to like it even better with nothing underneath later."

He dips his head to kiss me. Before our lips connect, we're interrupted by footsteps echoing on the tiled flooring.

"Ty! Where the fuck are you guys?" My brother's voice bellows. "James and I are heading out."

Figures. Chase has given us our blessing, and he *still* manages to kill the mood.

Hand in hand, we cut through the parking lot to Tyler's SUV. Chase's black truck is idling beside it. Even though we're both headed to our mom's place for family dinner, my brother insisted on taking his own vehicle. I'm not sure I want to know why. If they show up late, it'll be painfully self-explanatory.

"Are you nervous about meeting my family?" I ask Tyler. I wish my mom could've come with us to watch tonight, but with her ongoing cancer treatment, she's susceptible to infections and can't be around large crowds.

He pulls open the passenger side door for me. "Nah. I'm looking forward to it."

For the first half of the drive, we listen to a spicy audiobook we started together earlier this week. It grows more and more heated, doing the same to us. Then I realize we need to calm down before we can be functional around other people and we switch to playing more twenty-one questions—which might as well be renamed infinity questions at this point.

"Question fifty-one," I say, dialing up my seat heater to maximum. When it's cold, I like to roast my entire body through the leather; it's the only effective way to warm up. "What position would you play in hockey if you couldn't be goalie?"

Tyler runs a hand along his jaw. "That's a tough one. I like the idea of preventing goals, but scoring would be fun."

"You can still score later tonight."

He laughs at my bad joke, shaking his head. "Fuck, I love you." Shoulder checking, he switches lanes in advance of the exit coming up. "Question fifty-two: What's on your travel bucket list?"

This one is easy. I have a Pinterest board full of pictures from Santorini. The rugged cliffs; the azure sea; the beaches filled with lava sand and pebbles; and the cliffsides with whitewashed architecture. It's my secret honeymoon dream destination. If we ever get married, it's where I'd want to go.

"Greece. Definitely Greece. Santorini has these amazing cave hotels with swim-up pools and it looks super romantic. What's yours?"

"I'm on board with that. Spain is up there for me too. Maybe Portugal. We'll check them all off eventually, but we can start with yours."

A warm, fuzzy feeling settles in me at hearing that.

Moments later, he eases his car up the driveway to my mom's sprawling white house and shifts it into park. When we get inside, I hand my mother the flowers and wine we brought. She sets them aside, then proceeds to hug me for at least two solid minutes, fighting back tears.

"Sera."

I fight to breathe as she squeezes me tighter. "Hey, Mom."

We haven't seen each other since I told her about my BRCA results on the phone. It crushed me to hear the guilt in her voice. I spoke to her again after my genetic counseling appointment, but there's not a lot to say. Very little can be done at this stage other than plan for the eventualities in the future. I've done what I can in that regard, and now all I can do is make peace with it. At least I have a good support system now that I've told everybody.

When she finally releases me, I introduce her to Tyler, and she hugs him too. She's a hugger at the best of times, and she's extra emotional in light of everything else going on.

"Can we help you with dinner?" I ask.

"No, no." She waves me off, sniffling. "Go show Tyler around, and I'll call you when it's done. Where's your brother?"

You don't want to know.

"On their way. I'm sure they'll be here soon."

I lead Tyler up the winding wooden staircase to the second floor, past the spare bedroom and Chase's room, all the way to my old bedroom at the end of the hall. Unsurprisingly, it's painted hot pink and it's covered in posters, still the epitome of a teenage girl's room—just the way I left it.

He picks up a photo of me in a tutu from when I was five. "Aww. You used to dance?"

"Not well," I admit. "Chase got all the coordination and athleticism in our family."

While Tyler is scanning through the other photos scattered along my dresser, an email pops up on my phone, and I glance at the preview. My heart stops. I read and reread it, confirming I'm not hallucinating.

"Oh my god." My voice climbs to a squeak.

"What?" Tyler's next to me in a flash. "Is everything okay?"

To say he's become a little overprotective lately is an understatement.

I tilt the phone screen to show him. His brow furrows as he reads the message, and his face erupts into a huge smile.

"Holy fuck. That's amazing." He wraps his arms around me, picking me up off the ground. "I'm so proud of you, Ser."

Chase and Bailey show up not too long after, and we sit down for dinner once my stepfather, Rick, gets home from work. I wasn't the biggest fan of his in the past, especially when I was a teenager, but he's stepped it up a lot since my mother got sick and he's grown on me. Grudgingly.

Ever the hostess, Mom has set up the dining table with a crisp linen tablecloth, candles, and her good china. We dive into her roasted chicken and potatoes as we go around the table catching up and making small talk. Tyler fits right in, and I'm struck by how easy it is to have him here. How easy it is with him in general, really. I never thought it could be like this with someone.

When the conversation dies down enough to give me an opening, I summon my courage.

"I have some news." Everyone looks at me, and my anxiety spikes. "I won a writing contest, and one of my poems is going to be published in an anthology from *Revolve Magazine*."

Beneath the table, Tyler squeezes my knee affectionately.

Bailey clamps a hand over her mouth. "Oh my god, Sera. That's huge. *Revolve* is really a big deal. I have a few friends who submitted for that contest."

"I didn't know you still wrote." Mom gives me a warm smile. "That's wonderful, honey. I'm proud of you."

"That's awesome," Chase says, spearing a potato with his fork. "Aren't you glad you got dragged to all my games when we were kids? Really paying off now."

I stick my tongue out at him. "You would try to take credit for it."

"I'm just kidding, Sera. It's fucking cool."

Our mother gasps. "Language, Chase. We're at the dinner table."

I can't even attempt to hide my laugh. At this point, I'm not sure how she hasn't given up on his potty mouth. It's the definition of a lost cause.

"Can we read the poem, Sera?" she asks, returning her attention to me.

I hesitate because the subject matter is still a little too raw, and it feels akin to pulling back the curtain on my brain. "I'll send it later and you can read it when I'm not around. Does that work?"

Understanding crosses her face. "Of course, sweetheart."

We linger at the table, talking over dinner and dessert—including two pieces of my mom's famous homemade raspberry cheesecake for me. Mom hugs me approximately ten more times on our way out the door, fussing over me, then tells me how much she loves Tyler. Hearing it makes me happier than I expected.

Tyler's arm slides around my waist as our boots crunch over the snow on our way to his car. It's a crisp, cool evening. Out in the country where we are, the stars blanket the sky, far more visible than in the city back home. We come to stand beside his running car, and he tugs open the door for me.

"Thanks for coming tonight, Hades."

"Thanks for inviting me." He pauses, grinning. "Well, technically, Chase invited me. But I'm going to pretend you wanted me here."

Rocking onto my tiptoes, I kiss his cheek. "I definitely did."

◆ ◆ ◆

"Is this what you had in mind?" I ask Tyler.

He comes to a halt in his bedroom doorway, clutching a glass of water in each hand, and stares at me standing before him in nothing but his red jersey. Doesn't blink. Doesn't move. Doesn't say a word.

I think he might be glitching again.

After a beat, he recovers and closes the door behind him. Then he crosses the room to me in a few broad strides, setting the water aside on his nightstand.

"It's exactly what I had in mind. You're fucking perfect." Large hands scoop me up and lift me off the ground, carrying me several steps to his bed. I sink into the mattress as he places me down beneath him, his hair tumbling over his forehead. He's broad and lean above me, a sinewy frame sculpted from hours on the ice and at the gym.

"Seeing you out there tonight was everything, Tink." His eyes trace my face in that thoughtful, pensive way of his. "I love you."

I swear, my heart grows a little more every time he says that to me.

"I love you," I tell him.

Threading his fingers through the roots of my hair, he dips his head, and his lips crush mine, claiming and possessive. My palms glide up his bare arms, surfing along the curves of his muscles to grip his shoulders. I wrap my legs around his waist, reveling in how our centers perfectly align, and when I shift beneath him, he draws in a sharp breath, hardening even more.

Tender kisses land on my neck, his lips hot against my skin as his hands slip beneath the fabric of the jersey. It's not long before all of our clothes have been abandoned on the floor and we're completely naked.

Tyler sits back on his knees before me, pumping his length with a hungry look on his face. "Play with your pussy for me."

Our eyes stay locked as my fingers slide down my stomach, reaching lower until they find my swollen, aching clit.

"*Oh.*" Pleasure rockets through me, and a breathy moan slips through my lips.

He lets out a low, almost pained sound. "Keep going."

I do as he says, working in small circles as the pleasure blossoms in my core. It's both torture and relief; he's so close and he's what my body really wants.

Fisting his cock, he draws closer until he's hovering over me, kissing me again.

"I'm on birth control," I pant, my hips instinctively arching to meet him. "I haven't been with anyone else."

Tyler groans and looks down, grazing my slick entrance with the tip. "I haven't either. I haven't even looked at anyone." He drags his cock along my slit, watching for my reaction. "Ask me to fuck you."

My lower back arches, seeking his body, and I whimper. "Please fuck me."

He tsks. "You look so pretty when you beg."

We both cry out as he thrusts forward, sinking deeper until he reaches resistance. Tension coils in my center when he begins to move, rolling his hips with divine precision, nudging a spot only he's ever found. Somehow, knowing there's nothing between us drives me even more wild.

Sweet bliss washes over my body, and my toes curl, a needy whimper falling from my lips. The way he moves is a revelation. Everything he does is the perfect blend of gentle and rough, giving and taking. It's slow, languorous fucking; an unhurried exploration of each other's bodies.

He pins my wrists above my head with one hand, going deeper. "This tight little pussy is mine."

I gasp as another shockwave of pleasure rocks me. "What about your cock?"

"It's yours, Ser. Every inch belongs to you."

Slowly, he pulls back until we're nearly separated, and I feel empty at the sudden loss of his girth. I watch his six-pack flex as he drives forward, filling me completely. Pleasure lights me up from the inside out, and I moan, hitching my legs tighter around him.

Releasing my wrists, his broad palm slides beneath my lower back, lifting me to him. When he pumps into me, I arch against the pillow with a wordless cry. My eyelids flutter shut at the new sensation, my fingernails biting into his lower back. Wave after wave crashes over me, blurring into one. I cling to him as everything grows hazy, and I begin to lose myself in him.

After holding back at first, he gives me everything, thrusting harder and faster until we're both hovering on the brink. His mouth collides with mine, capturing my cries, and our kiss turns sloppy, desperate. He picks up my leg, wrapping it higher around his torso, and his next plunge fills me so deeply that I feel him everywhere.

Euphoria short-circuits my brain. "Come in me. *Please*."

When he drives into me again, he hits exactly where I need it most. I become weightless beneath him at the same time he shudders with a groan, his body tensing over mine.

"Goddamn it, Ser." I feel him throb between my legs with release, and he drops his forehead to mine, winded. Seconds pass, and we stay tangled together, breathing heavily. "You've unlocked another cheat code. I'm fucked."

"I promise to only use my powers for good, like when I'm already coming."

Tyler laughs, kissing my shoulder. "It's a deal."

We reluctantly pull apart and he cleans me up before we get ready for bed. By the time we crawl back underneath the covers, it's late. My body is tired, my heart is full, and all I can think is how lucky I am. After feeling lost for such a long time, now I know exactly where I'm going.

"Question fifty-three." He pulls me to him with my back to his chest, pressing his lips to the base of my neck. "Do you have any idea how much I love you?"

"As much as I love you?"

"More. I would do anything for you, Tink. Name it and it's yours."

EPILOGUE

SERAPHINA

THREE-ISH YEARS LATER...

Of my twenty-three years on this planet, this has got to be one of the most embarrassing moments I've had.

My hands tug at the denim, but it won't budge. "Ugh!"

"What's wrong, Tink?" Tyler walks around the corner, toweling off his wet hair. He's wearing nothing but black boxer briefs, and even though we just showered together, his lean, toned body briefly distracts me from my predicament.

I'm standing in the middle of our walk-in closet trying to get dressed. Emphasis on *trying*. The jeans I've been living in for the past two months are suddenly several sizes too small. I got a little overzealous trying to force them up, and now they're stuck halfway up my thighs.

That's right. I'm trapped in my pants. It looks every bit as ridiculous as it sounds.

"Can you help me?" I gesture to myself. "I don't want to lose my balance trying to get these off."

It's a valid concern given how clumsy I've been this pregnancy. Over the past few months, I've broken two phones, sprained my big toe, and spilled Chanel Rouge Noir nail polish all over our off-white carpet. I also shattered a glass yesterday when I turned around and knocked it off the counter with my belly.

A smile emerges across his lips and he sets aside his towel, walking over to me. He scoops me up effortlessly, carrying me to our bed. If he notices my weight gain, he doesn't let on. He's been amazing in a number of other ways during this journey, including holding my hair back through morning sickness, tolerating my weird cravings, and humoring my aversions—even when I had to ban coffee from the apartment for a month because the very smell of it made me sick.

"This is ridiculous," I mutter. "What would I have done if you weren't home?"

He chuckles, gently lowering me to sit on the edge of the mattress. "We'll get a chair for the closet."

"I'm officially boycotting denim."

"Also a valid solution." Kneeling in front of me, he gently peels the jeans down my thighs and sets them next to me on the bed. He cups my belly, his warm palms molding around the curve. "You're beautiful."

I glance down at his hands resting on my bare stomach. They used to eclipse my bump, but my bump is rapidly catching up.

Pregnancy symptoms hit me early and haven't subsided. Six months in, I have to pee constantly, I'm exhausted but I can't sleep, chicken tastes weird, and now that I'm past the morning sickness stage, I have killer heartburn. According to the internet, that means our baby is going to have a full head of hair, but that's little consolation when I have to sleep upright.

I might be a little cranky too. Just a tad.

"I'm enormous."

"You're supposed to get bigger, Ser." Tyler caresses the swell of my skin with his thumbs, planting a kiss above my navel. "I love your belly. That's my baby in there."

It's hard to stay cranky when he says things like that.

He reaches past me and grabs the tub of mango belly butter off the nightstand, unscrewing the lid. I heave a sigh of relief as he rubs a dab into my skin, instantly relieving the dry, itchy skin that's been plaguing me lately.

I run my fingers through his still-damp hair. "Thank you."

"Always." As he moves on to the other half of my belly, I scan the array of tattoos inked into his upper body, zeroing in on the Tinker Bell artfully blended into the rest of his sleeve. She's been drawn to look like me. He got it when we were apart during my fourth year of college, and he picked the left side so it would be closer to his heart.

It's even harder to stay cranky when I remember that.

My gaze travels lower, to the list of dates etched along his lower ribs on the same side. My birthday. The date we met. The date we moved in together permanently after I graduated. And a blank space below for all the milestones to come.

"I love you." My chest pulls tight as tears spring to my eyes. I'm so lucky. I couldn't have asked for a better life partner. We just got back from a babymoon in Greece, and I'm more in love with him than ever.

Welcome to pregnancy. It's an emotional smorgasbord.

"I love you. Both of you." He plants another kiss on the top of my belly, then one on my cheek. Pushing to stand, he offers me his hand to help me up. While not strictly necessary, it's definitely appreciated. "Let's finish getting dressed and go for a walk, wifey. Some fresh air will do you good."

Though we might as well be married, technically we're not engaged yet. It's my fault; I said I didn't want to plan a wedding in the midst of a pregnancy and a move. I regret it now, because house-hunting has been a total bust.

Heading back into the closet, I pick out a stretchy black maternity dress. There's less chance I'll get trapped in it later—but with the way my luck is going, it's still a possibility.

The elevator brings us down to the ground floor, and we step out onto the street, greeted by warm spring air and the noise of New York City. I love it here: the cars, the noise, the chaos. Something about it makes me feel alive.

Tyler threads his fingers through mine, steering me on a now-familiar route through our neighborhood. We start near our favorite deli, pass the yoga studio I attend several days a week, and approach the only dry cleaners he trusts with his custom suits. On the far side of the block is Lily's Ice Cream, which I've frequented an embarrassing number of times since we moved to the area.

Sadness glimmers within me as I steal a glance down the street. "I'm still bummed about losing that place."

After months of searching, we finally found the perfect place a few weeks ago. A sprawling brownstone over twice the size of our current apartment. Five bedrooms, four bathrooms, tons of living space. I have an entire Pinterest board full of inspiration saved for it, including the exact shade of pink paint I want in my office and the perfect white kitchen to recreate.

Sadly, it's a seller's market. By the time our broker submitted an offer, it was already pending. I was heartbroken. I still am. Hormones might be a factor in how hard I'm taking it. Tyler was disappointed, but not nearly as sad as me. I have the emotional resiliency of a toddler these days. I need naps and frequent snacks like one too.

He squeezes my hand. "We'll find something soon, Tink. I promise."

I guess it wasn't *perfect*. The interior was dated. It needed some paint and renovations. Still, that knowledge is little consolation when the things that can't be fixed—like the location and the bones of the place—were solid.

Panic looms in the back of my mind. "What are we going to do with the baby?" My nesting instincts have kicked into overdrive. We picked a small apartment knowing it would be temporary, and without a permanent place, I feel unsettled.

"We still have time. He's not going to be here for a few more months."

When we come to a halt at the corner, I turn away from the street in question, tugging Tyler with me.

"Come on," he says softly. "Let's grab something from Lily's."

Tempting, but making it there requires passing by the brownstone.

"Maybe another time."

"I'll get triple chocolate and share with you," he offers.

It's a dirty trick. Triple chocolate is my second favorite, which means I can get strawberry cheesecake for myself and then eat half of his. The temptation is almost too much to refuse.

"Fine." I can't avoid this street forever. Much as I like to contribute to the local economy, it's hard to justify ordering dessert delivery several times a week and guilt-tipping the courier $20 because it's only two blocks away.

As we pass the row of brownstones that house the unit we lost, I make a point to look the other way. Tyler slows to a stop and steers me directly toward it.

"Let's go look for a sec."

"What?" I protest. "It's not—we can't. The other buyers got it. There's been a sold sign out here for two weeks." It's gone now, so the new owners must be moving in soon.

He ignores my objection, gently steering me up the steps. Once we're standing at the front door, he pulls a key from his pocket.

"What are you doing?" I ask.

Instead of replying, he unlocks the door and motions for me to go first. I step inside, and all the air leaves my lungs. It's even more beautiful than before. The walls have been freshly painted a creamy white and the hardwood floors gleam, newly refinished.

It's everything I'd pictured in my head.

I look back and forth between the interior and Tyler. "I'm confused."

"The other sale fell through," he tells me. "It's ours."

"Ours?" My throat tightens, and hot tears fill my eyes.

"The sale closed two weeks ago. Then I called in some favors and got a couple of trades in here to do the work so you wouldn't have to worry about it. All we need to do is hire movers and we'll be good to go. Your mom said she'd come help us get settled before the baby comes."

"You're kidding." I blink back the moisture blurring my vision, threatening to overflow.

"Dead serious."

"I can't believe you didn't tell me." I sob a laugh and throw my arms around him.

He squeezes me, being mindful of the belly. "You were so crushed the first time. I didn't want to get your hopes up until I knew we'd get it for sure. There was a bit of a bidding war."

"Bidding war?" I'm not sure I want to know the details. We can afford it, but the initial asking price involved a lot of zeroes.

I'm a sniffling mess as he leads me through the rooms one by one. All of the details are perfect, down to the hardware on the doors.

We step into the kitchen, which looks like a completely different house than before. Last time I was here, it was full of dark wood and even darker green tile. Now it's bright and airy, filled with white cabinets, trimmed marble countertops, and accented by glossy tile backsplash. It's so beautiful I'd live in the kitchen itself if given the chance.

"You stalked my Pinterest, huh?" I ask Tyler.

He grins. "Every board. Come on, let's go look at your office."

Fingers intertwined with mine, he leads me upstairs, and we take the first bedroom on the left. It's the smallest one, which frees up the remaining bedrooms for the rest of our eventual children—should we even stay in New York City that long. With his career, there's no way to predict.

The office is equally amazing. A fresh coat of soft, warm pink adorns the walls, and a row of newly installed white built-in bookcases sits along one side. Once I throw in a desk, it'll be exactly what I always wanted. It's the perfect place to finish my manuscript before the baby comes.

"Thank you." I turn to Tyler and stand on my tiptoes to reach him, brushing my lips to his. "This is amazing. I love it. I love you."

"I love you," he murmurs. "So much."

He gently releases me, kneeling down as he does. At first I think he's tying his shoe, but then I see him pull something out of his pocket.

Pregnancy brain has me a little slow to catch up, and it takes a second for me to register what he's holding. Between his thumb and finger is a massive cushion-cut pink diamond set on a thin rose-gold band. It's stunning and exactly what I would have picked.

"Question one thousand one hundred sixty-two," he says. "Will you marry me?"

"Hades," I whisper, choking back a sob. "Of course I will."

I give him my left hand and he slips on the ring easily, evidently having sized it for my swollen pregnant fingers. Holding it out, I admire the way it sparkles in the light. Did I mention it's massive?

Tyler stands and draws me to him, kissing me softly. "I love you."

"I love you." My tears start to overflow again. I'm overwhelmed in the best possible way. "Thank you. You didn't have to do all of this for me."

"I would do anything for you, Tink."

Bonus Chapter #1
WINNING

TYLER

"Daddy?" Bauer's tiny hand tugs at mine.

I kneel, bringing the two of us to eye level. His sandy hair is tousled, he's got a red marker smudge on one cheek, and he's wearing a replica of my New York jersey. It's one size too big, nearly down to his knees.

He's the cutest toddler around. Not that I'm biased.

"What's up, buddy?"

He raises his arms. "Carry?"

At two, he's more than old enough to walk around himself. But someone once told me there will be a last time you pick up your child, and you won't know it was the last time. It's stuck with me ever since. Plus, those big brown eyes peering back at me are impossible to say no to.

I hoist him onto my hip, balancing him with one arm, and carry him into the primary bedroom where Seraphina is getting ready. With her back turned, you wouldn't even realize she's pregnant. Then she reaches for something on the marble counter and her belly comes into view. My heart swells as I look at her. Love doesn't even come close to capturing it.

She glances at us through the mirror as she fastens her earrings, and her mouth pulls into a smile. "There are my boys."

"Doesn't Mommy look pretty?" I ask him.

"Pwetty," he echoes approvingly.

"Thank you." Seraphina bustles up and smooshes his cheeks, planting a string of noisy kisses on each one. "You're going to be good for Grandma tonight, right?"

He nods. "Yeah!"

It's easy to be good when Grandma is a pushover. Tonight will surely consist of more treats and television than is developmentally advisable, but she adores Bauer, so I can't complain. Watching a two-year-old overnight is no small feat, and I appreciate that we have Seraphina's family nearby to help us out. It helps that the league's awards ceremony this year is being held in New York City, so we didn't have to travel to attend.

I examine Bauer a little closer. He still smells like sunscreen from when we were at the park earlier, and he's more than a little messy from our adventures around the city. I'd love to know where kids get all their energy from. We spent the day outside of the house to give Seraphina a break, and I don't think I sat down more than once.

"Can your mom give him a bath before bed, Ser? I think he got chocolate ice cream in his hair."

She laughs. "I'm sure that can be arranged."

We say a quick round of good-byes before I grab our overnight bags and we get into the car waiting outside. Seraphina is more upset than Bauer is at the prospect of spending a night apart. She works from home with her writing, and while we have part-time childcare, she and Bauer are attached at the hip most of the time. That's also why she's nursing heavy amounts of guilt about the new baby arriving in a few months.

The limo pulls away from the curb, and I turn to her. "You look amazing, Tink."

Her dark purple dress hugs her body perfectly, contrasting against her fair skin. But it's her face I love the most. She's so fucking beautiful I want to pinch myself every day.

"You clean up pretty well too, Hades." She angles her head, fussing with my tie. Her eyes lift to meet mine, questioning. "Are you nervous?"

"A little."

Her lips tug. "You're not breathing."

At her reminder, my chest expands with an inhale. She's right; I wasn't. I've been nervous ever since I learned I was nominated for goalie of the year. It recognizes the goaltender adjudged to be the best for a given season—in other words, it's a huge fucking deal. Once upon a time, winning this was a childhood dream of mine.

All the other nominees are formidable, Caleb Brown included. After I beat him out for New York's starting goalie, he ended up in Tampa, but we're nearly tied in terms of statistics.

I've mentally prepared myself to lose, and I've made peace with it. I'm having a hot season, but the competition is stiff.

"Is it hot in here?" I ask, craning my neck in search of the climate control.

She glances over my shoulder. "The thermostat says sixty-six degrees, so I'm going to go with no."

"I'll be fine. How are you two doing?" I rest my hand on her small bump.

"Pretty good. She stopped using my bladder as a punching bag and that was much appreciated." Her mouth scrunches. "I'm worried about Bauer, though."

"He's living his best toddler life with your mom, Tink. Promise."

"I know." She sighs, resting her head on my shoulder, and takes my hand in hers. "Tonight will be fun. I can't remember the last time I was out with a group of adults and got to dress up."

"Exactly. Been awhile since I had you all to myself too." Though with how tired she is lately, there's a reasonable chance she's going to pass out cold from exhaustion. With as much as I travel, I appreciate even sleeping in the same bed together. An empty bed is one of the worst parts of being on the road.

"I went to bed extra early last night, so I'd have more energy to stay up," she says, as if reading my mind. "I want to celebrate, because I think you're going to win."

I glance down at the platinum wedding band on my left ring finger. "I'm leaving with you, so I already did."

We check into the hotel quickly before driving to the venue a few blocks away. After a quick walk on the red carpet for photos, we go inside to mingle over cocktails. I grab Seraphina a pink mocktail from the bar and a beer for myself, then find her in the crowd where she's talking to Siobhan.

Chase strides up with a very pregnant Bailey in tow, flashing us a grin. He thumps me on the back harder than necessary because he likes to take advantage of the fact that he's family and I can't kill him. "Ready to take home that award?"

"It'll be a pleasant surprise if it happens. You ready to present?"

"I'm always ready."

Seraphina points at him with her glass. "There's something highly ironic about *you* presenting the award for best sportsmanship and gentlemanly conduct."

I suspect that's why the league did it—having one of the biggest antagonizers in the league present it is their own little inside joke.

"It'll be even funnier if Ward wins," Chase says.

"I think he will," I tell him. "He's the favorite by far."

Dallas reappears from getting his drink at the bar, and we take our seats in the auditorium to watch this year's opening act. It's a country band, and Seraphina hums along with every song.

While the host is entertaining enough and the program runs smoothly, I grow increasingly restless as the night carries on. The award I'm nominated for isn't till halfway through the program, which makes for a long time to wait.

Finally, Chase leaves his seat to present the award that comes before mine. I'm not a fan of being the center of attention, but he's clearly unfazed as he strolls on stage and comes to stand before the microphone. In fact, he almost looks like he was born to be up there.

After cracking a few jokes at the nominee's expenses, he unseals the envelope and slides out the card.

"This year's award goes to . . ." He pauses, laughing as he reads it. "Dallas Ward."

I knew it. He's the most squeaky clean player in the league, and everyone knows it.

Dallas glances at us with pure shock across his face, and Siobhan's face lights up, her eyes welling with tears.

"Congrats, Ward. You deserve it," I say as he slips past us down the aisle.

He gives a brief, witty, and perfectly on-brand acceptance speech before returning to join us. Time slows to a crawl as the next presenter takes the stage. Every word he says seems like it's being played in slow motion. When he slips out the card and reads it, I'm certain I'm hallucinating.

Did he just say my name?

"Ty." Seraphina nudges me.

"Did I win?" I ask her, still in disbelief.

She presses her lips to my cheek. "You sure did. Now go up there and get it."

As I push to stand, a million thoughts swirl through my mind. Winning something like this is a type of recognition most players never receive. It's everything I worked for—or so I once thought. But what really matters is the woman sitting next to me. Anything in addition to that is a bonus.

Bonus Chapter #2
DONE

SERAPHINA

My boobs are leaking.

This is pretty par for the course postpartum. Normally it isn't a huge deal, but right now I'm wearing an expensive wedding dress and I'm about to walk down the aisle in front of more than two hundred guests.

"Ser?" Tyler pushes open the door, breaking into a tentative smile when our eyes lock. Technically, it's before the wedding, but right now, I don't care. I need him. "Bailey said you wanted to see me. Is everything all right?"

"Yes. I mean, no. We're great. I'm not having cold feet or anything. I'm just feeling frazzled with everything going on." I gesture to myself frantically. "And now my boobs are leaking, and I'm scared it's going to stain my dress and—"

He presses a finger to my lips, silencing me. "Slow down, Tink. Let's handle one thing at a time, okay? What can we do about the leaking?"

The one thing I hate most: the dreaded pump. Nursing is fine, but that electric torture device is another thing entirely.

"Pump, I guess?" I say reluctantly. "Give me a minute and I'll be right back."

Because there's no way I'm doing that in front of my husband-to-be while I'm wearing a lacy white dress, I make him wait in the other room of our honeymoon suite, then stick the milk in the fridge for my mom to grab later. It takes the edge off my discomfort, but I'm still nervous about walking down the aisle.

Tyler is sitting with an ankle crossed over his knee, waiting for me in the living area. I was so worked up that I completely failed to register how hot he looks in his wedding tuxedo. There's something about the tattoos and formal tux combo that's working for him. And for me. He's definitely getting some wedding night sex later.

"Okay." I square my shoulders and clear my throat, standing in the doorway. "Can we start over? Let's do our first look again."

He crosses the room to me, breaking into a broad smile as he runs his hands down my sides, giving me a once-over. "You look fucking amazing, Tink. It's unreal how pretty you are."

Warmth creeps across my cheeks; even after all this time, he can still make me blush.

"Thank you," I say, looping my arms around his waist. "You look pretty handsome yourself."

His hand cups my chin, tipping my face up to his, and his expression softens. "Are you feeling any better?"

Just having him here has taken most of the edge off. We'd been separated for the last day and a half by wedding obligations, spending time with our respective bridesmaids and groomsmen, entertaining family, and doing everything *but* spending time together. Ironic, given the purpose of a wedding.

"A little. Today has just been a lot, you know? A lot of people, a lot of things to be done, and a lot of stress."

"I get it." He nods. "When you get out there, just keep your eyes on me. The ceremony will be quick, and after that, things will be more fun. Not to mention, then you'll be my wife."

Giddiness courses through me from head to toe at those words.

"I love the sound of that."

"Me too. And I love you. So much." He dips his head to kiss me. The second our mouths meet, all of my worries vanish, and my lips part, granting him access. We both draw in a breath as his tongue sweeps against mine. We're probably messing up my makeup, and I don't even care.

Breaking apart from our kiss, he skims his lips along the edge of my jaw and travels lower, sparking a craving that's gone unfulfilled for several days.

"How much time until we have to be out there?" I ask him, arching my neck.

"A little over an hour," he murmurs, nipping at my collarbone.

"If you can fasten me back into this dress after, then you can take it off right now."

He husks a laugh. "Done."

Bonus Chapter #3
MADE IT

SERAPHINA

"I'm nervous."

My agent, Tatiana, fusses around me, straightening my outfit. "Don't be nervous. You'll be great."

I'm due to go on national television in four minutes to be interviewed about my latest book of poetry. It's my third, and to say it took off unexpectedly would be an understatement. It went full-on viral and hit various bestseller lists. I'm still trying to process it. It's been wonderful, but it's also been a lot. With the attention has come a fair amount of hate, and it's hard not to let that get to you sometimes.

"Remember what we said," she tells me.

Stick to safe topics. No politics. Don't be controversial. Smile. Be gracious.

"I will."

After another lipstick touch-up and some smoothing of my hair, I'm ushered out onto the set for my first big interview of my career with Shannon Summerside. Her show, *The Vibe*, is the staple of American daytime television; she's basically the next Oprah. Landing this spot was a huge win for my career.

She greets me warmly as I sit down across from her, and we launch into an introduction of who I am, what my latest book is, and a bit about my family. While I try to play along like Tatiana instructed me, I'm always a bit edgy when talking about the kids, because I don't like them being thrust into the public eye. Tyler's had a couple fans who've crossed the line into scary territory, and I value our privacy and safety above everything else.

"How do you balance motherhood and your career?" Shannon

asks, moving into her next line of questions. "Especially with a husband who travels like yours does?"

This question always irks me. It isn't inherently bad; it's that people don't ask men the same. Mothers are assumed to be the default parent. Truthfully, that isn't the case when Tyler is home. He's as involved as I am, if not more.

"I always find it funny no one ever asks Tyler the same question." I can practically hear Tatiana's head exploding from where I'm sitting, so I quickly pivot. "But we have a part-time nanny, and my mother helps out as well. I'm very fortunate, and I have a lot of help. I want to be crystal clear about that, because there's no way I could juggle everything on my own. When Tyler is home, he's a wonderful partner and a hands-on father."

She gives me a smile that verges on forced. "I see. You're very lucky then."

"Very," I agree.

"Let's touch on your ADHD for a minute," Shannon says, crossing her legs. "It seems like such a common diagnosis nowadays. Don't you think everyone is a little ADHD?"

Now *my* head is about to explode. Shannon is young enough that she should know better than to buy into some of the old-school type of thinking and stigma around ADHD. At least, you'd hope.

Drawing in a breath, I search for a diplomatic response. "No. It isn't ADHD until it causes a certain level of impairment in your functioning. It impacts my life in ways neurotypical people don't experience. For instance, I get overwhelmed when I have too much to do, and then I get stuck unable to do anything. I also struggle to finish tasks, even if something is 80 percent complete."

"Mmm-hmm." She nods. "You don't think that comes down to more of a self-discipline issue?"

I bite my tongue, channeling every shred of my patience. Thank god I have two young kids who've strengthened it over the past few years.

"I don't. It's not the same. Think of it like living parts of life on Hard Mode, even when medicated."

The interview shifts into talking about my BRCA diagnosis before wrapping up with an opportunity for me to plug my local book signing next month. Shannon poses several other irritating questions in the process. By the time I step offstage, I'm both annoyed and thankful I didn't lose my temper completely. I'm not sure I was as personable as I wanted to be, but she didn't make it easy.

Tatiana speed walks up to me, her eyes wide. "Sera . . ."

"Don't say it, Tati. That wasn't my fault."

She sighs. "I know. You handled it well. I'm going to give a list of firm instructions for any interviews going forward."

My shoulders slump with relief. "Thank you."

When I glance behind Tatiana, I spot Tyler off to the side, and my heart flutters. He's wearing Calliope in the baby carrier, holding Bauer's hand. There's something incredibly sexy about a hot, tattooed guy holding a baby and standing with a cute little kid. It makes me want to make more babies with him immediately. Which is probably the plan in the near future.

I walk over to them, giving each a kiss hello. "I wasn't expecting to see you here."

"They wanted to come say hi," he tells me. "I thought we could catch a ride with you home. Or maybe go out for lunch to celebrate."

"Lunch sounds nice," I say, taking Calliope's chubby baby hand. At six months old, she's in the cute baby sweet spot. She's interactive, giggly, and so much fun. "How's your day been so far?"

"Good!" Bauer chirps. "Daddy took me to McDonald's for breakfast. Then we went to the toy store, and he let me pick out three things."

The last thing Bauer needs is more toys. He's the first grandchild on Tyler's side of the family, and my mom loves to spoil him. As it is, his room could probably double as a toy store showroom. I secretly donate stuff from time to time and he doesn't even notice.

"Did he now?" I nudge my husband.

Tyler shrugs, because he's terrible at playing bad cop. "Calliope needed a new Wubbanub, and things sort of spiraled from there once we arrived."

"Let me get changed and I'll meet you back out here in a few," I say.

Tatiana talks me down as I get back into my street clothes, and I'm much calmer when I meet them near the exit. Bauer is playing with a Transformers toy I don't recognize, and I assume it's one of the three purchased earlier.

Tyler pushes the door open, holding it for me. I take Bauer by the hand and usher him out onto the street. When I step outside, the full reality of the interview hits me, and I groan.

Turning to face my husband, I ask, "On a scale of one to ten, how badly do you think I botched that interview?"

"Are you kidding, Tink?" He squeezes me. "You nailed it."

"I said things I shouldn't have."

He laces his fingers with mine as we walk. "You said what you were thinking, and that's why I love you."

We stroll a few more blocks until we arrive at one of our favorite Italian restaurants, a family-friendly place owned by a couple who knows us by name. They fawn over the kids before bringing Bauer crayons and a sheet to color, leaving us to decide what to order. I take Calliope from Tyler and nurse her, perusing the menu with my free hand.

My phone lights up with a notification, and I move to lock it because I try not to work much during family time. Before I do, I can't help but read the message preview.

Tatiana: You hit it. Top 10! You're number 4.

Oh my god.

My throat tightens, my eyes flooding with moisture. I stare at her message, reading and rereading it. This was a big, hairy, audacious goal of mine; one you set and never think you'll hit.

I'd been floating around the bestseller lists for a couple of weeks, but never this close to the top. I've never broken into the top ten. I didn't think I ever would. Even on my darkest days, when I felt like quitting, Tyler insisted it would happen.

"Ser?" He touches my arm, ducking his head to catch my eye. "Is everything okay?"

I swallow, blinking back happy years. "Yeah. Tati said I hit—I hit number four."

He grins. "I always knew you would."

Bonus Chapter #4
THE BEST THING

TYLER

I had no idea how chaotic Thanksgiving would be with six kids running around our place. Or five kids, rather, since Hendrix isn't exactly running yet.

Bailey tsks. "Your son is showing off again, Chase."

"Can't imagine where he gets that from." Seraphina rolls her eyes, shifting to burp Hendrix on her shoulder.

Chase smirks. "That's your nephew you're talking about, and he's just skating."

"No . . ." Bailey cranes her neck. "He's *definitely* showing off."

Even though he's the younger of the two, Chase and Bailey's son, Gabe, is currently skating circles around Bauer in our backyard rink. He's a hockey prodigy in the making, and he reminds everyone of it often. Bauer is pissed—that much is clear from his body language. From where we're sitting in the living room overlooking the yard, I can't hear what they're saying, but they're exchanging words.

"We're gonna need to work on Bauer's mindset," I tell Seraphina. "Love him, but he's a sore loser." He wants to play goal like I do, and we're in for a rough ride if that's the case.

"You think?" She shakes her head. "He tipped over the Monopoly Junior board when he lost last week. By the way, where are the girls? I haven't heard a peep from them in ages."

"Last I saw, Reese, Tatum, and Callie were all playing dolls quietly in Callie's room." Bailey points down the hall to where the bedrooms are.

Seraphina huffs a laugh. "I swear they're wired completely differently."

Loud shouting carries inside from the backyard, and I look over to see Bauer and Gabe engaged in some kind of standoff. Bauer is gesturing angrily, and Gabe is shaking his head.

"Let's go play referee, Carter." I stand up and smack Chase on the back of the head as I pass by.

Once we get outside, the tension between the kids abates, and we play a bit of shinny with them until it gets dark. Having several acres of land has given the kids enough space to run free and enjoy being outside more than the city, including the full-sized rink and a massive yard for summertime activities. We still kept our other place, though, so we have the best of both worlds.

When the floodlights kick on, I take that as a sign it's time to wrap it up and we herd them inside. They're too tired to fight anymore, which is a bonus.

The house is dark and silent as we step into the living area. Two kitchen cabinets are left open, which makes me smile. Seraphina must've been in here getting some water or tea before bed.

Faint giggles echo from Callie's room, a sign the girls are probably tucked into bed and talking until they fall asleep, like they always do. Bauer is still grumpy, so I forgo his usual bedtime bath and change him into his pajamas before we get Seraphina to say good night. We find her in our bedroom, fast asleep on top of the covers. In the standing bassinet next to her, Hendrix is out cold too.

"Sorry, bud. Your brother's been keeping your mom up a lot at night. She'll see you in the morning," I tell him, steering him to his room. I read him a few bedtime stories before tucking him in, then switch on his Twilight Turtle before I shut off the lamp.

Chase shuffles in with Gabe a moment later and tucks him into Bauer's bottom bunk. As we leave the boys in their room, we overhear them talking and laughing, a sign they've mended their earlier dispute. I can't decide if Bauer and his cousin are too alike or too different; they're more like brothers than cousins, and they butt heads a lot.

Seraphina is nursing Hendrix when I walk back into our room. Her satin robe is pulled open to reveal a black tank top, slid off one shoulder, and the lamp is dimmed to its lowest setting.

"Hi," she says softly. "He just woke me up. I'm assuming I missed the tuck-in?"

"Yeah, but he's with Gabe and I think they're having fun together. Easier to bond when you feel like you're breaking the rules by staying up past bedtime." I study her face, noting the bluish-purple circles under her eyes. "I'll get up with Hendrix tonight, Tink. You need some rest."

"What? No," she protests, switching sides with him. "You have to go back on the road right away, and you need your sleep."

I lower onto the bed next to her and extend my legs, reaching for the remote to switch on the fireplace mounted on the wall across from us. "I'll be fine. I'm not the one who's been kept up for weeks on end with a colicky baby." That's one thing I hate about being away; feeling like I can't pull my weight at home, and it all falls on her shoulders.

"I think the end is in sight. Bauer was like this, too, and he got better around this age."

"Either way, I'll grab a bottle from the fridge and let you sleep." In a way, I don't mind those middle of the night feedings; probably because I'm not home to do them very often. There's something peaceful about being up with a baby when the rest of the world is asleep, snuggling them in the silence. Or while they scream, which has been the case with Hendrix lately. I know it'll pass, and he might be our last, so I try not to stress over it too much.

When Hendrix is finished nursing, he starts to fuss, kicking his legs.

"Let me have him," I say, beckoning with my hands. Seraphina hands him over and I prop him onto my shoulder, immediately rewarded with a burp so loud it sounds like it came from one of the guys on my team.

Then I cradle in my arms, taking in all of his tiny baby features as his eyelids grow heavy with sleep. Soft, downy brown hair. Long, dark lashes. Tiny baby nose. Cute little lips that I'm pretty sure are the same as Seraphina's. Chubby cheeks.

Right now, his eyes are gray, but with how young he is, it still could change. Bauer's shifted to rich brown like Sera's, whereas Callie's stayed gray like mine.

"Isn't he cute?" Seraphina coos.

"The cutest. I could stare at him all day." There's something about that new baby smell too. I have the most inexplicable urge to sniff his head constantly.

She draws in a breath, hesitating. "Are we done, do you think?"

"Done having babies, you mean? We still have a few years left before we really have to decide, Tink. There's no need to rush. Everything worked out with the kids, and now you have the luxury of some time to think it over."

Sadness wraps around my throat. It's a powerless position to be in knowing the only thing I can do is take care of her after the surgery someday. I hate knowing she'll have to go through that. I wish I could take on the burden for her—wish I could do something, *anything*, to change this terrible certainty that's been staring us in the face for years. I know it's the best course of action, though. I'd do anything to spend the rest of my life with her.

"Yeah." Shifting, she slides beneath the covers and snuggles up to me. We're silent for a few moments while Hendrix dozes peacefully in my arms. The fireplace dances across from us, flames glinting against the crushed glass.

In this moment, everything is perfect.

"You're such a good dad," Seraphina says softly. "I'm lucky to have you."

"I'm the lucky one. Look at everything you do for us. I'm gone half the time, and you take amazing care of the kids, handle the household stuff, and have a kick-ass career. Sometimes

I feel like you must be superhuman." I think about that all the time. She's so strong, and she handles everything with such grace.

"Mmm." She hums. "Maybe we're both lucky then."

I press my lips to her forehead. "Being with you is the best thing I ever did, Ser."

PLAYLIST

Theme: "Moonlight"—Chase Atlantic
1. "Head Up"—The Score
2. "Cool Girl"—Tove Lo
3. "more than friends"—Isabel LaRosa
4. "My Mind & Me"—Selena Gomez
5. "Tarantino"—PLVTINUM
6. "Right Here"—Chase Atlantic
7. "Fix You"—Coldplay
8. "For Me"—Lo Nightly
9. "Eyes On You"—SWIM
10. "Three Feet Away"—Vanglowe, Quantum
11. "Chemical"—Post Malone
12. "Sleepy"—Ashley Kutcher
13. "chaotic"—Tate McRae
14. "Demons on the Side of My Bed"—Teflon Sega
15. "Heartburn"—Wafia
16. "We Go Down Together"—Dove Cameron, Khalid
17. "Easy"—Camila Cabello
Epilogue: "One Life"—Dermot Kennedy

ACKNOWLEDGMENTS

To my husband, for loving me in sickness and (mental) health, being my hockey fact-checker, and listening to me rant and rave about all things indie publishing. And to both of my sons, who are the reason for everything I do.

To all of my writer friends, because writing is a lonely endeavor and you keep me sane. Alywn, without you, this book would never have made it. I can't express how thankful I am for all the time you spent with me on this, even while we balanced our crazy time zone differences. Sonali, thank you for talking me off the ledge at the eleventh hour and being one of my biggest cheerleaders.

Thank you to Autumn and Wordsmith Publicity for being endlessly supportive with this release.

And to all of my readers, without whom any of this would be possible.

ABOUT THE AUTHOR

AVERY KEELAN is an award-winning author of sports romance and contemporary romance, a lifelong hockey fan, and a die-hard coffee lover. She writes swoon-worthy happily ever afters with hot hockey heroes, snarky banter, and enough steam to fog up a mirror.

With undergraduate degrees in commerce and psychology, Keelan specialized in government policy and legislation in a previous life. She lives in Canada with her husband and their two children, along with two spoiled rescue cats who like to sit on her keyboard at inopportune times.